Beyond Red Lines

Pierre REHOV

PROLOGUE

January 1991 – French Army disciplinary camp, somewhere in the southwest.

"To begin prone shooting, assume position!"

The sandbags smelled damp, and they were murder on the elbows. The plastic underhelmet was keeping them warm despite the light drizzle pitter-pattering on the tarp. Theo felt ridiculous, his emaciated body swimming in his threadbare uniform. There was an odor of humus and crushed chestnuts mixed in with the smell of gunpowder from the previous shots.

"Load arm!"

Afterwards, no-one would remember who'd been assigned to dole out the ammo to the shooters. Five bullets per man. In time with the others, Theo inserted his magazine, then cocked the bolt handle in one smooth move. The well-oiled breeches snapped, almost as one.

"Facing your respective targets, call out: sighted and ready!"

"Shooter number one, sighted and ready!"

Antsy kid. A February recruit. Never seen a rifle, but a good sport. Always ready to chip in on detail, all on the sly.

"Shooter number two, sighted and ready!"

Stocky. Country boy. Raised rough. Hunter and poacher. Two or three incidents with him during weapons cleaning. His favorite game? Cock a rifle, Western-style, soon as he saw a rookie. One time, the shot had gone off, fortunately without injuring anybody. He'd only gotten confined to barracks for a month. The colonel was a hunter too.

A three-voice crescendo.

"Shooter number three… number four… number five… sighted and ready!"

Inseparable since they'd enlisted. The oldest in the company. Ever since the section chief had cottoned on that they were better off kept together, they didn't make trouble for anybody. They handled their guard duty, laughed at the same jokes, and spent their downtime playing tarot.

"Collin! I said, call out, sighted and ready!"

The instructor reached Theo at the same time as his barked shout. He swung his boot down against his ankle, and his eyes filled with tears. Raising the sight line of his rifle, he called in a choked-out voice,

"Shooter number six, sighted and ready... End of the line!"

At the other end of his scope, he could make out his target at two hundred yards. Minuscule.

The rest of the company was lollygagging, twenty-odd juveniles putting on nonchalant airs, leaning their backs against the wall of the building. One guy, one gun, one guy... Two days' confinement for a firearm on the ground.

The instructor stepped over them with an overbearing air. The stragglers followed him. The officer appraised each one and turned back to Theo.

"You must be fighting fit after two months in the hospital, Collin. No more slacking off. It's a turkey shoot, now."

Number five chortled. Without even seeing him, Theo could guess at the second lieutenant's satisfaction. His helmet was heavy and his stomach was cramping. He'd gotten up late, and he hadn't been given a choice between cleaning the latrines and chowing down breakfast.

The instructor stepped a yard out and issued his order.

"Now firing at two hundred and fifty yards, five rounds, one at a time, start firing!"

In answer, he got three immediate discharges. Theo quivered. Despite his fertile imagination, he hadn't managed to get a waiver. Two months in a military psychiatric hospital had gotten the better of his taste for freedom... and of his dread.

His desertion as soon as he'd stepped out of the hospital had gotten him a temporary assignment with a disciplinary battalion, which could even lead to a sojourn in Iraq. This was only the beginning of his ordeal.

"Collin!"

Yet another bellow. He cocked the lever. He needed to pull the trigger. Was the butt steady enough? There was so much talk, despite the anti-kickback system on these FAMAS's... What if his shoulder didn't hold up to the shock? He held his breath; the target appeared closer.

The discharge took him by surprise, but he didn't feel any pain. The casing surged out of the ejection port. Theo once again blew the air out of his lungs and pulled. The fifth casing soon ricocheted onto the soft ground, still smoking.

"Shooter number six, finished shooting!" he reported mechanically.

A series of discharges followed. Five shots. Then five more. Theo looked at the instructor in surprise. Had they reloaded without his realizing? He had very clearly taken his first shot well after the others. The second lieutenant charged over to him.

"Monkeying around again," he screamed. "You shot all over the place just to mess up Army equipment. On your feet when I'm talking to you, Collin!"

Theo stood up, taken aback.

"Second class Collin, at attention!"

He snapped to. They didn't like asylum seekers all that much in the French Army. That went double for fakers, who were deemed cowards. And conscription would, for years still, be part of the cultural foundation of a society that wasn't much inclined to replace its diplomatic tradition with any sort of a defense effort. But now wasn't the time to lay out this sort of an argument.

The instructor was getting a kick out of having him in his grasp now, under his complete authority. He knew everyone would look the other way if he found any a good reason for punishment. Ever since Theo had slipped the fatigues back on, he was headquartered somewhere between the head and the mess. With, for a bonus, the officers' boots to shine post-marches.

"Run over to the targets. And bring them here. On the double!"

To please him, Theo tried to execute an about-turn by the book, but his feet got tangled up. The others looked on sadly.

"Collin!"

A fresh bark.

"You'll show me your target first. If I don't see a hole, you're gonna be standing in for it!"

He snickered, pleased with his little witticism. Theo took off at a trot.

The rain was now falling resolutely. On the shooting range behind him, a second group was getting into position. A conscript was opening a new crate of magazines. The targets were still two hundred yards out. The mere thought of being in the brig once more, with nothing to do but think, was making Theo nauseous.

He closed in on the ditch that separated the targets from the field. During intensive training, one guy would hunker down in there and change out the targets in between each drill. In one leap, he was over on the other side.

Number one wasn't bad. Three holes, not too far apart. He grabbed the target and put a new one up. The following four, a half-dozen holes between them. Pretty mediocre. For a split-second, he entertained the notion of changing out his target for number one's. He reached his arm out and froze in his tracks.

Five centered holes. Barely two inches between them. Not possible! They must have left an old target up. Theo looked closer. Given the falling rain, it should have been soaked. It looked the same as all the others. These really were his bullet holes.

The intercom hissed to life. He darted into the ditch.

"You coming in any time today, Collin?"

"Coming, lieutenant."

He crossed the range right back again at a run, clutching that all too precious paper under his arm.

The second lieutenant peered at him suspiciously.

"You gonna claim this is really your target?"

"Yes, lieutenant."

The shooting had picked back up again and they could barely hear each-other. A private first class was holding on to Theo's rifle.

The officer seized it abruptly.

"Hand me a magazine.

The young conscript darted over to the munitions crate, as obsequious as anybody two days out from a leave. The squad leader picked up an empty casing and stepped away from the range. He propped it onto the parapet.

"The Marine Parachutists have the good rifles," he said, making his way back to Theo. "The ones we use here are for rookie practice only. Badly serviced, badly calibrated. Not one of them is accurate."

He slid the clip in.

"They all fire to the right..."

He cocked; took aim.

"Or to the left."

He pulled the trigger. The casing took flight, and the discharge dissipated into the din.

"This one seems to fire straight," he said, taking out the magazine.

He looked at Theo, furrowing his eyebrows, and ejected the cartridge that was still chambered.

"Five times, two hundred yards out? Come this way."

He propped himself in front of where the new row of shooters was standing at attention.

"Collin, go stand in for De Sotto."

Theo wordlessly headed to the range. Persuaded he'd gotten lucky the first time, he knew that even if spaced out his shots, he wouldn't get the same result. But the hardest part was over with.

"Next group, get into position!"

The forty or so youths making up the section gathered around the sandbags. The officer threw the rifle, which Theo caught midair. Arms long at his sides, head held high, neck stiff as a board, the marksmanship instructor bellowed out,

"If I ever ask you for a weapon one day, that's how I want to get it. Lively. Same thing among yourselves. A FAMAS is for throwing.

"If you've got a bunch of Arabs on your tails, you're not gonna see your buddies so they can hand you one nicely. Drop it out here, your ass gets the brig. Drop it in a firefight, your ass gets the dust."

There were a couple restrained chuckles in response. A few years back, he'd explained during instruction, Soviet Russia had been the default enemy. They'd taken that mantle from the Germans, who had themselves replaced the English.

After the Berlin wall came down and the Soviet bloc collapsed, France no longer had an established enemy, and its involvement in Operation Desert Storm hadn't yet resurrected this indispensable if fluctuating concept.

But as far as the second lieutenant was personally concerned, he made it no secret that he thought the Arabs – no matter their country – were a bunch of raggedy freaks that needed to be flushed out and smoked, before they ended up wiping their asses with the French flag.

He asked them to take a count, then bared his teeth in a predatory smile.

"For prone shooting, assume position!"

After they all loaded, he pulled out a pair of binoculars from his sack and ordered them to fire at will.

Just like the first time, Theo thought the target looked closer. He was no longer afraid of the kickback. The report boomed out, and Theo instantly understood that the bullet had struck true. He knew it without even seeing the target.

The casings flew out. Two, three... The trigger snicked on empty.

"Mother of God!"

Raising his eyes, Theo met the second lieutenant's stupefied gaze. His shoulders had stooped, and the binoculars were dangling from his nerveless arm. It was as though one of the bullets had hit him in the back.

The silence was so deep that they could hear one of the soldiers strike a match. The recruits had gathered in close and were now pressed in a swaying group, feet firm on the ground, all faces turned towards the target area, expressions frozen in astonishment. The officer got a hold of himself.

"Where'd you learn how to shoot?"

Theo got up, leaving his rifle propped onto its bipod. A handful of seconds had turned him untouchable.

"I never learned," he replied.

"Don't give me that nonsense, Collin. Nobody's ever hit a target two hundred yards out on their first try. Have you been practicing long?"

"This is the first time I've ever laid hand on a weapon, lieutenant."

His face hardened.

Thirty pairs of eyes were now collectively pinning Theo. Standing in a semicircle behind the instructor, "his" section was looking at him like he was some kind of strange animal. The deserter, the failed discharge, an elite shooter.

"You're taking me for a ride!"

The second lieutenant had pulled himself together. A glow had lit his gaze for a brief instant, while he'd analyzed the incident and drawn the conclusions that he attributed to an unexpected clarity. Theo the ace sharpshooter fazed him, but Theo the liar he could accept. He went on to grill him for a couple of minutes, before coming to the only obvious conclusion: this young misfit was a miracle.

That entire day was then dedicated to him. The second lieutenant sent a P4 dispatch rider to the barracks before lunch. The firing range was 30 clicks out, a distance covered by truck. They only saw the messenger again around fifteen hundred hours, alongside the captain in command of the training division. During that time, Theo had spent sixty cartridges and drilled twelve targets without straying once.

A consummate firing officer, the second lieutenant had calculated his MOA[1], which wasn't done at two hundred yards, and concluded that his shooting surpassed what the ordinary soldier could produce at fifty yards out.

Their rations had been handed out at noon on the dot: pâté, single-serve ready meal, fruit paste, chocolate tablet, and ration bread.

---

1   The tightness of the shot grouping.

The weather had cleared as the clock struck two. Despite a timid shaft of sunlight, breaths and plumes of cigarette smoke looked alike. Engrossed in the mystery of such an unexpected show of skill, the second lieutenant had forgotten to prohibit smoking.

Every bit as surprised as the others, a young Breton redhead named Kernian had come by to question how sincere he was being. His repeated assertions that he'd never touched a gun before hadn't satisfied the guy, and he'd walked away from Theo in cold suspicion. An NCO ultimately took charge of the section and they were taken away to another, empty shooting range.

It took yet more cartridges to fully convince the captain — a man of short stature, whose deeply-lined face was contorted in a continual grimace of pain, and whose tailored uniform clung to his body so closely you could have seen the play of his muscles under the fabric. The showcase only came to an end at nightfall. The captain approached Theo then and spoke to him for the first time.

"You claim never to have learned how to shoot."

Standing at attention, arms and shoulder in pain from his grip on the rifle, he once again repeated his assertion.

"Would you be willing to swear it on the Bible ?"

"No, captain."

He speared him with a glare and turned to the second lieutenant, a sly look on his face. Theo immediately went on.

"I... I'm not religious, captain."

His voice softened, then, his tone turning almost amiable as he spoke.

"You already knew you had a gift, Collin: that of getting yourself into trouble. You uncovered a second one today."

He unsnapped his holster open and handed him his gun.

"This is a MAC 51. You've only shot that rifle. And prone. Ultimately, even if you are lying, you've never given this one a try. Let's step in closer to the targets."

Theo fell in behind him. Despite the ten or fifteen years separating them, he was having a hard time keeping pace in the fading light. Fifty yards out from the target, the captain turned back towards him. His face was implacable.

"You don't like the military, Collin. And I don't like young folk like you. You have no guts. Training may give you discipline, but it'll never turn you into men. Take the safety off..."

He pawed at the cold metal of the gun, hands trembling, and released the slide on instinct. The captain stepped in close enough to brush up against him. Theo was half a head taller than him, but that was hardly enough to instill any confidence. He was spurred by one obsession: avoid the cooler; and so, obsequiously, he lowered his gaze.

"Fire at will!"

Clumsily, Theo pointed the muzzle towards the target and pulled the trigger. Nothing happened. The captain snickered.

"Pull back the slide. Chamber a bullet. Collin, you're already dead."

"I apologize, captain, nobody's ever taught me..."

8

The officer yanked the semiautomatic out of his hands and got into position. Legs spread, facing the target, the arm holding the weapon pointed down alongside his body. Not bending his elbow, he brought the gun up horizontal to his line of sight.

"Got that? Hit six rounds for me and I'll give you seventy-two hours."

Theo mimicked his position. The promise of a three-day leave suddenly had the gun feeling a lot lighter. This would be a first for the disciplinary battalion. Without catching his breath, he pulled the trigger six times. As if he'd been practicing from the cradle.

The captain reached out a hand and grabbed the gun, holstering it with the barrel still scorching.

"What do you think, Collin?"

"I don't know, captain. I don't get it."

"There any family history of this?"

"No-one, captain. Nobody's ever used a gun."

"No need to go look at the target, is there? Six rounds in."

"I reckon, captain."

He made a surprising move, then. He put his hand on Theo's shoulder and patted it.

"I'd have much rather it had been some daredevil. One of those guys who enlist to see some action and become heroes out of a sheer survival instinct. Cases like yours are pretty rare. You're gonna undergo a very special kind of training. That's going to require you to sign a VLS[2]."

His voice firmed up.

"And you're going to consent, Collin. Your record's so thick that your year will be a living hell if you set so much as a hair out of line. No leave, no visits. And three months from now, moldering in the brig, you're going to spend every second regretting that you didn't sign certain paperwork. Have they told you about me?"

"I don't know who you are, captain."

"I'm Captain Meyrek; remember that name. Whatever happens, your fate now hangs on my will. Do you understand that, Collin?"

He showed his assent. What else is there to do at nineteen years of age, after you've spent the first few years of your life fleeing from weapons, from combat, and from conflicts of all kinds?

Hackles raised, the captain saw it fit to tack on,

"Up until this day, you were a loser. You're going to become part of the elite, and your handling will fall to me and only me. Any objections, Collin?"

Theo wavered for a moment before replying.

"At your orders, captain."

"Good. When you get back from leave, come straight to my office. Go on, now. The truck is waiting on you."

---

2   Voluntary long enlistment: a voluntary commitment to extend one's military service beyond the ten-month legal enlistment period.

Pink Floyd was belting out a *Wish you Were Here* that crackled pathetically over Kernian's old cassette player. The overhead lights in the room went dark for a few seconds to signal that curfew was imminent.

Theo crossed the barracks in a daze, shivering even as he slid under the covers. All around him, the bustle was dying down. The last of the cigarettes were being put out. Bit by bit, the twenty-odd conscripts sharing the same foul air as him dragged their feet over to their beds.

"You hear what they did to Germont yesterday morning?"

An unknown voice was recounting the exploits of a pack of jokers against the unit's punching bag. This time they'd pulled some kind of a dirty trick that had ended up with the hapless recruit standing in the courtyard at three in the morning, nothing but his briefs on, waiting for the raising of the flag.

The soldiers were engaging in a jolly chorus of har-hars and whoop-whoops when the door flew open to reveal chief Valentin. The covers folded over as one and all voices went quiet. He barreled into the barracks and came to a stop before Theo's bed. It was his night on guard duty.

Valentin was a cartoon character, like something torn right out of the pages of a comic book on the Legion. Hulking, blond hair in a tight fade. A square face with an obdurate chin, and furnished with a minuscule nose that looked as though a mischievous Mother Nature had propped the appendage on at the last minute. His gaze swung between distrust and impishness, with the occasional glimmer of sadism. In his three years' active duty, he bragged that he'd negated nearly two thousand leaves.

"Collin, attention!"

From his mouth, the order came out, "Co'i', atte'tio'!" Theo obeyed, in his shorts. Terrified and frozen.

"You've got a quarter hour to get into full battle gear. Fatigue 107 tonight. That'll teach you to lick boots for three days' leave."

"But, sergeant, all I did was..."

"Shut your mouth, Collin. I can still take you down. Even if you're leaving the training company on Tuesday." His voice suddenly veered towards hysteria.

"Our asses are at war. Three months from now, half of you in this room will be learning how to count in dead towelheads, and it's runts like you that real soldiers are gonna have to depend on for backup. Shut off that fucking radio or Imma hurl it out the window."

Pink Floyd had moved on to the *Dark Side of the Moon*. Kernian hurtled toward the radio.

"At the ready in fifteen minutes, Collin!"

The lights turned off as soon as he'd stepped out. Seated on the edge of his bed, Theo stamped down on the urge to cry. This thing that was happening to him was beyond his comprehension. This gift that had suddenly put him under the barracks' microscope was too heavy a burden to bear. One of Germont's torturers sing-songed in a half-whisper.

"Who was it who went and signed? Collin."

"Who's gonna get it mighty fine? Collin," another chortled in response.

"The delete shooter," the first one snickered.

He would have loved it, in that moment, if he'd had the guts to get up. To shut them up, using his fists. But violence terrified him, in any shape or form. He pulled on his woolen socks and his fatigue pants.

"Collin…"

It was Kernian.

"What did he say to you, the cannibal?"

"Who's *the cannibal*?"

"Meyrek. At the shooting range, what did he ask you to sign?"

Theo wiped at his eyes, hoping the semi-darkness would cover him, before pulling on his regulation T-shirt.

"Nothing much. A VLS plus six, to start with…"

"What? You signed on for six more months? But you hate the army!"

"It's a very long story. He wants to put me through some kind of special training. He gave me seventy-two hours because I plugged six holes with the handgun. I'd never fired a gun before, Kernian. I swear to you. And since then, he won't get off my back."

"Now that you've signed on, we're gonna stick together. Is it true the VLS's are gonna be joining the others in Iraq?"

"I have no clue. Why do they call him *the cannibal*?"

"He's a former legionnaire. They say that he and his brigade got lost during some covert op in Chad or Angola. Four days without food. They came across some maverick and showed him a good time, African style.

"Meyrek gave whatever was left of him to his cook. His guys were more the roots-and-leaves type, but he made them eat with him. They say he kept the brain for himself."

He snapped his belt and got up.

"You've been reading too many comic books, Kernian."

A week later, Theo was breaking his left femur and tibia on the obstacle course. The captain had demanded that he jump from the top of the ladder. The signing of his VLS, scheduled for the following day, was postponed.

He was laid up for two months, plus an extra month's rehab. During his stay in the hospital, the enlistees in his unit had joined the conscripts in Rafah, in northern Saudi Arabia. Kernian had been among them. They tried to pick his training back up, but his leg was weak.

Towards the end of February, the head medic informed him that their battalion had taken part in the capture of As-Salman airport, alongside the 4th Chasseurs regiment. He would regularly give him news from the Iraqi front — at least, whatever he had access to himself, which wasn't all that much. Theo wondered how much of that was about laying a guilt trip on him. So he was the one to let him know, on the 3rd of March, that a ceasefire had been signed by General Norman Schwartzkopf at the Safran base.

Kernian was one of the few declared missing.

On September 30th 1991, he was discharged of all his military duties with no grade or distinction. He'd only done his legally-mandated ten months, and he had just turned twenty years old.

His records were filed. Captain Meyrek alone kept track.

Chapter 1

April 23rd, 2003

The war hadn't yet defaced Erbil, a small city of over a million inhabitants that spreads out its circular expanse into the only non-mountainous area of Kurdistan. Further out and to the south, around Bagdad, or over to the west in Mosul, the battles still raged out, despite the resounding victory of the anti-Saddam coalition and the conquest of the capital city 14 days earlier.

It was sometimes difficult to know who was fighting whom: Westerners versus Arabs, Ba'athists versus dissidents, Sunni versus Shia; but life went on as before in Erbil, at the foot of Qalat, the ancient fortress that overlooks the central bazaar quarter, as it did in the outlying neighborhoods of Ainkawa, which are for non-muslims only, minorities that are often ill-treated and thus all the more closely knit.

Erbil was Howard Beck's first destination, and he only had a few clicks left to go, while, on his left, the sun was already setting, skimming the flatland and the dunes.

The two Humvees borrowed from the 1st Battalion 10th Marine Regiment that were acting as his escort had been keeping his vehicle in a perfectly straight convoy ever since they'd left the northern suburbs of Baghdad. More often than not, the shape of the road merged with the desert, and the hours they'd spent on this trip had quickly robbed him of all sense of time.

Outside, around noon, the temperature had reached 122 degrees. It was still 113 towards the end of the day, which was enough to wonder how the rare camel drivers they'd crossed paths with even managed to survive, to say nothing of those gangs of kids that would leap out, out of nowhere, and make the head vehicle swerve and swerve.

The kids had no fear. They hailed them with huge cries of joy, some of them waving American flags drawn crudely onto old sheets, others bounding right onto the middle of the road.

Those were the ones to watch out for. The Iraqi "resistance" had no qualms about using them as bomb planters, and more than one escorting NCO had paid with his life for being unaware that these ragged kids were blissfully willing to sacrifice themselves for what amounted to a single dollar in cash.

Using kids for combat! Beck would never reconcile himself to that. Never mind that it was the most widespread atrocity across Africa, the Middle East, and in just about every war zone where his duties as a CIA field agent had tossed him over the past ten years.

His driver turned to him as the first lights of Erbil came into view.

"I don't know how we're gonna find the Parliament building with the crappy old maps they hand us out. But there's no way I'm stopping to ask for directions."

From afar, the walls of the old fortress where Alexander the Great had suffered his worst defeat seemed to be steeping in a cloud of carmine and ochre dust; its hazy outline stretched out heavily, as though crushed by the heat. It was overtaken only by a cluster of minarets, out of which the tallest dome rose some fifty feet, all lit up a blazing green.

The convoy entered the city right at *adhan,* the call to prayer, and an intonation rose up from every mosque and was soon picked up by other voices, all as vibrant as the stagnant air, and every bit as timeless.

Allahu'akbar... God is greatest...

The streets, wide enough to accommodate several lanes of vehicles, were lined with low houses, between which a male multitude meandered despite the pressing call of the muezzins, while a swarm of teenagers on sputtering motorbikes aligned themselves with the convoy, all howls and laughs. The driver opened the window and yelled at them to move away. A wave of heat instantly slammed into the airconditioned vehicle.

"Shut that," ordered Beck. "It's useless. Even if they spoke English, they don't give a damn."

The lead Humvee turned right, escorted by several tiddlers, each bearing two kids astride. Signs in Arabic and in Kurdish, languages that Beck understood and could read fluently, indicated the Salahddin University in that direction, and the Parliament building straight ahead.

They drove around the dried out fountain inside a little square that was teeming with people, and for a smattering of seconds, the call of the muezzins was drowned out by sweeping cries.

"Americans! Americans!"

"Looks like they're glad to see us..." uttered the driver, all smiles.

"You been touring the Arab countries a long time?" Beck asked.

"No, Sir. Just a couple weeks..."

"Then you should learn not to put stock in these ebullient cultures. Today, we're freeing them from Saddam; in a few months, they'll want nothing more than to get rid of us."

Howard Beck finally opened the sealed envelope he'd been holding close since they'd set out. It was a routine mission yet again. He'd been instructed to find one Major Len Sutton, serving with the Delta Force, at the Arbil Tawar hotel, not far from the Kurdish Parliament building.

Sutton was a training officer, an expert in combat under extreme conditions. There were however only two months left until he was discharged, and in that time, he was meant to evaluate the potential of the Kurdish combattants alongside Beck.

The Major's service record was admirable. West Point, the Marines, then Fort Bragg. During the decade bookended by the two Iraq wars, he'd risen up the military ranks at lightning speed.

Beck furrowed his eyebrows.

Strange that qualifications like that hadn't lead Sutton to reenlist. By assigning him an evaluation report in a secured zone, the Chief of Staff was sidelining him, as though to keep him safe right before he left. And who did they send to play nanny to him but Howard Beck.

The CIA and the Delta Force didn't always necessarily get along. The latter all too often criticized the former for getting bogged down in endless bureaucratic twists rather than getting out in the field. Beck shrugged his shoulders and let out a slight growl when he saw the rest.

"Holy shit! They're seriously using me as a babysitter!"

A small memo tacked onto the file added that he also had to consent to the presence of a Wall Street Journal reporter, Jamie Turrow. According to his resumé, the journalist had spent three years in Tehran before getting sent to Jerusalem by Fox News, and then transitioning into print journalism. An old hand.

At least he wasn't part of these wide-eyed rookies who parade in front of the camera in bulletproof vests, and then piss their tailor-made cargo pants at the first discharge. In his articles, Jamie Turrow blended a pragmatic viewpoint with a good field knowledge. He had also written a historical essay, the title of which stirred something in Beck's memory. "The Old Man on the Mountain." He must have come across some critique of it.

He suddenly raised his head.

"Honk your horn, they're going the wrong way!"

The driver instantly obeyed. The lead Humvee abruptly hit the brakes.

"It's over on the left, at the end of this street," Beck went on after unscrambling a road sign.

A few moments later, the three vehicles were parking in front of the Arbil Tawar hotel, a squat edifice squeezed in between two buildings of another age. Two armored vehicles with machine guns on the roof were guarding its entrance. The youths astride the motorbikes scattered as though they'd gotten a signal.

The Humvees were arranged in such a way as to guard the door that Beck got out through. The CIA agent stretched delightedly before darting into the hotel; its faintly-lit front gave him an impression of adequate comfort.

He was brought back down to earth upon taking in the ravaged lobby, with its mostly overturned furniture and its main desk destroyed by blows with an ax. A decrepit fan was acting the part of an air conditioning unit, and despite the thick walls, the heat was almost as oppressive as outside. In one second, he found himself covered in sweat. An officer by the bar, escorted by two soldiers and a civilian, put an end to his conversation to come greet him.

"Howard Beck? Major Sutton… Have you seen the state of the palace? It's like this everywhere. The little guys are getting even. Too bad they're mostly

14

coming after the hotels and boutiques. If we can't manage to train them up a police force, there won't be anything left to sell in this country…"

Beck held his tongue. It was always the same old tale. An armed conflict generally arose after years of accrued frustrations, led to a turnaround, and the same old injustices picked right back up, only with the roles reversed.

"At any rate," the Major went on, "we aren't sleeping here. I've gotten fresh instructions…"

"Thanks for the good news," Beck grumbled.

"Yeah, you sure do look worn out, buddy. Sorry, but the Kurdish chiefs need to join us back in Mossul. The Chief of Staff won't stop playing hide and seek with them."

The two men were the same size, and no doubt the same age, but the Major's military appearance gave him an edge over Beck, who won out in the stoutness of his build. Despite an otherwise pleasing appearance, he readily admitted he was less than fit.

The Major, on the other hand, had athlete written all over him. Beck respected the frank if glacial gaze, and the straightforward smile of a man used to be in charge, who didn't abide either lies or compromises.

"We do still have time for some *kubbeh* soup and a couple pitta breads," the Major added before turning toward the civilian who was coming their way. "And here's Mister Turrow, our assassin expert…"

The journalist's face looked familiar. Symmetrical features, an intelligent forehead, tanned skin. The textbook cable news correspondent. He held out a firm hand to Beck, who experienced instant recall.

"Your book. "The Old Man on the Mountain." It was that treatise on Hassan-i Sabbah's sect?"

"The leader of the *Hashshashin*, that's right," Jamie Turrow admitted in an appreciative voice. "That's where the word "assassin" comes from. Flattered you're familiar with my work…"

"The civilians who join the armed forces in combat zones have a reputation for knowing just about anything," the Major asserted with a wink. "And I don't mean the reporters…"

Escorted by the Major's guards, who'd been joined by Beck's driver, the three men made their way to a smaller, slightly less ravaged room, where a couple of tables had been set, with a bottle of sparkling water on each one, and a pile of steaming flatbreads next to them.

The servers were dressed in the Kurdish fashion, in baggy pants and flowing jackets. They gathered in around the Americans with an enthusiasm that wasn't feigned. Bowls of soup and ramekins of finely-diced salad were brought to the tables.

"This is a local specialty," intoned the Major, who enjoyed playing host. "*Kubbeh* means meatballs. They're terrific, you'll see. And besides, that's all they've got tonight."

"You make do in war," gritted out Jamie Turrow, raising his glass of water.

A feeling came over Beck like he was living this same scene out for the hundredth time. A hotel that was requisitioned by the army (the owner was generously compensated), a few officers who were enthusiastic and cocksure, some soldiers to guard the entrance, an intellectual, occasionally a woman, and the scene would re-form endlessly, whatever the country.

With this heat, he'd just have liked a little cold one, and the water they'd set on the tables didn't exactly instill the most trust. The Major raised his glass in turn, and the three men clinked glasses.

"*To the end* of this war," ventured Sutton. "Like all the others…"

Beck couldn't hold back a smile. Soldiers always drank to the war ending, doctors always drank to diseases ending, and no doubt plumbers raised their glass to water leaks and clogged pipes ending. He was yearning to question the Major. Occupational hazard. The reporter pre-empted him.

"As far as you go, it'll be the end of the line soon," he started. "You're back to civilian life in two months?"

The Major stirred slightly in his seat, his face impenetrable. But Beck thought he could perceive a sudden embarrassment in the motion. There was always something surprising, if not suspicious, in the retirement of a great warrior.

"I'd gotten the impression that your column was focused on the Kurdish combattant training; I hope you aren't secretly writing my biography."

His tone of voice was just the right amount of dry. Turrow conceded the point, his nose shoved into his bowl of soup.

"Any story has its guiding thread and its B-plot…" he uttered.

It was like a moment of perfect clarity for Beck. There was nothing more he needed to know. Evidently, the Major was not headed back to a civilian status.

He would not be the first high-ranking officer to move from an official elite unit into something off the books. He tried to picture Len Sutton wearing business casual, sporting the ubiquitous black sunglasses that the movie industry traditionally bestows on Secret Service agents.

As far as the Major went, there weren't many options. White House and Presidential Security, FBI Anti-Terrorist Units, or a CIA Operations Unit. Neither he nor the WSJ correspondent would be able to learn more during this dinner. Sutton – still flawlessly playing the part of the host – steered the conversation in a different direction.

"I read your latest article, the one on the internal factors that could lead to the West being defeated. Good insights! They can't ever be overstated…"

Then, turning to Beck,

"Our friend here is amazing. Actually, if I hadn't read some of his articles, I'd have never consented to his presence here. The media already tears us to enough pieces without needing us to give them more ammo. You'd think our wars are always dirty and dubious, the complete opposite of our enemies' strikes, which are obviously justified by their poverty and our misdeeds…"

"That's the exact theme of my article," whispered Turrow in a tone that was meant to sound modest. "But it's actually not hard to understand what causes this inadvertent betrayal…"

"I haven't had the pleasure of reading your work," interceded Beck. "If you could enlighten me?"

That was all Turrow needed. What was the use of being a professional wordsmith if you didn't leap at every opportunity to share your thoughts? He quickly laid out the viewpoints in his column. There were three major trends ostensibly leading to the fall of the West.

Pacifism, or the idea that handing the aggressor a bunch of flowers was enough to reason with them. An almost religious sense of self-hatred, conveyed by the loathing of a capitalist system that was at the root of all materialism. And a superiority complex that included a paternalistic drift, and its immediate impact, manifesting through a form of protectionist contempt towards those civilizations that were perceived as inferior.

"In short, it's Vietnam syndrome combined with the myth of the noble savage. No savagery committed by the other side could possibly justify our intervention. In a story about cops and robbers, it's trendy to make the bad guy sympathetic; and if he happens to assault sweet old ladies, it's obviously the rotten system that's at fault. But this is a debate that's been going round and round…"

The journalist set his bowl of soup down with a smack of his lips. He'd managed to drain its contents even as he'd talked. Beck had barely touched his, finding the soup too bland and too spicy all at once. There were only spoons and forks on the table. No knives.

He tore a chunk of pitta bread and dipped it into his cucumber, olive and tomato salad. The clock was ticking. If they wanted to catch at least a couple hours' sleep in Mossul, they needed to cut this dinner short.

"I'm more interested in history than in the tide of current opinion," he disclosed. "One day, I'd love to read your book on the sect…"

"The asssassins!" Turrow instantly exclaimed. "But it's not just history. You dive right in! This sect has never been so relevant; listen to this!"

His eyes glowing, and mopping up the last dregs at the bottom of his salad bowl with an abundance of bread chunks, he summarized the essay that had gotten him a prize from the New York Times, an outstanding occurrence for a journalist that the great broadsheet considered a conservative.

Hassan-i Sabbah, the Old Man on the Mountain, had been made famous by Marco Polo and his chronicles. The mountain in question was Alamouth, found in Afghanistan, some place north of Iran.

"That would have been an ideal hiding spot for Ben Laden. You have no idea how much history is repeating itself!"

Sabbah would recruit young boys, orphans for the most part, or else bought from their parents. After weeks of harsh instruction, during which they were beaten, then trained up, then tossed half-dead in squalid cells, he would have them drink a brew he'd concocted himself, a mixture of hash and herbs.

The kids would fall into a deep sleep, following which they'd be carted into a magnificent garden that was carefully tended to by Hassan himself. There, as soon as they awoke and for the duration of a whole day, nymphets and young boys would introduce them to every pleasure of the flesh. At nightfall, they would be drugged once more, and then thrown back into their cells.

"When they came to, Hassan-i Sabbah would make them believe that, through his powers, he'd shown them a glimpse of Paradise."

A Paradise of the flesh, within a verdant universe, and every bit as real as what the Quran and all the Imams described, Turrow enthusiastically went on. From then on, all the young recruits needed to do was blindly obey their leader and they would inherit an eternal Eden after their deaths.

That was how the Assassin sect was born. Hash-drinking killers. The Old Man on the Mountain, so called because he'd been believed to be immortal, kept up their training to the point where he made those young adults into the most efficient and most ruthless killers of his age. They'd been feared by the entire Orient, and being in his good graces, even for a second, was better than being his enemy.

"He was simultaneously the first all-out terrorist, a mercenary, and the forefather of the 72-virgins myth that encourages all these young Muslim fanatics to blow themselves up aboard buses or in front of nightclubs, in our days," added the journalist. "Unfortunately, such tantalizing myths are hard to kill, and they spread like wildfire."

"Their trouble," the Major concluded as he stood, "is that if God exists, he's neither a whorehouse owner, nor an orgy organizer!"

He turned towards the waiters and inclined his head in thanks, together with an accent-free "*shukran habibi.*" The guards instantly sprang into action. Perimeter surveilance. Convoy readiness. Mounted cannon positioning and engine starting.

Whistle signals combined with specific gestures indicated that the perimeter was secure. Several soldiers equipped with bulletproof vests came up in a half-circle in order to shield the exit of the three-man group. Beck's vehicles were now accompanied by the two armored cars, an armored personnel carrier, and the Major's all-terrain.

"Who are you riding with?" the latter asked Turrow.

The journalist took in Howard Beck's sullen air and opted to be in Sutton's company.

"Fantastic!" ribbed the Major. "Instead of dozing quietly on the way to Mossul, I'm gonna get myself interrogated."

"If you'd rather he came with me…" ventured Beck.

The journalist shook his head. He could only be enticed by the Major's volubility, whereas Beck's duties constrained him to excessive discretion.

"Without meaning to be rude… Besides, I'm too worn out to keep making a pest of myself."

The convoy moved off as soon as the men had gotten on board. Beck got two soldiers on his hands, one of whom took a seat next to him in the back, while the other sat in the front. The sky was starless and the night a deep, dark black.

A blackout, frequent in northern Iraq since the conflict had broken out, had just plunged the neighborhood into complete darkness. Even the minarets of the old citadel were no longer lit. Reaching the end of the street, the lead vehicle sped up, and the convoy crossed the town in a rush, all lights beaming and horns blaring with every encounter.

As luck would have it, Beck's escorts weren't the chatty type. He leaned his head back against the seat. His mind started drifting to other horizons, to other missions. He'd enjoyed the few moments he'd spent with the Major, but their brief dinner had only served to establish contact. The real work would begin the following day at dawn, with a private briefing followed by a meeting that the Kurdish leaders would attend.

Nothing much would happen there, and the Major would undoubtedly not have the time to accomplish his mission in two months. But it was still a better deal than the hunt for WMDs that Howard had been taking part in since he'd come to Iraq. The consensus among all the reports was that the weapons had existed, but they had long been stowed safely away in Syria.

The hundreds of liters of deadly gas and other chemical and biological weapon stocks that had been developed by the Iraqi researchers could only have vanished into thin air inside the minds of the liberal opinion-makers and the European governments.

But the administration lacked proof, and if Iraq was vast enough that some underground remainders could exist, there was no doubt that the Ba'athist regime had forged an alliance with its Syrian counterpart in this matter.

Beck had consequently been thanked for his failure by way of this pre-retirement mission.

He fell asleep thinking that the two months to come would certainly give him enough time to get back into tennis, or at least jogging. Despite himself, he was envious of the Major's figure…

The sudden brake, coupled with his driver's curse, startled him awake. The two soldiers had already seized their handguns. Through the windshield, Beck could make out the dark shape of a truck that was stopped across the middle of the road.

"What's going on?"

"That heap of junk is blocking our passage."

The two armored vehicles had already gotten into a combat position, machine guns on stand-by. The driver of the first vehicle, head poking out the door, was swearing a blue streak in Arabic at the truck driver.

There was enough time for Beck to take in the shitty accent and the clumsy syntax, as well as a road sign indicating that they'd gone seven kilometers outside of Erbil. A short flash lit up the night, then a second, followed by two explosions.

The deflagration lifted the first armored vehicle, while the Major's car litteraly took flight. A spray of glass shards and metal debris rained down on a scene that was suddenly lit up like the midday sky.

Beck's windshield shattered into pieces that embedded themselves into the faces of the driver and the soldier posted in the front seat. By some stroke of luck, he was untouched. Orders rang out, drowned out by cries.

The counter from the second armored car was immediate, and the hard staccato of its machine gun soon muffled the roar of the flames and the shrieks of pain. The truck driver started dancing, while his bullet-riddled vehicle was sinking onto its punctured tires.

Out of sheer reflex, throwing caution to the wind, Howard immediately surged out of his car to rush towards the carcass of Sutton's SUV, now turned into an inferno. There was nothing he could do. The terrorists, who'd undoubtedly already disappeared behind the multitude of dunes out in the desert, had been aware of their target, and they hadn't missed.

Beck gave the order for them to stop shooting. There was no other ranking officer to escort him. In a matter of seconds, everything had come crashing down.

His mission. Sutton's career. And that of the journalist who, a few minutes earlier, had made the worst choice of his young life.

The message kept displaying at steady intervals. Given the nature of the work in progress, this was beginning to feel like a wisecrack. The wind was blowing against the double-glazed tinted windows, and from this height, the New York City lights no longer shone out.

April 24th. This is the first day of the rest of your life. Be happy!

Irked, Gregory Cheston pushed a button, and the message vanished.

The first day of the rest of my life… Who on Earth could have come up with something that stupid?

The news of Len Sutton's death had landed on his desk just as he'd been about to head out and up to his rooms a couple dozen feet higher. It was two o'clock in the morning, and since then, the computer had been churning massive amounts of data, analyzing military records by the tens of thousands, and enjoying a level of access to that type of information that the Pentagon could hardly even dream of.

The death of that officer, fallen in the line of duty in Iraq, was a statistical data point for the military, a tragedy for his family, but most especially an ugly setback for the organization that Cheston was in charge of.

Gregory Cheston cursed the military regulations that had constrained him to postpone hiring the Major by two months. Without this matter of an early retirement, he'd never have taken the risk that had now directly resulted in a need to replace such an invaluable element.

He got up, and his huge steps carried him across his expansive office with its picture window overlooking Manhattan. This was his routine. The way he thought. All he'd have had to do was slink into his private elevator and he could have performed his routine up in his apartment, located two floors above, but he subconsciously felt the need to pace this office from one end to the other. Be at the heart of his empire.

Down below, across forty-five stories, a multitude of computing centers assembled the daily entries from three multinationals in the chemical, electronics, and weapons industries. The staff, handpicked carefully, was accustomed to an impersonal and paranoid setting, while the day and night teams came in one after the next.

Civilian dress required, no outwardly distinctive marks, everyone knowing their teammates but no-one beyond that. The biometric scanners that acted as keycards made any foreign ingress impossible. No visit, be it organized or off-the-cuff, was authorized.

This definitive fact was all the more amazing considering that this didn't involve a bunker in the middle of a desert, but instead a harmless office building with its foundations implanted among all the others in Manhattan. The entryway was done in genuine Carrara marble and displayed the three companies' logos on a polished copper plaque, plain as could be. The main one: E.C.TRONICS.

A huge reception lobby lead to a fleet of elevators that worked by groups of floors. Nothing unusual there. All the office buildings on the island worked by the same system.

All the same, this prevented the staff on the lower stories from crossing paths with their colleagues farther up...

After long minutes' straining, the computer finally wrapped up its task. Cheston requested a print-out, and a hundred and eighteen-page report landed on the carved ebony desk with legs that sank voluptuously into an oversized Baluchi carpet. This part of the building was completely out of the reach of mere mortals, and all the more so to the staff occupying the lower floors. An elevator led up to it straight from the basement.

The contents of the report represented a summary of the files collected by the computer. The first twenty-seven pages compiled a list of names of diverse national origins, all followed by one simple mark: "Negative."

Next came another series of names, accompanied by short biographies. A brief perusal of this second list was enough to reveal that each of the identified individuals was a decorated officer in his country's armed forces, and boasted an impeccable service record. The better part of them had been highly decorated in combat.

To conclude each summary, the computer had been content to issue one single, enigmatic remark: "Outside the scope."

The names were listed alphabetically, spanning thousands of miles from one row to the next. Moscowitz came before Mulligan, the information regarding ensign Tzi-Xiao of the Chinese People's Army followed the biographical details of Commandant Thibault.

But it was the final sheaves alone that justified the scope of the data dredging, the capacity to compute and centralize deployed by the organization that had devised this service. Sixty pages were devoted to just three men. A Swede, a Chilean, and a Frenchman.

Gregory Cheston paused a beat before grabbing his phone. A female voice answered.

"The computer's given us three," he said.

"I know, I got the same. Don't forget what you promised."

Cheston sighed. Sadly, he knew all too well. The result of a moment of weakness. But it was too late to back out.

"So, have you made your choice?"

"Of course. Can you extract the Frenchman's file for me?"

He might have known. But he'd still held out hope.

"And here I'd thought maybe the Swede…"

"Don't backtrack on me. *You promised…*"

That girlish little voice, tacked on after the husky tones of an ailing young woman… Cheston had never been able to resist.

"And besides, I like the French guy's nickname!"

Beyond the storage and analysis capabilities of a machine built to emotionlessly evaluate a choice on the basis of abstract psychological data reduced to a simple numerical formula, the charismatic power of a nickname had just cast the decisive vote in a decision that was going to upend the lives of numerous human beings.

According to that same report, the incident that stood at the origin of that nickname had occurred in Chad, in an extreme life or death situation. But no board of inquiry had managed to rule on any sort of recurring propensity for cannibalism.

Chapter 2

Juliette was stretched out across the bed, her ankle anchoring the bedsheet that was mostly spilled onto her clothes on the floor. Her body was moist. The fluttering, dying light of a candle was casting shadows on her pale, pale skin, like a shadow theater playing between the folds and wrinkles of the pillowcase.

Despite her unaffected pose, there was a sense of sophistication to it that made her nakedness feel demure, as though there was something of this showcased figure still left to uncover. Scarcely audible, the final notes of Rachmaninoff's *Piano Concerto n° 2* faded into nothing on the turntable.

Theo, she thought with a smile, had a gift for making the least-original of scenarios blood-stirring, and she caught herself yet again savoring these precious moments, where the two of them were able to turn the banal into an inexhaustible tenderness. She felt good.

The shower was running in the bathroom. She was usually the first to get up while Theo tended to doze off. But when their enjoyment of each other had been vigorous and unbridled, like tonight, she preferred to stay like this, with the memory of his flesh still lodged deeply inside her loins. She hardly moved, for fear that this feeling, sweeter as it was than love, might disappear. Her skin still tingled from it.

She ventured a hand downwards, was fast frustrated by her fading desire, and just as quickly gave up on the idea of stoking her passion back into being. If the years of their marriage had dulled neither their chemistry nor their faith in one another, the routine of a shared existence, as enjoyable as it may have been, had gotten the better of their "second round."

Theo came back into the room, still dripping, a towel wrapped around his waist. He walked around the bed to rifle through his clothes, carefully stacked on a chair, as he always did. Eyes at half-mast, Juliette scrutinized him as he moved around the room. Still in shape, she mused as she looked his figure over. A tiny hint of a paunch, but passable. If only he'd start doing some kind of sport...

"What are you looking for?"

He smiled, not looking at her.

"I knew you weren't really sleeping."

"If it's a cigarette you're rooting around for, you know the rule…"

"Yeah, I know. We have been married seven years, honey… Ah, there it is…"

With a triumphant gesture, Theo wrested a small package out of the pocket of his jacket. Wrapped in a pink ribbon, the object had the shape of a box and was barely bigger than a couple inches each way. Juliette felt her cheeks heat. She blushed at the slightest hint of emotion.

"Is that for me? But… why…?"

Without a warning, Theo threw himself backwards with his full weight, landing in the middle of the bed and moving to cuddle his head into the hollow of Juliette's shoulder. The move made the towel fall to the floor, leaving him completely naked. But Juliette couldn't stop staring at the little object her husband was waving in front of her face, clearly a hasty wrapping job by his hand.

"Nothing outstanding, don't get excited," he let out suddenly. "It's the…"

His gaze caught the mounting excitement in Juliette's eyes. Her flushed cheeks. In a second, as an icy hand began gripping his nape, he realized what an enormous blunder he was committing. The date. Juliette would never, ever, ever-ever forgive him…

Obviously, it was their wedding anniversary tomorrow, and if he'd wanted to do a nice thing for her, he was now a second away from Juliette discovering that the box could not have been farther from containing the jewelry that she undoubtedly expected. What was more, it wasn't exactly a box. And the wrapping, done in his style, should have certainly alerted her to it…

"It's not… just… I mean… I didn't forget about tomorrow, but this is…"

Too late. With a fevered hand, Juliette had already torn through the ribbon and wrapping paper.

"You told me you needed one," Theo stated sheepishly. "Your old one had stopped getting a good signal…"

Juliette, looking puzzled, was taking in a mobile phone that displayed the logo of the company her husband worked for. A company gift. And not a top brand, either.

"Tomorrow," mumbled Theo, "I made reservations for…"

"Don't worry about it, it's great, thanks."

Juliette got up to take her own shower.

At around four in the morning, a soft noise woke Theo. He pricked up his ears, listening for the creaking of the hardwood floor beneath the bedroom carpet. As discreet as the footsteps of a faltering and ungainly small animal. Theo smiled and pretended to be asleep. In no time at all, a tiny, warm body slid between the sheets, right between him and Juliette. He waited for his daughter to get into her resting position, then spoke to her in an amused and fake-irate voice.

"I thought you weren't going to come out from your bedroom tonight," he murmured.

Making as though she hadn't heard him, with that talent that all small children have to skirt around awkward situations, Katia whispered to him,

"You and mommy did weird stuff."

Theo caught the tip of her nose between his thumb and forefinger and twisted lightly.

"Who taught you to talk like that, you little monster. Don't tell me your mom did."

Her answer was made of pure false innocence.

"No, daddy. You did."

Theo grabbed one of his daughter's plaits and pulled on it gently.

"Well, don't ever repeat what I say. And now shush, you're going to wake your mom up."

"But I'm sure you guys did weird stuff."

With that, she burrowed under the pillow with a self-satisfied chuckle. Three minutes later, she was asleep. Theo sighed.

"And to think, she's only turned six!"

The day started with a drizzle, despite the weather forecast announcing a late but sure start to spring.

Paris was gloomy this late March. Theo's only solace was that the rain was preventing him from keeping a promise he'd made Katia. Obviously, the prospect of teaching her how to rollerblade on the Trocadero plaza as soon as the weather turned warm was almost urging him to wish for a long winter.

That would teach him to play Poker Slapjack (a card game similar to War where the loser owed the winner a forfeit of their choice).

"You can put away your camera," he told Juliette as he looked at the flower boxes dripping out on the balcony. "Today isn't the day you're going to immortalize me making a fool of myself."

Juliette was clearing the remainders of breakfast from the kitchen table. Clad in a T-shirt and boxer shorts, she looked ravishing, her natural allure only enhanced by the tousle that a night's sleep had added to her curly hair.

"It's only a matter of time," she said. "You don't actually think she's going to forgive your gaming debts just like that..."

"Come on, though," Theo exclaimed indignantly, "can you picture me in roller blades? At my age!"

Laughing, Juliette came and cuddled up against him.

"My decrepit old husband… You should have just not taught her how to play!"

"She's lucky, and besides, she cheats. Just, whatever you do, don't get her up. As soon as she sees it's raining, I'll be roped into a PlayStation tournament."

Juliette walked away from him and closed the pantry, pushing hard against the squeaky door. There was a soothing blandness to their perfectly ordered apartment that belied the classy building that it occupied.

That was all down to her husband's slightly extravagant side. He'd opted for appearance over comfort, and chosen this three-room apartment for the nice neighborhood, despite its smaller surface. Zip code over square footage. With how much she hated messes, she spent hours and hours outside her job trying to keep some tidiness in their interior design. Not the easiest task with a lively and imaginative little girl.

Pensive and smiling, Juliette went on, as though to herself.

"She's good at everything. And I'm so proud of her for defeating a former sniper."

Leaning forward slightly, Juliette teased her husband through the curtain of her hair, then brushed back a stubborn lock.

"That's gotta sting, right?"

"Let me remind you, I was *never* a sniper… And besides, it doesn't count when you're shooting aliens!"

Mechanically, he grabbed a pack of cigarettes that languished on the corner of the table, then thought the better of it when Juliette met his gaze.

"I think Katia is even more gifted than I am, if I'm honest. Without that stupid military service episode, I never would have known a thing. She's got a real knack for ballistics. Have you ever seen her throw a candy wrapper anywhere but in the bin? I wonder where she gets that from…"

"Old grandpa Collin, without a doubt," Juliette replied. "I always thought your grandfather's piercing gaze and his dexterity with gadgets were amazing. Circumstances must have prevented him from uncovering his talents. The way you did."

"Fat lotta use I'm making of them!"

Juliette wiped her hands with a dishtowel and took a seat.

"At least you have the ability to impress your daughter on a gaming console."

"Without a question," Theo rejoined. "But that's where it stops."

"No, you dummy. You're an amazing mathematician, a super gifted computer scientist, and a pretty great husband for your advanced age… And if you keep that up, I'm going into greater detail on just what it is you do real well, and it's gonna make me get racy."

Theo, who'd come closer to her, stepped around the chair…

"About that, what if, instead of talking about it…"

"Morning daddy, morning mommy."

Their blonde little slip of a girl picked that moment to appear in the doorway, her eyes slumberous.

"Daddy, are you doing weird stuff to mommy again?"

"Theo, do you see what kind of an image of us you're giving our daughter," Juliette said indignantly, extricating herself from him. "And how about you start by watching your language!"

Katia leapt up onto a chair, sat down cross-legged, and grabbed a spoon that had been left on the table.

"So, how about that breakfast?"

This time, Juliette got mad, all while tamping down on the urge to laugh instilled by this naïve caricature of Theo's.

She administered a quick smack to his hand, which incidentally had no effect.

Theo shot a surreptitious wink his daughter's way and got a mischievous smile in return. He tried to imagine the incredible woman she promised to become, with every bit of objectivity he could muster.

She was cute as a button. Her slightly upturned nose, a Collin feature, gave her still-babyish face a softness that the penetrating, almost burning light of her gaze invalidated with irony. At six years of age, Katia blended the disarming charm of a little girl and the feminine impishness of that first brush with coquetry.

It had taken one lecture from his wife as she rebuffed one of his amorous advances for the child to remember the expression that she'd used. "Stop it! What if she wakes up? She's gonna think you're doing weird stuff to me." Katia hadn't been asleep. And since then, she'd shown that she knew how to place words in their appropriate contexts...

Certain that her father's unblinking gaze betrayed some deep thoughts that she was the subject of, she bestowed him with another bewitching smile.

"Say, daddy, do you think it's gonna be nice out today?"

Juliette plopped a giant bowl of steaming hot chocolate in front of the girl.

As she did so, Theo noticed the grimace she sent his way. Around the child, he and his wife had come up with a sort of coded "gaze language." For a long time now, eyes meeting coupled with a slight smile meant, "You're about to get suckered. Let's see you get yourself out of this one..."

"I don't think so, sweetheart," he replied. "It's raining."

He leaned down to give her a kiss.

"The rain won't stop me from getting the paper," he quickly added. "Do you want me to get you a magazine?"

Katia thought intently, her forehead furrowed. Then, gesturing expansively, as though she were counting them on her fingers, she started listing an impressive amount of titles, complete with order of preference, and covers to steer clear of – because she had those already.

Outside, the rain had just stopped.

The first time he'd seen Juliette, during a student party, Theo had briefly felt dazed by her scintillating femininity, by the perfection of her features, but most especially by her naturalness, her slightly lost air, before he'd seen her disappear...

He'd been in his final year at the Supélec; she'd been majoring in civilization history. By all accounts pursuits that had no reason to bring them closer together, from either a geographical or a theoretical perspective. But in the heart of Paris, over in the Latin Quarter, parties were run without discrimination.

A friend of Theo's, the son of a divorced Belgian diplomat, would gladly put his father's staff apartment at the disposal of all the different partiers who made up his inner circle. A computing student just like Theo, meant for a career in engineering same as him, the diplomat's son nevertheless lived far off the campus in Gif sur Yvette, where most of the partygoers came in from.

With the consular officer gone one out of every four weeks, his huge residence with its balconies overlooking the Jardin du Luxembourg, one of Paris's rare green lungs, had reached a well-deserved level of fame within student circles.

Juliette had come alone. All night, she'd seemed to be bored. Holding herself a little back from the other students, she'd favored everyone who approached her with brief, subtle smiles, without getting any more involved. Fearing that he'd strike out if he approached her, Theo had gone after another girl that evening, one who'd been less pretty, less distant, apparently easier.

He would learn, years on, that Juliette hadn't looked at him at all, hadn't even noticed his presence. But that was one of those things that solid couples confided in each other. It took time to work up to that sort of a confession. For just as he'd forgotten her, destiny was seeing to it that he'd get a new chance.

Born into a family of modest means, Theo had been in his mid-teens when he'd lost his father. Nothing had hinted, an hour earlier, that this man in his prime would succumb to a heart attack in the street, right in the middle of a conversation with one of his coworkers. Theo had felt that loss like a sort of divine punishment, without being able to define its cause, and he'd shrunk in on himself in an expectant, self-rejecting attitude. The only outcome of that had been a series of academic failures, up until he'd been called to serve the flag.

At nineteen, with no college education to his name, there had been no escape for him. His several months in the service had been a shock. Not violent by nature, rather retreating and lacking in self-assurance, his nightmares had since made him relive the trauma of that trek through a warrior world, where some quirk of fate had made him a hero for a day.

As soon as gotten he'd his freedom back, he'd picked his studies back up with an unimaginable frenzy. His last gift from his father before he'd passed away had been an old laptop, which Theo had spent hours and hours on, hoping he'd lose himself and forget even as he dove into the twists and turns of computer code. That was it; he was going to be a computer engineer.

Fortune smiled down on him when he was revising for his baccalaureate while taking long-distance classes. A start-up was looking for a programmer to intern with their graphics department. That same day, in late June, Theo learned that he'd passed his scientific baccalaureate, the hardest of the versions, with honors, and that the start-up where he'd spent the past six months climbing up the ranks had nailed its IPO. The only thing left for him to do was to revise for the Supélec admission tests, which he would soon pass, the first step in his upward spiral.

Two years later, the company, where he'd now become a part-time software developer, got acquired by a Japanese group, and would carry out massive layoffs as part of a restructuring and relocation plan. As compensation, Theo was granted just enough money to wrap up his studies. Just barely enough…

A classified ad had put Theo along with other students on a movie set. The producers needed a significant number of young extras, and those who got cast were summoned to the Porte de Saint-Cloud, at the Trois Obus café. They then got loaded up into several vehicles and dropped off in the park of a castle in the Chevreuse valley.

Some of the hopefuls lost their brand-new calling over the course of their six-hour wait in the freezing cold, during which time no-one seemed to spare them a thought. All the while, the film crew had been feverishly carrying out several barbaric rites, going from the complicated creation of a mount meant to support one of the cameras and its operator, all the way to the incessant to-and-fro of one of the "heads" who, exposure meter in hand, had kept metering every inch of set that had a chance of being in the frame. Every ten feet, he exclaimed "That's over!" or "That's under!", then he ordered a few extra K's with ample gesticulations.

Inside the castle, the director and the main cast remained out of sight.

Snubbed by the "professional" extras, sidelined by a too-busy technical crew, not a groupie by temperament, it didn't take long for Theo to move away from an ebullience he felt a stranger to, his curiosity quenched by the long minutes spent in wait, hopping from foot to foot in the meager hope that he'd warm himself up.

At lunchtime, the sandwiches they handed out were gulped down in no time, there was still nothing coherent going on, and Theo was thinking that he'd clearly given them enough for the two hundred franks he was supposed to be paid.

He'd already moved pretty far away from the castle, the alleged filming location, and he was still hesitant on whether to disappear completely, not knowing how to get back to downtown Paris beyond taking the local train to Gif, when his attention was caught by a strange rustling and giggling. Behind a copse, a man wearing makeup and half-lidded eyes had rapturously abandoned himself to the doubtless just as made-up lips of a brunette in a hoodie. Their breaths drew strange spirals in the air, as though they were aflame, prone amid the dead leaves.

Mechanically, Theo raised himself on the tips of his toes. It barely took him a second to realize he embodied the typical voyeur. Two hate-filled gazes pierced him as he stumbled, trying to turn himself around.

"The hell's that whack job doing?"

Swiftly readjusting himself, the actor took a few giant steps around the copse and hurled himself at Theo. He was well over six feet. A hulking, meaty mountain topped with a puce face and a pair of steaming nostrils.

"So, we like to peep? We enjoying the show? You don't have anything else to do?"

Before he could even reply, Theo got treated to a powerful push, so forceful he felt it rattle right through his spine before he fell backwards like a felled tree. Seen from below, the man seemed even more imposing. He burst out laughing, all his anger melted away.

"Do you know what you're sat in? A pile of shit!"

Theo made to get up.

"Stay there. Sit. And stew."

Satisfied with himself for his so-called witticism, the actor laughed uproariously. Behind the copse, the girl had made a furtive escape. Slightly dazed, Theo tried to apologize.

"How was I supposed to know..."

"Jimmy! Who are you tormenting now?"

A feminine voice had cut in on them, amused but full of authority. Turning his face, Theo could see a rather pretty figure in slim jeans, and he felt all the more pathetic. The girl came closer and held a hand out to him.

"Don't worry," she said. "Women are the only thing Jimmy here fears. Except for when they're busy worshipping him."

Theo once again gave himself over to his amazement. Beneath a mop of blonde hair, he recognized the young woman from the student party.

His smile beaming, Jimmy went away in search of his friend with the welcoming lips.

"I dunno if he's your boyfriend, but he's in deep shit," he said as he turned his back on them.

Theo got up.

"Did he hurt you?"

"No, I'm fine, I mostly just look like an idiot."

Feeling shabbier and shabbier, Theo dusted himself off with a sweeping, falsely nonchalant gesture. A few leaves came loose, while others stuck wetly to him. Recalling the actor's last words, he contorted himself suddenly, wanting to check the state of his pants.

"Don't worry. You fell just to the side. Not only is he a thug, but he always makes the dumbest jokes."

She flashed a row of neat, straight teeth, a warm smile to go with those eyes that sparkled with tenderness.

"And I actually can't even stand him, either!"

Theo smiled back at her. A sudden burst of activity on set had made them both turn around. The whole entire crew had just gathered around the director.

"I guess we have to go back," Theo said.

"Not me. My job is done."

"You're not an extra?"

"Nope. I just give the costume designer a hand during rush days. It's kind of an internship."

Theo felt his heart soar. He looked at her watching him and, yeah, no doubt about it, there was a hint of amusement there. She gave off this kind of soft resolve, an eager warmth, but at the same time a very slight aloofness, like a veil over her laughing eyes and welcoming smile. The flawless ambiguity of the mysterious woman, unattainable and yet so near. He heard himself ask her, only to instantly feel immeasurably trite:

"Now that you've saved my life, how would you like to come with me to the nearest café? I have to clean myself up. And we could get ourselves warmed up."

She wavered.

"Weren't you here for a job?"

"They'll make do… That charmer, Jimmy, made me rehearse my scene, and I have a feeling I'm not made for the part."

For a split second, the veil lifted from the young woman's eyes. They left the frenzied set behind, but Theo didn't regret it for one moment.

That was the last time he had the opportunity to be on a movie set. Her name was Juliette, she loved Rachmaninoff's works, and in particular his second piano concerto.

Chapter 3

Despite the dismal quality of the video feed, the visceral fear submerging the prisoner was striking. His legs lifted by a gnarled rope with one end tied around a ceiling beam and the other end around his ankles, he swung upside down with his hands tied behind his back, hanging like nothing more than a chicken.

A shadow moved into the camera's field of view, briefly obstructing the scene. As it moved toward the prisoner, the figure took shape. The image focused in on his back, clad in a beige tunic. A head adorned with a balaclava. A fist gripping a knife.

The man in the balaclava came to a stop level with the prisoner and grabbed him by the hair to bare his neck. The rest of it only lasted an instant. The blade glinted like a flash before disappearing from sight.

All too clearly, a furious cry immediately drowned out the agonized cry, and was picked up by several men who were out of the frame.

"Allah U'Akbar! Allah U'Akbar!"

Howard Beck was still chewing on his sandwich. He suddenly realized he was eating, and spat out the last mouthful into his hand.

"I warned you, it's not a pretty sight," said the tech from in front of his monitor.

Over on the screen, the video kept playing. The makeshift cameraman had zoomed in on the tormented man's face. Beck pressed the space bar to freeze the frame, persuaded that pleading, panicked gaze was searching out for him personally.

"It's the first time they've hung one by his feet," noted the tech. "It's gotta be some special message."

"It's always a special message when it's meant for us," ground out. Beck

It was three o'clock in the morning at Langley. Howard, on duty that night, knew what was left for him to do. First, he needed to verify the information;

then, wake the agents in the Central Asian divisions and the NCTC; and lastly, get a report ready for them asap.

It would then fall to them to prepare their own summary reports to send out to the heads of the two Directorates, Intelligence and Operations, who would in turn address memos to their commanding officers, the Director of the CIA and the DNI[3].

It was not to be a tranquil night at Langley. But tranquility had lost all meaning for Beck since he'd gotten back from Iraq, even if his bosses, following an assessment of his trauma and despite his protests, had pulled him from the field while granting him a promotion. He grabbed a cardboard folder.

"Here," the tech said, holding out a cup. "You forgot your coffee."

"Thanks." Beck grimaced. "But I'm using this thing as an ashtray."

The tech's eyes went wide as saucers. Same as with every other administrative building, smoking was formally forbidden at Langley, in the daytime as at night.

"Only in my dreams," added Beck, tossing him a wink.

He spared a brief thought to the program he'd set for himself once he was off-duty the following day, though he could muster no regret. It was already Friday. He'd been banking on a weekend of lounging around and working out. The Major's memory was still with him, and he saw it as paying him a tribute that he'd managed to gradually tone his body. Naturally, he could have never held a candle to Sutton. But his physical appearance had improved dramatically.

What was the name of that hotel in Maryland where he'd booked a room? Some horseback-riding, the shooting range, the sauna, the swimming pool, a nap, some DVDs, a bit of jogging… and Jenny at his side. A one-nighter, certainly. But he'd taken pleasure at the thought of spending forty-eight hours away from it all, in the company of a pretty, young woman he'd be seeing for the second time. He'd have to cancel, now.

Before leaving his desk, Beck slid a copy of the video into the cardboard folder he took with him. The only writing on the folder: Operation Buridan.

The start of this new mission had overlapped with the Iran crisis. As if the United States didn't already have their hands full on two fronts, between Afghanistan and Iraq. Here came their sworn enemy, the most totalitarian and aggressive government on the planet, outside of North Korea, expressing an underlying will to enter the nuclear arms race.

Beck had just come back from Iraq, and he'd been denied the coveted position of permanent delegate to the embassy in Tel Aviv. His supervisor had recalled a key detail in the agent's file: before he'd taken an interest in the Oriental languages, Beck had done his undergraduate in Physics.

---

3   *Director of National Intelligence*: The head of the American intelligence community. The head of the CIA was also the director of (the whole of) the intelligence community, the DCI: *Director of Central Intelligence*. The two positions were split following the *Intelligence Reform and Terrorism Prevention Act* in 2004.

32

"Tel Aviv? What the hell do you think you'd be doing over there, pal?"

Beck had had a hard time admitting that, after his stay in Iraq and the overly long time he'd spent in the Arab world, he wanted nothing more than an assignment in his favorite part of the world, if somewhere where his immediate environment wouldn't have him only been pretending to be a sympathizer. As though he'd been reading his mind, his boss had gone on.

"Besides, if you like Tel Aviv, you'd actually be useful to them by taking on the Iran case."

The obstinacy with which the president of the former Persia was pursuing his ambition to set up a uranium enrichment program was an incredibly serious threat. According to a top-secret file, Ahmadinejad belonged to an Islamic sect that believed in the destruction of the world as a harbinger of the Last Judgement. A paradisal afterlife that only true believers could attain, and that he wanted to hasten the coming of.

"Next to this guy, Hitler was a cakewalk." So the whispers went in the CIA hallways. "At least he didn't have TV or the internet to broadcast his views."

It was in those same hallways, in the ingenious minds of the Special Activities Division, that Operation Buridan had seen the light of day.

The key difference between the uranium used in nuclear powerplants and military-grade uranium resides in its level of enrichment with isotope 235. The ratio of U235 in the rods used in non-military reactors sits at around 12 percent, whereas the fissile material intended for nuclear warheads is enriched to 93 percent.

The issue, then, was simple: whoever claimed they wanted to pursue nuclear development towards peaceful ends could all too easily, with a few adjustments and a bit of patience, divert this power to military uses, all while covering that endeavor up.

When it came to the Muslim world, Europe and the UN were harder to bring around than a cuckolded husband. When it came to the latter, at least, nothing was more effective than a good photo of the hotel and the lover.

The operation had all the earmarks of a classic sting. Since Ahmadinejad claimed he wanted to gain nuclear capabilities for non-military use, the best thing to do was catch him red-handed. And, towards that end, to organize the delivery of certain all-too-coveted items to his Pasdaran.

While Beck was busy laying down the fieldwork, the Agency's best strategic minds had to concoct a whole fake network of illegal fissile material from scratch. Nowhere but in the former USSR could they have found nuclear weaponry apt to scamper. That improbable connection had been the most difficult to set up.

Next, they'd needed to recruit. Candidates had been difficult to rustle up. They'd needed to speak Russian at the very least, if not Farsi also. They'd had to have spent at least six months at "the farm," the CIA training ground, and needed to be able to withstand several forms of torture, including the worst of them all, which was physical torture, despite all wide-held beliefs to the contrary.

They also needed to know how to ride a donkey, since that would be their ride and their means of carrying the fake nuclear weapons from buttresses of Kopet Dag to the Khorasan Province, beyond the Iranian borders.

That part, of course, had not been Beck's to manage.

The doors to the secure conference room opened with a sucking hiss. The Agency's bigshots made their way out one after the other, all of them wearing the same shuttered expression. Howard Beck fell into step with Paul Murphy, his new supervisor, the head of the NCTC, the CIA's antiterrorist unit. The meeting had been wrapped up in record time, which had taken Howard by complete surprise. He waited until the bigwigs were far enough away before he started grilling Murphy, who answered him without breaking stride. His past in the military had left him with a pace that was hard to follow.

"You didn't have much to go on, to call a meeting at this level. What'd you expect?"

"One of our guys getting hanged upside down and bled out like a pig may not be much in this day and age, but I was still hoping for more responsiveness."

"Howard," inquired Murphy, "how long ago did they give you the Buridan file?"

"Before you got here, Sir. Soon as I got back from Iraq. Going on 16 months now."

"And did you know those two men well?"

"We weren't close or anything. Doesn't mean I'm not the one who's gonna have to notify their next of kin."

They'd arrived at a new restricted access area, one Beck didn't have the clearance for. Murphy's office was at the other end of it. A glass cage that the push of a simple button could instantly render opaque. He shook his head and put a hand on Beck's shoulder.

"End of the road for you, unfortunately. I'll see to it that you get another file. As for the next of kin, don't worry about it, I'll take care of it."

"That can't happen," Howard said obstinately. "Tradition demands that…"

"Let's set tradition aside this time. Operation Buridan ended in tragedy. I'll put together an investigative committee and get in touch with the next of kin. That's how the Director wants it done, at any rate…"

Inwardly, Howard shrugged his shoulders. If the Director himself wanted it that way, it would happen if the Earth stopped spinning. Just like that, the chain of command superseded all other considerations.

He suddenly felt tired. Exhausted, even. It was almost like he was cursed. All it took was for him to get assigned to a mission, and it ended in failure and tragedy. Murphy was most likely right. He might as well drop Buridan and everything it entailed. To his shame, a sense of relief went through him at the thought of dodging the difficult task of notifying the families.

As per Agency standards, his next op would be even more run of the mill. Soon, if this went on, he'd be assigned to the building's maintenance and sanitation services.

There was no time for him to get one word out. A small, pudgy, balding man had shot out of the elevator and made a beeline for Murphy, hand stretched out.

"Took you long enough," commented Murphy.

The new arrival briefly took Beck in, looking like a dealer evaluating new horse flesh. Then he turned his attention to the head of the NCTC, answering him.

"So did your meeting. They told me about it. Well, I wasn't about to cool my heels in your office…"

Beck finally managed to put a name to the face bearing the man's tormented and unfriendly features. Joseph Feldman. If the guy had recognized him in turn, he didn't let it show. A brief nod of Murphy's head put an end to their conversation, then he escorted Feldman into the high-security area, looking just as sullen.

Howard had happened to cross paths with Feldman multiple times, back when he'd been on assignment in the Middle East. A chameleon man, as the Agency liked to call this type of person. Affable, all things considered. A man whose business acumen had enabled him to infiltrate the highest military levels in Baghdad. Feldman had initially been recruited for his command of Farsi and Arabic, as well as for his skills as a manager and negotiator. He knew how to use his rough appearance to dissimulate the avarice of the businessman that he was above all else.

With him as their go-between, the US government had aided Iraq in its war against Iran, by supplying it with tactical weaponry and munitions manufacturing technology. That was an entirely different time, and some within the Agency still spoke with disgust about the cynicism of the Reagan administration, which had fixed it to simultaneously supply Iran, through their main ally, Israel.

The war between Iraq and Iran had caused over a million deaths.

People here still remembered the Iranian children sent barefoot into the minefields, their key to Paradise hanging around their necks. In the Muslim world, a child's life, assessed in terms of potential damage dealt to the enemy, was worth a lot less than a man's, and perhaps even than a woman's. They'd leapt onto the American mines, mixed in with the improvised Iraqi ones, while the Shiites fought back in the name of Allah, hurling U.S.-made munitions that they thought they'd gotten from the USSR.

By some miracle, Feldman hadn't been caught in the Irangate blowback.

As a matter of fact, he'd even climbed higher up the Agency ranks, all while keeping his official role as a wheeler and dealer who was well-versed in the trade of weapons and military supplies.

Despite the feigned smile that Feldman wore while in his presence, the thought of seeing him maneuver on US soil had left Beck with a feeling of deep discomfort. The same feeling had just come over him again. What business could Feldman possibly have with the head of the NCTC?

The elevator doors opened to reveal a young analyst and a smiling girl that Beck had never seen before, probably someone assigned to data entry. The two only stopped kidding around when he stepped inside the car with them, and they greeted him deferentially. Beck took his attention off them and dove back into his thoughts.

Going by the latest intelligence gathered on the situation, the ECHELON program had picked up the transmission of the execution video of one of the three agents involved in operation Buridan, video that had been making the rounds online for going on four hours, now. The NSA had seen fit to instantly transfer a copy of it over to Langley, while their own teams were trying to analyze the video and follow its trail back to the machine that had uploaded it, somewhere in the Middle East.

Another thing they were up to speed on, thanks to the latest satellite imagery, was the movement of their mule-back procession along the mountain ridges, towards the Iranian border.

The three agents must have been intercepted either a little before or a little after the border. But with no-one claiming responsibility for the act and given the ritualistic nature of their murders, it all pointed to his agents not getting arrested by either soldiers or border patrol.

Granted, the Pasdaran, the Iranian Revolutionary Guards, were no strangers to kidnapping and hostage-taking operations, but solely on the other side of the Iranian border. The intel was already six hours old, and nobody had the slightest lead as to the perpetrators of this massacre.

More worrying still, given that the operation had been set up in keeping with the separation principle – only one department involved at a time – how had Operation Buridan been exposed? The question was twisting Beck into knots as he made his way to the offices of the Central Asia division. Wouldn't that make Paul Murphy and the big boss himself just blow their tops, if they knew how near and dear to his heart Buridan was.

Beck had barely made it past the entryway into his office before he was accosted by a tall, lanky guy brandishing a stack of papers.

"Sir, there's been a new development. The NIO[4] has just sent these images over. A Crystal took them, precisely three hours ago."

Frank Hoffa, the chief IPA operator, cleared a corner of the table with a single sweep of his hand, then unfolded the images captured by the KH-12 satellite. Despite the phenomenal resolution of their eye in the sky, only an imaging specialist was capable of deciphering these photos. Of course, anyone could recognize an aerial view of an arid landscape. A couple bushes. And, as a layperson, nothing beyond.

Beck leaned over the print and waited for Hoffa's explanation.

"See here," he began, pointing his pen at a lighter area of the shot, "these two kind of rectangular areas?"

"Yeah. They look like boulders."

"At first sight, given their size, there'd be nothing setting them apart from plain old rocks…"

---

4 National Imagery Office.

Beck waited for the follow-up.

"Aside from their shape."

"Their shape?"

"Yes, sir. Look closer. For a start, both those "rocks" are rectangular, far too sharp-cornered. Wat's more, they're exactly the same size, even if it's not immediately noticeable in the photo."

"And you're concluding?"

"Well, they're not boulders. You're looking at what's left of two dummy SADMs."

"You're positive?" Beck went rigid.

"Yep. They left them where they were... You'll notice that they took their mules, though," said Hoffa, mockingly.

Beck paid that little shard of irony no mind. He'd already come to other conclusions. Theirs had been left where they were. His men could have fallen prey to plain old local scumbags, if it hadn't been for the video.

'They didn't even go to the trouble of hiding the SADMs, or even burying them...'

Except, of course, there was the video. So they were indeed dealing with terrorists. Ones with enough intel to root their guys out as US agents. And with enough familiarity with nuclear technology to tell a fake "briefcase" apart from the real thing. Which seemed unlikely to the point of impossibility, even for nuclear experts, without carrying out a thorough analysis of the briefcases' makeup and contents.

'They even had a bit of fluorescent paint smeared over on their bottoms, just enough to set off a rudimentary Geiger counter.'

"They should have hid them. At least to keep up appearances. They take out the three agents, but they leave the gear behind. Something doesn't add up in all this."

"I mean... when they figured out they'd gotten a bunch of duds, maybe they just..."

"If they'd thought they were getting played, they would have just shot them where they stood. It's obvious they're sending a message. And it's meant for us specifically."

"What exactly do you mean by meant for us specifically?"

"It's a local custom. They're messing with us!"

Beck hated admitting it to himself, but he was starting to seriously entertain the possibility of a leak.

In other words, a mole.

Chapter 4

Commander Meyrek landed at JFK on the fifteen-thirty hours Air France flight. He was discovering New York without excitement, though he still regretted being unable to stay for more than twenty-four hours. With a snowball's chance of being able to return for a long while.

The arrivals security check took place with a meticulous slowness that he wasn't used to, and he was forced to trundle along the corded-off areas alongside the three-hundred-odd other passengers that had been stuffed into the Airbus with him, all under the somewhat pitiless gaze of the TSA officers. Ever since nine-eleven, the entry requirements for the US had gotten considerably more stringent, and fingerprinting as well as photo-taking had become mandatory upon touching down on U.S. soil.

None of his identification papers bore mention of his rank in the French Army, which he'd only retired from four months ago.

He was already feeling the full effect of his jetlag. Few men had shaved during the flight. Economy class tended to haul more tourists than businessmen, and the non-resident aliens were manifesting their impatience in a markedly European way.

As unlike him as it was, Meyrek had given himself over to the neglect begotten by his travels. His cheeks were shadowed with grey. He was sorry that the need for his trip to be anonymous had to go hand in hand with this discomfort.

He cleared the security checkpoint and retrieved his suitcase.

There was no-one waiting for him at Arrivals. They'd set up a different kind of rendezvous.

His long military career had gotten him accustomed to these precautions, which generally stemmed from pure routine. A soldier did not travel first class. A retired officer did not drive around in a limo. And so it was without reservations that he took himself to the foot of the Rockefeller Center, where a cab driver with sketchy English dropped him off after a noisy trip in a car with shot suspensions and the stereo blasting Oriental music at full volume.

Meyrek took a seat on one of the benches loomed over by opulence, his mind empty, his battered suitcase set between his legs, just as instructed. An unbroken stream of yellow cabs trickled slowly before him, the traffic punctuated by the sound of honking horns. To his right as to his left, the same hot-dog, pretzel, drink, and assorted kebab vendors all boasted "allal" meat.

At nineteen-thirty hours – half-past one in the morning to his internal clock – he left his bench and slowly made his way to 6th Avenue, a couple blocks down. On the corner of 48th Street, a black limo, an unremarkable car in here the business capital of the world, slowed down to match his pace. He opened the door, slid into the cream leather seat.

Despite his perfectly honed reflexes, Meyrek was overcome by something like a flinch when he discovered the creature that was picking him up. It wasn't a midget. Nor was it a Lilliputian. The word dwarf would have described this simian character, had it not been for the fine, even features. The feet didn't reach the floor of the vehicle, and an enormous hump distended an abdomen clad in impeccably-tailored clothes.

Once he'd adjusted to the darkness inside the vehicle, Meyrek discovered with even more astonishment that it was a woman. The strange and unpredictable result of some genetic upheaval had brought an aberration into the world, a beauty in a grotesque hodgepodge. Eyes like two embers bore through him.

"Gotten over your shock yet?"

The voice was low, hoarse, like an imprint of suffering. Commander Meyrek didn't rise to it.

"Do you think all these precautions were really necessary?"

The creature – he could think of no other word to describe it – let out an ironic giggle.

"I'll leave you to imagine how discreet a meeting at the airport would have been. Besides, all these precautions do add a bit of spice to our jobs, wouldn't you say?"

The limo had just reached Central Park, and was now overtaking a row of multicolored carriages. Impassive, the horses were snorting one after the next, expelling vertical puffs of air from their nostrils and into the growing darkness.

"What am I to call you?" asked Meyrek. The midget wriggled in her seat.

"What everyone does. Marylin!"

She adopted a grotesque pose, one ripped right out of the covers of women's magazines, flinging an otherwise captivating smile towards Meyrek, which only deepened his unease. That was of course the intent.

"Well, what did you expect? Monstrous deformity goes hand in hand with obsequiousness and unquestioned allegiances. Remember your classics. You know, all those spy novels where the big bad antagonist inevitably wants to take over the world. Do you smoke?"

"No, thank you."

"Marylin" extracted a cigar from a case built into the armrest. She lit it with decadence, drawing on it with a slow blink.

Meyrek watched her silently. Suddenly, with a reptile agility, she darted out her arm and rammed the glowing tip into the commander's hand. He bit back a cry of pain, overcome with confusion. A fraction of a second went by; then, with a restrained motion, he ripped the cigar out of those pudgy fingers and rammed it in turn into the expensive leather interior of the luxury vehicle.

She burst into laughter.

"Good," she said. "Very good, commander. That's exactly the kind of style and class we need. You've passed this little test with flying colors, and I have to tell you, it was of my own doing. What do you think?"

"About?"

"About men who hit disabled people, by which of course I mean women. I really was expecting more violence… Ah, here we are!"

Distrustful, Meyrek silently stared at his wrists, holding himself rigid in preparation for another potential extra test. His gaze turned to the driver. But there was no way the guy could see them through the two-way mirror separating them. Not slowing down, the vehicle made its way through a security gate as it opened, and into a huge parking structure.

"I think you have such a funny nickname, commander. Maybe someday you'll tell me all about the glorious circumstances that bestowed it on you!"

"That must be written in my file," he retorted dryly.

"Marylin" swept a voracious gaze over him.

"Then you'll tell me all about the taste!"

The limo came to a stop on the third basement level. The door opened, revealing two men and a wheelchair. Marylin wriggled and writhed her way out.

The commander made to help her.

"No. Don't. You can see that neither of these men is moving. My legs work just fine, no matter how ashamed they are to be propping up this body."

Straining on her pudgy arms, the young woman arduously made her way to the wheelchair. Without a word, the two men flanked her while they waited on Meyrek. Under the lights of the parking garage, even Marylin's unspoiled face held something monstrous. Her very white skin had taken on a light greenish cast, as had the figures of her bodyguards. An acrid smell of disinfectant blended in with the odor of gasoline and exhaust fumes, putting Meyrek in a vaguely nauseated state.

"Oh, commander," she began. "Starting right now, since you've just set foot in this parking garage, you have a new rank. From now on, I'm going to have to start calling you Colonel."

"Those were the terms."

"Wait until you see your army!"

Marylin's laughter reverberated through the corridor. She turned her back on him, and the group moved away towards the elevators.

The ringing made him jump out of his skin. Crouched next to his desk, Theo Collin was trying to plug in a coffee maker that Juliette had gotten him. As usual, the espresso pods didn't match this brand of percolator.

He picked up.

"Theo, can you stop by my office toward the end of the afternoon?"

Nicolas Serry, the general manager of E.C.Tronics France, had an authoritative and refined tone of voice that Theo had come to know well since he'd been named manager of the international conglomerate's research department. Nonetheless, a crumb of a detail caught his attention. Serry only rarely called him by his first name.

"That should be doable."

"Great, then shall we say six thirty? Be there. And let your wife know you're gonna be home late tonight."

Coming from anybody else, tacking on that last bit would have sounded like a condescending show of politeness. Out of Nicolas Serry's mouth, there was nothing more to it than a preoccupation with crossing all the t's and dotting all the i's. Theo automatically asked him what file he should bring along.

"No file. This meeting doesn't concern ongoing business."

Theo was flabbergasted. Rarely did they hold meetings outside working hours, since Serry was fanatical about planning; it was the very quality if not flaw that had gotten him put in charge of the French branch of E.C.Tronics.

In his book, there was nothing about overtime that went hand in hand with a real need for improvement, so much as with a need to pick up the slack on some inefficiencies that the company, more so than the employee, was to blame for.

His detractors claimed he was what would happen if a hooker had a baby with a computer. Why a hooker? For his sentimental side, of course!

E.C.Tronics France was built in the image of its leader, at least insofar as the concept of it, as well as the services it provided. Associated with several global entities, the company only sold highly specialized software and expert systems, a booming sector that the old hardware monoliths hadn't managed to keep in their monopolistic grasp. E.C.Tronics's mission statement was to provide true artificial intelligence to machines. Paradoxically, this intelligence was nothing more than a functional derationalization of their own architecture, based on chaos theory and fuzzy logic.

Theo's position within E.C.Tronics was privileged. Combining the aptitudes of a computer analyst with a high degree of inventiveness, he supervised adaptive programming, and essentially worked on the algorithmic transcription of cognitive processes meant to lead to self-learning machines.

That had led to him developing an extremely adaptive program that effectively enabled several small computers running on different operating platforms to be turned into a single virtual superstructure.

By plugging into a massively parallel architecture that greatly magnified their individual computing power, these machines became an aggregate capable of rivaling the great supercomputers and their teraflops. The program was able to autonomously remodel the entire network architecture in such a way that it constantly optimized its processing speed with each PC that stacked up onto the initial structure.

The system had potentially infinite applications: a couple dozen personal computers could have quickly defeated *Deep Blue* in a game of chess, and beaten the greatest chess masters' Elo rating. It was impossible to define the theoretical limits of a thousand or so interconnected workstations.

But, more prosaically, this software, which could have made the lives of meteorology institutes the planet over, had gotten confined to the realm of strategic analysis. Its technology had been stamped "Strategic Secret," and not a single word was heard about it anymore.

The program had been named Enterprise 17. Naturally, E.C.Tronics held all rights to it worldwide – under strict government control – and Theo had immediately been promoted to a high position within the group, all for a piece of software and technology that officially didn't exist.

"Don't worry about me," answered Juliette tenderly. "Maybe you're on track for a promotion."

Theo found himself daydreaming of it. The coffee maker brought him crashing back down to the real world when he tried his luck with it again. Unlike computer programs, coffee pods weren't interchangeable from one brand to the next. Luckily, he always had a spare shirt in his office.

Nicolas Serry's office was a masterpiece in functional simplicity. For all that, it still gave off a welcoming vibe. Its unadorned picture window, lacking the customary greenery, was framed by minuscule downlights that bathed it in a soft light.

Paris appeared through it, as though recreated by a genius painter of a hyperrealist bent.

The desk itself, a huge mahogany slab, only took up a small part of the vast room. It seemed to be floating in the air, supported by slim, nearly invisible titanium bars. Two computer terminals bookended a switchboard. Behind the chair, several flatscreens were set into the wall, making up a harmonious whole with the whitened beech doors hiding mounds of documents.

The safe looked like a bar, and the bar looked like a safe. Several leather chairs created by some Japanese designer surrounded the conference table. Two rows of bamboo grew against the stone walls, framing a small, minimalist cabinet, on top of which stood some very seventies-style horses by Dalí.

Above the lounge area, which was made up of a sofa, a coffee table, and two armchairs, there was an astonishing sculpture of a blown-up computer with its parts covered with melted aluminum.

Nicolas Serry was seated on the sofa, facing a man who couldn't be made out from the doorway, aside from a bald pate atop a pair of wide shoulders.

Serry got up to greet Theo, who was taken aback by the unusual lack of formality to this meeting. The lounge area was for clients only. Not for partners.

The general manager of E.C.Tronics was over an inch taller than Theo. He wore his grey hair close-cropped, and the icy blue of his cold gaze bolstered his military look. He held out his hand.

"Theo, let me introduce you to Mr. Feldman, whose position in New York is the same as mine here."

The man in question turned around, and Theo instantly found him unpleasant. The expression on his face was reminiscent of a sick sea lion, with an endless forehead that was creased into folds. A clever gleam shone in his small eyes, behind their multifocal lenses.

Theo stepped forward, and Feldman got up. Standing barely earned him an inch in height.

"Pleased to meet you, Mister Collin," he said in flawless French. "I'm very honored to make the acquaintance of the man behind Enterprise 17."

"Have a seat," ordered Serry. "Mr. Feldman is going to take you through the purpose of our meeting, and I think you'll find this conversation to be of some interest."

Quietly, Theo sat down in one of the armchairs. He poured himself a cold tea, and politely declined the ice that Serry was holding out for him. Feldman wouldn't stop watching him with his sly gaze.

"Mister Collin," he said at last, as Theo brought his glass to his lips, "do you like traveling?"

Theo smiled, taken aback.

"Who doesn't?"

"Well that's certainly a suitable answer. But when I say traveling, I mean more of a long-term trip."

"I assume you're familiar with my file, my home life..."

"Yes. I know. You have a wife and a young daughter. I was not referring to them. All men have attachments beyond mere family life. A hobby. A squash club. A political affiliation. Season tickets to the Opera. Machinery... You get where I'm coming from, don't you?"

Theo turned to Nicolas Serry.

"I'm not sure I understand, sir. What do these questions have to do with the professional meeting you called me in for?"

"We're getting to that, Theo. I believe Mr. Feldman wants to get a bit more insight into you before cutting to the heart of the matter."

Theo took a second sip of the fragrant tea. Feldman seemed to be enjoying himself, although nothing showed on his face outside of that annoying gloom.

"I live a very simple life," admitted Theo with a sigh. "My wife and daughter are the only thing I care about, and I have nothing really keeping me in Paris. If you intend to offer me a job at one of the other European branches..."

"What if I said Mexico?"

Theo registered the words. Feldman stretched his face into a smiling grimace.

"Your psychological profile reveals you to be of a rather calm disposition... if not an outright retiring nature. Nicolas here even seems to put some stock in your discretion. Which is an indispensable trait as far as what we need. Would you be ready to accept a transfer that translated into a significant promotion, without anyone but your closest family knowing about it?"

Theo felt his heart rate speed up. Feldman had cut to the chase. Clearly, and for reasons beyond him, the management of E.C.Tronics was thinking of giving him a significant promotion by transferring him to a new satellite branch of the business. He took a moment to picture Juliette's reaction if he told her they'd be moving. Nothing would delight her more.

"Given the right offer, you can, of course, be assured I'll keep quiet."

"Very good." Feldman seemed relieved. "First of all, you should know that as soon as you accept my proposal, your pay is going to triple on the spot." He took a beat to scrutinize his reaction. Theo had a hard time keeping his cool.

"However, before I say anything more to you, I'm going to need to ask you to keep this interview completely under wraps. No matter how innocuous some of my words are going to seem to you.

"The job I'm about to propose to you aligns perfectly with your skills. All you'll need to do is consider cutting yourself off from your friends and acquaintances for two years' time. This will entail the same sort of sacrifice from your wife.

"Officially, you're going to be transferred to New York City. In actuality, your new position will take you to Mexico. Should I go on?"

A surreal feeling had now taken over Theo.

"I'm keeping to the confidentiality clause so far."

"Very good. Let's move on to the practicalities, and dive into the strictly professional portion of this meeting," said Feldman, standing up. "I believe that's something best settled around the conference table."

In the hour that followed, Feldman monopolized all speech, only rarely interrupted by brief questions from Theo. Serry didn't utter a peep, which was unlike him. But then, this meeting had nothing in common with anything he'd been part of before.

And yet, on the face of it, Feldman's offer looked like any other transfer accompanied by an unexpected raise. It wasn't even registering with Theo that the raise in question signified triple his pay, plus all expenses paid. In two years, that would mean more money than he could have hoped to save up over the course of his whole lifetime.

At the start of the year, the construction of a gigantic computer research center, equipped with the latest innovations, had wrapped up in the middle of the Mexican Sierra. Feldman's explanations, sanitized to an almost obsessive degree, revolved entirely around the technical details defining Theo's new job, without revealing anything beyond the indispensable about the new center.

When he asked whether it was a question of expanding E.C.Tronics's activities, Feldman told him that any link between the center and any other existing companies was held in absolute secrecy. He added that even the existence of the structure would be kept confidential for two years – the length of his contract.

"Don't ask me any more questions for now," added Feldman, thus forestalling yet another question from Theo. "The information you'll be required to process there is extremely sensitive, and it describes a reality you can't begin to imagine."

"I haven't agreed to anything yet," stated Theo when Feldman broached the matter of his departure. "I'm thinking I have a whole lot of personal matters

I'll need to settle. No-one can just disappear like that, completely without a trace, even as a matter of security.

"Besides, I do have some more earthly concerns. Such as my daughter's education, for instance. She's only just started going to school. Or my family, for that matter. I may not see them all that often, but I still..."

"We've already taken all these matters into account," Feldman cut in. "The necessary conveniences are, of course, available over there, for your wife as for your daughter. As for any communication you would wish to engage in with your loved ones, it will be handled by our services."

"By mail?"

"Yes. And any replies will come to you by the same means. Emails are forbidden, and all traffic between the internal network and the outside world is kept under constant surveillance, as a security measure.

"Since the matter has come up, we do need to address one final, indispensable constraint, if one that you might find rather worrying."

Theo tried to comfort himself with a show of feigned good mood.

"Go ahead. I'm ready to hear anything, now."

"You're going to have to make the necessary arrangements to ensure you have no reason to physically communicate with the outside world for the entire length of your contract. Because from the moment you're joining the center, neither you nor your family will be authorized to leave it until its existence has been made public."

Serry took over then and finally let Theo know that he had twenty-four hours to give his final answer, time enough to talk things over with his wife. The meeting came to a close. Theo left the office and the two men behind.

"There is one thing I don't get," inquired Serry after he'd left. "There's no shortage of qualified engineers in New York, and Collin doesn't even speak English well. Why him?"

"Enterprise 17," replied Feldman. "They want to have the software developer on hand."

"That's not good enough. Do you have any other explanation?"

"It seems that Collin has been selected due to certain qualities that don't transpire from his professional file. It's the responsibility of his new supervisor. That's all I know."

No sooner had he stepped out of Nicolas Serry's office that Joseph Feldman forgot everything about Theo Collin. Recruiting wasn't within his remit, and when he'd first gotten the request concerning the young computer engineer, his first instinct had been to forward it to the Paris office.

And then he'd gotten that phone call.

Feldman was a cautious man. That was what had enabled him to survive and, for the past sixteen years, play a game that would have taken others down within months.

This particular April, Feldman had needed an urgent excuse to make his way to Europe. He knew his movements were being watched, as were those of everyone involved in the current operation. His relationships with various government agencies did not shield him from any ill-timed investigations, no more so than his position with E.C.Tronics did. And his usual job of special middleman gave more arguments than necessary to his detractors. Of which he certainly wasn't lacking.

And so this recruiting assignment in France had come at just the right time. Even though his final destination was Rome, where he intended to make his way as quickly as possible.

Feldman had reached the Trocadero esplanade and was getting ready to flag a cab when he became aware of the staccato vibration in his coat pocket. He quickly grabbed his phone, simultaneously signaling the cab driver to wait for him. His Nokia display showed six missed calls.

"I was getting ready to hang up again," went a voice thickened by a heavy accent.

"I'm getting out of a meeting," retorted Feldman. "I'll be on a plane in two hours."

Arabic exploded at the other end of the line, a language that Feldman spoke fluently. A fine drizzle was beginning to come down, spreading its lustrous sheen and beads of glitter across the esplanade, between the Homme museum and the Maritime museum. Meanwhile, the first streetlights were starting to come on, greeting the oncoming dusk. Feldman shoved himself into the waiting taxi and hung up at the same time.

"Gare du Nord," he told the driver. "That is where you take the Eurostar, yes?"

Fine, so he was no longer going to Rome. At the end of the day, his reasons for making this trip to Europe hadn't fundamentally changed.

Juliette had seated herself on the bed in the lotus position, which was how she arranged her body whenever she had a problem to solve. Stretched out in front of her, his head supported by a pillow he'd propped onto his elbow, Theo would have given entire minutes of his life for a cigarette.

This was their "confab" position, as Juliette called it. She was of the mind that all important discussions needed to take place in the bedroom. And it bore reminding that the word "congress" originated in an old medieval custom, according to which conjugal inability had to be attested by the city dignitaries before the marriage could be annulled. In short, discussions took place in bed, and not in the living room or the kitchen, which were meant for the small-fry kinds of joint decisions.

Theo could not tamp down on his agitation as he watched his wife. He'd disclosed everything to her in one breath, and was now waiting for her to share in his enthusiasm.

"There's something about this whole thing that doesn't sit right with me," she said at last.

Theo straightened up. The break was over.

"What? I delve into the smallest details of a confidential meeting that could lead to a once-in-a-lifetime promotion, and the only thing you can say to me is that something doesn't sit right?"

"I don't know. It all seems too good to be true, and the rest of your story sounds like a crappy spy novel. And what about my parents, think about not talking to them for two years. They're not exactly young anymore. We can't just up and disappear like that…"

"I'm sure these safety regulations are stringent on purpose at the time I commit. Once we're there, we'll be able to work something out. Who would picture a computing center without phone lines."

"About that," Juliette went on. "You're being asked to keep our destination a secret, when by all accounts there should be all kinds of ways to communicate with the outside world. Don't you think that's fishy? How do they plan on stopping us?"

Theo shrugged his shoulders. Whole hours of his life for a cigarette!

"Don't go all paranoid on me now. Serry was at that meeting."

"You told me yourself that he didn't particularly seem to know what was going on.

"And Katia? How are we gonna put her through school? What friends will she have over there? You're not cognizant about what kind of a shock such a change would be for her."

Theo smiled.

"You know full well she's at an age where she'll be able to adapt to anything. And it's quite the opposite. I think this trip could only fire up her imagination. I mean, damn it, Juliette! Mexico!

"Over here, we have crappy weather. Our apartment is barely bigger than a shoebox. I work myself to the bone and we can barely make ends meet. And it's a situation that could easily last ten years."

"You've already made up your mind, haven't you?"

"I won't make any decision without your full approval."

Juliette uncurled herself and stretched out beneath the sheets.

"Let me sleep on it," she said, "and go to the kitchen to grab a bite. I bet they didn't even give you a sandwich."

Theo got up, feeling confident. He knew his wife well enough to be sure that her thinking things over usually resulted in a positive decision.

Joseph Feldman was the first one out, as soon as the doors to the Eurostar slid open with a whistling, pneumatic hiss. He looked at his watch: eight fifty-five. The train was right on time.

He swept a slow, measuring gaze over the Waterloo Station platforms, attempting to make certain he'd been neither followed nor watched, before making his way towards the central walkway. He then fell into step with the Monday morning throng, walked past the newsstands, went straight to a baggage locker. He pulled a key out from inside his coat, and inserted it into the lock, the picture of calm. From the depths of the locker, he pulled out an attaché case.

Next, he made his way over to the men's room. After pushing the latch, he turned his focus on opening the briefcase. Inside it were a British passport, another locker key, and a membership card bearing the logo of an "Action

Gym – Leeds." He shoved the passport into his inner jacket pocket and placed the card and the locker key back at the bottom of the briefcase.

He got out of the restroom almost as soon as he'd gone in, and he made his way over to a car rental agency.

The receptionist greeted him with a professional smile.

"I have a car booked," stated Feldman, flashing a passport.

"Mr. Berko? I have your booking right here. There's a Ford Mondeo ready for you in the parking lot," she told him, holding out a form. "If you wouldn't mind signing here…"

The sedan came to a stop a handful of hours later, pulling up a couple hundred yards from the Leeds "Action Gym," a large, grey, two-story building with a loud yellow logo painted on its wall. The driver slid inside, showed his pass to a bleached-blonde attendant in her forties, then took the stairs after the way to the lockers had been pointed out.

Once on the second floor, he went through a door, landed in a hallway leading to a light-filled room with a hardwood floor dotted with little blue plastic mats on which female bodies of all shapes and sizes sweated to a beat of "…and one, two, three, and turn…"

Feldman kept going, and entered the men's changing room. He made sure he was alone, then opened his briefcase once more to retrieve the small key, which matched a locker that he soon picked out from the bunch. He then began undressing, carelessly tossing his clothes. There were several items waiting for him in the locker when he opened it. Swimming trunks, a towel…

He took in the final item with acute apprehension.

An electric stun baton.

Feldman had already had the pleasure of feeling the effects produced by the discharge of this innocuous-looking device, and the mere sight of this defensive weapon made him blanch. But the clock was ticking, and there wasn't a minute for him to lose. So he seized the swimming trunks.

The item was just his size, distended by the stomach of a slovenly man in his fifties. The double glass doors opened on a deserted, run-down pool. It would be at least an hour until the next water aerobics class. Feldman made his way to the edge, then caught sight of the ladder leading down into the highly chlorinated water.

He thought it preferable to inch in. *'Might as well spare myself the extra shock,'* he told himself.

He swam at the surface for a couple of seconds, then decided to proceed to a few racing breaststrokes, as per the instructions he'd received. That way, there would be no part of his body had hadn't come into contact with the water.

He soon got out of the pool, then headed back to the changing room without coming into contact with a single living soul. He dried himself off, then opened the locker once more and grabbed the stun baton with a trembling hand. Next, he locked himself into a shower stall, took off his swimming trunks, hung his towel, and started to think.

"Ah, but if I don't do it, nobody's gonna know…"

Then, the doubts started creeping in. He shot a look towards the ceiling. No cameras. He opened the stall door. Nobody there. But the worry niggled on. Maybe someone, somewhere, was watching him.

"And if I don't follow their instructions to the letter, it all goes to pieces… Nothing's set in stone. There's no other way… Come on, just grit your teeth. The effect wears off quickly… Now!"

A crackling could be heard. A pale light sparked for a moment under the stall door. The smell of ozone filled the room and overrode the chlorinated reek that had dominated the space until then. Berko, his muscles seizing, his teeth ready to crumble under the pressure from his jaws, kept on digging the stun baton into is hip. Under the onslaught, his body gave out on him, and he relieved himself against his own leg, before slumping down.

Two scant minutes passed. Feldman regained consciousness, panting. He found himself seated in the shower cabin, his body soiled, blood flowing from his scalp. He must have hit his head against the wall while under the effect of the electric shock.

He let go of the stun baton with a grimace of disgust, then ran warm water over his skin. Either his next contact was hugely paranoid, or he liked toying with him. Feldman cursed him inwardly. His skin burned where he'd discharged the baton.

When he opened his locker, it was to find that all his clothes had gone missing, replaced by a midnight blue three-piece suit that appeared tailored to him. His briefcase had also been moved, undoubtedly to scan it. Feldman got dressed, grumbling all the while. Clearly, nothing was being left to chance!

In the right jacket pocket of his suit, he found a business card advertising a strip club, a "Ladies" in the inner suburbs of Leeds. If this wasn't too much; but did he really have a choice?

He exited the building into pouring rain and shielded himself with his briefcase. At this time of day, city traffic was bearable again. Behind the wheel of his rental Ford, he managed to quickly locate the "Ladies" club, squeezed into a grubby alleyway somewhere at the most populated outskirts of the Leeds suburbs.

Feldman headed right for the bar, not sparing the slightest glance to the Asian beauty in a micro G-string undulating to the reverberating base of The Prodigy.

"Where can I find Tarek?"

"There's no Tarek 'ere," retorted the bartender, an ageless man with unkempt hair, a cigarette stuck to the corner of his lips. "Who're you, then?"

"I'm Berko. I'm supposed to meet Tarek right here."

"Berko? Never 'eard of you. Stay put; let me check."

The bartender stepped away for a moment to get on the phone. He stood with his back turned the whole time he talked. Berko kept his hands flat on the bar, not even sparing a bit of attention to the waitress with the augmented chest who came by to caress his bald dome.

"D'you know, I have a soft spot for baldies, love? They say it's caused by excess testosterone… Why, it gets me running just thinkin' about it."

"Sorry, but I don't have the time," he retorted laconically.

"What… Can't spare five minutes for a pretty blonde like me? You know, I'm sure you and I can…"

"You, clear off," barked the bartender. The girl slinked off straightaway, showing her displeasure with an obscene gesture.

"Still no Tarek here." The man grimaced as he tipped his chin to point out a row of booths. "But if you wanted to give your eyes a treat, you'll find the 5 to your liking."

The room Berko stepped into was round, housing a big, tattered pleather bench seating four men who were having heated words. Silence fell instantly, and two of the guys came his way. He held his arms out to the sides as soon as they did, waiting for the henchmen to get the pat-down over with.

One of the two men who'd remained seated got up and made an inconspicuous exit. The last man stayed as he was, legs crossed, and merely leaned forward to grab his coffee cup. In the muted light, his short beard bore a curious red color, same as his short hair. His white shirt, buttoned all the way up to the neck, gave him a clergyman's look, at instant odds with the impressive number of rings that adorned the fingers of his right hand.

"Changed your name yet again, Feldman? What a droll little treasure hunt. I wonder how you even come up with all these names. And since we're on that, why Berko this time? I am curious…"

Feldman couldn't help himself from scanning the figures surrounding him, as if the mention of his real name would conjure an evil specter from the empty stage, where the mirrors reflected each-other to infinity.

"I pick them at random. Nothing over two syllables, so I can remember them better."

"Very good," snickered Tarek. "And what have you got for me today?"

Feldman inched his fingers into the pocket of his jacket while the bodyguards closed in on him once more. He extracted a minuscule thumb drive. Tarek's eyes glittered in the half-light.

"Is that it?"

"Come now, Tarek; you know the saying: the smaller the gift, the more priceless the contents…"

Tarek placed his coffee cup back down and swung his gaze from one of his associates to the next.

"Is that a saying, then?"

"I heard it straight from a woman's mouth. My wife's. Did you want to take a look at the contents of this drive, or would you rather we just kept chatting about what may or may not be on it?"

Tarek nodded his head, suddenly more serious than the clergyman he appeared to be. Instantly, one of his men pulled an ultra-slim laptop before him.

"Well, well, let's see here…"

Mere moments later, after Feldman had connected the thumb drive, the wallpaper depicting a vague landscape of the moon was replaced by a series of numbers that soon settled into one blank space followed by a question mark.

50

"The code," demanded Tarek.

Feldman leaned down to nimbly punch in several letters. The screen turned white. Then, a plain line appeared.

"What do you think of our new rendezvous spot?" asked Tarek, as though the information being displayed held no interest for him.

"Is that Saudi humor?"

"Who would think to look for faithful, observant Muslims in a place such as this one, hmm? You never know. The sight of a bare woman might make our eyes fall out of their sockets, or turn us to pillars where we stand, as with Lot's wife in Sodom… Although, things are looking a little quiet, don't you think?"

Tarek patted the fake leather of the upholstery next to him, as though directing a dog.

"Come, Feldman, take a seat, stop and smell the roses; we're fulfilling a sacred mission, all will be forgiven after."

One of the men pushed the button on a little doorbell near the one-way glass that separated them from the stage. Soon after, a very curvy brunette dressed in a Scheherazade outfit, a sequined bikini under a collection of swaying veils, started undulating between the mirrors. In one abrupt motion, Tarek swung the computer Feldman's way.

"And this, then, what is this supposed to mean?"

Over on the screen, it read:

"White Cells – Business Plan".

The temperature in the room had dropped a couple more degrees. Beyond the purr of the air conditioner, colonel Meyrek was intently listening to the cries and exclamations that his career in the military had gotten him used to. Curt orders, indistinct grumbles, panted breaths.

He perked up his ears. Much like the instruments in an orchestra, footsteps crunched on sand with a specific rhythm all their own. Parade step or goose step, the disorganized rush of combat exercises. New cries. Insults. Whatever abuse it took to trigger hate. Fear. Aggression. A will to dig deep. To push the body beyond its farthest limits rather than stand down. As though every step became a battle to survive.

He counted to ten. Out in the distance, the snick of breech blocks sliding. A hundred bodies diving onto their stomachs as one. Then, the staccato of automatic rifles.

Stretched out on his cot, settled in the one somewhat comfortable room on base, despite having opted for the sort of Spartan bunk he was used to, he was able to follow along with the day's training by sound alone, issuing the orders in his head before they happened, so sharp he could time every single maneuver as it occurred.

Meyrek wrapped up his "siesta." This half-hour's rest he gave himself every day during warm-ups got him ready to emerge, after, like a conductor coming into rehearsals after the entire orchestra had already tuned their instruments.

When the automatic fire died down, he got up, unplugged the air conditioning unit, and opened the window wide behind its bars.

Scorching hot air streamed into the room.

Theo never would have imagined there were so many formalities to check off before breaking it off with a country. Not due to any bureaucratic trivialities – supported by E.C. Tronics, he'd been able to settle everything with the tax man, get his visas, and expand his social security coverage in a matter of hours – but due to the reality of separating himself from each and every component of his daily life.

It took two appointments to break the lease on his car; selling off all their furniture took him and Juliette two good weeks. Saying goodbye to their friends and their families took over practically every evening they had. At last, in their final week, with their empty apartment becoming uninhabitable, they had to move in with Juliette's folks.

Throughout those two months of frenzied bustle, Katia and her dad were gripped by the same enthusiasm, the same childlike excitement at the thought of their imminent departure. (The child thought they were going to America, which was a crucial half-truth.) Juliette, for her part, far from sharing in that euphoria, had become careworn and irascible.

The imminence of their departure caused a lot of fights, with Theo getting criticized for making his decision too lightly and persuading her using arguments that she hadn't had the time to weigh properly.

After all, despite their financial straits, their family life brought them enough joy and satisfaction to more than make up for their financial worries! As for their meager earnings, Theo would just have to get his head around the fact that she'd get a job again, once Katia was old enough to go to school.

Juliette was afraid. Afraid of the unknown, and of these events that were going to turn such a morally comfortable life upside-down. Marrying Theo had given her a feeling of safety, not because he gave off any kind of protective energy, but in actuality because his weakness gave her a shield, convincing her that he'd never go into bad deals head-first. Against all expectations, however, it was just this character flaw of his that would soon be separating them from everything that comforted her.

One day, following one of their particularly nasty fights – Juliette had ended up locking herself in the bathroom, refusing to talk to him, and truth be told ashamed that she'd been finding herself short on arguments – Theo had asked Nicolas Serry to grant him a meeting.

He was hoping, without truly believing it could be done, that he might still be able to change his mind. Serry very quickly disabused him of that. When he'd signed his new contract, Theo had effectively quit his job at E.C. Tronics France. Hiring him back was completely out of the question now, having already found his replacement. At the end of their very brief meeting, Serry saw fit to add that not being dependable was one of the flaws that just couldn't be tolerated by a group with the standing that E.C. Tronics had.

Theo walked out of the meeting with his mouth tasting like ash. He thought it prudent not to share his negative impressions with his wife.

Nevertheless, his enthusiasm bounced back when, at the end of the first month following his signing on, he got his first new, triple paycheck. Feldman had been true to his word.

Reconciled, the worst of the crisis now over, they celebrated the happy event with a lavish dinner at Lucas Carton, one of France's most refined and emblematic dining establishments, where a wealthy suitor had once invited Juliette, back in college. A date she'd had to cancel on, stuck in bed with a nasty prelude to the flu.

It was to recall that particular rivalry that Theo had picked this place to celebrate in, not without a touch of provocative irony.

Helped along by the champagne, feeling euphoric, Juliette went so far as to start making a couple plans for when they were coming back and would have all that money at their disposal.

"We'll see about all that when we get back, but for now, here you go…"

Happy to be able to recreate an old cliché in a fancy restaurant like this, while the sommelier and the maître d' kept trying to outdo each-other in determined obsequiousness, Theo slid a long velvet box across the white tablecloth and between the silver flatware. This time, its contents were anything but a marketing support.

The look in Juliette's eyes flickered when they came to rest on the string of gold and pearls that was nestled in the velvet.

"And now what am I supposed to say?"

A waiter had stepped in closer to refill their glasses. With a barely-there gesture, the maître d' signaled for him to wait.

"Lots of things," retorted Theo bemusedly. "That you're sorry, that I'm always right, that you're happy, that you adore me…"

"And that I love you, right?"

"That, too," went Theo as their fingers met and held between the crystal glasses.

"So then," murmured Juliette, "shall we drink to Mexico?"

"And to all that money!"

As if by magic, their glasses, which had been almost empty not a moment ago, filled up with sparkling pink liquid. Despite her apparent unpretentiousness, Juliette had always had expensive tastes. It was a penchant that Theo was proud to know he could finally live up to.

Chapter 5

The front of Howard Beck's desk was covered with a spread of documents, archive copies, and photographs, reams and reams of them taking up all the space leading to his computer keyboard. Most of these documents came from the other departments, in particular from the third floor.

There, some sixty-odd agents, assigned to internal affairs, carried out a thorough, year-long surveillance of the agency's every office worker, operative, or field agent, in a bid to guarantee the huge building was completely safeguarded against any outside incursions, even potential honeytraps.

It was a laborious undertaking, and one that hadn't prevented traitors or double agents from infiltrating the service every now and again. It was Langley's worst nightmare. Over on Beck's floor, a feeling of full-blown paranoia had settled in following the failure of Operation Buridan.

The men's waxen complexions and dark undereye circles, mirrors to his own tormented countenance, attested to the number of sleepless hours that had driven Beck and his team straight into a dead end all the same. And the latest report to date, the one provided by the Turkmen administration, added to the overhanging confusion by its utter vacuity.

You'd think, according to them, that the three slaughtered agents had died in some indeterminate accident. Two scanty pages summed up the case, and the local field office, restricted to an overwhelmingly passive role, hadn't gotten anything more out of them than the vague promise of a potential investigation that would, of course, never take place.

The days, then the weeks gone by were bringing Howard closer and closer to the oblivion that would soon claim these three men who'd been his responsibility. But dying in combat was one thing, and Beck, like any handler, was deeply aware of the state of war that each new recruit consented to enter as soon as they joined the Agency.

Being massacred in front of a camera, so that jihadis the world over could delight in the spectacle for years to come, was something else entirely.

Beck wouldn't stand for it. This wasn't the first time that men on his team had lost their lives, and he himself thought he'd gotten a miraculous escape after such a close brush with death back in Iraq. But unlike the armed attack that he'd survived, the indecency of these images that he'd spent hours taking apart was still haunting him at night.

In his most sordid nightmares, he even took his men's place, only to wake up panting for breath and covered in sweat, spending whole seconds convinced that the wetness covering his body was from his own spurting blood. The Erbil muezzin would then sing out "Allahu Akbar," and a noise like an explosion would come from the knife at his throat.

This morning, however, two memos drew his attention. The first came from the third floor and went over the entire chain of command of Operation Buridan. If there was a leak, then just like in plumbing, the best way to root it out was to follow the pipes. The documents that the memo referred to were all classified.

Still, used to the way the Agency bureaucracy worked, Beck instantly uncovered an anomaly. Approval for his mission had come all the way from the top, a break from the routine that demanded approval for a field operation from just a department head.

This precaution dated back to the Nixon amendment and the Reagan purges, following which the CIA had found itself unauthorized to carry out any sort of assassination, be it tactical or strategic. Like any administration would, the Agency had reacted by putting in place safeguard procedures that worked like reverse umbrellas.

Obviously, this detail revealed nothing more than the state of emergency that the Agency had entered ever since Iran had shown its resolute willingness to become a nuclear power. The director himself sometimes rubber stamped a sensitive operation. As for assassinations, they were now organized and carried out by other countries' secret service agencies, such as the Mossad, who was renowned for its relentless efficiency.

It was this last thought that led Beck to look at the second memo. This one came from the fifth floor, from the strategic counterespionage division, a service that was in direct contact with the FBI. An agency that, unlike the CIA, had domestic dealings only.

The collaboration between the two agencies had been stepped up since the implementation of the Patriot Act, which had been necessitated by the terrorist threat now hanging over America.

It wasn't a rarity, these days, for files related to homeland security to be shared between the two agencies, a routine that would have undoubtedly made it possible to avoid the tragic events of nine-eleven. Two months before the attack, the Mossad had warned the CIA of a large-scale terrorist operation, but the FBI had refused to listen.

On that note, the letter H for "Hebrew" referred to a recent espionage attempt in which there was no doubt as to the involvement of the Israeli agency.

Beck smiled. His country and Israel sometimes acted at total odds, so divergent were their interests despite their being natural allies. This time, the case had to do with an attempt to backdoor into "sensitive" – read military-grade and top-secret – software with the help of a plant in one of the subsidiaries of E.C. Tronics, one of the many privately-held companies subcontracted by the Pentagon, as by the CIA.

Sighing, Beck shoved the third-floor memo away. It was too depressing. For a couple of minutes at least, he needed to think of something else. Inside the folder bearing the letter "H," he found a code that enabled him to access all the information from his computer.

The plant's name was Vince White. The subsidiary with the leak was OptroNex. And, of course, White had been manipulated by a woman. The case had been temporarily assigned the label "Misc-Civ," meaning as of yet, no legal measures had been taken against this White.

A detail startled Beck. The plant's handler was an agent he knew of by reputation, without ever meeting him before. Avi Haim. This guy was the closest thing to his own counterpart inside the Mossad, and Beck had had no idea that he'd been in D.C. these past few months.

Like him, Avi Haim had been put in charge of the Iran dossier by his country. So then what was he doing spying on a private American company?

Howard Beck took a deep breath in and settled himself into his chair as best he could before diving into White's full deposition.

Vincent White, real name Vincenzo Bianco, was the son of an Italian Jew who'd emigrated to the United States in the sixties. Enzo was born here, on American soil. All of Enzo's childhood, which he'd spent in a small village in Michigan, had been defined by Italian culture. His mother had never missed an opportunity to play a piece by Puccini on the old stereo system her husband had given her for their tenth anniversary.

Growing up, Enzo had quickly realized he was different. Not being a WASP – white he may have been, but not an Anglo-Saxon, nor a protestant – with his Italian-sounding name, he'd had to endure bullying, put up with nicknames from his playmates, and silently suffer for belonging to a minority that was thought highly of everywhere else, but not there, in that protestant school, the one closest to their house, where he was nothing but a wop. Fortunately, none of the children knew he was a Jew.

His father hadn't been fooled. A sensible and very observant man, he had quickly understood that his son was scientifically gifted. And if he wanted to give him his best chance to climb his way to a higher social status and to go to college, a name like Bianco would be a handicap, he had naively thought.

And so the Biancos formally requested to change their names, just before their son went to middle school. The Biancos became Mister and Missus White. "What's in a name?" the father had asked at the time. After all, his own father had done exactly the same thing, in his day.

That was how the family of Saul Weisz had transformed into the family of Paolo Bianco. Names could change as far as how they were written, as far as they were pronounced, but not as far as the meaning that they carried. A meaning that made him predisposed to "laundering," Vincent had always told himself, with a touch of humor.

And, to be sure, once he'd become Vince White, Enzo had excelled academically and ended up getting into Caltech, where he'd easily gotten a degree in computer engineering.

Not a bad-looking guy, in that introverted Italian sort of way, he would take advantage of his new status from then on, not only to assert himself as far as his academic achievements, but also to work his way through a string of conquests, being predisposed to a sort of spontaneous hedonism. The name change had brought him nothing other than the confidence he'd been missing, but that was something it would take Vince years to understand.

Soon recruited by Intel, where he worked for four years, Vince would go on to get hired by OptroNex, a subsidiary of the mighty E.C.Tronics that specialized in the development of optronic devices for use in weapons systems.

"Are you really called White? How bissare, you really do not look anything like your name."

That had been the first thing his department head, Ephraim Rozenwald, had said to him after they'd been introduced to one-another. Rozenwald had a funny way of pronouncing his z's, which came out s's, like the opposite of a lisp.

"I would really rather be called Vince, if you don't mind, Mr. Rozenwald."

The small, slightly plump man with the gaze brimming with mischief and good humor gave him a long look, an enigmatic smile dancing at the corner of his lips. Within OptroNex, Ephraim Rozenwald was hailed as a genius. His organizational skills, his infallible instinct for project development, and above all his uncommon kindness, his indefatigable geniality, had earned him the nickname "Mr. Nuclear Fusion"… With the fusion pronounced fission, as you might well guess.

"Go on, you can tell me," he'd breathed to Vincent in a mischievous aside before pointing out his office. "I'm sure we wouldn't have to go too far back to find some Weiszes in your family. Either Weiszes or Levans[5] …"

Vince had frozen in place, blushing, before bursting into laughter.

From then on, the two men had forged a strong friendship, while Ephraim had made it his mission to progressively bring the one he now considered a protégé back on the path to Judaism.

"You don't have to learn the Kabbalah or the Talmud. That's even more complicated to master than nuclear physics. But at least come spend the *Shabbat* with us tomorrow!"

At first, Vince was difficult to persuade. The Jewish faith was as foreign to him as the German language, which his family had spoken not two generations earlier. His nature tended towards rational skepticism, and certainly didn't lend itself to rituals or to accepting dogma. His father had kept him well away from something he'd considered a vice and a weakness: religion.

A paradox of the Bianco-Whites, who held their share of superstitions and naïve beliefs despite it all. Did his own mother not refuse to do the laundry on nights of full moon? Did his own father, iconoclast in chief, not take absurd detours to avoid crossing paths with a black cat? But no religion at home. None of that for the Whites!

---

5   Like Weiss in German, Lavan is Hebrew for white.

But here was a kind of magic that his father hadn't prepared him for: that which permeated the warm and timeless atmosphere of a Shabbat evening with the Rozenwalds. From that first dinner, Vince didn't look back. Ephraim introduced him to his wife and daughter as a "Jew who thought he was a goy."

"Put this on your head," he told him kindly while loaning him a kippa. "It will make you look a little bit more who you are."

"And what is that supposed to mean?"

Ephraim's daughter, Lisa, instantly intervened in Vince's favor.

"Pay no mind to my father's teasing, that's only his way of telling you he likes you."

But Rozenwald wouldn't have been Rozenwald had he not slid in a mischievous aside.

"The great Freud had an expression that thousands of psychiatrists the world over are still trying to interpret today: "I must arrive to where I am." It is a phrase I understood a long time ago. What you are always catches up with you. *L'chaim,* Vince; *l'chaim.*"

And thus, holding up their wine glasses, the two specialists in applied computer science drank "to life," in keeping with the best of the Hebrew traditions. That evening, Enzo Bianco felt a bit less Italian, a bit more American, and, for the first time, a little bit like a Jew…

Over the months that followed, Vince saw more and more of the Rozenwalds. Of course, that earned him increasing scorn from some of his colleagues, who saw his attitude as nothing but a heavy-handed maneuver meant to suck up to "Nuclear Fussion" and get into is good graces, so that he'd be appointed his successor when the time came.

That reminded Vince of the jibes he'd been the target of some fifteen years earlier, back when his name had still been Bianco. But this was old ground, a familiar enmity that now only made him smile. Far more bearable an ostracism than the emptiness he'd flirted with just a few months before. Vince was a loner at heart. Thanks to Ephraim, he was becoming a little less of one every day.

The spring of his first year with the subsidiary of E.C.Tronics, Vince was invited to take part in the *Passover Seder* at his new friend's home. Lisa Rosenwald too had invited one of her close friends to the celebration. Her name was Rebecca[6].

An Israeli who had recently settled in the United States, Rebecca Bruhl was a trilingual secretary with the Israeli embassy. Her skin very fair, her figure slim, and a pair of intensely black eyes under a thick, silky, luxuriant mass of dark brown hair, she exhibited the sort of reserve and refinement that were rare for a *sabra* who'd been raised rough in the Land of Canaan. Two years' military service hadn't whittled away a softness that bordered on shyness.

Vince was instantly charmed by her clear, expressive eyes and the high cheekbones that framed them, leading to a wide smile that bewitched by its frankness.

All through the evening, Ephraim made as if he couldn't tell anything was going on. And Vince couldn't see, beneath the table, Lisa's hand grip and

6 The Key to Rebecca, a spy novel by Ken Follett.

squeeze her mother's, like two partners in crime moved by the charming spectacle put on by their two single friends.

As the night came to a close, Vince offered to drive Rebecca home. In the doorway, while the women were saying their goodbyes in the living room, Ephraim placed an almost paternal hand on Vince's shoulder.

"I can see right through you, Vincent. Be careful with how you treat Rebecca! Do not forget. She isn't one of these *goya*... You know already that I like you, but if you show her any disrespect, you will have me to contend with..."

Faced with a speechless Vince, he felt compelled to add:

"...That is to say, you are a big boy, now. You know what you're doing... Don't hold it against me if I'm saying this to you... After all, I'm just an old *schmuck*..."

"Don't worry about it", soothed Vince. "I do want to do so many things with her, but I don't have the slightest intention of being disrespectful to her in any way."

"In that case..."

Ephraim treated Vince to a wink. He turned his head toward the inside of the house.

"Rebecca? Your devoted admired is going to freeze out on the stoop if you're going to be chatting to my wife for much longer..."

Rebecca lived on the second floor of a former Victorian residence that had been divided into luxury apartments. Vince dropped her off on her doorstep, intrigued but mum about the fact that she was living someplace this prestigious. An embassy secretary should not have been able to afford anything close to this zip code; but no sooner had the thought come that he'd told himself her family had to be well-off.

He didn't even try to steal a kiss from her, which was pretty out of character for him. Just as he was getting ready to head back out to his car, Rebecca slid her scarf over his head and pulled him in towards her, fervently pressing her lips to his. There went her *sabra* side. A kind of determination that would often leave Vince panting.

Still overcome, his lips still moist from the taste of the beautiful Israeli, he tried to clasp her to him beneath the portico, on her stoop, but Rebecca moved away from him straightaway with a little laugh that was conspiratorial and already a little teasing, too.

"I'd invite you up for a drink," she said with a pout, "but I have to get up very early tomorrow – there's a very important meeting at nine o'clock. They would not look too kindly on my showing up with bags under my eyes... And besides," she added impishly, "I think Ephraim wouldn't understand why we went so fast..."

She scribbled her cell phone number on the torn-off corner of an envelope and held it out to him before closing the door behind her. Vince stood there in the doorway for a moment, staring at that piece of paper. Then he shoved it into the pocket of his coat and cheerfully made his way back to his car.

Vince had never fallen in love before, with the obvious exception of the first misunderstood stirrings in his teenage years. Deep, abiding, total love was going to be a new experience, one that he would progressively give himself over to until he lived it with abandon.

In Rebecca, he would discover the alter ego he'd pictured to himself for years and years, a son of immigrants who'd had trouble integrating, too fragile to get involved, too self-assured to admit it. The Israeli woman wasn't an affair. In his mind, she was taking the shape of a waking dream.

There was nothing Rebecca didn't know about Washington, as though the young woman had spent the better part of her life there, and not in the working-class neighborhoods of Tel Aviv, where she was from. She happily guided him through the secret spots, the places where she loved to wander, from the banks of the Potomac river to the National Mall, from the Natural History Museum to the rostral columns at Union Station, with a soft spot for Arlington, the essence of the American soul, which she said she felt attached to.

The second floor of the Georgetown Victorian soon became the love nest cushioning this dream built from different feelings ranging from the fear he'd see her disappear from his life at any moment, to the almost juvenile enthusiasm Vince felt at the sight of her naked body. Love turned to passion. Three months on, Vince could no longer picture his life without her.

That was when the Israeli woman decided to press her advantage. Vincenzo Bianco was hooked.

That night, the pleasure they'd taken from each other had been particularly intense, and the sight of the young woman's shadowy silhouette where she stood naked in the window frame, before the halo of the streetlights outside, brought something like a sob to his throat. A mild, moist, sweet-tasting sensation, granted by a feeling that, right then and there, he swore to himself he'd never allow to disappear.

Rebecca smoked on occasion. Rarely in an enclosed area. Still, she'd gotten up to root around for a cigarette and came back to sit down next to him, the glowing end of the smoke dancing close to her face.

By the look on her face, which he felt more than he saw, Vincent understood that she had something serious to say to him.

"Vince," she said, taking his hand. "We won't be seeing each other anymore."

Vincent would have leapt, had this pronouncement not outright paralyzed him. His fingers tightened around Rebecca's.

"What are you talking about? Has something happened… Have I done…"

"No… no, darling. It has nothing to do with us. I was given orders yesterday. I'm going to have to leave the US."

Vincent sighed, his chest caught in a vise of fear the likes of which he'd never known. Things were already looking better than a breakup.

"How long will you be gone for?"

The young woman's voice softened to an impossible degree.

"Forever, Vincent. I must return to Tel Aviv. My mission here is over."

"Tel Aviv? OK… That's not the end of the world. I am capable of taking a plane. I could even…"

Rebecca brought her face close to Vincent's. In the moonlight, two silver trails trickled beneath her eyes.

"Things aren't that simple. I'm going to be assigned elsewhere, effective immediately… I don't know where, and even if I did, I wouldn't be authorized to tell you."

A panicked fear took over Vincent. He chose to kid his way out of it, that seemed the best way to banish the glowering ghosts that were clamoring around the bed.

"Oh, right, I get it, you're Mossad, and your code name is Rebecca !"

He gave a faint smile, which froze when he saw the expression on the face of this woman he loved more than anything.

"I'm not with the Mossad, Vince. I work in the civilian sector. And I failed with you."

Beck found this part of the deposition particularly intriguing. At the time of his arrest, White had still had no idea whom his betrayal had benefitted.

Bit by bit, the words that followed chilled Vincent to the bone. He could no longer move, or speak, or try to make the slightest joke to lighten up the suddenly stifling atmosphere in the bedroom, where all magic had vanished.

Rebecca explained to him how she'd been recruited by an international agency that, while preventing certain technology from making it off Israeli soil, simultaneously tried to lay hands on foreign inventions before they could get patented.

No, she did not work for the Mossad. It was worse, and far less glorious. Industrial activities comprised the extent of her work. And Vincent had access to several secrets that had the bosses salivating.

Vince swung from lethargy to fury. He suddenly got up and started picking up his clothes.

"Industrial espionage! Tell me I'm having a nightmare! You used me…"

"No, that's just it, and that's exactly the problem. Don't be angry, come sit back down."

Rebecca then told him that her mission had been to get close to him. Her friendship – a true one – to Ephraim's daughter had made her task easier, and she'd had two months to convince him to cooperate.

"But I just didn't ask anything of you, do you see? I didn't try anything with you, and I failed my mission. And do you know why?"

Vincent White was weak. Rebecca could have been the Devil made flesh, all he needed was one thing, to hear her say the words that next streamed from her mouth like the sweetest music, like a balm over his deepest wounds. Rebecca had failed, because she'd fallen in love with him. How do you betray the one you love?

Deep down inside, the young woman, who felt true friendship, and even some affection, for the man she'd so adroitly turned, could only curse herself as she heard the phrase that she'd been waiting for.

"What can I do to stop you from leaving?"

Over the course of several months, Vince strove to piece together the disparate computing elements that were involved in the development of an ultra-sophisticated stealth software that targeted satellite sensors. OptroNex was at the forefront in this domain, even though Vincent himself worked on other projects. That was what made things difficult.

The security system that was in place to protect OptroNex's innately volatile data included routine body searches and several X-ray walkthrough gates that everyone needed to pass through when entering as when exiting the premises.

No sooner had she gotten his assent that Rebecca introduced him to a middle-aged man with a heavily receding hairline and a face that vaguely resembled a historical figure, one that Vince initially had a hard time putting his finger on.

"Meet Avi Haim," said the young woman once Vince had joined them in the booth they'd been occupying in the bar. "He's going to walk you through everything…"

She was smiling sadly, and, in a flash, Vincent recognized who the man across from him looked like. David Ben Gurion, the founder of the State of Israel. But a Ben Gurion whose black hair was nicely cut, and who was saddled with glasses.

"I'm glad that Rebecca managed to get your cooperation," the man said without preamble. "Let us begin by going over some of your habits."

Avi Haim wanted to know everything. Everything from the brand of clothes and watch that he wore, to what his favorite breakfast looked like. For well over an hour, he made him describe the routine that took him to OptroNex every day, and made him picture himself leave the buildings at nightfall. He took no notes.

Every now and then, he put a stop to Vincent's explanations, pulled a face, looked at Rebecca, then started questioning him again.

"How long have you had your car for?" he asked towards the end of what was becoming an exhausting interview.

"Very well." He wrapped things up. "A German car, that's just what we need. You're going to be handing Rebecca your spare keys, and we're going to take care of the rest."

Vincent had owned a Golf for the past four years. The small blue car had an electronic starter that was programmed to a matching key. The exchange took place the following day, and Rebecca taught him how to slide open his new key so he could extract the minuscule 8-gig thumb drive that was concealed inside.

"When this will all be over," promised Rebecca, "we'll be able to think about our future. I'm sure that Haim will help us out. After all, nothing's really keeping you in Washington. You'll see, in Haifa, we've got a one of a kind technology center, the Technion."

Vincent couldn't have cared less. During the weeks that followed, he focused all his energies on the "mission" he'd been entrusted with, and every evening he would cart out his little double-ended thumb drive brimming with new data. The only thing that mattered now was the night to come. Their two bodies entwined with such ardor that, at that moment, nothing in the world seemed able to split them apart. Ever.

To White's, and by extension Avi Haim's, extreme misfortune, the employee walkthrough gates at OptroNex had been changed without his paying it any mind, and replaced with cutting-edge technology that was able to analyze the metal weight of everything it scanned down to the milligram. But had it not been for the extreme vigilance of a tight security crew, the car key would have undoubtedly never revealed its secret. It had taken a zealous agent undertaking a comparative analysis between his own kit and that of every staff member of OptroNex for the anomaly to be rooted out.

Vincent White had been arrested, still in possession of certain data, as he'd been hanging around outside Rebecca's house. By the sheerest of coincidences, she had been delayed at the embassy that evening. As soon as White had been arrested, she'd vanished into thin air.

Beck closed the folder containing poor White's deposition, knowing that the guy would pay for being a puppet by a long prison time. He dithered for a beat or two, then picked up his phone.

The receptionist at the Israeli embassy told him in flawless English that military attaché Avi Haim wasn't in that day, but that she would be happy to take a message for him. It was with an almost savage joy that Beck stated his identity and his position within the CIA.

"Military attaché… My ass!"

Chapter 6

The contrast between the New York and Mexico City airports was staggering. While the whole of the US aviation system was like a well-oiled machine, with the planes performing a flawlessly choreographed dance out on the runways, the Mexican folklore had even seeped its way into the capital city's skies.

Between the construction of the second terminal and the airport modernization works, organization had fallen to the wayside. The contents of three ultra-full long-haulers were meant to spill into the narrow access point of a corridor in the process of being renovated. At the other end of it, a half-dozen impassive guards, stood in front of a kind of green sentry box, were stamping passports without tossing a single glance at the passengers holding them out. The walls of the terminal were painted the same color, and the reflected neon lights made everything look sickly, emphasizing everyone's defeated mien and exhausted air.

"American, *señor*? Ah, French! Welcome to Mexico."

Once past border control, they had to wait another half hour for their baggage to arrive. Porters with foreheads beaded with sweat babbled incessantly while standing on the lookout for potential clients.

The arrivals from Dallas were jostling those from Rio, while the bags from the Air France flight, meant to come on belt 3, finally made their appearance, amid much blaring of sirens, two numbers down.

No sooner had they recovered their bags that some travelers, whole families at a time, rushed towards the gates, forging a path between the mounds of suitcases that were strewn all over the floor, adding to the general confusion by calling out to each other at the top of their voices, afraid they'd otherwise get lost.

It all felt like a fun fair, like a good time, like happy chaos. Despite a semblance of air conditioning, it was hot and humid. Juliette and Katia were at the end of their rope. Theo was holding back his laughter. At last, they were outside.

"Here we are," went Theo. "No second thoughts?"

A molten lead weight had just dropped onto their shoulders. Smack in the middle of the afternoon, the sun was beaming down, its glare implacable in the high, rarefied air. Outside the terminal, the fairgrounds atmosphere seemed to have gotten worse. A snaking line of old green Beetles wound its way into the traffic stream, while the drivers clamored one by one to get potential customers, to grab their suitcases and shove them as they could into trunks and onto roofs.

"Yeah. I'm already giving a second thought to that air conditioning," sighed Juliette. "Even though it didn't work."

In the huge parking lot that overlooked the airport, few were the vehicles that bore license plates. Theo would later learn that, in Mexico, the police had stopped handing out citations for traffic violations, because everybody had stopped paying them years ago. They had switched out their notepads for screwdrivers and simply took the license plates off illegally parked cars.

Unfortunately, nobody went to pick those up, either, and the metal plates were sold by the precincts by the ton.

"*Taxi, señores?*"

A small, stocky man with glittering eyes had sneaked his way through the mass of other cab drivers, shoving them over without compunction. Without waiting for an answer, he'd grabbed Juliette's bags with a firm hand.

"Hey, wait a minute!"

Theo grabbed him by the sleeve. A smile shone on the Mexican's face.

"*Taxi? Sigue-moi.*"

Theo grabbed hold of his suitcases, and Juliette took Katia's hand. They followed their improvised guide, who had already left them several paces behind.

"Theo, look at that!"

Just a couple yards away from the door they'd exited through, the column of cabs was getting checked by two police officers. The front passenger seat of every vehicle had been taken out.

Every now and again, one of the drivers would call some of his colleagues to push his little Beetle outside the queue. The air-cooled engine was easy to maintain, but had a hard time handling long idling times during heatwaves.

Most of the passengers on their flight had formed an orderly queue, and the cars loaded them up one by one.

The small Mexican was leading them in the opposite direction.

"Hold on a second," said Theo. He pointed his finger at the taxis. "*Aqui?*"

"No, *señor. Yo, taxi independiente.* Come with me, I make good bargain."

"OK, let's follow him," Theo told Juliette, who was starting to look worried. "Not too far. Katia's worn out."

The man stopped. He came back to Theo and grabbed two more suitcases, despite his protests. He now vanished under the weight of the bags. Gesturing, he signaled to him to take his daughter into his arms and leave Juliette carrying a single vanity case.

Thus loaded up, the small group set off again. They crossed a utilitarian-looking square that had known an attempted beautification by way of several flower beds and a few flamboyant bougainvillea. A Mexicana Airlines A320 Airbus was making its landing approach, its white fuselage gliding just a few dozen yards above their heads.

After several minutes' walk, they ended up in a small street. A cobbler was fixing a pair of shoes in front of his shop.

Two children, seated close to him on the ground, were looking through a tattered comic book together. They paid them no mind.

"*Aquí*. My car!"

A Chrysler that must have been twice as old as its owner and seemed ready to blow out its last breath at any moment. Most likely red in color, the body paint was eclipsed by a thick layer of dust and dried mud. The two right-side doors were mismatched, and a string held the trunk closed. The driver thanked the *zapatero*, earning a sullen gesture in reply.

"This is unreal," whispered Theo, breathless. "We're not getting in there, no way that car can run!"

Smile not dropping from his face, the Mexican tenderly patted a fender. Squinty from the sun, his eyelids were like two slits revealing a glittering, impish gaze. Between his smooth cheeks and the deep grooves furrowed into his forehead, it was impossible to guess at his age.

"This is a very good car, *señor*. Every day, I bring tourists. And I am the best driver in Mexico. Fifteen American dollars for the city center. All good?"

"No, I'm sorry…"

Juliette cut her husband off.

"Listen, we've come all this way. You're not gonna make us go back to the airport now. Let's get in and hurry to the hotel."

Suddenly worried, the driver leapt back into the fray.

"Fifteen dollars? Too expensive. Ten dollars?"

"OK," went Theo. "Ten dollars if we get there alive. The *Camino Real* hotel."

Cheered back up, the man untangled the string that held the trunk closed and hurled the suitcases inside.

"*Camino Real* hotel," he said. "Very good. Right in the city center. Best hotel in Mexico."

Katia jumped down and hurried over to the car. Before settling in, she turned towards her father.

"I don't get it," she said. "He doesn't just not talk like us, he doesn't even talk like the people on the plane. Are you sure we're in America?"

If the brakes on the cab were questionable, the comfort level of the interior inexistent, the suspensions out for the count, the smell of the old seats barely this side of bearable, the engine itself had lost none of its vigor.

They crossed the city at a furious speed. Several times, they missed pedestrians by a hair, largely by alerting them at the last minute by way of violent honks. Most of the near-victims had been policemen, who seemed particularly targeted by the driver when they had the insolence to be in his way.

Around the tenth red light they ran, Theo stopped keeping track. Katia alone enjoyed it all immensely, laughing uproariously at this mad rush that her parents couldn't put a stop to despite their loud protests.

"Don't be afraid," he soothed them. "Here, everyone drives like this. But me, I'm the best!"

By some miracle, they made it to their hotel after crossing the Paseo de la Reforma at around 50 mph, despite the pretty heavy traffic.

"Here you are, *señores*. Your hotel."

Apoplectic, Theo got out of the car and waited until he'd gotten all his bags before holding out a ten-dollar bill without a word – or a tip.

"If you want to visit Mexico…" began the driver.

"Thank you," Theo cut in. "We'll manage without you."

Laughing, the man slammed his car door and left in a cloud of exhaust smoke.

A multitude of little details betrayed the age of the *Camino Real*. But its resolutely extravagant design enabled it to do justice to its reputation as a high standing hotel. The room, which had a large balcony and a small adjoining living room, came fully equipped. Flat screen TV, minibar, air conditioning…

Juliette threw herself on the bed.

"I don't even know where we are anymore," she said. "I don't know what day it is, what time it is, either here or in Paris. And I really don't care. I'm dirty, but I don't wanna get washed up. Whatever happens next, I'm sleeping now."

Without even taking off her clothes, she hurled her shoes across the room and slid between the sheets.

"Don't even wake me up for the next three days at least."

Theo put Katia to bed. She was in no better shape than her mother. Then, he shut the heavy drapes and slid out of the room on tiptoe.

Inside the living room, he carefully read the instructions explaining how to use the phone and dialed a local number.

A voice answered him in Spanish. Theo introduced himself.

"We've just gotten here," he said.

"Very well, *señor*. You can rest until tomorrow. We'll be in touch late tomorrow morning."

Theo felt tired. A seven-hour flight to New York, a restless night spent at the airport Sheraton (they'd felt frustrated at not being able to visit the Big Apple, but their itinerary had been tight and all their seats had been booked from Paris). The next day, a shuttle had picked them up at dawn and dropped them off at the terminal where their flight to Mexico took off.

All he needed to do now was wait. He knew their trip wasn't yet over, and that they would undoubtedly need to grab another plane, since the Center was located somewhere in the western Sierra Madre, almost 1300 miles from Mexico City. An astonishing route, with a journey of another several hours in store…

Despite the barrage of explanations as to the necessity of keeping the Center shrouded in mystery, Theo felt a little unsettled by this paper chase that he didn't really see the need for.

He opened the picture window and looked in wonder out at the old city and its show of contrasts under a dreamlike haze. Beneath his feet crawled heavy traffic, and the downtown high rises in the oldest capital city of the New World drew his gaze to the strange, Aztec-style edifice that loomed over the horizon: the imperial residence of Chapultepec.

"Mexico," he murmured, as though to persuade himself that he was truly there. "What in the world am I doing in this country with my wife and six-year-old?"

The thought gave him vertigo. All of a sudden, after he'd made his decision swept up in the euphoria of it all, and his excitement for this adventure had made all rational thought take a back seat, he suddenly felt the weight of his own responsibility.

No, this commitment was no joking matter.

All the precautions that had been taken to cut them off from their loved ones, and from all the safety nets they'd built for themselves throughout their lives, suddenly no longer seemed like such a game. He'd signed on for two years. And maybe more, he mused, quivering. Would these two years prove enough for Feldman and his employers, whose identity he actually didn't even know?

Beneath a glorious sun, leaning against the guardrail of a balcony on the eleventh floor of a luxury hotel, staring at the ruins of the old city of Tenochtitlan, Theo felt utterly alone.

And utterly defenseless.

The table was covered in multicolored dishes with lilting names like hymns to the sun: *enchiladas, tacos, guacamole, chili con carne, tortillas, chili…* A small band was playing between the rare patrons, intoning a long lament tinged with languor and heartbreak. The temperature in here was mild, while outside it was set to break new records.

Theo hadn't had any breakfast, having woken up too late, yanked out of bed by the phone ringing.

He'd merely had the time to get dressed and grab a cab to the rendezvous set by his contact, leaving Juliette and Katia to their lollygagging.

Because of the time difference, he'd fallen asleep before sunset, only to wake up for the first time a little after midnight. He hadn't been able to fall back asleep until dawn, and even that had been troubled by anguished dreams, nothing tying them together if not a suffocating feeling of imprisonment.

Juliette had been through the same. Less constrained by a schedule than her husband, she'd treated herself to a sleeping pill, utterly determined to snap back into shape as fast as possible so that she could face whatever was coming next.

Theo, who had been expecting a very official meeting, had been pleasantly surprised to find the small restaurant inside which his contact was waiting for him. The man recognized him as soon as he stepped through the doorway.

"Mister Collin, pleasure to meet you in this small *cantina*." His French, although heavily accented, was almost flawless. "It's one of my favorite places in Mexico. And I'm not just saying that because I own it. I thought it preferable to invite you where I feel at home rather than at one of my offices. Follow me. You are at home here."

Recognizing in that the colorful and emphatic spirit of Mexican hospitality, just as he'd imagined it, Theo had delightedly let himself be led, decided that from then on he would take full advantage of the good times that his "mission" would grant him.

It was with the same warmth that his host had introduced himself:

"Pedro Tamazula. Truly delighted. I am very glad to have you."

No sooner had they sat down at their table that they'd been surrounded by prompt servers who, unasked, had set down two margaritas in glasses that could easily have doubled as goldfish bowls.

Theo felt relaxed. The hushed atmosphere of the *cantina*, with its stucco walls and its heavy, walnut-stained wooden tables, was comforting, and had managed to instantly remove him from his cares, while his insecurity had given way to curiosity.

His Mexican contact gave off a cheerful and contagious intensity. He too was dressed in the European style, in an off-white suit and an open-collar white shirt. His one concession to the local fashion was a pair of white cowboy boots. He looked like any other businessman in his fifties, despite his pomaded hair and small, Clark Gable moustache.

"Let us drink to your arrival in Mexico, land of all the gods and honor."

Theo had brought the glass to his lips, out of politeness, meaning to keep a clear head.

"You don't like plain margarita? Would you want me to have them bring you something else?"

"No, thank you. It's very good. Sadly, I'm running on an empty stomach and still suffering from jetlag."

"Of course. I understand. I too get jetlagged very easily. And my travels have me endure it all too often. If you would like a fruit cocktail, we have a house special…"

"Thank you. Truly. I will have what you're having, but in moderation."

The Mexican had laughed.

"Then I will do the same. But our way with moderation is not so European."

He had drained his glass in one move, then watched Theo with an enthusiastic grin, showing off teeth too white to be real, laugh lines bisecting a face weathered by the sun.

Without bringing any menus, the waiters had then engaged in a saraband, underscored by the music, piling mounds of food on the table, laying each one down with a small, artful bow, in a manner not unlike Oriental receptions. Just for that moment, Theo saw himself like a maharaja; or, better yet, an emir.

After he'd finished his cocktail, Tamazula gestured to one of the waiters, who hurried over to their table.

"Would you care for some wine, or would you rather some Mexican beer? I import an excellent Cabernet Sauvignon from Napa Valley. I do not mean to offend, but it holds its own against many vintages I've had the opportunity to try during my stays in your country. I also have some more modest local vintages, but I do strenuously recommend the Cabernet…"

"I'll follow along with your suggestion."

Tamazula gave an order in Spanish. A moment later, their glasses were full of a rich, red liquid, while Theo's cocktail was vanishing from the table. He had to admit that the wine was exquisite, as fruity as it was sunny, with an oaky aftertaste that defined its whole body.

"You speak excellent French," he said as he set down his glass. "Where did you learn it?"

"It was a long time ago," began Tamazula, adopting a nostalgic air. He savored his wine in little sips, as he would have if it'd been a piping hot soup.

"My father already owned two restaurants. He sent me to study hospitality management, thinking I'd prove more useful to him that way than if I learned physics or medicine." He dipped a taco in guacamole, then into the spicy salsa, before greedily stuffing it into his mouth.

"He wasn't wrong. In fact, the man died during his stay in France." Tamazula crossed himself while murmuring a few unintelligible words. "There was barely time for me to come back for his funeral and to take over his business.

"Since then, I stay in France on business sometimes."

Theo had finished his wine glass without realizing it, and it surprised him to see it full once more. His head was spinning a little. He started to nibble at the food.

"You like my Cabernet, eh, *amigo*. The sun is what makes it so lush. Believe me, wine does not take well to sea shipping… Once it's made it to your country, Californian Cabernet is a very sad affair.

"But you have given up on your moderation," he added impishly. "*Bravo*. Your glass is empty."

Theo was wolfing down, now. The food was just the right amount of spicy, if a little fatty for his tastes. He helped himself to generous servings of fajitas, enchiladas, and other stews with mouthwatering odors and utterly devastating flavor.

The whole of the meal went on just as tranquilly, with Tamazula proving to be charming and very courteous, carrying their purely touristic conversation and spicing it here and there with some personal opinions and anecdotes.

When Theo showed signs he was full, Tamazula gestured economically. Instantly, the waiter dance picked back up, and the table was cleared in the blink of an eye. The band stopped. Tamazula extracted a leather case from his jacket, and two cigars out of that. He held one out to Theo.

"Here. A genuine Cuban cigar. You'll soon see there are a few advantages to being on this side of the Rio Grande…"

Theo's stymied gaze swung back and forth, from the cigar to his host.

"Of course, it is true; you're French. Unlike our American friends, you are not so bound by this embargo…"

"That's not quite what I meant. I wasn't really expected to be getting this warm a reception…"

Tamazula took the time to roll his cigar against his ear, to light it, and to take a draw.

"You are starting to wonder? What is the first question to come to your mind? Why have I been received by an opulent restaurateur instead of one of those technocrats I'd been expecting? Or perhaps, what is the relationship between him and this Center I am supposed to go to?"

"I have to admit, the unusual aspects of this mission have been a constant surprise."

Tamazula burst out laughing.

"Mission? You sound like a mercenary! But at least you are still polite. Others who have sat at this same table were less patient than you!"

"Mister Tamazula," Theo broke in, "you have done your best to stir my curiosity, and I can indeed say I don't really understand what's going on. I was supposed to be hired for my analyst skills. The work I do is highly specialized. When and where do I get to meet the members of my team?"

Tamazula took a long drag of his cigar, stoking up the mystery he was so gleefully building up. Close to the door, the musicians, who had packed away their instruments, said their goodbyes to him, then walked out of the restaurant. The room was now empty.

"Are you quite sure that you were hired as a computer specialist?"

The Mexican's glowing gaze had come to rest on Theo.

"You don't yet know what place the Center will hold within the future of our civilization. That's why my words seem obscure to you. Just as you must be having a hard time making sense of all these precautions being put in place to send you, and others, right in the middle of the Sierra Madre with the greatest secrecy. Still, you volunteered."

"I took this job for the money," argued Theo defensively.

A dangerous glint came over Tamazula's gaze. Then his expression shifted, once more giving way to that chubby, good-natured businessman he'd started the meal as. The Mexican set down his cigar, the better to shift his hands apologetically.

"Very well. Excuse my manners, I get so easily carried away by my taste for mystery. That's something typically Mexican, you know!

"What you call the Center is a research base located in the heights of the Sierra Madre. It will be revealed to you before the week is out. People more qualified than I, who will fully satisfy your curiosity, and who will lay out your task for you much more clearly than I would be able to."

"At the base!" snapped Theo in agitation. "When I won't be able to turn back anymore. When I'll be completely cut off from the outside…"

"Those are the rules of the game. I'm sorry."

"Well then, give me some explanations. What's the organization we're going to be working under? Is it legal? Why haven't I been met by anyone official? And these allusions to a task that won't necessarily involve analyst work? Good God, I have the right to know!"

"Listen," said Tamazula in a tone of voice that was meant to be reassuring. "I'm going to try and make you see the reasons why the base must exist..."

He cut himself off, then went on, looking cheerful.

"But first, did you know that one of my best friends was French, just like you?"

"Please, get to the point."

"I'm getting there. Allow me to tell it to you in my own way."

Theo sighed and acceded with a nod of his head.

"I met him while I was studying in Paris. He belonged to those great provincial upper classes, and he had the soul of an entrepreneur. In just a few years, he was able to turn a small inheritance into enough profit to make him one of the key financial players in his region."

Tamazula paused for a beat. He lit his cigar once more and tossed a look toward Theo, who was having a hard time keeping a lid on his impatience.

"He was safe from everything, after that, barely forty years old and achieving all his ambitions. Even so, intuitively, he felt that his world was going to change. Oh, not his very own. But he had gleaned an essential matter: that this social order he was so fond of, this world of freedoms and opposition and secularism and individual freedoms, that it was all splintering apart.

"He called me and he asked me: "Pedro, in your opinion, how many years are we from a world war?"

"I told him that, no matter how rich he was, it was a pity to waste his money on long-distance calls to talk nonsense. But he was being serious: "Pedro, you feel safe over in Mexico. Do you think "they" will be attacking you one day? That won't ever happen. You've seen how things are in Europe, "they" come from all over, "they" think they can do as they please, "they" act like they own the place now"…"

Tamazula broke off once more, the better to grab Theo's attention.

"We have been living with this threat for so many years that we've grown used to it. My friend had his little theory, and as they say, just because you're paranoid it doesn't mean you don't have enemies, isn't that right?

"That day, I listened to him predicting a whole host of catastrophes. Secular governments being toppled over, terror attacks, nuclear proliferation. And this same "they" that kept passing his lips over and over, without further clarification. All until he reached his conclusion, which freezes my blood when I think of it today. "You'll see. It was Pearl Harbor that escalated the Second. One day, a massive attack on US soil will signal the start of the Third – and the worst!""

Theo incredulously shook his head. He'd expected some speechifying, but certainly not to hear Tamazula unload a bunch of apocalyptic-flavored barroom talk.

"World war three?"

"Yes," stated Tamazula. "It's been nearly twenty years since that talk. Long before nine-eleven, long before Al Qaida was even a thought.

"A few weeks later, my friend was headed to New York on business, with a layover in London, with his family in tow. He had the bad sense to get on board a certain Pan Am flight, on precisely December the 21st 1988. Does that ring any bells?…

"Their mangled bodies were found somewhere around Lockerbie, in Scotland. That was not the start of the war, to be sure, but it changed a great deal of things for me…"

Theo sighed.

"I am very sorry about your friend. But I'm not interested in political fiction. And I don't see what that has to do with the Center."

"Come now, *amigo*. Try to read a bit between the lines. I can tell you nothing more.

"My friend was certain that the Soviet Union would collapse and that the third conflict would oppose the north to the south. He feared the Americans' isolationism and the Europeans' typical cowardice. But having his own fortune enabled him to conceive of other ways to protect himself.

"Back during the Reagan administration, people were already talking about the need to put a part of our defense in private hands. What is the best safeguard of a free world? The interests of bankers and magnates!"

"Do you mean to say that the Center…"

"I don't mean anything at all," Tamazula cut him off. "I have tried to expose some principles to you. Or do you believe that a chemist or a physicist is not kept in the dark when he is transferred from one company to another?"

Tamazula stopped talking. Theo understood that was as much as he was going to get out of him. And the reality he was now glimpsing summoned a far worse feeling of vertigo inside him than the previous evening, when that first lucid flicker had struck him out on the balcony of the *Camino Real*.

"And if, at the end of these revelations," he ventured, "we came to agree that I'm not really your man?"

"You're not anyone's man, Mister Collin. You are nothing but a computer scientist who got a promotion in a foreign land on behalf of a company who employs him. You are not being asked to buy in. Merely to slot yourself into a puzzle."

Tamazula checked his watch. His gaze regained its jovial and considerate expression.

"It's grown late. And the temperature outside must be stifling. I'll have you dropped off back at your hotel, that way you'll be able to enjoy my limousine. I recommend you take a good nap, for when we are tired things often seem darker.

"Plane tickets will be left for you in your hotel room, and you will leave for Chihuahua the day after tomorrow. Take the day to tour around a bit with your family. Why don't you go visit Chapultepec Castle and its park; I'm sure your wife will find it delightful.

"And this evening, take her out to dinner in the old city, around the Zócalo. You cannot, sadly, get to know Mexico in just a few hours, and my own schedule doesn't leave me the slightest bit of time to be your guide."

Tamazula took in Theo's bleak look.

"One last bit of advice. Remember that you made a commitment. Don't do anything you might regret."

The interview was over. Theo got up from the table. He was ashen. Tamazula stood up in turn and went up to him to put his arms around him. With one pull, he held him against his chest.

"Come now, *amigo*… Enjoy your stay. Enjoy life, enjoy the sun. She is short, life… very short."

Juliette was radiant in this little mauve top that Theo had never seen her in, and this little white skirt that showed off her legs well above the knee. Her hair was a voluptuous, golden fall. She and Katia seemed excited as could be. They threw their arms around Theo's neck like he'd been gone for weeks.

Mechanically, he took his daughter in his arms. The French doors to the balcony were wide open, and the built-in radio was blaring out some fiery music, enhanced by trumpets and a Spanish chorus.

"It's amazing. We've just ate the hugest meal poolside, and the band wouldn't stop serenading us. Your daughter even fell in love with the singer. And this weather... I feel like I'm floating."

"Daddy," asked Katia, "is it true in Paris people are asleep and it's night?"

Theo gently set her down.

"Of course, since your mom said so."

"She ate at least two pounds of fruit," said Juliette tenderly.

She kissed Theo, then twirled to send her hair flying.

"I washed it with chamomile and let it dry in the sun. Do you like?"

"Me too," interjected Katia. "We went to the hotel boutique, mommy bought a lot of stuff…"

Juliette suddenly noticed Theo's worried look.

"How did your meeting go?" she asked in a less lighthearted tone of voice. "Were there any issues?"

Theo took off his jacket and tossed it on the couch in their small living room.

Hopping on one leg, Katia made her way to the bedroom.

"I wanna show you what mom got me."

"Hold on a bit," went Juliette. "Daddy wants to talk to me."

Katia put a stop to her dancing right in the doorway.

"I think your face looks funny," she said. "You'd better go outside in the sun."

"That isn't such a bad idea," acquiesced Theo.

The hotel pool was huge. Its streamlined design looked like a heart with three compartments with a sort of island in the middle that housed a bar. Behind it bustled several smiling waiters, passing multicolored cocktails down to the swimmers sitting on submerged benches.

A few clients were polishing off their late lunches in the shade of the brightly colored bougainvillea that were arranged into pleasing groves. The tropical foliage seemed to be subject to constant care on the part of the *Camino Real* staff, and the whole of it gave off a feeling of languorous stillness that put Theo at ease for a very brief moment. Juliette took his hand.

"There's two lounge chairs over there. We can just ask for an umbrella."

Katia was already gamboling towards the water.

"At least take your shoes off if you want to dip in your legs," cried her mother.

They stretched out in the sun and were instantly joined by a harried waiter. They ordered two fruit cocktails. Theo dismissed the idea of getting a parasol.

"Just what paradise is made of, right?" commented Juliette.

Theo resumed his serious air. He waited for their drinks to get there, then sidled closer to his wife.

"I think I got us into a hell of a pickle."

He told her all about his lunch with Pedro Tamazula, down to the last detail, knowing how Juliette was able to keep a clear head about the most complex situations. Tamazula's words, evasive as they'd been, had offered plenty of explicit subtext.

He shared with her his own interpretation of things, and waited for her to share her thoughts. The time for fighting was over, and Theo knew that she wouldn't hold it against him now for not giving more thought to her warnings.

"What do you intend to do?" she contented herself to ask.

"I don't know. The worst part is that I still have no idea what's being expected of me."

"That seems pretty straightforward. It sounds like E.C.Tronics is getting mixed up in planning or building a paramilitary base. Why Mexico? That's a first great question.

"It also sounds like their fixation with secrecy has some funny roots. Your Mexican sounds more like a mobster than a businessman. But the real mystery here is, why come to you? There's other analysts out in the world…

"Do you think it has anything to do with Enterprise 17?"

"I was dumb enough to get you and Katia mixed up in this whole thing."

Juliette was moved by her husband's distraught look. She blamed herself for not being strong enough to impose her will and prevent their leaving. Though for this part, Theo had left the choice up to her.

She angrily recalled her own attitude over the two months leading up to their departure. Rather than harass him as she had, swinging between bad moods and temperamental excess, she should have supported him, tried to find out what precisely was being cooked up.

But how? They'd both gotten caught up in the same trap. Theo wouldn't have held a grudge for too long if she'd vetoed his surreal promotion. Deep down inside, she too had wanted them to leave, only she'd found it easier to let him bear the full weight of that responsibility.

Well, the dream had just come true. They now needed to do all it took to keep it from turning into a nightmare.

"Let's calmly think this through," she said. "We have enough information to try and guess at what sort of thing we're going to be getting mixed up in. After all, we're still free, and the *Camino Real* is hardly a Central-American gulag. It's very likely that your work will keep you safe from any kind of political compromise. I have a hard time believing there's a clandestine organization…"

"I also thought that E.C.Tronics was sending me out here on some government's behalf. How could I have been so stupid!"

Theo went quiet. On the edge of the pool, Katia had spontaneously taken her dress off and jumped into the water in nothing but her underwear, to fond laughter from a handful of tourists. Excited by that clamor, the hotel parrot, set up on a perch shaded by a parasol, wanted in on the fun.

In a stentorian voice, it called out the first bars of the *La Cucaracha* chorus. The tourists clapped. A young woman in her twenties, clad in a Brazilian G-string, moved towards the bird, taking care to make the swing of her hips as provocative as possible. She held out an olive to it. The parrot spat. A new, and louder, wave of laughter followed.

Juliette couldn't hold back a smile.

"Chihuahua, that was Pancho Villa's town, isn't that right?"

"It could be," replied Theo. "Why? Do you want to draw an allegory?"

Juliette drank her glass down in one swallow and straightened up in her seat. Her face suddenly took on a new determination.

"Theo," she said. "Let's get out of here. Let's pick up our passports from reception. Settle our bill and let's head back to France right away. There's got to be a direct flight out tonight, or maybe tomorrow morning.

"We'll give those extra paychecks back to E.C.Tronics, and you'll tell them that you changed your mind. Tell them whatever. That I'm pregnant, that you can't handle this weather. We'll figure out a reason.

"Let's hurry. I'm now absolutely certain that we shouldn't go any further with this. Nobody's gonna be able to come bother us. We don't know anything, or anybody…"

Theo felt much brighter. She was right, of course. As things stood now, who would believe him if he decided to reveal the existence of the Center? "The base on the high plateau." That sounded like a video game title spawned from the deranged imagination of a little programmer who was hard-up for adventure.

What else did he know? Practically nothing. The western Sierra Madre were bigger than several French departments put together. Whatever link there was between E.C.Tronics and some organization that he didn't even know the name of? His allegations wouldn't hold up to a disavowal from such an important company. He'd been tested. It was an exam he'd failed, and that was that.

If he'd been wrong not to trust Juliette's instincts, he wouldn't be making that mistake twice. And if he had to borrow money again, so be it. If he had to be jobless for a few months, so be it. The safety of his wife and child came first.

Flee Mexico. Get back to his life. Show back up before his loved ones and everyone else who could offer them protection.

"OK," he said. "Phone the airport and see what you can learn. I'm gonna get our passports back. If there's no plane before tomorrow, we'll get another hotel."

At the edge of the pool, Katia was pulling up her underwear, which had distended from the water. She called out:

"Dad, mom, look at me! I'm diving!"

Clamping one hand against her nose, she launched herself into a mighty cannonball and then resurfaced, the picture of delight…

The heat had reached its peak, and the shadows cast by the odd cactus had been reduced to mere spots that even a lizard couldn't have found shelter under. The red rocks of the trail were too hot for the *peones*, their feet hardened by calluses, to tread without shoes.

In the clear sky, the ever-present vultures circled around, looking for carcasses. Some of the *rios* of the Sierra Madre had dried up several months too early, making life difficult for the desert regulars. The slight breeze that stirred the dust atop the cracked ground had fallen, dropping its dried grass sculptures like so many faux shrubs sparsely lining a road to nowhere.

The air had become unbreathable and burned the lungs of the man who had ventured into this hell two days ago now, with only a scrap of a shirt, which he'd wrapped around his head, for protection against the sun. Sweat and dust had hardened his makeshift hat.

The exposed flesh of his back and shoulders had grown covered in blisters. His feet, otherwise protected by a pair of stogies, had doubled in volume, and each step he took pulled a moan of pain from him. His body was nothing but an open wound, and his brain had taken refuge inside a sort of waking coma, a blessed unconsciousness that enabled him to keep moving forward, to keep getting up after each of his ever more frequent falls.

A step. Another step. He was no longer sweating. The water inside his body had dried up like the *rios*, and his parched tongue had welded to the roof of his mouth.

'I'm going to die soon,' he thought.

And the thought sparked no feeling inside him. He was in a volcano. Its lava was flowing through his veins. In Mexico, man and nature are one. His mind had dissociated from his body when the cactus had broken under his heel, yielding a flesh as withered as the rock it had grown on.

The man collapsed with a spray of dust, and his muscles, his clothes, blended in with the desert, becoming a new hillock that life was draining from like blood from an artery.

A huge vulture circled the motionless body. It was far larger than all those that had been following his inescapable torment for hours. The beating of its wings gave rise to a deafening noise, and its shadow stretched out over several yards. The man struggled to get up. Die standing, at least. Only get devoured after his soul left his body.

The helicopter blades came to a stop with a sharp whistle.

"He's still alive, Colonel."

"I can see that. Unless dead men walk in this country."

Colonel Meyrek jumped down onto the burning stone. Several yards out, the staggering silhouette was trying to get away in a last, desperate effort. Meyrek unholstered his gun.

"Hand me a canteen."

A soldier tossed one in his direction. Meyrek caught it midair.

"Mister Fleisher," he cried.

The silhouette stopped walking. Somewhere inside the man's brain, that name still held a semblance of meaning. He turned around, and his reddened eyes made out nothing save a shadow close to the immense vulture.

"Mister Fleisher, might you have forgotten to bring some water with you when you left us? Unless your canteen dried out as you walked. Mister Fleisher, can you hear me?"

Water! Even more so than his own identity, that word triggered a reawakening of his conscious inside of Fleisher's numb mind. Water. It was mirages fading a few steps out, the candelabra cactuses turning to fossils in the sun, the *rios* abandoning their beds until the following rainy season, the carcasses of animals dead from not reaching the end of their quests.

"Water!" uttered Fleisher, no sound issuing from a throat turned to desert sand.

He started walking again, in the opposite direction. Forgetting why he'd run. Forgetting the vulture and what that voice was to him, that voice that had been able to tame him with one word. A huge hope engulfed him.

The colonel unscrewed the cap on the canteen and turned it upside-down.

"Hurry now, Mister Fleisher. Run. The water is. Run. Soon there won't be one drop left."

Driven by the last of his instincts, Fleisher quickened his pace, like a puppet with broken joints, his legs refusing to carry him despite a last-ditch effort of will.

"Faster! The desert is drinking it up."

Fleisher got within fifteen feet of the colonel. Three-quarters of the contents of the canteen had already spilled onto Meyrek's boots.

"Oh, I am sorry," the man said. "You got here too late."

He lapped at the last hint of moisture that hung from the flask. The other man fell to his knees on the ground and began sobbing softly.

"Take him back to camp," the colonel ordered his men. "And leave him in the courtyard for a few more hours, without water."

Without sparing a glance to the wretch at his feet, he got into the chopper and ordered the pilot to head back to base.

Meyrek loathed deserters. They were stupid creatures – and worse yet, cowards. But they would all ultimately understand that it was useless to try and run.

Chapter 7

Juliette had carefully folded and packed all their clothes in the suitcase containing their meager effects. Katia had rinsed and dried herself off, and now wouldn't stop protesting.

"Why can't I stay in the pool? And why are you packing? We aren't leaving?"

Finally, faced with her mother's silence, she'd begun to cry.

"I don't want to go. Why don't you say anything?"

Despite her worries, Juliette had had to calm her down. She'd finally managed to get in touch with someone at the airport and had learned that the next direct flight to Paris would be operated by Aeromexico the following morning at seven. She'd instantly booked three seats.

As she was hanging up, Theo burst into the room. In an instant, Juliette understood that fresh problems had cropped up.

"They won't return our passports."

"What?"

Juliette had shot her question out like an exclamation.

A ball of anxiety settled in her chest.

"I don't know what they're plotting. They told me this whole story about how with our room paid up until tomorrow, they've sent our passports to the police station to get them checked. Supposedly that's routine."

"But that's a lie! We've never had that. In any country."

Theo crumpled onto the bed.

"I know. Everything I said fell on deaf ears. Only the hotel manager is authorized to hand them back to us."

"Well then, go see him."

"He won't be in until tomorrow morning."

Juliette felt herself get submerged by panic. It was in a choked voice that she quickly went on.

"Theo, we've gotta get the hell out of here. We've gotta move fast and we've got to do it now."

Her voice turned shrill. Theo sadly watched his wife's face grow twisted. He tried to adopt a firm and soothing tone.

"I know what else we can do. Don't get worked up. I'm going to head over to the French embassy with our I.D.'s and declare our passports lost. We'll get a safe-conduct if I tell them we have to be back in France immediately. What time's our flight?"

"Tomorrow, very early."

"Fine then, we'll take the earliest flight we can make. I'll settle the hotel bill and we'll go sleep wherever. In a rental car if we have to. I'll go to the embassy first thing tomorrow. Calm down."

Katia had watched her parents without a peep. In a small, worried voice, she asked:

"Is it bad?"

Theo hoisted her on his knees.

"Don't worry, sweetheart. Daddy's got some problems at work. We're gonna have to go back to France in a hurry. But we'll come back real soon. Just promise me that you'll be good until tomorrow when we get on the plane. Can you do that for me?"

She burrowed her head in the hollow of her father's shoulder and consented with a timid "Yes."

The manager of the *Camino Real* returned to his office towards the end of the afternoon. He quickly took care of some supply issues and got ready to carry out a staff inspection. That was when his gaze was drawn to two passports placed inside a locker. Taken aback, he flipped them open and then called the receptionist.

Why hadn't Mr. and Mrs. Collin picked up their I.D.'s? Embarrassed, his employee told him that the clients had just left the establishment, and that he hadn't been able to stop them.

"What are you talking about!" shouted the manager. "They're guests of *señor* Tamazula's. Why would they leave without their passports?"

Alarmed, he learned that the police station had called towards the start of the afternoon, specifically requesting that the clients be held there until the next day at least. The receptionist had found no better solution than to confiscate their passports, using a routine check as an excuse.

Incensed at the thought that clients might have gotten treated like that in Mexico's greatest luxury hotel, and under his supervision what was more, he yelled into the receiver for a few moments before furiously hanging up. He then dialed Tamazula's direct line to make his apologies.

"Do not worry," replied the other man. "I am aware. I am only sorry that they settled the bill themselves when they were my guests. Tomorrow morning, someone will be by to pick up their papers and return them to them… Yes, of course I know where to find them. That call from the police was most certainly a mistake!"

The hotel manager dabbed at his forehead. The air conditioning unit in his office was running at full blast. But the droplets of sweat that he felt beading on his face had nothing to do with the temperature inside.

The French embassy was located on the Campos Eliseos, the Mexican Champs Elysées, just across from the Chapultepec zoological garden. Despite the raised security level, the soldiers from the contingent posted at the entrance seemed to have quickly adapted to the Mexicans' blissful nonchalant nature.

Seated in one of the seats in the public waiting area, Theo had been waiting for over an hour for the person at the reception desk to forward the paperwork he'd filled out when he'd gotten there. Several times now he'd reiterated the urgent nature of his request. Fifteen odd people, out of which one French couple, were waiting around with him.

"I'm sorry, *señor*," the employee had retorted. "Only the vice-consul is authorized to deliver any authorizations to cross the border. There is nothing I can do."

Theo had to make his way to the French General Consulate, located at number 32 on Lafontaine street. At the end of another hour's wait, a balding, elegant man kindly received him at last; without beating around the bush, he asked him if he'd reported the loss to the local authorities.

"No," answered Theo. "The problem is, my wife's father is seriously ill, and we need to get back to France quickly. We haven't had the time to file any reports. Our plane leaves this afternoon."

Finally, after filling out a sworn statement and producing his and Juliette's I.D.'s, Theo got three consular safe-conducts.

Relieved, he left the consulate to wishes of a speedy recovery for his father-in-law.

The day before, they'd managed to find refuge in a small hotel on the *calle* Bolivar, not far from the Salto Del Algua subway station in the San Geronimo neighborhood. For the price of a few U.S. dollars – a particularly prized currency in Mexico, it seemed – the concierge had consented to rent them a room without having to register their passports.

Theo hurtled himself into the first cab he could hail and shouted out the address to make himself heard over the racket from the engine.

Calmed down at last, he delightedly patted the pocket where he'd stashed the authorizations from the vice-consul, picturing Juliette's relief when he'd brandish them. His only regret was not having phoned her from the consulate.

It was useless to waste the time to look for a pay phone now. With these formalities out of the way, they could finally call their families and let them know they'd be back early, without worrying them too much. The plane was taking off in a few hours.

Lost in his optimistic thoughts, he even let himself be exhilarated by the reckless maneuvering of the cab driver, who did full justice to his profession's by now established reputation.

The sky had become slightly cloudy. Theo looked at his watch. There was just time enough for him to grab his girls and race to the airport.

The taxi got slowed down by a truck that was loaded with bottles and had a half-dozen beaming kids hanging off it. They took a one-way street the wrong way to clear the obstacle.

At last, they made it onto *calle* Bolivar, and the driver agreed to wait for him in front of the hotel.

It was no longer the same concierge. Theo greeted him mechanically. The room was on the second floor. He climbed the stairs and reached the landing in four giant steps. The door was locked. He knocked. Silence.

Stunned, Theo checked the door number. It did in fact read nine. He knocked again.

No answer. Juliette and Katia must have been waiting for him at the bar. Or on the patio.

At reception, he saw that his key was hanging on the hook.

"*Dónde está la señora del número nueve?*"

The porter jerked himself out of his torpor to answer.

"She's gone, sir."

"Gone? Gone shopping?"

"No. Gone. With the little girl. The room has been paid."

A wave of terror overwhelmed Theo. He stammered.

"That's not possible. I'm her husband. The *señora* from number nine. She was waiting for me."

The man lifted his shoulders.

"I don't know, *señor*. Two men came to pick them up. Your wife left with them."

"But, look, you must be making a mistake. My wife's blonde, with long hair. She's French."

"Yes. I know. That was her. With the little girl and many suitcases."

Theo felt himself teeter. The taxi driver walked in right then.

"Any luggage to carry, *señor?*"

Theo didn't even notice him.

"How long ago?" he went on to ask.

"About an hour," the man in front of him replied. "Ah, that's right, I was forgetting. They left an envelope for you."

"Do you need help with anything?" interjected the cab driver again.

The concierge held an envelope out over the counter. Theo feverishly grabbed it and tore into it.

"*Señor,*" uttered the cabbie once more, this time impatiently. "Do I wait for you or not?"

Theo seemed then to realize he was there. He rooted through his pockets for some money and held out a random banknote for him.

"Oh, *muchas gracias.*" The Mexican backed away with a rapturous smile. He'd just made ten times his fare in tip money.

Inside the envelope, there was only a plane ticket and an address. The *El Presidente* Hotel. Chihuahua. In a weak voice, Theo requested the phone.

Tamazula picked up on the second ring. His voice drained of all benignity once he recognized Theo.

"Where are they?" he yelled.

"You did not act reasonably, *señor* Collin. Your departure from the *Camino Real* worried us greatly. Why did you book plane tickets to Paris?"

"Return them to me," thundered Theo, "or else I will call the French embassy, the police, I will reveal to them your dealings, I will tell them about the base…"

"That attitude will get you nowhere," Tamazula calmly broke in. "They have both left for Chihuahua, where you will soon join them. You did find your ticket, did you not?"

"What did you do to them? How did your men convince my wife to follow them?"

"Do not be worried. Your wife was every bit as mad as you are, and we had to administer a tranquilizer. I think that from now on it would be far more clever of you to scrupulously respect your commitments."

"You have no right," gritted out Theo. "You have no right."

"We have this right," snarled Tamazula. "You are the one who did not obey the rules of the game. Our Organization cannot afford to have you return to France after everything that I disclosed to you."

"But I don't know a thing. Nobody would believe anything I said. I have no proof. All I'm asking is to leave here with my family. Let us go and you'll never hear from us again. I'll even pay you back your costs and the advance pay I was granted."

"Too late for that, Mister Collin. The base needs you, and they're waiting for you. Follow your contract and you will be in no danger. Neither you nor yours. *Adios, amigo…*"

Tamazula hung up. For a few moments, Theo was left prostrate before the phone. Outside the hotel, the cab driver patiently stood waiting for him.

The rain had started to fall once more. Fortunately, this greyish kind of drizzle was mostly made up of carbon monoxide, and it had for a side effect to diminish the particularly trying heaviness that thickened the air of this early New York summer.

Few of the rubberneckers crowded outside the entrance to the *Millennium Plaza* had had the foresight to bring umbrellas with them. They gathered together in dripping clusters, covertly trying to take refuge under a scrap of awning, pushed back by the security tape that allowed no-one close to the hall except the card-carrying clients, the members of the press, and the guests attending the special gala organized by the American Security Council[7] in close cooperation with its congressional lobbying arm, the National Coalition for Peace through Strength[8], jointly with the Council for National Policy[9].

---

7   A non-profit advocacy group.

8   Today the National Security Caucus.

9   A preeminent conservative networking group.

The personages invited to this event were the sort to stir up talk as they stirred the curiosity of the onlookers. Expected to attend were, among others, Vice President Theo Chertoff and the Secretary of Homeland Security, General Winclaub, alongside two hundred of the richest men in the world. The cost of attendance: ten thousand dollars a head…

It was the largest fundraiser ever organized by any association, and the dinner alone was expected to net ten million dollars in pure profits. A sum that was all the more fabulous since it was destined for neither humanitarian nor peacekeeping works, but, on the very contrary – and this was its novelty – for the resurgence of the American people's nationalism, and to caution against the arming of antiterrorist organizations. Hence General Winclaub's indispensable presence.

Dozens of camera flashes crackled upon the arrival of each limo, and two officers of the security service instantly rushed forward to cover the newcomers.

"No need to find a parking spot," announced Gregory Cheston. "Stay double parked and come pick me up in a half hour."

The driver acquiesced silently, and Cheston waited for a first security guard to open the door for him before he allowed himself to be escorted into the hall.

"Mister Cheston… Mister Cheston!" pushed a reporter. "What does the presence of E.C.Tronics mean for this gala? Is it a mere courtesy visit or does your company endorse the associations responsible for this fundraiser?"

A dozen or so mics were brandished in his direction. Cheston lowered his head, his face closed off, and wordlessly climbed the three steps leading up to the turnstile spilling into the great hall. Stung by his silence, the reporters got ready to resume their questioning, but there was a new sizzle of flashes and all of a sudden, the swinging horde of microphones lost all interest in him and heaved towards a new arrival.

Cheston took a quick peek over his shoulder. The door of a new limo had just opened, revealing the founder of Amway and owner of the Orlando Magic basketball team, Richard DeVos, whose face was lit by a personable smile, and who took the couple of steps separating him from the shaded area before allowing himself to be surrounded by the press corps, thus enabling Cheston to sidestep all uncomfortable questions.

"Is it true you're personally getting involved in General Winclaub's 2008 campaign financing?" Cheston heard.

He kept himself to a simple answer, adding a wink to his legendary smile.

"Don't spread the word around to the Democrats, they think I'm on their side…"

The reporter couldn't hold back a tinkling laugh. There weren't likely to be all that many democrats in the Millennium Hall that day.

"Mister Cheston, do you think the situation in Iran… Mister Cheston?!"

He held out his card to the buxom blonde dressed up like a combatant – combat boots, light helmet, "war paint" makeup – who was barring access to the reception area. She handed him a badge bearing the eagle insignia and bestowed a dazzling smile on him.

"Have a good evening, sir."

Shock flared through Cheston as he discovered the Renaissance salon, which had been turned into a vast convention hall for the occasion. Stands bearing the emblems of various associations were crowded around the perimeter of a huge stage, from which a speaker was giving the sound system a workout as he welcomed the newcomers in.

Between the stands there was the heavy traffic of a squadron of hostesses clad in fatigues, handing out flyers as well as free copies of *Soldier of Fortune*, the hitmen's magazine that had seen a towering leap in its print and distribution numbers.

Bit by bit, the salon was becoming crowded. The newcomers rushed around each stand as though they were booths at a funfair. The Victory badge was forty bucks, the U.S. Army Forever T-shirt (child-sized) sixty, and each item flew off the proverbial shelves like hotcakes.

"Gregory! This is a nice surprise! I was hoping you'd be stopping by this evening. Everyone's here... including the representatives of the Council on Foreign Relations, of course."

Cheston turned to face Joseph Feldman and greeted him with a slight nod of his head.

"I hope we'll be able to grab a seat at the same table," Feldman went on, looking cheerful behind his multifocals.

The small man barely reached his shoulders, and stood as much in contrast by his mien as by his bearing to the president of E.C.Tronics. Clad in plain casualwear, the latter cut an imposing figure by his natural ease and distinction, whereas Feldman, despite his tux, bore the burden of his dusty bureaucrat's appearance.

"I'm afraid not, unfortunately," politely retorted Cheston. "I won't be staying for dinner."

Feldman lifted an intrigued brow, then resignedly shrugged his shoulders.

"Sorry to hear that. You're going to miss General Winclaub's speech."

Feldman's squawky voice had always had the ability to get on Cheston's nerves. Tonight, more so than usual, he hated the circumstances that had made his presence at his side indispensable.

"I already know his speech," stated Cheston scathingly. "I got a copy of it this morning."

Feldman's mouth twisted. A tic. He was overtly stung that Cheston had been given an honor that he himself hadn't been granted. General Winclaub was the spokesman of fundamentalist Christian America and of the radical wing of the neoconservative "eagles." A movement that was gaining ground by the minute since the September 11 attacks, and that was trying, through efforts from its different constituting parts, to pressure Congress and the White House alike into adopting tougher measures against terrorism, Islamic for the most part.

"Did you hear they're trying to get a motion through Congress to legalize the private units under their control?" Feldman went on.

"They'll never get it," grated out Cheston, sweeping his gaze from right to left in the hopes of finding an escape from this conversation that was exasperating him. "Congress will never vote that kind of thing in, and you know why just as well as I do."

"But they've already gotten tougher measures into the legislation regulating the intervention of counterterrorist forces. You know as I do that the President has rescinded the use of executive order 12333[10] in the case of terrorist networks, and with the creation of the DHS, the... Gregory?!"

Cheston took several steps towards a stand that looked deserted, Feldman on his heels. The arrival of numerous groups had ended up filling the great room to bursting, and the speaker had removed himself from his pedestal, some military music taking the place of his welcome speech and punctuating the guests' motions, like the Red Cross dances back in the forties...

Several yards away, DeVos was trying to make his way through the throng of reporters and reach the banquet hall, smile not leaving his face. Cheston greeted the lost-looking hostess.

"Your stand isn't getting much traffic. You not selling anything?"

"No," replied the young woman, she too dressed as a soldier. "I'm collecting donations for a relief fund to help the families of Gulf war victims."

"Not a lot of success," interjected Feldman. "How much have you gotten?"

The hostess shook her head with a sorrowful look. She was getting ready to say, "Nothing." Cheston cut her off at the pass.

"Ten thousand dollars," he announced, pulling out his checkbook.

The young woman's lips fell open in a staggered pout. Feldman snickered.

"Oh, Gregory, that's you all right."

Very close to them, a young reporter had caught sight of the spectacle. She abandoned the chase after DeVos, who, as it happened, was done with the journalists, and she rushed over to Cheston, who was just about done writing his check.

"Mister Cheston, I know you've declined to make any statements, but please, my paper was one of the few to take your side after that incident with the nuclear plant in Des Moines.

"We've supported your foundation to finance medical research on the Gulf syndrome and veteran care at Bethesda, and I believe in fact that you were among the first to float the idea of private strike forces...

"Does your presence here mean that you intend to get your organization off the ground again despite the failure in 1993?"

Gregory Cheston affixed his signature, clear and legible, to the check that he let the hostess fill out, and slowly pirouetted towards the journalist. Feldman watched on, amused.

The failure in '93!' Cheston repeated inwardly. That had not been a failure, strictly speaking, and if the journalist had had the barest inkling of what the

---

10   Executive Order 12333, signed by Ronald Reagan on December 4 1981, was an executive order that, among other measures, forbade the US intelligence community from resorting to or perpetrating assassinations. An amendment by George W. Bush rescinded the limits of this measure when it came to terrorist networks.

86

real truth was, the halls of the Millennium Plaza would have witnessed the explosion of the biggest truth bomb ever launched before the public.

There had indeed been vague talks in 1993 to put together a small contingent of volunteers well-versed in hostage exfil and crisis rescue. This was not long after the failed October 3rd raid on the Olympic hotel – the refuge of General Mohammed Aidid, the head of the Somali National Alliance – during which the Rangers and the Delta Force, hemmed in among the populace, had lost nineteen men and two UH-60 Black Hawk helicopters. The pilot of the second chopper had been beaten and captured.

Cheston had considered going to his rescue by turning to this private elite unit. Information had leaked outside the Organization that Cheston had created and financed. The press had gotten wind of the emerging plans, and the US government had been forced to put pressure on E.C.Tronics to prevent Cheston from carrying out that operation.

As a matter of fact, and owing to the October 3rd tragedy, the US had almost instantly disengaged from the Somali crisis. The one positive note, the helicopter pilot had been freed eleven days later. Ever since, Cheston had officially withdrawn from military matters and dissolved his organization. Officially!

In actuality, the government had rather different plans for Cheston. But that was a whole other matter, and certainly not one the likes of which the president of E.C.Tronics could afford to reveal for a long while yet...

"I'm here this evening because I was invited," responded Cheston. "As a matter of fact, I will be unable to attend the dinner, which I regret. You can report that I'm here this evening as an observer, with no hidden agenda or secret angle, save for a certain amount of esteem for most of the members of this gathering."

"Allow me to belabor the point," the journalist went on. "With the exception of Ross Perot, your immediate predecessor, and someone who actually successfully pulled off a hostage rescue[11], you were the first to advocate for the privatization of counterterrorism efforts."

"Different times, different thoughts," Cheston retorted blandly. "The current government seems to be doing a very good job of things on its own, and still seems to be enjoying plenty of support. I believe tonight is proof of that. Now if you'll excuse me..."

Cheston slipped away. He'd seen enough. Pretty steep half-hour, even taking into account that fifty percent of his donation would be tax-deducted.

The journalist leaned over the stand and tried to glean the amount on the check from the hostess.

"It's pretty reassuring, everything that's going on, eh?" started Feldman, who had joined Cheston near the exit.

---

11   Ross Perot, founder of an electronics company tasked with building a modern social security system in the days of the Shah, has entered history for a private military operation called "Eagles," conducted on Iranian soil to free two of his company's employees, who had been taken hostage by the Khomeini regime. The rescue was successful.

"What is that supposed to mean?"

"It's a trend that's going in the exact same direction as our plans. Could you have pictured this ten years ago?"

Cheston handed his badge back to the receptionist and nodded briefly to a Texan billionaire he knew who was trying to make a discreet entrance with his wife. The man could have just as easily come to the event astride his horse, which surely wouldn't have been at odds with his fringe white leather jacket.

"Gregory!" he hollered. "Not leaving, I hope?"

"An urgent matter to take care of," demurred Cheston.

"It's been ages since we crossed paths. Good God! It's good to see you. But you're looking mighty ragged there, old boy. What'll it take for you to say yes to my invite? A week on my ranch, that'll cure what ails ya. Have you met my wife?"

Striving to mask his impatience, Cheston returned his smile and bowed slightly before the young woman whose attire was just as understated, and who sported enough ice to make her insurer break out in a cold sweat.

"I'm in New York for the week," the Texan insisted. "Maybe we'll be able to catch up."

"Certainly, gladly," ground out Cheston. "Let's talk tomorrow morning.

"We're staying in our apartment on Park. And in the Hamptons for the weekend. Same number. Go on, give us a call!"

Cheston made his final goodbyes and sidled close to the porter.

"Have my driver called," he requested. "He must be double-parked nearby."

He was looking forward now to slipping away before he crossed paths with any more acquaintances. Many of the guests were part of his network and he'd been lucky, so far, to only cross paths with one. He asked himself once more what whim had compelled him to come to the Millennium, even just for a half-hour.

Nevertheless, the important thing was that he showed up on the attendants list, and that the press had seen him there. For the rest, Feldman at least had the advantage of being able to represent him. Feldman, who was in fact still at his side, and clearly still waiting for an answer. His Texan friend had nearly made Cheston forget he was there.

"You must be pretty satisfied, right?" said Feldman when he could once again catch Cheston's gaze.

"I'm not following."

"America seems fully ready to accept White Cells, as of now… It's your theories…"

Cheston speared him with a gaze.

"We're in a public place, Feldman!"

"Come on, no-one can hear us…"

Through the curtain of rain appeared the white headlights of the long black limo that had dropped Cheston off in front of the hotel.

"Your car, sir," indicated the porter.

"Excuse me, Feldman. We'll see each-other tomorrow morning in my office. Try not to show too much largesse with the funds we've allocated to you for this association's "works." Just enough for us to be seen as having joined the ranks…"

"Where are we going, sir?" asked the driver as soon as he settled into the back of the vehicle.

"My daughter's," uttered Cheston. "Don't rush, I need to think."

He opened the minibar entrenched in the leather-paneled wall and poured himself a healthy dose of scotch in a glass he kept between his fingers, not even bringing it to his lips.

The streets of Manhattan, deserted because of the downpour, unfolded beyond the tinted windows. Cheston closed his eyes.

My theories!

Out of Feldman's mouth, the phrase had sounded like an insult. Cheston had the consistent feeling that he was always facing off with his destiny. Twice he'd been marked by it during his irrepressible ascent, and he knew that no leak could now erase the wounds lodged in his flesh.

Firstly, Des Moines. The nuclear power plant that his first company had been tasked with providing the security for… Des Moines, for which his daughter stood an implacable symbol that condemned a terrifying reality…

Cheston's hand began to tremble, as it always did, at the recollection of that memory. Ellen was the monstrous, accusing finger of past mistakes. The acromegaly had only set in late, as the doctors had been wondering about the abnormal development of her pelvic and hip bones. They had diagnosed her with a very rare form of pituitary cancer, inoperable and incurable. Progressively, the captivating little girl that he adored beyond words had developed that repulsively lopsided body, while Cheston's wife had plunged into a depressive, compulsive, and bulimic-anorexic state.

Cheston would wonder to his dying day if the cocktail of whiskey and anxiolytics that had finished her off had been the result of an accident or a deliberate act on his wife's part.

Then there had been, six years later, the establishment of that E.C. Tronics subsidiary on the outskirts of Kuala Lumpur. Two months after taking office, the manager and his young wife had been abducted by a commando of the Jemaah Islamiyah. His disappearance had only given rise to a few rounds of cynical commentary in the local press.

The Malay police had pursued a half-hearted investigation, despite the weight Cheston had thrown around, and it had yielded the discovery, six months later, of two horrendously mutilated bodies in the trunk of a stolen car abandoned not far from the American embassy. Following his arrest, Hambali, the architect of the southeast Asian Jemaah Islamiyah networks, had insinuated that one of his proteges had personally orchestrated that operation.

Out of respect for the memory of his managing director, Cheston had ordered E.C. Tronics Malaysia be shut down.

The two victims had actually been his half-brother, twenty years his junior, and his second wife, two months pregnant when she'd been abducted…

That same year, Cheston had been summoned to a bidding war in the sale of outdated US Army stocks. Outdated meaning six months behind in the arms race. The government had put pressure on him, meaning to use the opportunity as a way to recover a part of the "tax exemptions" granted to each company that was active in the military sector.

Well, it just so happened that E.C.Tronics was in covert possession of a weapons components factory. Seeker heads for missiles, detectors of all kinds, sensors, nuclear detonators, conventional programmable detectors, radar-integrable silicone chips…

Smack dab in the middle of the restricted area of the Nevada desert, east of the Mojave, escorted by an officer and a quiet, jaundiced-looking little civil servant, Cheston had discovered the most unimaginable of arms cemeteries ever to exist.

Covering hundreds of acres, rotting out in the sun, were alignments of entire squadrons of B-58 Hustlers, some old B-52's, C-130's, KC-130's and 135's, F-111 Aardvark fighters, F-5E Tiger II's, F-14 Tomcats, F-15 Eagles, H-3 Sea King choppers, CH-47 Chinooks, MD500 Defenders, Sea Stallions, Kiowas, and even a few old Bell AH-1 SuperCobras, personnel carriers, missiles, 20 to 50 mm machine guns, assault rifles, tanks, hand grenades by the ton, and anti-personnel mines for a buck each…

The government's offer had been simple. E.C.Tronics was to sign on to acquire all or part of the hardware on show and accept the eyewatering price requested by the administration… Up to them to resell them, even at a loss, or worse, for the going rate of scrap metal. The losses would thus be an elegant means to wipe off the fiscal debt that the government had looked the other way on before this downturn.

Against all expectations, Cheston had accepted the offer without the slightest attempt to negotiate.

He'd then had in mind one of the last things his brother had said to him. Worried about the growing violent unrest in Malaysia, he had asked him, not long before his abduction:

"You sure you wanna stay open? You've seen what's going on, the riots, the three families murdered last week…"

"We don't really have a choice," Cheston had retorted. "We have to stay active where circumstances are toughest. If we pull back, it'll mean that many years lost for our technology penetration strategy."

Cheston had then been a firm believer in positive colonialism, a notion that he'd concocted while trying to understand the history of the Roman empire and of its influence on less developed civilizations.

He'd even taken to dreaming of what the western world would be like if this empire, the ideas and technologies of which had been so advanced for their time, hadn't fallen to the barbarian invasions, to corruption, but above all to the inward spread of Christianity, so incredibly regressive at the time. His brother had known his convictions. He'd shaken his head, disillusioned.

"No matter what we do, we'll always be in the wrong. Our civilization is built on guilt, and so we will always lose our wars from within. Material comforts lead to doubts, and this idyllic world we're trying to build self-destructs even as it keeps progressing.

90

"Who's to say we have a right to drag civilizations that aren't ready for it into our world? People who have put God into all the shadowed corners of their knowledge so they wouldn't have to look too closely at them."

"I'm not sure I get your point?"

Jack Cheston had given himself over to prophesizing, then.

"It's our arrogance that gets us mixed up in things, Gregory. We want to know and have control over our destiny, and we're convinced everyone else wants the same thing. We're positive we're in the right because we believe in evolution, and we're persuaded that we're the tip of its spear.

"What do you think the reaction is gonna be from all those countries we pillaged in the past, and that we're now claiming to help? We spend billions propping up dictators, hoping we'll be able to sell their people computers and cars.

"The worst part is, we're acting in good faith. Good faith versus conviction. Material happiness versus a hope of eternal happiness. Answers to immediate questions, and which lead to even more difficult, more numerous questions.

"Going on as we have is tantamount to preaching the right to panic. You'll see, I can already hear the answer.

"In the ten years to come, terrorism and guerilla warfare are going to explode the world over, the way organized crime did during prohibition. And governments will be powerless to react, outside of negotiating and counting their dead…

"Our moral objectors will instantly take our opponents' side, that's just a Judeo-Christian reflex. You can't act against a hostile foreign body that grows inside as well as outside. Our democracies lack antibodies… They don't have any *white cells*…"

After his half-brother's death, Cheston had inwardly begun working on this "white cells" concept. Making antibodies. Those very same antibodies that his own daughter cruelly lacked to fight the disease that devoured her.

Due to his glory and his power, this was the least of the projects he could still support. Defending what he'd spent his whole life building. He had accepted the government's offer, but not with the intent to resell his arms. He now possessed the makings of a small army, and all he had to do was find himself the manpower…

White Cells had just come into being. The organization didn't yet bear the name.

"Would you like for us to cross Central Park, or would you rather I bypassed it?" the driver interrupted his thoughts.

"Bypass," sighed Cheston. "I already told you, I'm not in a hurry."

He sank down into his seat and closed his eyes.

A year after he'd bought the weapons, Cheston had once again been contacted by the administration, and this time a Langley official had requested that he rid himself of all heavy armament asap. The missiles and tanks in particular, which E.C.Tronics had immediately sold for a song through subsidiaries set up for the purpose. Several South American and African countries had been on the highly classified list that the company man had handed him with the following words:

"We're aware of your plans, Mister Cheston. We know what happened to your brother last year, and we're sure that a man like you isn't about to get over such a painful occurrence in a hurry… We'd even be willing to help you… if of course you agreed to obey certain rules."

And so Feldman had come into the picture.

"We're here, sir," the driver spoke again, breaking into his thoughts. "Would you like me to wait for you out here?"

"No," replied Cheston before knocking back the still-full glass of scotch he'd kept clenched in his hand for the duration of the drive. "Head into the parking garage and take the hour off. I may be a while."

Before opening the door, he poured himself a second glassful. It was like this every time he paid Ellen a visit… The only instances in his existence when Cheston lacked even the most basic courage.

The match had started over a half-hour ago and Ellen, furious to have missed the start because of an inopportune phone call, had her eyes glued to the giant screen of her Bang & Olufsen setup. She knew it was all fake, and that the heaving masses of flesh procured a show that was as carefully rehearsed as a circus act.

Nevertheless, their grimaces, the sometimes grotesque contortions undergone by these mountains of muscles and fat, their panting breaths, and their expressions of pain were in secret alignment with the realm of her unhealthy fantasies.

How could that not have been the case, however? She saw in those disfigured bodies a projection of her own anatomy, made sublime by the applause and cheers from the fans of this sport. Alas, what was strategic padding, limberness, and sometimes even gracefulness onscreen was called deformity, viscosity, and impotence when it came to her own flesh.

Ellen Cheston, aka "Marylin" – a nickname she had cynically picked out for herself as a teen, back when her legs still carried her weight and when even her father's fortune hadn't been enough to prevent the jibes – Ellen Cheston delighted in this spectacle with the same relish as that invited by a hard-core magazine.

Sprawled out onto a pile of cushions, she sometimes even lost herself in her own touch, briefly getting a taste of the sort of pleasure that was not in her reach.

"And the Apollo catches his opponent with a chop," went the commentator. "Oh, that's gotta hurt. Catching out the Cincinnati Butcher…"

Fascinated, Ellen stuffed a chocolate cookie in her mouth. A buzzer sounded next to her bed once more. Irritated, she lowered the volume and activated the intercom.

"It's me. Can you buzz me in?"

Over on the screen, a total turnaround. The Apollo of Maine, crushed beneath the Cincinnati Butcher's two hundred and fifty pounds, was attempting to use a thigh hold to free himself. Ellen started a digital recording of the match and turned off the projector. Gregory Cheston appeared in the entryway.

"Is this a bad time?"

Ellen's father wore a perpetual mantle of despondency. As though he alone bore the entire burden of his empire. New wrinkles creased his forehead every time he had to look upon his daughter. After every one of his visits, he tried to only keep the memory of her still-human face alive in his mind, lit by a maybe-affectionate smile.

"Never," she replied, camouflaging her irritation. "It's actually good to see you…"

Gregory briefly scrutinized his daughter, trying to discern a hint of irony within her frozen smile. Without waiting for an invitation, he took a seat at the end of the bed, before sweeping a gaze over the incredible picture the room made.

The most amazing objects were associated with very valuable furniture, imported from Europe for the most part, and devoid of any real usefulness. Ellen systematically bought any and all knick-knacks she liked, if only for a moment. Electronic gadgets, ornaments, automatons, and especially Aibos, Sony robot dogs, which she happened to dismember when she went into fits of rage, and which were sometimes left lying on the floor in pieces for days on end. Jewelry, never.

"I came to get your opinion," ventured Gregory Cheston.

Ellen gobbled up a fistful of candy.

"You in trouble?"

"Not really. Not yet. Just a bad feeling."

"Mexico?"

Cheston made an irked face.

"Which other of my businesses do you think I'd consult with you about?"

He softened.

"…Forgive me."

Ellen didn't seem affected by the hint of contempt she thought she'd made out in her father's voice. Of course, nothing bar the Mexican "base" could concern the both of them. It was actually the only occurrence that had managed to bring them closer together since her birth, and especially since her mother had died.

The only thing they talked about, at any rate. And Ellen took joy in this forced complicity. The base was the first project that she'd had the skill to insinuate herself into, quickly becoming indispensable in the eyes of the great Gregory Cheston, who abhorred following this operation too closely.

"I'm not sure we can consider the base to really be part of your business," she gritted out.

Cheston didn't rise to her words.

"Meyrek," he went on. "The Frenchman. You and Feldman alone were in contact with him. I'd like you to tell me about him."

"Have you seen Feldman already?"

"Certainly. He gave me a description that was as detailed and meticulous as a computer report. I know the man down to his slightest habits, his favorite brand of toothpaste, and what age he took his first mistress. Except, it's your impressions I'm interested in."

"What are you afraid of?"

Cheston mechanically dusted off his jacket. Ellen watched on, an amused glint in her eyes. She tried to move her stiffened right leg and had to stop in her tracks. She'd have needed to use both her arms to assist herself, heaving the bulk of her chest, and these inelegant movements would have cost her the feeble illusion of superiority she felt whenever her father came to her in her bedroom.

"Meyrek fits the profile," she commented. "He has that winner's rage. All his victories were something he first won individually against his own men before replicating them in the field."

"There have been too many deaths on base since he got there," uttered Cheston.

Ellen burst out laughing. A sort of comingled rattle and giggle. An unpleasant, grating sound.

"Is that why you've come? The man may just surpass his reputation. But, tell me, where is this sudden humanitarianism coming from? You're far from the only responsible party here."

"Ellen, the number of accidents that take place during trainings is far below the percentage we'd factored in. But Meyrek is carrying out executions; that wasn't in the books!"

"Well," commented Ellen. "What are you complaining about? All that does is confirm his abilities. Few accidents and an implacable discipline. That's what a bona fide military leader is made of. I don't get why you're worried."

"I'm not worried. So long as Meyrek works for us."

Ellen seemed to meditate on her father's last words.

"There were three options…" she said with a grimace. "You promised you'd give me final say."

"I got the new analysis reports this morning," said Cheston. "They reveal an impressive budget overrun…"

Ellen's gaze went unfocused. Cheston noted her sudden nervousness and marveled at it.

"I can't discount a margin of error, but we've reached seventeen percent. That's far too much. I can't wrap my head around it."

"Marylin" let a few moments go by without responding. She seemed plunged deep in thought, knowing her father was watching her carefully, studying each of her reactions.

"Tamazula doesn't have access to the accounts," she replied at last. "So there's no danger from that end. And as for Meyrek, each of his equipment orders is supported by a report…"

Ellen took a deep breath and straightened up at last, relieving her stiffened muscles.

"There's only one answer," she added. "Head out and see for ourselves."

Cheston hesitated.

"Who's to handle that? Feldman?"

"Don't worry," whispered Ellen, her eyes shining. "I make a lot of smoke when I travel incognito."

Once again, Theo had the feeling that he'd escaped a deathly rally unscathed. Landed at Chihuahua airport, he'd elbowed his way through the waiting crowd to avail himself of the first available cab, and he'd spurred his driver on by means of copious tips. Their speedy crossing of the town had still seemed unbelievably slow to him. His heart beat fit to bursting at the mere thought that Juliette and Katia might not be waiting for him in the room, and that the chase would keep going on.

The *El Presidente* hotel showed off the same luxury as the *Camino Real*, though it was more incongruous in this small town that mainly lived off farming.

Chihuahua was humid, and his shirt was sticking to his skin. Theo felt exhausted. He rushed to the front desk of the hotel and uttered his name. The receptionist shuffled through a pile of paper slips with exasperating slowness. Finally, just as Theo was feeling apt to scream out his rage and fear, she came back to him, all smiles.

"*Si, señor.* Some people are already expecting you. Your wife and your daughter, I believe. And a friend. *Bienvenido* in Chihuahua, and enjoy your stay."

In relief, Theo could have kissed the Mexican. She didn't understand his sudden enthusiasm, and her brows raised when Theo dashed towards the elevator.

"Hey! *Señor.* I did not give you the room number!"

Deep purple marks underscored Juliette's slightly lost gaze. Seated against the bed in a lotus position, she held Katia tightly against her in a naturally protective posture. The room's window was closed, and the air conditioning was chilling the space. Seated in one of the armchairs, a man Theo didn't know was calmly smoking a cigarette. He paid him no mind. Before Juliette could make the slightest gesture, Theo was already against her, kissing her.

An entire day had gone by since they'd been taken. Katia seemed to suddenly come awake. She leapt onto her father and squeezed him.

"Daddy, tell the man to go away. He made us come here. Mommy cried."

Juliette reciprocated to Theo's affections tenderly, but perhaps a little too unenthusiastically. This detached behavior was not like her. Theo suddenly became aware of the man's presence. He turned around and asked, in what he passed off for Spanish:

"What did you do to her to make her come with you?"

The man raised both hands to shoulder height in a gesture indicative of his ignorance. His fingers were yellowed from nicotine and his face displayed a strange good-natured look that scarcely fit with his duties. For the rest, he had the dark complexion typical of his country, and the same brushed-back, oily hair as most Mexicans.

"*Señor,* I have stayed with your wife and your little girl to watch over them until you got here. *Señor* Tamazula ordered me to drive them here nice and easy, not harm them at all. My friend and I did as he said."

He got up. In his confusion, Theo must have seemed menacing, as the Mexican saw fit to add:

"There is no need for you to get angry. The *señora* is very well, and I held the little girl's hand all through the trip. Ask them."

"Theo," went Juliette in a low and somewhat slurred voice. "Theo, tell him to get t'hell out."

The man's face lit up with a smile that he meant to be affable. The tone of Juliette's voice had Theo's blood stirring. The Mexican noted his worry.

"Do not worry. My friend gave her something to calm her down. After a good night's sleep, its effects will all wear off."

The phone rang. Theo started.

"That must be for you. *Señor* Tamazula was eager to know you'd arrived all right."

Tamazula didn't give Theo the time to talk.

"I believe this was a clear enough warning, Mister Collin. You've found your wife again, your daughter. You're in Chihuahua, so all is as it should be. Is everything well?"

Theo felt a torrent of curses crash against his lips. There wasn't a language in the world that seemed to him robust enough to put his rage into words. Tamazula had adopted a firm, honeyed voice. Theo wanted to shout. Katia was holding his hand. He erred on the side of caution. Almost babbling, he replied:

"My daughter is scared to death, and my wife is barely awake. Do you know the punishment for kidnapping in civilized countries!"

"Come now," gritted out Tamazula. "Such big words. I can imagine they're covering up an anger that you would rather not express. Once again, I understand. But look on the bright side. We are still keeping our commitments. You must admit that my kidnappers have been bringing you to rather pleasant places."

The Mexican's voice hardened.

"As of tomorrow, the base will get in touch with you. In the meantime, we will leave you alone with your family. I believe you're smart enough not to try anything else."

"Which means you're giving us free reign over our movements?"

"Yes. But make no mistake. We have no wish to see a repeat of the *Camino Real* incident. Your line does not dial out, and the local police is used to giving me a hand from time to time. So try not to get in touch with the airport or any car rental companies. Tomorrow evening, you will be assuming your functions on base and your bad mood will be forgotten. *Buenas tardes, amigo.*"

The dial tone came back on. Theo turned towards the Mexican.

"He said you can leave us alone."

"*Si, señor.* Those are the orders. I'm leaving right now. Good night, and I hope the *señora* gets lots of rest."

Before shutting the door, he turned back around.

"Ah, I almost forgot. If you need me, call room two seventeen. It's right across."

Theo collapsed onto the bed. He slipped his arm around Juliette, pressed a kiss against her hair. Katia, standing next to him, watched them shyly.

"C'mon, sweetheart. Come here."

She joined them. Calm descended on the room once more, and, by tacit agreement, they all kept quiet for a few moments. Theo was wrecked with remorse and had no idea how to express his simultaneous regret and relief.

Mechanically, he caressed his daughter's face where she'd snuggled in against his chest. Get a hold of himself, before all else, he thought. Let his courage and strength come in so he could impart them to them.

Now that he'd found them again, he felt confusedly as though nothing on Earth could ever take them away from him again. The fear he'd felt had been new. He'd been ready to face any danger if it meant Juliette and Katia could be kept safe from it.

His quiet little universe had blown up in a matter of days. His own courage, which he'd always believed he lacked, had just stirred awake, and the feeling was, despite it all, thrilling.

Lost in thought, Theo didn't immediately realize that Juliette had fallen asleep. He closed his eyes in turn…

"I'm thirsty, I'm hungry. What time is it?"

Theo woke up with a start. The lights in the room had stayed on. In the hollow of his arm, Katia was smiling as she dreamt. He sneezed, checked his watch. It said one-thirty. Finally, he saw that Juliette was watching him. Her gaze had lost that vacant, heartbreaking gleam, side effect of the drug she'd been given. She seemed serene, and Theo was overcome by a deep wave of tenderness.

"My love," he murmured.

She took his hand and brought it to her lips, squeezing it warmly as thought to reassure herself.

"Are you feeling better?"

"Yes, other than a slight headache and a huge case of the munchies."

"Ah, that was you talking. I thought I was dreaming."

"I'm sorry. Thankfully, I didn't wake the girl."

Theo pressed a kiss onto his daughter's forehead, very softly, then he slowly extricated himself from the bed.

"Come over on the armchair. She won't hear us."

Juliette followed him. Her clothes were wrinkled. She'd even kept on her shoes.

"There's a minibar. You want an orange juice? I'm going to call reception and have them send up some sandwiches or some fruit."

"Great idea. Hand me that water bottle, too, I'm completely parched."

"That's the AC," ventured Theo. "I think I caught a slight cold." He opened the bottles, poured himself a Coca-Cola, and looked for the AC thermostat, which he unplugged. Juliette drained the small bottle of mineral water in one swallow before sighing.

"I'm reliving it…"

She'd slumped down onto the cushion of a rattan armchair, her dress hiking up slightly and revealing her knees. Her bodice had come unbuttoned during her sleep. She wasn't wearing a bra. Theo felt himself stirred by the spectacle she was so innocently offering. He crouched down at her feet and put his head between her thighs. Juliette caressed his hair.

"Hadn't you said something about a sandwich?" she teased.

"That's right. I'll call them right now."

"No, hold on. The orange juice did me a bit of good. Stay like this for a bit."

Theo was simultaneously impatient and anxious to learn of her adventure, and of the frights she must have gone through. However, he dared not broach the subject just them.

Juliette's flesh was warm against his cheek; the light fabric of her dress gave off a slight fragrance, heady and natural. He let his hand stray the length of her thigh, sliding along her stomach, up to her breast, which he caressed softly. The moment was unique. He was rediscovering a woman who was his with the same emotion as the first time, and the quietude of a long compatibility.

All his senses came awake. He wanted to shout out his desire, his happiness to share this moment with her. Juliette's hand tensed against his hair. He pushed his face between her thighs, beneath the fabric, and teased his mouth along her skin. Juliette arched and sighed deeply.

She lifted herself up slightly when he pulled the elastic of her panties towards him. The material slid down the length of her legs, landed in a small, wrinkled heap on the polished marble floor. All her muscles tensed, coiled as far as possible, she let herself go while biting back her moans, despite everything aware of her daughter's presence there.

Theo felt her nails score into his shoulders. He stood back up.

"Come. We'll look funny if she wakes up."

He led her to the bathroom and carefully closed the door behind them. Juliette blew out a breath.

She slid the dress over her head in a single move, gaze laughing, and took off Theo's clothes herself.

"I've always had this old fantasy," she giggled.

"What's that? Tell me all about it and I'm on it."

"Make love in a bathtub filled with hot water while I'm with my husband in Chihuahua, Mexico."

Authoritatively, she turned the taps.

Katia was still asleep. Theo had wrapped his wife in a blanket and had, himself, pulled on a T-shirt and a pair of pants. It was nearly three in the morning. Outside, the cane toads sang out a hymn to love that heralded rainfall. The cicadas had gone quiet.

Crouched on the floor, close to the bed, Juliette had launched into the story of her kidnapping. Just after Theo had left for the embassy, two men had barged into the room and hurled themselves at Katia first, certain they would subdue the mother by grabbing the daughter.

Juliette had screamed. One of the men – the one Theo hadn't seen – had ordered her in English to keep quiet and follow them. Katia had struggled, worked up, and Juliette had hurled herself at the Mexicans, fists first. After a short struggle, the two men had overpowered and then drugged her.

Of her flight, she had no memory. In Chihuahua, she had come to not long before Theo had arrived.

"You know," she finished, voice once again choked by emotion from recalling the images she'd just retold, "I think that if Katia hadn't been there, they could have done anything to me without my realizing it."

She nevertheless recovered her smile and went on in an amused voice.

"Your daughter was far braver than I was. One of the guys got bitten bloody, the one who was trying to gag her. He also took one heck of a kick to the shin! I saw his face go all white.

"And then" – she tenderly gazed towards Katia – "she never stopped asking for you. The state I was in, I couldn't explain a thing to her. She was the one putting me at ease, almost. I mean, maybe I dreamed that part. But I think she kept telling me, "Daddy's coming, daddy's coming!"

She gently kissed Theo's lips.

"And then, you were here."

"Yeah," he grumbled. "Wasn't like I did much. Tamazula had left an envelope for me, I hopped onto the first plane, just as they'd planned. I was scared to death at the thought that they'd harmed you. For now, you two are the ones paying for my screw-ups. Some hero I am!"

The cane toads had quieted down. The sun wouldn't be long in rising. Through the curtains, the nearly total darkness of a starless night had made room for a somewhat greyish semi-darkness. Now and again, the brief intonation of a car horn or some tire screech pierced through the silence of the sleeping town.

"And now?" asked Juliette.

"I don't know. I fear we may be forced to follow their instructions. Whatever happens, getting separated is out of the question from now on. After all, their one objective is to drag me onto the base, and I don't believe you'll be in any danger so long as I play their game."

Theo ruminated.

"It's still strange," he went on. "The measures they're using to bring me to heel are utterly disproportionate. I'm nothing but a computer guy; they've got the means to manipulate thousands of them, and they're persisting in making me stick to an itinerary that takes one and the same path no matter what I do.

"They're trying to trigger something. What? I don't know. What was to stop them from drugging us both, when they found our hideout in Mexico City, and sending us straight to the base? Why force me to come here by kidnapping you?

"Why put us up in luxury hotels, guarded by thugs? There's no logic to any of this.

"Just like my interview with Tamazula. After all, if I'd been received in Mexico City by officials, even fake ones, I would have undoubtedly held on to my full enthusiasm. This is like they're enjoying this game of cat and mouse. I just can't figure out what they're expecting…"

"Your willing cooperation, I'm sure. It's the old carrot and stick method. The type of work they have in store for you must require the sort of efficiency that they know can't be gotten by force alone."

"No, Juliette. I'm telling you, thousands of guys are capable of taking my place, and would certainly do it willingly. Tamazula even implied that my professional skills would maybe take the backseat. There's something off about the way they're handling things. And I don't know what."

Katia let out a small cry in her sleep and fidgeted. Juliette went to tuck her in.

"We should try and get a little bit of sleep ourselves." Theo yawned. "You especially."

Juliette acquiesced. She crossed the room, still clad in her blanket, and helped herself to another drink from the minibar.

"That's right!" exclaimed Theo. "I forgot your sandwich again. I'll head down to reception and find you a snack."

"No. Never mind. It's too late. No-one will serve you anything. I'm going to sleep."

"They will," he insisted, getting up. "I'll slip the night watchman a coin. You'll sleep better on a full stomach. I won't be five minutes."

He grabbed the room key.

"No matter what, don't open for anyone."

A uniformed guard was dozing in a chair at the front desk. The hotel lobby was partially lit, quiet and subdued. For a second, Theo expected to stumble across several men, armed to the teeth, just like during the guerilla days, when Chihuahua had been one of their capitals. A welcoming committee recruited for his benefit, of course, its mission to bar him from accessing the kitchens. The man stirred in his chair.

"*Señor?*"

Theo shot a sympathizing wink his way and slid a few pesos across the reception desk.

"My wife and I couldn't sleep. Do you think you could find us something to eat?"

The cash had an invigorating effect on the guard, who promised to see to the problem immediately. He nevertheless asked him for his room number and headed towards the kitchens, a bunch of keys in hand.

Theo went to stand before a thermally molded map of Mexico, and mechanically identified Chihuahua on it. The border with the United States was only, what, some seven hundred kilometers out. He tried to guess at where the base was situated. The region was made up entirely of tall plateaus and mountain ranges, stretches of desert and widespread pastures. The base could be anywhere.

He walked around the lobby, peering at a few engravings, and even a display case full of fossilized reptiles. The double doors leading outside opened automatically as he got near. Theo stepped outside to smell the chill morning air.

The hotel opened onto a big avenue. A few vehicles belonging to the early-morning workers were already on the road. The pavement was wet. Had there not been the prospect of a future departure towards a place that he was now having trouble separating from the idea of a prison, he would have been wonderfully soothed by this daily tranquility. He returned to the lobby. The guard was waiting for him.

"Ah, *señor*. I thought you were gone. Here are some fruit, and some cold tortilla. There's still some left over if this isn't enough."

He'd been kind enough to wrap the food. The parcel seemed sizable. Theo thanked him.

"Your region seems very beautiful," he added, out of sympathy.

The Mexican's face lit up.

"Yes. *Muy bonita*. The most beautiful in the world. Lots of things to see. Is it your first time here?"

"Yes," confessed Theo. "And I don't think I'll be staying too long, unfortunately."

"That really is a pity, *señor*. I know Chihuahua well and I could have pointed you to places that tourists never visit. Inside the city and outside."

"Maybe next time," answered Theo before biting into an apple. He stepped away towards the elevator, professing his thanks once more, before he got held back by a sudden thought.

"You wouldn't have happened to hear about a new military base up north?" he inquired.

The guard seemed to give it some thought.

"No, I don't think so. There are barracks in Chihuahua, on the route to Cuauhtémoc, but they are very old. No. Aside from those and the Quinta Luz, I can't think of anything in the region that would fit the description of a military base," he added with a laugh.

"The Quinta Luz?" asked Theo.

"Yes. The hacienda where Pancho Villa lived. It is five blocks from here. You can visit it, and they even have the limousine where he was gunned down in 1923. When Villa lived there, it was surrounded by at least five hundred soldiers. But I was joking, señor."

Disappointed, Theo greeted him one last time, adding, out of sheer politeness:

"If I had a car, I'd stay a few more days to visit everything, following your recommendations…"

"You don't have a car? Why? Are the rental companies overbooked?"

"Something like that," replied Theo evasively, careful not to tangle himself up in a lie.

"But, I can help you with that, señor. Not a problem. My cousin is a mechanic. When tourists break down, he fixes their cars and rents them a replacement. I saw him yesterday, he had several left. It's a big garage," he added proudly.

Theo stepped back the way he'd come, forehead furrowed, suddenly less than eager to be back in his room too quickly. His pulse sped up.

"Does he live far, your cousin?"

The garage was on the outskirts of town, and a scant ten minutes were enough to get there. Theo had just concocted a very simple plan. He hurriedly went upstairs and explained it to Juliette.

It was, first of all, indispensable for them to rent a car, in any name but their own, and Theo was certainly counting on the guard being an unwitting accessory in greasing the wheels with his cousin. He'd go there with him as soon as his shift was over, at seven o'clock.

Juliette would wait until eight, not opening the door to anyone, ready to ask for help from reception in the event of an emergency. She'd then head down to the lobby. Odds were that Theo's disappearance would go unnoticed. All their bags would need to stay in the room. Theo would park the car a couple blocks from the hotel and would see them in the lobby.

It would then be a matter of slinking quietly away without giving the impression they were fleeing. If they were made out, they would undoubtedly need to provide explanations on the spot. That was a risk they had to take. In the highly likely case they were not, all that would be left for them to do was to calmly walk around the hotel, so as to pick out anybody who might be following them, then get to the car and flee towards the nearest airport, Nuevo Casas Grandes, which they could reach in five hours.

"From there," finished Theo, "we'll reach the US, thanks to the safe-conducts issued by the embassy."

"And then," asked Juliette. "Where do we hide?"

He seemed not to understand.

"Hide? But we'll be in the U.S. From there, all we'll need to do is return to France."

Juliette peered at her husband incredulously.

"Because you think being in France will be enough for us to never hear from them again?"

Theo shook his head, once more lost in thought. He certainly had no intention of going in blindly, and had, since their disappearance, considered all manner of potential scenarios, until he'd been concentrating so hard he'd gone breathless. He'd reached a nascent conclusion: Tamazula was trying to play in his own little sandbox.

The base, the Organization, whatever name they were calling the trap that was waiting for them up north, had been created by a multinational group that E.C. Tronics was part of, but the executive running of which they had been constrained to entrust to a local due to logistical concerns. In Mexico, the mafia was everywhere, as far up as the highest echelons of industry and finance. That was the image that Theo had of it, at any rate, undoubtedly inspired by everything he'd read from one of his favorite authors, Jim Harrison.

Tamazula had toyed with him, enjoying taking on the role of intriguing philosopher, but Theo's panicked reaction had caught him wrong-footed. From then on, only one thing mattered: getting back to the initial plan, making them follow the itinerary that he was responsible for. The hypothesis was thin, but it was the only one he had.

"In which case," he concluded after sharing his analysis with Juliette, "our best hope is returning to New York and getting in touch with E.C. Tronics..."

"And if you're wrong? If Tamazula is only following very specific instructions that don't necessarily preclude their using force against you?"

"Listen, my reasoning may be dumb, but we need to go for broke. We've been gullible enough so far.

"First off, we need to give detailed warning to our lawyer, as well as to my coworkers and our friends.

"Once they've all been apprised, we'll be in the clear. I'll explain everything to Feldman clearly, if I meet him in New York. Or even to Cheston. We'll become untouchable.

"No matter what, neither you nor I have any intention of getting ourselves locked up on that base if we can help it."

"Theo," said Juliette somberly, "you know our lives will never be the same after this."

He didn't want to allow himself to be brought down by this sentence and insisted, holding her by the shoulders.

"We don't have a choice, Juliette. Everything surrounding this base emanates fear, violence. That's not us.

"We'd be crushed before my contract ran out. Let's leave this country, and everything will seem healthier. If we need to fight, let's fight on our turf. Surrounded by our loved ones."

She caught his gaze with hers.

"You scared?"

"Yeah."

"OK. Go get the car. Katia and I will be waiting downstairs."

The plan orchestrated by Theo was going along perfectly. Using Juliette's maiden name, he rented a Dodge Intrepid, air conditioner working, in a very acceptable state. No-one seemed worried about their departure, and they left the last dwellings in Chihuahua behind them around eight-thirty. Juliette had managed to cram a maximum of changes of clothes in a small travel bag, and Katia, becoming alert to the gravity of the situation, was trying to temper her typical exuberance.

At the same time as the vehicle, Theo had managed to get his hands on a detailed map of the region, for which the night guard had provided enthusiastic commentary, extolling him to extend his explorations west towards the Pacific, to see the Tarahumara canyons, considered one of the wonders of the world.

He'd had to promise to stop over at the El Divisadero, an eminently touristic spot where a mirador had been erected to enable the contemplation of the Barranca del Cobre, the Barranca de Tararecua, and the Barranca de Balojaque, famous for their chromatic variations and their tranquil vastness.

In a bid not to disappoint, Theo had even taken a Ferrocarril schedule, absolutely regretting that he had neither the time nor the stomach to savor this touristic experience that even a month ago he'd have sold his soul to get.

Those itineraries would have taken them west. From his perusal of the map, Theo only recalled one thing: a highway was going to take them halfway to their destination in the north.

Comfortably settled in the back of the car, Katia was commenting on the stunning landscapes unfolding on either side of the freeway. Miles of pastures stretched out, with cattle grazing on them in their hundreds. The horizon was broken by mountains in shimmering colors underneath skies marbled by long, flimsy clouds.

In one hour, the temperatures outside had gone up several degrees, and Theo had needed to roll up the windows and turn on the AC. Tremendously preoccupied, inordinately tense, he nonetheless made a concerted effort to drive smoothly, observing the speed limits. He was having a hard time tearing his gaze away from the rearview mirror.

"We'll be driving along the freeway for another hundred kilometers or so. Next, at El Sueco, we'll head to the left. We'll only have another hundred and fifty kilometers of side roads to go before reaching Nuevo Casas Grandes."

Juliette was keeping her eyes closed.

"Daddy, look at the cows lying there, do you think they're asleep or they're dead?"

"They're getting some rest from the sun, sweetheart."

"Then why are they resting in the sun?"

"I read somewhere," Juliette broke in, "that car crashes were the leading cause of bovine death in Mexico." Theo took a quick peek at her; her eyes were still closed.

"What's bovine?"

"Cows, oxen, and bulls, sweetie."

"And they die in cars?"

Theo couldn't bite back a smile. Katia waited for her curiosity to be assuaged before returning to her contemplations.

"At least," went Theo, "she doesn't seem too traumatized."

"Do you think they've realized, by now?"

For the first time since they'd left Chihuahua, they were addressing the problem that was giving them no rest inside.

"Worst comes to worst," said Theo, "we'll find ourselves at the base, as planned. At least we'll have tried something. Together."

Juliette tenderly grazed his shoulder.

"You're right. Together. I'm still having a hard time processing that yesterday was real."

"Don't give it anymore thought."

There was enough gas in the tank to take them the three hundred kilometers that stood between them and Nuevo Casas Grandes. The freeway was relatively clear. For the most part, the few vehicles they overtook bore American license plates.

Keeping straight, they could reach Ciudad Juarez and cross the border at the legendary El Paso crossing. They'd then run into the problem of a car rented from an unauthorized company. Theo's idea was undoubtedly the best solution.

The dashboard clock displayed nine-thirty.

"Yes," muttered Theo. "They have to have realized. But this time it'll take them a while to figure it out."

"It only took them one night, in Mexico City," objected Juliette.

"There's a fifty-fifty chance they search for us in Chihuahua first," retorted Theo, brimming with confidence.

Face against the car window, Juliette kept mum. The landscape alternated between lush and verdant areas, if wholly dominated by a feeling of sweltering heat. Theo looked at his daughter in the rearview. The kid smiled at him. Still, there was a seriousness in her eyes that he'd never seen in her before.

"Stop worrying," he said, voice resonant. "Mexico is still a civilized country."

As though by a quirk of fate, the gloomy shriek of a police siren rent the stillness of the freeway at just that moment. In the rearview mirror, Theo made out an unmarked car, atop which a police officer had reached out through the window to affix a flashing light.

"Damn." Theo grimaced. "Damn. What do we do?"

On the steering wheel, his hands had begun to tremble.

The siren wailed out again, while the car flashed its headlights several times in warning.

"This is a nightmare," moaned Juliette, face crumpling.

Over on the backseat, Katia burst into sobs.

Theo pulled over on the first lane.

"No need to panic," he went, without much conviction. "I was driving too fast. We're most likely gonna get a ticket."

Juliette refrained from commenting. The needle had never strayed past 110, the speed limit.

Two police officers flanked the Dodge.

"*Control de identidad! Señor, por favor.*"

"Have we done something wrong?" asked Theo in the most detached way he could muster.

"*No, señor.* It's a simple check."

The other cop was walking around the vehicle, testing the tires with the tip of his shoe, checking the state of the license plates. Which was brazen, in Mexico.

"American?" the policeman standing next to Theo went on to ask.

He was tempted to answer in the affirmative, knowing the virtual immunity that *gringos* enjoyed in Mexico.

"No, French. On holiday."

The policeman remained implacable.

"Papers, please. Driver's license and passport."

Theo handed him his driver's license and the vehicle paperwork, including the rental contract, trying to skip over the passports. The officer didn't react.

"Where are you headed?"

"Up to Ciudad Juarez."

Juliette had slipped into the backseat and had taken Katia into her arms to try and soothe her.

The policeman leaned inside the vehicle.

"Your family?"

"Yes. My wife and daughter."

"Could you open the trunk, please."

"Certainly," went Theo. "But I don't understand. We're in a bit of a hurry."

"*Por favor, señor.*"

Theo exited the vehicle. The cop leapt back from it in a theatrical movement.

The trunk, needless to say, was empty save for a jack and some emergency tools.

The second officer opened the back door and made Juliette and Katia get out. The girl started to cry again. Juliette protested.

"We have to search the car," the Mexican retorted firmly.

Inside the police car, the radio crackled in Spanish. Passing them by, several vehicles slowed down, the people inside throwing curious glances their way. In a matter of seconds, beneath the glare of the sun, they were covered in sweat.

Suddenly, the second policeman, who'd gotten on his hands and knees to inspect the Dodge, let out a triumphant roar. Theo felt his sweat turn to ice.

A trap!

A stupid trap like in the corniest cop shows. The policeman got back up, brandishing a clear plastic baggie. The contents were white.

"Oh, no!" uttered Juliette.

Imperturbable, the Mexican unsnapped his gun holster and pulled his weapon on Theo.

"Against the car," he said, suddenly agitated. "Right now!" Juliette threw her arms around her husband's neck.

"No," she cried. "No! It wasn't us. You did that on purpose. You just put that there. It wasn't us."

The second officer yanked her roughly away. Katia grabbed onto his uniform jacket, squealing. The Mexican made a threatening motion.

"Katia, stop it. Stop!"

To avoid any ill-advised actions, Theo carefully complied. Katia instantly grabbed onto her mother. The two cops only had Theo in their sightlines.

"Hands behind your head, stomach up against the car. Spread your legs."

Theo was patted down roughly. The second Mexican opened the plastic baggie and dipped his finger into the white powder. He tasted it.

"Cocaine!"

There must have been thirty grams there. Roughly five thousand US dollars.

"*Señor*, your vacation is over."

Juliette and Katia were sobbing. Protesting would have been futile. This time, the base had them. Hands and feet tied. Laconically, Theo answered all their questions, as though accepting of the role he'd been cast in this sordid scene.

He was handcuffed.

The first cop got in touch with a police station – made up or real – then signaled for Theo to join him in his car. His wrists were cuffed to the door.

"And my wife, my daughter?"

"They will stay in the other vehicle. My colleague will drive them."

"No, please. Don't split us up."

"Those are the rules. *Señor* Collin, you are going to be in big trouble. Carrying drugs through Mexico has a very steep price."

Theo watched him. A tiny, nervous man starting to go bald, he was scrupulously following orders. Taking his role so very seriously. Suddenly washing his hands of the weight of this farce, persuaded that his own import shielded him from the consequences of his actions, Theo burst out into nervous, almost hysterical laughter.

"You poor bastard!" he lashed out. "You stupid goddamn chicano! You know full well I wasn't carrying anything at all. I'm sure there's flour in that baggie of yours.

"Go 'head. Bring me in. Drive me to your fake little police station and let's get this over with! But what if we called Tamazula right now, huh? That would speed things up…"

He spat at the officer.

The man lowered his gaze. Juliette and Katia hadn't missed a second of the scene. Suddenly, the slap rang out. In a sudden surge of energy, the police officer hit him with all his strength. The blows, delivered with his open hand, started to rain down on his face and his neck. Wrists immobile, Theo couldn't dodge a single one.

Juliette screamed, hammered against the car window.

"*Bastante*," admonished the second cop. "Enough. *Vamos!*" He grabbed Juliette by the arm and pulled her away from the vehicle.

"Theo!" she yelled. "You hurt him, you bastard!"

Inside the car, the violence had subsided. Lips swollen, Theo smiled at his wife.

"Keep calm," he said. "I'm fine. I'm OK." He pushed his face against the glass pane.

Katia joined her mother. The two of them looked at him lovingly.

"We'll make it out of this," he went on, sobs thickening his voice. The officer started the car.

The two cars drove single file on the freeway for a dozen kilometers. They took the first exit.

From the backseat of the Dodge, Juliette and Katia watched Theo unblinkingly through the rear window. There were no words being exchanged between him and the policeman.

In the end, the second vehicle overtook the Dodge and the Mexican told his colleague:

"Keep driving to the station. I have to get some gas."

A few kilometers on, they pulled over at a gas station. The Dodge sped past them and Theo lost sight of his wife and daughter. His heart twisting in his chest.

Serpientes vivas y muertas.

The inscription was translated into English and indicated that the snake museum could be visited for ten cents. Most gas stations in the region boasted these kinds of attractions.

The attendant couldn't have been older than ten, and he wouldn't stop scratching his crotch as he pumped the gas.

Next to the Coca-Cola billboard, a mangy old dog agonized in peace. The little Mexican questioned the officer, staring curiously at Theo.

"*Quien es? Un bandito?*"

Not replying, Theo's driver got out of the vehicle and went inside the gas station in search of the men's room.

"What did you do?" the kid asked again, his fingers still scratching away.

Theo smiled at him.

"If I tell you nothing at all, would you believe me?"

"Oh, no, *señor*. If you didn't do nothing, the police don't arrest you."

"I'm thirsty. Can you get me a Coke?"

The kid hesitated.

"That guy will pay for it. With the gas."

"No, I can't. He won't pay. He'll say he didn't ask me for anything."

Theo showed him his wrists, and the handcuffs.

"Then take some money, from my pants. And buy yourself something to drink as well."

The little Mexican's face lit up.

"I can not drink. And keep the money?"

When the policeman came back, the small attendant was holding the Coca-Cola can to Theo's lips. He wanted to curse at him, but settled for shrugging his shoulders.

"I'll pay for the gas," he said. "Not the drink."

The kid showed off a smile half full of teeth.

"You don't want to visit the snakes, *señor*? I have several horned vipers. I'm sure you'd find them interesting."

He seized the several pesos handed to him for the gas and started scratching once more.

"Good luck," he said to Theo.

From wide and clear, the small, shoddy road turned winding and steep-sided, hugging the contours of a rugged environment, suddenly leading to narrow ledges dropping into deliriously beautiful canyons. Very partially paved, it climbed in hurtling, bumpy twists, the wheels of the vehicle spraying countless dusty pebbles in a cloud of ochre smoke.

The policeman began to show clear signs of nervousness. He glanced at Theo often, as though afraid his prisoner would be escaping. There had been no words exchanged between the two men since they'd set off. Theo's anxiety had given way to a fuzzy languor. The handcuffs, the smell of foul sweat given off by the Mexican, the jolts of the vehicle seemed to him too unreal to still trigger the slightest feeling inside him.

The car cleared the pass. The road started to descend.

Screeching brakes. At the sharpest point of a bend, a semi-truck stopped right at the ledge was making it almost impossible to pass. The cop swore.

He maneuvered carefully, slipped the wide carriage of his vehicle between the sides of the truck and the steep slope of the mountain.

"*Maricón! Hijo de puta!*"

Theo was distractedly monitoring the maneuver. Suddenly, he hailed the policeman.

"Look, smoke."

Thick black plumes were drifting upwards from the precipice, concealed by the imposing size of the truck.

A man appeared from the side of the road, bare-chested, upper body gleaming with sweat. He planted himself in front of the car, windmilling his arms. Panicked.

"*La policia! Madre de Dios.* Quick, help me. An accident!"

The cop pulled the handbrake and hurtled himself out of the vehicle. Theo felt his breath seize in his lungs.

"A terrible accident, *señor*. The car. In the ravine. They were going too fast. Much too fast."

Theo twisted his neck, trying to see farther, his movements hampered by the handcuffs.

The truck driver was pointing his finger at the drop. The cop burst back into the car. He unclipped his radio unit to call for assistance. Theo's breath was lead.

"I am sorry, *señor*. It's the Dodge."

"The Dodge," muttered Theo. "The Dodge?"

Dazed, it was beyond him to grasp the meaning of those simple words just then. Then, suddenly, harrowing reality dawned on him as though the world around him had just gone ablaze.

"Juliette? Katia?"

He thrashed like he was possessed, gouging his wrists on the steel of his shackles.

"Let me loose, right now. I want to see them. We have to help them!"

In a desperate motion, he tore the door handle off, rending the pleather across several inches, scattering the screws inside the vehicle. The policeman didn't have the heart to stop him.

"We have to do something," moaned Theo, already running towards the ledge. "They're alive. This can't be happening. Juliette!"

His final word was swallowed up by a cry, propagated by the echo.

"No!" he howled again. "No! No!"

The cop seized him before he could hurtle himself into the ravine, ready to try the impossible. Thirty feet below, the distinctive back of the Dodge was edging out from an inferno. An explosion threw the hood into a bush.

"Don't go down there," cried the policeman. "It's too late!"

Theo crumpled to the ground, his hands fisting the earth. He vomited long streams of bile, getting it all over his clothes, his forearms, and his cuffs.

"Why?" he moaned, tears streaming down his face. "They hadn't done anything. Why?"

The truck driver was giving more details to the cop. The Dodge had been coming downhill too fast. He'd nearly hit them, and had swerved at the last second. The driver's reflexes had been bad; losing control of his vehicle, he'd careened over the ledge.

Theo suddenly stood up, a heavy boulder gripped in both hands. He advanced towards the policeman, eyes mad.

"You killed them. You and your schemes!"

Without realizing it, he'd slipped into French. The cop sidestepped, yanked his gun from its holster.

"Remain calm, *señor*. Please."

The truck driver had edged around Theo, cautiously. There was something surreal about the scene. The inferno. The huge truck with its vertical exhaust looking like a chimney. The gun in the Mexican's trembling hand. Nature, all still…

"That's right, go ahead," yelled Theo. "Shoot. That what you want, *maricón*? Shoot. I'm going to end you."

He stepped forward again. Nimbly, the driver had edged close to him. The officer's finger tensed against the trigger.

Theo felt a weight impact against his skull. For a moment, he was convinced a bullet had struck him.

His sight went hazy. He collapsed. His forehead violently hit the ground.

"Why do cows die in car crashes?" asked Katia.

Theo laughed.

"In car crashes? But there's no such thing. All cows work on the base. They provide milk. When they have no more milk, they get killed, they get carved, and they get eaten."

"You shouldn't tell her that kind of stuff," grumbled Juliette. "Look, now she's crying."

"That's OK," retorted Theo. "Since we're in Paris."

Chapter 8

Howard Beck cut his daydreaming short, noting that an Audi had been tailing him for just about ten minutes. From his first training session, it had been drilled into him to notice this kind of thing. And given how closely the hulking German sedan was sticking to his bumper, the driver wasn't even trying to pretend.

Howard pushed down on the accelerator.

He saw the grill of the Audi kiss the pavement and grow bigger in his rearview. The driver seemed to be the only one on board. Howard opened his glove compartment and extracted a Glock 17 that he stuck under his thigh. Then he downshifted and pulled into the left-hand lane, still speeding up.

The speedometer was indicating seventy miles an hour. Very quickly, he got it up to a hundred, nearly double the speed limit on the freeway. The vehicles on the right lane were disappearing as fast as they appeared. But behind him, Howard could imperceptibly see the aggressive black hood edging closer to his trunk. The engine of his Chrysler was of course enhanced, but clearly not as powerful as the one in the S4 that was trailing him. This was a game he knew he couldn't win.

Without warning, he darted into the right-hand lane, smashing on the brakes, and he settled into a minuscule edge between a huge Cherokee and a Nissan minivan. His pursuer overtook him and did the same thing a couple vehicles down the line. Howard slowed down some more, attempting to put as much distance as possible between the two of them.

It started to rain.

Beck drove past an exit, and decided he'd take the next one. Traffic was getting heavier, and he tried to make out the black sedan among the myriad glowing red taillights, without success. He took the next exit, then, a few miles down, and saw the Audi, idling on the shoulder, clearly waiting for him. Howard hadn't managed to shake him. He gave himself over to the inevitable and pulled over in turn, a couple yards down. Eyes fastened to his rearview, he cut off the engine, then grabbed his semi-automatic again and waited.

A stocky figure exited the S4 and nonchalantly made its way toward him, hands clearly visible, no apparent weapon. Beck noticed that the features of the approaching man were familiar. When the stranger knocked on his window, he recognized Avi Haim.

"And here comes the Mossad," he gritted out, smiling joylessly.

Howard lowered his window, not truly sure what to expect from the Israeli. In a split second, he saw his file, his service record, flash before his eyes. Their conclusion defined him as an "old-school" agent, active in the field and always at the forefront during arduous negotiations.

"Mister Beck," began Haim in an affable tone, "we need to talk."

"And you couldn't find a better approach than a high-speed car chase?"

"You're right," retorted Haim ironically. "But you're the one who called me. Perhaps I should have dropped by at Langley and asked your secretary for an appointment. Wouldn't you rather we talked somewhere dry, over a drink?"

The Webster's bar sign was a four-leaf clover, the shamrock typical of all Irish pubs. The paneling had dulled with age, the felt on the pool tables was threadbare, and the hammered bar top betrayed its advanced age. But the hushed ambiance in the darkened alcoves, suitable for trysts between couples eager for privacy, suited the two men all the more since, at the end of that day, the pub was practically deserted.

The owner of the place, who could have passed for Victor McLaglen, seemed to know Haim, as he greeted him with a brief not of the head before withdrawing into the customary silence. Without conferring, the two agents ordered a pint of Beamish, which the Irishman slid before them. They then got settled on a bench.

"I believe I heard that your service has just suffered a terrible setback," whispered Haim, letting out a sigh like a big, contented cat between two gulps of stout. "Please know that you have our sympathies. It is always regrettable to see an ally lose men during an operation that is of particular interest to us."

"You chased me down the highway to offer your condolences?"

"Certainly not. But the failure of your operation has made quite the stir in the region. You managed to bring Iranian surveillance in a state of alert not just at the borders, but domestically as well, and our embedded agents must now redouble their efforts to maneuver safely. I must assure you, we sincerely mourn your failure... Buridan, that was the name of a famous ass, was it not?"

Beck kept his own counsel.

"What a quaint idea, to name a field operation after such a common animal... But regardless, our archive work was carried out using that denomination."

"Archives serving what purpose?" gritted out Beck.

Haim moistened his lips with a grimace before replying.

"My mother always told me, "That which is necessary to your survival, you do not ask for, you take!""

"Your mother was an Auschwitz survivor. These are different times."

"Are you so sure?"

Haim went on.

"Far too often, your government has put its immediate interests, in particular financial ones, before the security of my country. And yet isn't it strange: America's enemies have always fundamentally been ours, as well. Nazis, communists, and now fascist Islamists… That speaks volumes about our common values, don't you think?"

Beck let out a small laugh, like a squeak.

"Why do I get the feeling I'm gonna need to sit here and take all your philosophical crap if I want to find out more…"

"Come now, Howard, you called me. Otherwise I would not have come your way. I imagine the White case made some waves, even within your service. But that is not the purpose of our meeting, not precisely…"

The two men watched each-other for a few long moments. Behind the bar, the McLaglen clone was on the phone, a glowing cigarette at the corner of his lips, underneath a sign declaring smoking forbidden. From the backroom drifted the muted noise of pool talk, punctuated by the clacking of the balls across the felt. Too far off to make out a single word.

"You are convinced a mole betrayed you," uttered Haim at last. "And what wouldn't you give to find out who…"

Beck hunted for a way to regain his composure. He'd have expected anything, but not the Mossad taking such a close interest in the failure in Islamabad. But perhaps that explained Avi Haim's presence in Washington. An agent of his caliber had no business being in a friendly country, excepting if a still-warm lead had brought him there. It remained to be seen what precisely brought this and the White case together. He chose to respond in a natural, slightly irked tone.

"Two men died a terrible death, the third is missing, and the little snuff film they made of them is still being broadcast online. Certain sites have even become specialized in this kind of spectacle, and it has the Islamists going wild.

"One of the three guys was married. If the man responsible is here in Washington, somewhere, you bet I'd like to have a couple minutes alone with him!"

"Oh," – Haim raised his hands in a fatalistic gesture – "he's not necessarily in Washington right now. You know full well that your capital is no longer very fashionable in our circles… Would you be willing to make an exchange?"

Beck was used to this kind of subterfuge-laden conversations, where every morsel of information had to be yanked out with plyers, in a mutually suspicious atmosphere, under the cover of the warmest friendliness. It was the only game to play between the agents of allied nations, among which competitions at the individual level were often fought out for the most noble of reasons.

The Israeli secret agencies had been burned more than once in the past by the attitude of their American counterparts, who all too often displayed a troubling naiveté when it came to their common enemies. The CIA had a reputation for its multitude of dropped balls, and its covert interventions in western politics had ruffled more than one set of feathers, at all levels of power and opposition. It was laughingly said that they were always running behind, still fighting communism when Islam was already a truer threat and proving it out in the field every day.

As for the Mossad, they were a microscale expression of the tortured soul of the country they served. The slightest error could prove fatal: Israel did not have the luxury of suffering a single defeat. It remained to be seen what Haim really wanted. Because there was no doubt in Beck's mind that the Mossad never moved its pawns forward just because. If his Israeli counterpart was talking about an exchange, that meant he was able to deliver on his side of the deal.

"Give me just a little bit more," ventured Beck, "and I'll see what I can do."

"Intel for intel, a man for a man…?"

"…And a tooth for a tooth," finished Beck through gritted teeth. "That's from your Talmud, unless I'm mistaken? Come on, Haim, let's drop this little game. Give me enough to be able to ascertain how good the intel is on my own!"

"Very well. This may take a while. Do you want another beer?"

Beck sighed. Not waiting for a response, the Mossad man began describing a sting that an Israeli team had put together in Rome, London, and Paris several months earlier. The goal had been to cut the funding of several terrorist cells, which had their roots in the very heart of Israel, in Jerusalem East, at the source. The current popular doctrine at the "Institute" was "follow the money, find the enemy."

It was an open secret at best that, using their alliance with the all-powerful United States as a cover, the Saudis gladly played both sides, using their covert contacts to maintain a level of insecurity that favored oil prices, while making use of a religious cause that was beyond the understanding of even the best western analysts.

In this little game of replete cat and mischievous mouse, the Mossad was often at an impasse, hoping to come across an Islamist viper's nest so as to finally flush out some rich Riyadh bankers, with the CIA's full knowledge. Money flows were the life blood of a shadow body with nebulous tentacles.

During this sting, the *katsas*[12] crew had spotted the intriguing plot of a man who was well-known to the service. In principle, said man had no strategic reason to be in contact with their surveillance target. Per information obtained during classic exchanges, the CIA had no ongoing operations in that theater.

"You're lucky," finished Haim. "Few Saudi businessmen are connected to Iran. This man is one of them. And the first meeting with the one we believe to be your mole took place two weeks before the incident that troubles you."

"Do you have any proof?"

Haim hitched his shoulders up.

"Our materials are not always as sophisticated as yours, but as you know, we have a gift for infiltrating anywhere. Espionage is still the work of men, Beck. It takes the arrogance of some of your bosses to believe that wars can be conducted between electronic devices, as though it were a gaming console."

---

12   Katsa – Active MOSSAD agent.

"Very well, then what do you want in exchange?"

"Something not too complicated. There are rumors of an operation that your agency is connected to. An off-the-books scheme…"

"I'm not aware of any such business."

"Come, Beck, this is no longer a question of donkeys or fake warheads. "White Cells," does that mean anything to you?"

Beck's face clouded over. For a moment, he had hoped that Haim would ask him for the list of CIA agents embedded in Lebanon, or the bank account numbers of Muslim "charity" organizations being monitored, their purpose often being to siphon funds off to Hezbollah or to Hamas. Something negotiable, following some equivocation. But a parallel operation being conducted under such a code name was absolute news to him.

"Genuinely, Haim… I'm not read in," he confessed.

The Israeli watched him attentively. The expression on Beck's face was unequivocal. He was torn between disappointment and curiosity.

"Ah! There it is. This then is one of those operations requiring a very high clearance level. The last one of those that reached our ears, Operation… hmm… Merlin, if my memory serves, ended in total failure."

Beck settled deeper into his seat. Haim appeared to like demonstrating his knowledge, but not boastfully, in a manner akin to an old professor delivering his academic litany for the thousandth time.

"In February 2000, you sent a Russian scientist who had recently emigrated to the United States to deliver the plans for a TRA 480, a nuclear detonation system, to the permanent Iranian representative to the IAEA. The Russian's mission was simple: pass himself off as a greedy scientist selling to the highest bidder by producing plans – already doctored by the engineers at your Sandia laboratory – as a show of good faith. That way the Iranians would have proved that they were trying to get the bomb…"

Beck was waiting for the other man to finish telling his story, his gaze fastened to the bottom of his glass.

"But the snag," ground out Haim, "is that your scientist tried to go above and beyond in proving his credibility as a spy apprentice. So he went overboard and included a short note signaling that there were mistakes in this plan he was handing over.

"No sooner than that, a member of the Iranian mission hopped on a plane to Tehran, and their engineers, aware of the deliberate mistakes baked into the plans, had only to root them out, and thus get a fully operational equivalent of the TRA 480," he wrapped up with an amused smile.

"Yes," conceded Beck irritatedly. "I've heard about that."

Haim's cheerful mien gave way then to a grave countenance.

"Quite funny, yes. Unless you're Israeli, when you know that Tehran already disposes of vectors with a wide enough range to be able to aim a rudimentary bomb at Tel Aviv, and can equip it with your detonator. For you, it's a failure. For us, however, it is a threat."

Beck was more and more irked. As Haim delivered his usual paranoid Israeli oration, he was trying to recall the slightest hint of watercooler talk that could have led him to this whole "White Cells" business. He struck out. Yet the mole's identity would remain a secret unless he had something to provide in exchange. He was in danger then of missing out on this deal.

"Give me a couple of days," he said at last. "I'll see if I can unearth something."

"I'm sure you can do better than that!"

Beck stood up. Haim slipped a twenty out of his pocket, which he slid under his beer glass, and a cell phone, on which he tapped away. A few seconds later, Beck's own phone started to vibrate.

"No need to pick up," said Haim. "Merely call the number on your screen when you have an answer."

Howard straightened up, said a terse goodbye, and made his way towards the door. Halfway there, Avi called out to him.

"Howard? I nearly forgot. There is one small thing we'd like to ask of you. Concerning Vincent White, is there anything you can do?"

Outside, through the man-high window separating the pub from the street beyond, the rain had turned into a deluge. Beck lifted his shoulders.

"What do you want, that we set him free? How is he connected to this other business?"

"There appear to be several multinationals involved in White Cells," said Haim. "OptroNex among them. But that information requires verification, of course. White, after all, only got himself mixed up in some industrial espionage, my agency is not concerned with that."

"Obviously…"

"If we could prevent a repeat of the Pollard business, that would be great," said Haim, closing the collar of his coat against the chill. "Twenty years you've been holding on to that poor joe and that we've been getting ourselves marches on every anniversary…"

Beck held the door open for his colleague to go through. He couldn't stop himself from snickering in his face.

"I might have known you weren't getting mixed up for altruistic reasons."

The Chrysler had been pushed to its limits, under the pouring rain and unmindful of the speed cams. Beck soon got back to the "farm" at Langley, cleared the security checkpoints, crossed the lobby, trampling the CIA sigil stamped into the marble without even paying it any mind, then stepped into an elevator.

He first made his way to his office, and started with a search through the Agency files.

"white cells"

No files matched the search term. He tried several operations, including a full decryption, without any results. His own clearance unfortunately did not enable him to go any further, and he knew that certain "special" operations weren't even stored electronically.

His watch showed twenty-two hundred thirty when he exhausted all avenues available to him.

Beck picked up his phone then and tried several office extensions before he ended up getting Foster, a level two agent that he knew for having sometimes accompanied him to a baseball game, the one thing he knew the man to be fanatical about outside of his commitment to the Agency. Stunned to hear his voice so late – especially from an internal number – the man immediately tried to talk sports with him. Beck cut him off.

"I just need to know if Murphy's around. If not, who else you've got on your floor. I need a level three or four."

Beck waited a beat, nervous, and almost let out a sigh of relief upon hearing Murphy's voice. Ten minutes later, he was being seen inside the "aquarium," a glass room impervious to all waves that every Agency department was equipped with, and going over his conversation with Haim down to the slightest detail.

For a start, he forebore to allude to Haim's main demand, waiting to gauge whether the head of the CTC had any real interest in his intel, and how seriously he took the *katsa*. A demand for a two-bit spy, an opportunistic traitor, to be freed was hard enough to swallow as it was.

Paul Murphy had spent enough years heading the action division to immediately grasp the import of what was going on. He let Beck talk without cutting in, and waited for the debrief to be over before he unleashed his rancor.

"The FBI has Vince White, Howard! Not us. I don't need to remind you that we aren't supposed to operate on American soil. This falls within the Bureau's purview, not ours."

Beck pushed his hands against his eyes for a long while. He stared for a moment at the head of the CTC, who was standing upright before him, tie undone and fists against his hips.

"This is intel we can't pass up. Paul, we've gotta be realistic. We don't have any leads. And if the Israelis have managed to ID our mole, they admitted it was through sheer luck. We can't afford to waste days and months before we get our hands on him.

"Not to mention that, with every day that goes by, this guy can maneuver right here, with impunity. God only knows what other op he might blow for us."

Murphy turned towards the window, acting like he was contemplating the rainy vista outside.

"The price is unacceptable."

"The fee is non-negotiable," pointed out Beck.

"White… He's untouchable! The FBI will never let him go. For a start, even the press doesn't know …"

"There's gotta be some way to persuade them…"

"Not at my level."

"And if you were to ask the right person?"

Beck kept a close watch on Murphy, trying to discern the internal thought process that had overtaken the head of the CTC behind an apparent impassivity. Finally, the latter sighed.

"I may have someone who owes me a favor… It's far from a sure thing, and the director will still need to sign off on it… I do wonder what business the Mossad could have with a guy like that. They didn't make as big a deal about Pollard."

Beck felt that the time had come.

"Actually, this isn't the only thing they're asking for. But I must admit I didn't understand their first demand."

It surprised him to see Paul Murphy go white as he disclosed the Israeli's main request. Beck, who had so far only felt a perfectly natural curiosity, suddenly found himself on his guard.

"No-one's in the know," spat Murphy in a glacial tone. "How could word of this op have reached the Mossad?"

Mechanically, Beck patted his inner jacket pocket. Old smoker's reflex that he hadn't contended with in a long time.

"Paul, what if you told me a little more about White Cells?"

To his immense surprise, he saw Murphy pick up the secure phone, and heard him proclaim in an arctic voice,

"Officer, we're at code 9. You have one hour to set up a meeting for me."

In seventeen years, this was the first time that Beck saw the Agency's highest-level emergency procedure being implemented.

The "aquarium" was also called the "fishbowl" by the agents, who were beyond uncomfortable with the impression of complete isolation bestowed on their systems by the composite cage especially constructed not to let either images or waves through. Instead, it was itself flooded with beams that were modulated electronically in real time so that no detection system, not even one as cutting-edge as micro lasers, could intercept the communications within.

Complex technology to hide a most simple concept: a voice is nothing more than a sound beam that, like all waves, strikes the walls that stand in its way as it propagates. No chance for your garden variety human being to discern the slightest hint.

But for a microphone system based on technology derived from laser telemetry, one that picks up the vibrations reverberating through the walls, this sound flow that is for all intents and purposes inaudible becomes as deafening as an earthquake. The mic acting the part of a seismograph or hydrophone would make it possible, after a screening, to hear the slightest word being said.

A simple phone call had gotten the emergency committee together in the middle of the night. At the far end of the table sat the deputy director of the Directorate of Operations, as well as the head of the CPD, the Counterproliferation Division. At the other end, Paul Murphy of the CTC waited patiently alongside Beck, who was certainly the least-ranked attendee.

The members present at the meeting were not all CIA. A representative of the National Security Council was also there, as well as an NSA big shot. It hadn't quite sat right with the NSC representative that he'd been disturbed from his first sleep in the middle of the night. But this was an emergency situation, as Murphy had impressed upon him.

"Gentlemen," he'd begun as soon as the four men had settled in, "I must regretfully inform you that "White Cells" is no longer a secret."

Beck, discreet and silent as someone of his rank had to be, had had to wait for the usual procedures to be put into place, everyone needing to proffer proof of their identity, even though they'd all known each other for a long time.

At Paul Murphy's request, a sworn secretary had placed a sealed folder before each man, extracted from his own safe. Beck had needed to wait until he was authorized to open his, after Murphy had pleaded his case by explaining the reason for his presence at the meeting.

"The fact that the Mossad has information on the mole before we do obviously takes second stage as far as our concerns," Murphy had gone on, punctuating his phrases with slaps to the surface of the conference table. "The only question at hand is: how did they catch wind of such a highly classified, off-record thing?"

Beck had avidly perused the top-secret file, and, while everyone had taken their turn meandering down conjecture lane, the sound of their conversations had seemed farther and farther away to him, while the blood had drained from his face.

There were only few elements in the file, with the exception of the op description itself. A bit of correspondence. The first report written up six years earlier by a certain William Jarmush, a name unfamiliar to Beck. The profile of a famous multibillionaire, Gregory Cheston, an informatics mogul whose companies were spread out in a tentacle-like grip of the five continents.

And, most especially, the technical summary signed by the director of the CIA himself, recommending the highest possible Top Secret classification. Only the Kennedy assassination and black site prisons had ever been granted such a confidentiality level. Under this classification, the President of the United States himself could deny being read in, and therefore fully benefit from the process of plausible deniability.

The description was plain and unembellished, and contained few arguments, as though it pertained to an established fact: the democratic western world, the explanation essentially went, was going through an unprecedented crisis in the face of a multi-headed and polymorphous enemy. Future wars would no longer be territorial disputes, and alliances would no longer be established between nations, but according to spiritual beliefs.

Field wars, the prelims concluded, could do away with official armies, the role of which would be relegated to deterrence, not unlike a nuclear arsenal. Faced with a lawless enemy, democratic laws became a handicap, a millstone, a toy that profited the other side.

To combat the viral proliferation of terrorism, the immune system of the democratic body needed to change tack, and to that end change form while the virus used up the body's own leukocytic reserves to disable its functioning.

120

Only putting together an elite army that resembled a clandestine Delta Force and worked according to the same multicellular model could counter such a debilitating strategy, with its underhand alliances and its daily increases in terrifyingly effective attacks against civilian targets the world over. An apolitical army. A stateless army. A lawless army.

Beck had the abominable privilege of holding between his fingers what was undoubtedly the most explosive document of the 21st century.

"Beck, where'd you go?"

Murphy's voice rang out in the sudden silence.

"It's done, you've read it," he went on. "Pull yourself together! You're now among the half-dozen men inside this agency who've had access to this information."

"If I read that right," said Beck, "you authorized the creation of a military force that neither the President nor Congress has any oversight over..." He slowly rubbed the bridge of his nose, then went on in a nearly toneless voice. "An army not subject to the will of the people, for the purpose of defending it..."

"Mister... Beck!" Broke in the head of the CPD – a man in his fifties with eyes of such a light blue that he might have seemed blind if not for the glimmer dancing in his watery pupils. "Your boss asked you a question. No-one here is in need of your melodramatic commentary! When are you supposed to meet this Haim again?"

"I suppose he'll be expecting a call as soon as I know more."

"Very well, as of this moment I suggest you stick to answering our questions!"

Howard Beck acquiesced with a pensive nod. Like all field agents, he hated the bureaucratic conception of the Agency, built like a solidly sealed hierarchic tangle. If he approved of the notion of interdepartmental segregation, he railed against the way that decisions impacting human lives were often made from the comfort of a cushy office with a picture view, with no input or consent from the concerned parties.

"With all due respect, Sir, to the extent where the information has trickled down, it is my duty to provide a street-level point of view. As a sworn agent, I will uphold my sworn duty of confidentiality; but from a personal standpoint, I'm stunned to learn that the Agency I work for could have taken measures that run counter to the Constitution."

"Beck, enough!" intervened Murphy. "Everyone here values the way you think, but we've gone beyond parlor talk, don't you think? We've got a crisis to solve. Let's get back to work."

Howard dithered. He didn't have too much choice, however. He could keep expressing his disapproval, and put not just his career on the line, but maybe even his life, if he followed through on his thoughts.

It wouldn't be the first time that a field agent disappeared, "fallen in the line of duty," that duty being the preservation of the Agency's secrets. He wouldn't even be granted the honors due his rank. A discreet burial following a nondescript accident, though his family would get a pension despite it all. At best, he'd get transferred out to a high-risk area, Iraqi Kurdistan being particularly in right now.

All the same, he was having a hard time coming to terms with the contents of the folder he still held in his hands. Seventeen years in the service of the CIA had accustomed him to all manner of extremes, his baseline being that of a lover of freedom such as it was immutably guaranteed by the constitution he defended.

"So," thundered the head of the CPD, "are you in, or do I call Security?"

Howard Beck closed the folder and slid the legal pad meant for his use in front of him. It was gonna be a long night.

Chapter 9

"Every one of them will be operational in under eight months."

"For now, they look rather like zombies," countered Ellen Cheston.

Colonel Meyrek protested.

"You can't judge a man after a day's training. Especially here. Stick around for twenty-four more hours and you'll gain a full appreciation for their new abilities. Tomorrow, at dawn…"

"I'm not here to sit through a military parade," Ellen dryly cut in. "You said eight months. That is what we were hoping for."

She teased the curtain of the Mercedes back into place, cutting herself off from the rest of the world, face dripping with sweat despite the AC in the vehicle. There was a fine layer of ochre dust on the car window, painting the landscape and the men in the sepia tone of an old film. Inside, everything was high end. Outside, a stretch of hell.

This had been a very particular reviewing of the troops. The limousine, delivered by special helicopter that morning for the sole purpose of shielding Ellen from the unflattering gazes of a crowd of exhausted men scattered into discrete rows in the base's vast main courtyard, enabled her to zigzag incog among the troops, something she particularly enjoyed.

A small Learjet twinjet had landed on a prepared landing strip between two prefab hangars a little after noon. "Marylin" had made her way straight to the barracks housing Meyrek, who had spent the past three hours neglecting the two thousand-odd well-supervised men stationed out in the sun at his discretion. Meyrek had nicknamed that day's exercise "motionless abnegation."

After having consulted the entirety of the files relaying the progress of the on-base activities, Ellen had finally deigned to turn her attention to the human end.

The Mercedes had then wheeled slowly between the rows of worn-out men, its tires stirring up clouds of dust, the recruits staring with wary eyes at the metal monster that reflected nothing but the fiery glare of the sun from its chassis and its tinted windows.

Two men had fainted before the vehicle reached them. The colonel's instructions were specific: under no circumstances was anyone to intervene.

The Mercedes hadn't slowed down for the prone bodies, "Marylin" content to keep counting.

Their BDUs were similar to the desert fatigues worn by the marines. There were reddish tints to the volcanic soil. A short distance away, the heat given off by the ground distorted their figures, creating mirages of twinkling water where four thousand boots splashed.

It was a parade ground that was only missing a flag.

"Did you know that the slush funds of eight multinationals got swallowed up by this project?" hissed Ellen.

Meyrek settled deeper into his seat. The contact with the leather was unpleasant to him. "Marylin's" presence, repugnant. He loathed the idea of needing to review his men from inside this incongruous haven of luxury.

"Soldiers have a reputation for being bad with money," he retorted. "I am supposed to be training soldiers who haven't, for the most part, gone beyond street fighting. You asked me to make a unit out of illiterate yokels, and an elite corps out of thugs. I should not have to worry over material concerns."

"I agree entirely. I am merely noting that you're not skimping out on the human matter. If these reports are to be believed, your weekly total varies between one and three dead… which we are constrained to replace."

"I'm assuming there's nothing selfless about your remark."

"This project is selfless," retorted "Marylin." "As such, the efforts we will expend to see it through will be turned towards that purpose."

"Listen," gritted the colonel, "spare me your crap, OK? I'm getting paid a lot of money for this job, and I'm supposing your recruitment methods are excellent. Your companies have spent hundreds of millions of dollars to make this camp a reality, and you entrusted it to me. That wasn't so you could wave the bill for your extra spending in my face today. A few thousand dollars to replace some missing men aren't a problem for you. So?"

Ellen got a faraway look in her eyes. For several moments, she might have been thought asleep. Suddenly, she pinned Meyrek with her gaze.

"We have gone dramatically over the allotted budget, and my father is beginning to suspect something. That's the reason for my visit to the base."

Meyrek's face flushed, and his mien turned into a menacing rictus. For a moment, Ellen thought he would leap at her. She was surprised to hear his voice, strangely calm.

"Don't tell me I'll have to take care of this kind of matter as well… I never approved of the second camp being built, and I'm even more against it now. The base we're on now should be more than sufficient for your plans. Why not give up on the other one?"

"Colonel, some things are beyond you! You're right, you should stick to your duties as a soldier."

Ellen once again mopped up the sweat that was running down the bridge of her nose.

"My report will show that, thanks to the increase in your staff's pay, the growth in strength, and Tamazula's extra spending to search for recruits, the army is evolving at a rate that is more than satisfactory. Which may even enable us to consider moving up the active phase of the operation…

"Alas, no amount of training can ever replace conviction. And I see nothing in this camp that could inspire the abnegation we will soon be asking of them."

Meyrek burst out laughing.

"You want to create kamikazes, madam "Marylin." Fanatics that will fight with your companies' logo tattooed on their chest? You're hoping I'm creating a common cause for them, a religion perhaps.

"But I am only here to teach these men to give their lives for no other reason than the orders they'll get. You should have hired an ayatollah if my instruction methods appeared insufficient to you. Not a soldier."

Outside the vehicle, surreptitiously supported by his closest comrades, a tan boy in his early twenties was about to collapse. Despite the sun, his complexion was waxen, huge beads of sweat standing out on his brow.

Meyrek signaled for the driver to stop the car.

"Look at these men. I'm able to recognize every one of them, though they are in their hundreds. I know their pasts by heart. Eighty percent of them no longer have a family. They let themselves be taken in by promises, and they have nothing to defend save their skins. To survive, each one of these men will do whatever it takes. They will go beyond their own imaginations.

"Look at him. A Guatemalan, recruited by Tamazula. He was convicted of rape, and he wouldn't have gotten more than two years in prison. He preferred to "enlist." Several of his compatriots made an attempt to escape after a week of training. He couldn't follow them, because he twisted his ankle.

"I used these escape attempts to instill terror in them all. You will witness the result. You will behold just how you can fight for nothing."

Meyrek opened the car door. Blistering hot air streamed into the vehicle. Instinctively, Ellen hid her face away behind one of the files perched on her knees. Meyrek reached the first row. The recruits automatically adjusted their positions. Without the support of his comrades, the young man staggered. He nevertheless remained standing.

Meyrek harshly bellowed at him in Spanish. Several supervising officers had immediately joined him, arms in a firing position, ready to intervene at the slightest signal. Meyrek got himself a rifle from one of them and emptied it of its cartridges. He placed it in the soldier's hands.

Tears flowed down a face barely out of adolescence. On the verge of collapse, he tried to beg the colonel. The latter dryly repeated his order. The boy silently nodded his head.

Meyrek slid back inside the vehicle.

"Since you're getting back to your plane, I've arranged an escort for you. This young Guatemalan is at the end of his rope. As are most of these men, actually. Four hours in the sun, upright, no moving and especially no water.

"He will nevertheless run behind your car, an eight-pound rifle in his arms, for as long as his legs will carry him. Had I not stepped in, he would already be lying there, in the dust, relishing the bliss of a loss of consciousness."

"What did you tell him, to make him obey you?"

"He had a choice between escorting you, with the vehicle driving at a moderate pace, or getting his feet tied to the bumper. In which case, the car would have driven a good deal faster."

"This rather cruel experiment does nothing to prove his combat prowess."

"I asked you for eight months to train them for combat. For the moment, watch him survive. That is phase one."

Meyrek cracked open his window and called out to the nearest officer.

"Have them break ranks, hand out water generously, and take the weakest to the infirmary. Tonight, improved fare for everyone, and rest."

The Mercedes set off, followed a couple yards out by the young Guatemalan.

"Eighteen miles an hour," Meyrek told the driver.

He turned towards Ellen.

"In your opinion, how long will he last? The boy hasn't had any water since this morning."

Face twisted in pain, holding his rifle with both hands, the soldier was swaying. The Mercedes was pulling away from him.

"Drive slower, let him catch up."

In front of the vehicle, the men were slowly scattering towards the mess. Their gazes, heavy with reproach, were converging towards the invisible interior of the vehicle.

"Terror and hate, isn't that right?" whispered Ellen.

"The perfect analysis," assented Meyrek. "The two drivers of old-school military training. Imagine this hate potential that I'm allowing to fester inside each of them.

"The terror I inspire will never allow them to rise up against me. But it will grow, for months on end. Up until the day when I will give them a weapon and a target. Then, their hatred will explode. Alongside the preservation instinct, it is a soldier's greatest motivating force. Stop!"

Behind the vehicle, the boy had just collapsed.

"You didn't make a bet," commented Meyrek coldly. "A pity. He lasted for five minutes."

The Mercedes had barely pulled past the edges of the camp.

"Injustice must, however, be meted out at appropriate doses."

The colonel heaved himself out of the vehicle and made his way to the prone man. To Ellen's great surprise, he hauled him onto his shoulders and turned back towards the base. Two guards came running to his aid. Meyrek entrusted his burden to them.

"Still alive," he announced, resuming his seat next to Ellen.

She made no comment.

The twinjet, its nose in the wind, was already prepped for takeoff. At the bottom of the ramp – in actual fact, a slide equipped with a winch – the attendant had already unfolded the wheelchair.

Meyrek exited the vehicle first.

Just like in the New York parking garage during their first meeting, Ellen declined the colonel's help and settled herself as comfortably as she could in her invalid's chair.

The sun was dipping low, casting the shadow of the mountains all the way to the runway. A light breeze was finally making the air bearable.

"Most touched by your visit," growled Meyrek.

"From now on, IT connections will be the main way we'll keep in contact," replied Ellen. "The organizers of this operation are eager for reports."

The attendant hooked the cable to the back of the wheelchair and handed Ellen the remote.

"Speaking of, that French computer engineer who was supposed to take over the service, is he here?"

Meyrek screwed up his eyes, his gaze seeing far beyond "Marylin's" monstrous body.

"Not yet. We've had some difficulties with him."

"I hope they're taken care of," spat Ellen in a glacial voice.

"They are."

"Mind telling me why you were so set upon recruiting him?"

"Chance," uttered the colonel enigmatically. "Chance! As well as a certain gift of his that I'm aware of."

Ellen pushed the button on her remote, and her seat began its slow ascension.

"In our Organization, chance is called probability. It is calculated and controlled."

Theo came to. A red-hot poker was embedded deep in his skull, shredding his brain. He tried to lift himself up on an elbow, mind empty, and his vision went blank. For a moment, he thought he was losing consciousness again. He wondered what illness had struck him. Prone once more, his vision cleared, and his eyes were struck by a blinding glare. He closed them again.

Suddenly, in tandem with a huge wave of nausea, his memory returned in full.

Theo howled.

His cry dwindled to a gurgle as his stomach seized spasmodically. His mouth filled with bile. He turned his head to one side in a sudden motion and let his throat expel the bitter, sour liquid.

His soul crazed with pain, he couldn't prevent the discharge of his body, wetting his thighs, soiling their undersides. Like an agonizing animal. For long minutes on end he let himself go, having lost even his shame, even his basest dignity; then, his flesh finally settled, he sobbed.

He could utter nothing but his wife's name. His daughter's. Unable to believe that he had not just come awake from a long nightmare, expecting to see their faces through his tears.

At last he twitched a leg out, slid it slowly towards the edge of some sort of bed. This simple movement tore moans from him. The room was lit by a ceiling light. Grey walls, crisscrossed with huge cracks. A second bed, empty, similar to his. The rest of the room, bare of any furniture.

Theo managed to sit up in his own filth. He'd been stripped of all his clothing. He rubbed at the painful spot on his head and discovered a bump under his sticky hair. He took in his reddened fingers, cursing the one who'd knocked him out for not ending his days.

The door opened to reveal a small, rotund woman with a pockmarked face. She was wearing a questionably clean blue blouse, and her small, lively, perpetually moving eyes lit up when they landed on Theo.

"You're awake," she said, rolling the r. "Thank God. You have been asleep for hours. Hours."

She came to a stop a couple steps from Theo and watched him.

"You're all filthy. A lot of pain, *no*?"

She went on to exclaim in a Mexican dialect that Theo couldn't make heads or tails of. Then she took his hand.

"Come with me. I will give you a little wash."

He resisted. Gently, she tried again.

"You are hurt. I must clean your head. Put a bandage. But first you must take a shower. Here, it smells bad. You have a visit soon. You must wash."

"Leave me alone!"

"*Que dice usted?*"

Theo roughly jerked his hand away, eyes crazed. Her tone utterly commiserating, the nurse tried to calm him down. Overcome with a demented inspiration, Theo grabbed the nurse by the collar and, slowly, despite her cries, pulled her to him. She shrieked, tried to get away. Theo gathered all his strength, forgetting about the pain in his skull. Slowly, he brought her towards the bed, bowed her spine until her face dipped into the fecal matter.

The hapless woman heaved. Her calls for help echoed through the room. Satisfied, Theo let her go at last. The Mexican hurtled towards the door, her blouse, her face, and even her hair smeared. She pinned a murderous glare on him and ran out as fast as her legs could carry her.

Theo heard her yelping fade down the corridor. A moment later, two pairs of arms seized him and dragged him unceremoniously out of the room. The last dregs of his strength deserting him, he gave in.

He was taken down a long hallway into a huge shower room. The attendants, literal behemoths, threw him down onto a tiled floor. Immediately, an ice-cold stream of water hit him full blast.

Theo felt his blood rush through his veins, the pulse at his temples speed up. The feeling, unpleasant at first, became invigorating. The suffering in his scalp lessened a bit. Suffocating, he tried to get up. One of the men brutally shoved him back down, while the other one turned up the water pressure.

Through the water stream, Theo heard another shower turn on, and a female voice grumbling curses in Spanish. Despite the cold, despite the trickle of blood he saw streaming before his eyes, Theo smiled a demented smile.

His head was wrapped up after he was given an X-ray. He put on some kind of pajamas reeking of crappy detergent. His bed had been made, the room ventilated. An attendant brought him some soup and watched him the whole meal through. He devoured a crusty morsel of rye bread. His blood pressure was taken. He allowed an unknown substance to be injected into the vein in his left arm.

All these treatments were proffered without a single word. Then, he found himself alone.

Roughly an hour must have gone by. Theo had managed to doze, his rest unsettled by obscure dreams that startled him awake. The door opened once again. An attendant stepped to the side to make room for an average sized man with dark hair threaded with grey. His stature was impressive. That of a man used to physical exercise. His posture was tense, as though his muscles, corded, were ready to uncoil and spring into action at the slightest warning.

There was something vaguely familiar about the man's face. Steel-grey eyes, machete-carved features. The nearly invisible scar of an old gash bisected his forehead, starting from his left eyebrow.

The man closed the door and approached Theo with a feline gait that was at odds with his stocky build. He took a seat on the second bed.

"I am sorry for what happened to your family."

He spoke French without the hint of an accent. That level of proficiency, it was undoubtedly his mother tongue. Theo did not respond.

"I could tell you that you and I share responsibility for what happened," the man went on, "but neither you nor I were on that road when the incident occurred. I would rather chalk this accident up to a twist of fate."

"Who are you?" asked Theo.

"Fifteen years," murmured the colonel. "Can you cast your memory that far back?"

"I don't understand."

"Who am I?" said the man, as though he hadn't heard him. "Today I am in charge of this base. A place that few know of, truth be told, which makes it all the more interesting."

He stared him down.

"You haven't really changed. That same anxious look in your eye, but a bit more maturity about the face. I expect time hasn't had the same impact on you."

"Good grief," grumbled Theo, infuriated, "are you going to tell me who you are?"

"François Meyrek," replied the colonel. "Does this name still mean something to you?"

Theo rooted through his memories. He saw himself, aged twenty. Going into military service, after so many efforts to avoid it, the disciplinary battalion, with the threat of Iraq. His recollection sharpened. Suddenly, he cried out, stunned.

"The captain? Captain Meyrek?"

Meyrek nodded.

"Colonel Meyrek… It's been some time."

Theo felt himself plunge into madness.

"What are you doing here?"

He recalled then what his former captain had just disclosed. He was in charge of the base! The realization hit him like an uppercut. His head spun.

"You're the one who had me brought here?"

The colonel stood up, mechanically rubbed at an imaginary wrinkle in his impeccable jacket.

"The people in charge of this Organization don't like me saying the word chance. Their computers make it more… biddable. Only it is by chance that I came across your name as I sifted through the data. Also by chance that we had the same employer. Still by chance that some of your computer findings matched their needs…"

"What needs? What use could I be to you?"

Theo straightened up on his bed, too stunned to react. Standing, the colonel was barely an inch taller than him. Despite the painkillers, the pain in his skull throbbed with every beat of his heart, as though an invisible finger was pushing against the wound. Theo clung to that pain: this was life, a life now devoid of hope. His suffering was the one solid thing he had, the sole thing he owned.

"I want to know what you expect from me, Meyrek! Your obstinacy cost my wife and daughter their lives." Theo's voice broke. He took a deep breath in and raised his voice. "I demand that you tell me what I'm doing here, right now."

The colonel suddenly stepped in close. A dangerous gleam shone in his haze.

"You don't demand a thing, Collin. Have you forgotten who you're talking to?"

Theo looked at him, taken aback.

"But, you're insane!" he whispered.

"Let me walk you through this," growled the colonel. "You've lost your job, your country, your family, and I'm the only thing standing between you and something worse. You've lost your identity, Collin!"

"What are you saying?"

"There were three bodies in that car," announced Meyrek. "Officially, the third party was you."

It took Theo a few beats to comprehend the significance of those words. The scheme was a classic, effective, diabolical. He could do nothing but look at the colonel, mouth gaping. The expression on Meyrek's face was that of a reptile facing its prey. Theo was livid. Still, he declared in a whisper,

"I don't know what kind of ridiculous plan you cooked up in your sick brain the day you found me. But you're right: I'm dead. So go ahead, have your fun, *Colonel!* Nothing can get to me anymore."

Meyrek shook his head with an amused smile. Inside his mind, Theo's mere presence had turned back the clock fifteen years in one fell swoop. Faced with this broken man, he had absolute power. Was that not the very essence of what an officer was?

"In a little while, you will be a member of one of my elite units," he said, straightening up. "You'll be quick to learn what I expect from you."

"Meyrek… you're certifiable!"

"For the time being, I'm your superior officer! You will address me by rank!"

Tears sprang to Theo's eyes. In possession of his full faculties or not, the colonel was nothing more than a block of marble. The weight of his despair was making it hard for him to discern what was a game and what was sincere in Meyrek's behavior, but Theo hadn't yet reached the acceptance stage. He clung to the idea that he was living a nightmare. Everything was going to work out. Obviously, no god would allow such a misfortune to strike him, not something so absurd. In a quivering voice, he inquired,

"And… If they were still here…?"

"We would have had room for them. There is female staff on base…"

"Even my daughter?"

The colonel did not reply. Theo was insistent.

"What would you have done with my daughter?"

"That," said the colonel, "is a question I cannot answer today."

He looked at his watch.

"You're going to spend the night in this infirmary. Tomorrow, you will be driven to the base."

Meyrek adjusted his jacket, signaling the conversation was over. When he reached the door, Theo called out to him.

"Meyrek!"

The colonel spun on his heel.

"Whatever cause you're fighting for, and I can imagine it couldn't be farther from glorious, you'll never have me. You hear me? Never. You can torture me, put me through hell; I've already endured the worst. Not one of my bullets will hit their target if you make me shoot. Not unless, one day, my target is you!"

The colonel shrugged.

"We'll see!"

He slammed the door. A few minutes later, an attendant was leaning over Theo and injecting him with a tranquillizer.

He slept.

Chapter 10

The man was bald and clad in a green shirt. His hands were callused. His breath reeked.

"One hundred and fifty-nine pounds. Height, five foot ten. The body mass index is insufficient. Take a seat… Reflexes are normal. Open your mouth… Optimal masticatory coefficient. One bridge.

"Relax your face. Slight yellowing of the sclera. Gallbladder insufficiency. To be monitored. Lie back…"

Completely naked, Theo silently obeyed. The room was cool, and being inside it, even for a few moments, was a blessing. At least it meant an escape from the furnace outside.

The doctor was examining him with an interest that was completely devoid of sensitivity, dictating a medical record to his assistant – hirsute virility given a female form – that would soon be logged into the computer.

"Normal blood pressure. 120/60. Sit up fast. Poor blood pressure control. Slight anemia. Soft stomach. Clear lack of physical exercise. Supple cutaneous tissue. No premature aging. Subject appears slightly young for his age. Spread your legs slightly…"

He slipped on a transparent glove.

"No cruro-genital ganglions. Stand up and turn your back to me… Slight curvature of the lumbar spine. Insufficient back muscles."

The doctor drew a bit of blood and handed him a sterile container for a urine sample. Theo withdrew behind a screen. The nurse set the vial on a shelf. He was then X-rayed.

"Good. Return to the other room. You can get dressed."

Theo put on his regulation DBDU fatigues, shabby but comfortable, and a pair of combat boots.

The nurse watched him wordlessly. She flipped her notepad closed and exited the room with the vial of urine.

Outside the window, beyond the bars, nature unveiled a bounty of colors and contrasts. Volcanic desert stretched out to the rocky peaks that blotted out the horizon with the solemn grandeur of their silhouettes.

Orders muffled by distance streamed in from outside. The troops were back.

Theo finished buttoning his shirt.

"You'll need to put some weight on fast. About fifteen pounds."

"Oh yeah?" gritted out Theo. "And grow how many inches taller?"

The doctor didn't dignify him with a response. He sat down behind his desk (army surplus, like the rest of his furniture) and bent his head over his notes, no longer paying Theo the least mind.

The man remained standing, expectant, not showing the slightest hint of curiosity. A mirror reflected his image back at him. He was holding himself stooped. His features were drawn and his eyes, expressionless, were underscored by great purple marks. Unconsciously, he lifted his chest.

The phone rang.

"Colonel Meyrek is expecting you outside his barracks," the doctor told him. "Two men will take you there."

The base stood on several acres. Designed according to the principles shared by all barracks. The buildings were surrounded by a twelve-foot wall covered by barbed wire and inlaid with guard posts. The western buildings, separated from each other by eighty feet of clay, housed the men's quarters. Eight-bed rooms for the "elite" sections, and sixteen- or eighteen-bed dorms in the other buildings, all one story high.

To the east, beyond a central courtyard six hundred feet wide, the mess, the infirmary, and the officers' mess.

The munitions store, the helipad, the computer center, and the officers' quarters were located to the south-east, clustered together in a secure military area placed under heavier guard. All made from red bricks, the top of the buildings covered with earth and growing sparse dry grass and the inevitable cactuses.

The plateau, for its part, went on for miles. The only way to access it was a mule track that could be taken by ATVs. From a hundred yards up, the base melted into the landscape. Hard to make out, even on satellite photos. The only thing left to hide was the signs of life, of human activity and vehicle movements.

But the Organization's backers had set their consultants on the task from the very beginning, and an ingenious if costly solution had been designed and implemented at the heart of the base's computer center. As far as an imaging satellite was concerned, this remote corner of the planet was nothing more than a torturous, untouched landscape, shielded by a thick layer of fog.

The garage took up the fourth corner and housed a score of 4WD APCs, several Land Rovers, a dozen HMMWV, also known as Humvees, and the Mercedes that Ellen had left behind. There, too, a guard post stood at the entrance.

Theo had arrived by chopper at dawn. A laconic officer, American, accompanied him. No words had been spoken during the flight. They'd reached the base in half an hour.

Shortly before landing, Theo had made out a gigantic network of camouflage netting laying in part on the tops of the surrounding trees, consolidated by a structure of hastily painted cables and metal braces. There was no way for Theo to know that he was flying over a pasteboard reconstruction of a town, at the heart of which maneuvered several hundred men.

Before the spectacle of this vast net, Theo had the odd feeling he was hedgehopping above an emerald sea, its netted surface dotted with leaves and twigs. He wondered what it could be covering.

A long, silvery glint followed him for a moment, giving him a partial clue. Beneath the nets, the glare of the sun was reflected in the mirrored surface of a huge stretch of water, out of place in the middle of the desert: an artificial lake.

He got dragged to receiving. Just like fifteen years earlier, he was subjected to the indignity of the regulation haircut: clippers shearing him to four millimeters on top, two on the sides.

After a frugal, solitary meal, he'd been left to stew in his room until his medical visit.

For four hours, Theo had remained seated at the edge of his bed, his gaze drifting far beyond the whitewashed wall.

Like a machine, he had followed the man tasked with escorting him to the infirmary…

The colonel was waiting for him, flanked by two officers. The markings were standard, for a nationless army, and Theo recognized the three captain's stripes and the sergeant's braid.

His watch had been removed, but it was chilly. Outside, the shadows stretched out like colossal smears. It was probably six o'clock or thereabouts.

"Collin," began Meyrek in a very courteous voice, "let me introduce your two superior officers. Captain Novak and sergeant Garroni. The working language, considering the different nationalities at play, is English. You can understand bits and pieces. Enough, I'm certain, for what will be asked of you. Well, Collin?"

Theo, standing before the three men, was still.

"Won't you salute, Collin?"

"Salute? According to what protocol?"

"Great question," hooted Meyrek. "Your mind is still ticking, despite all appearances. As commander of this base, I've held on to a few nostalgic attachments. Legion conventions have been adopted for protocol. Collin, attention!"

The affable tone had suddenly turned biting. Theo remained motionless. Meyrek laughed again.

"I guess we'll skip that step. Sergeant Garroni will be your formal instructor. You're in for a treat. His mission is to turn you into an athlete in less than six months. Think you can make it happen, sergeant?"

"He looks younger than he is," replied the officer. "Not too fat, shows some spirit. He can be a real fighting machine. With some effort, of course…"

"Very good." Meyrek seemed delighted. "Captain Novak is in charge of training. Sergeant Garroni is in charge of a section. An elite section, Collin! We separated our most gifted recruits in there before your arrival. You'll soon be proud to be among them."

Through the wide-open gate of the base wafted a cadence call chanted by hundreds of boots. Two four-row phalanxes of men were returning from training.

We're headed out to combat
With no skin in the game.
We don't fight for no country,
And don't salute no flag.
Our only goal is freedom,
And that's what we'll defend.
No love, no hate, no nation,
No morals to offend.

Sung in atrocious French, the base anthem was a hodge-podge of accents with an almost superhuman percussive strength. A cloud of dust created a sun-streaked halo around the huge gathering. They kept their pace until they reached the center of the courtyard, their movements punctuated by brief orders. Theo, stunned, couldn't suppress a snicker.

The song came to a halt.

"What do you think?" asked the colonel. "I wrote the words myself."

Novak and Garroni had come to attention. The sergeant had parents from Belgium and from Bordeaux. Novak came from Hungary. But inside this piecemeal army, with all its disparate parts, everyone wore the same uniform.

"This is some kind of joke," whispered Theo. "You can't seriously imagine…"

The men put their rifles on the ground.

"The time has come for you to give us a demonstration of your talents," the colonel went on in a flat voice. "Your instructors would like to judge the perfection of your shooting for themselves. It's the ideal time. The sun is casting the kind of shadows that heighten contrasts."

Theo stiffened. Meyrek pinned him with a vigilant gaze.

"What's your weapon of choice?" asked the sergeant. "Rifle or automatic pistol?"

Theo stared the colonel down. The latter's face was lit up by a smile.

Strangely, he was devoid of any feelings.

"I've already told you," he said. "That is a satisfaction you'll never get from me."

Novak took a menacing step forward. Meyrek stopped him in his tracks.

"You're refusing to obey?"

It was more a statement than a question.

"Go ahead," gritted out Theo. "Hit me with your disciplinary measures. I'm ready. Years in the army are sure to have taught you all kinds of ways to break men. What'll you start with?"

"Collin," murmured Meyrek in a honeyed voice, "I would advise you to grab a weapon."

"Your mistake, colonel, is that I'm not one of your men."

The two officers slid a stunned gaze towards Meyrek, expecting a violent outburst. The man merely watched Theo tranquilly. Bit by bit, the courtyard had emptied out.

"Sergeant, it's time to start this man's physical training. I'd advise you to work on his breathing."

"A dozen laps to start with," said Garroni enthusiastically.

"Hands tied behind his back to teach him to stand up straight."

The sergeant raised a worried brow at his superior officer. He extracted a piece of string from his fatigues.

"Behind his back, colonel? He won't make it six laps."

"Do as I say, sergeant!" thundered Meyrek. "You can shove your compassion."

He turned on his heels and disappeared inside one of the barracks. Novak watched the sergeant for a few moments, then stepped away in turn as soon as Theo had been tied.

"Elite shooter, my ass," grumbled Garroni.

A platoon made up of ten men, all laden with backpacks, streamed out of a dorm. Without sparing Theo a glance, they rushed towards the main gate, followed by the curses of an officer rolling his r's.

"The main courtyard is four hundred yards by two hundred," remarked the sergeant. "A twelve-hundred-yard perimeter? That's a good ten miles you've gotta haul ass. In two hours, you could have some chow."

"And if I refuse?"

"Listen, you little shit, let me explain something to you once and for all. I don't know why you're here, and I don't give a damn, either. Me, I enlisted, and this army is as good as any.

"If I was you, I'd grab a gun, do the colonel a favor, and save yourself a ton of trouble. Either way, you'll break one day, and sooner than you think. Now, you're gonna run. It'll help clear your head. Or else, I'll call Novak back here; there's no-one more persuasive than him."

He wrapped up his words with a jackbooted kick to Theo's kidneys, to give him the start signal. The last flickers of light were beginning to steal a blush over the sky.

Theo took a deep gulp of air and started his run.

136

"Enter!"

The door opened to reveal captain Novak. Meyrek readjusted the knot on his tie and checked his holster. He'd traded his fatigues for a dress uniform with gleaming stripes.

"The helicopter is ready, colonel."

"Good. Lead the way."

As he crossed the courtyard, he slowed down for a moment to watch Theo. He was running the last few yards of his imposed race like a drunken automaton, half upright, half on his knees, spittle at the corners of his lips. The position his arms were in prevented his lungs from filling all the way. After just a few minutes, his breathing had become short, like molten lead dripping down his trachea.

Nonchalant, sergeant Garroni stuck to his side and counted his laps. He pulled him upright when he caught sight of the two officers.

"This is the third one, colonel. He's been walking like this for ten minutes."

Indifferently, Meyrek kept going and climbed into a Humvee. There was already a soldier behind the wheel.

"Pretty breathless," noted Novak.

The vehicle sped off, moved past the two men, and headed down towards the large hangars.

The chopper appeared swamped by the surrounding vegetation, the incongruous lights of the landing strip blinking out in the middle of nowhere. Irrigated by a *rio* nestled into the limestone hillside, the southern area offered the lushness of a nearly tropical vegetation as a contrast to the arid highlands located a scant few miles from there.

"I hope the pilot has been screened for discretion," fretted Meyrek.

"No need to worry, colonel," retorted Novak. "From now on, he alone will operate this transfer. There's no chance he'll disclose the existence of this strip to anyone at all."

Meyrek stepped down. Three outlines sharpened in the halo of the signal lights, then darkness submerged the landing strip. Light dots, flashlights, swept over the engine as the rotors came to a stop with a final whistle.

"Welcome, Colonel."

The voice might have been effeminate. Novak, side by side with Meyrek, lit his own flashlight. The face of a young woman appeared in its beam. She was in uniform, and flanked by two men.

"Let's go," said Meyrek. "I don't have a lot of time."

Silently, the welcoming committee did an about-turn, and the two officers followed them along a winding path carved through the trees, leaving the pilot to stand sentry before his machine. Several minutes' walk brought them within distance of a complex of buildings surrounded by a wall.

"The last barracks are ready," commented the young woman. "We had them furbished this week."

They went through a gate and, in passing, got saluted by two guards bearing Kalashnikov assault rifles.

"AK-47's?" noted Novak, stunned.

"I'm aware," the colonel replied tersely.

The young woman turned. She watched Novak worriedly. A black strand of hair fell into almond-shaped eyes. She had an almost archetypal oriental face, aside from her rounded cheekbones, characteristic of Caucasians, and her very white skin.

"Yes. We've got AK-74's, too. And even a few Nikonov AN-94's. Weapons rarely reach their officially-intended recipients," she noted. "AK's see a lot of insurgencies and terrorist organizations."

Her eyes blazed. She picked up her pace.

The two men escorting them opened the gates to the first building. A song suddenly rose out in the twilight. A reedy rhythm like a nursery rhyme. The young woman stepped aside to let Meyrek and Novak through. Inside, several dozen mess tables were lined up like pews, overlooked by a huge desk in a setup reminiscent of a press conference.

A few soldiers were prowling between the rows. It was hot and it smelled like soup.

Sitting docilely, obediently reciting an anthem they undoubtedly didn't know the words to, two hundred children were waiting for permission to start their dinner. The oldest among them were not yet fourteen.

"Tamazula sent us twenty-five this week," their guide commented proudly.

Right then, one of the monitors noticed the small group from his place at the conference table. He stood up suddenly and shouted:

"Attention!"

His voice rose over the song, which instantly came to a halt. As one, the two hundred children stood up from their seats. Meyrek turned towards the young woman and smiled.

"Very good, captain Khouri. They've made some progress."

The woman's face remained impassive. Her gaze alone, as it had swept the room, had darkened.

Eliane Khouri had been "approached and auditioned" by one of the Organization's recruiting officers, back when construction on the two bases hadn't yet wrapped up. A Lebanese Christian, she'd fled to France after a Hezbollah assault on her village, during which her father and sisters had been massacred. She'd only just escaped the slaughter, taking refuge in the old pantry of her birth home, behind crates of tools and cleaning products that the Islamist militia members hadn't seen fit to root behind.

That night, half her village had been exterminated. It happened often; the world was silent about it. It was in vogue to make westerners believe that Christians and Muslims got along like houses on fire in the land of Cedars, going so far as to sweep the millions of exiled Lebanese under the rug, alongside the forced conversions, and the regular pogroms organized after Friday prayers at the mosque.

A counter-offensive had prevented the Hezbollah millitants from finishing their work, and Eliane's house had, by some miracle, not been set ablaze. At dawn, Christian militia members had found her, still in the same position, voiceless in horror and fear. For over four months, she'd been unable to say a word, despite the lavish care she'd gotten at the hospital in Beirut.

She'd been nineteen at the time.

Her uncle, her only close relation who was still alive, had extended his hospitality in Paris. Eliane had neither accepted nor declined. At the time, she'd been spending her days at the window in her room in the psych wing of Beirut hospital, barely eating, watching on the television as the influence of Damascus over her country spread and grew.

Her doctor had been of the opinion that the only way for her to emerge from her lethargy was by being with family, and he'd answered for her, explaining that Eliane could not express any will of her own, for the time being, but that he was personally in full favor of the idea.

A week later, Eliane was being greeted by the brother of her departed father at Charles de Gaulle airport.

She'd then shared a room with her cousin, a student the same age as her, and she'd found herself showered with affection and constant attention. Little by little, she'd started talking again. She'd begun by giving polite thanks for her food, then sought to help her aunt with the minor chores around the house. Her cousin showed her around her new city, introduced her to friends, took her to the university, and Eliane lost the mad light in her eyes.

Six months on, she'd regained some weight, showed interest in her outfits once more, and even dedicated a quarter of an hour every morning to putting on makeup.

Eliane was pretty. Her cousin's friends began courting her. Among them, a Lebanese law student managed to get her, now and again, to smile.

Eliane started leading a normal life once more. One evening, for the first time, she managed to tell him about the events of that terrible night when she'd lost everyone dear to her without rhyme or reason. Farhoud had listened compassionately. He already knew the story.

The following day, Farhoud took her to a meeting of a mouvement he was involved with. Eliane suddenly found herself immersed in this intense, romanticized atmosphere that had shaped her childhood. The vehement speeches held by amateur lecturers reminded her of the things hinted at by her entourage back in her village.

Paris was no more at peace than Lebanon.

New motivations suddenly fueled her existence. As though to make up for her long period of silent introspection, Eliane dedicated herself to the movement body and soul. Their objectives were to intercept all actions leading towards the "Syrianization" of their land. Returning Lebanon to its status as "Switzerland of the East" was a flame that she meant to keep burning by whatever means necessary, violence included if that was what it took.

After all, the Hezbollah Shia were supported by Syria and Iran. Why not look for allies of their own, in Europe as in the Middle East? France could turn out to be overflowing with relevant opportunities, provided the necessary energy and expenses were spent.

In a matter of weeks, Eliane became a fanatic of the counter revolution. She quickly broke up with Farhoud so she could unleash a sexual appetite that she meant to pour herself into as intensely as she did her political life.

Her uncle saw fit to rent her a studio apartment and get her hired as a medical secretary by one of his doctor friends.

It relieved him to know that he was thus preventing his own daughter from being influenced by his niece, over whom he'd lost all control.

Before long, she even stopped paying them any regular visits, too busy with her activism. Over the three years that followed, she made several trips that listed Lebanon as their official destination. She always left contact information behind for her uncle, so he could get in touch.

But the one and only time he tried to do so, the number she'd left him turned out to be out of service. She only came back three months later. And when he asked her for news from Beirut, she was as evasive as could be. Her uncle found that suspicious, but his refined Eastern manners told him it was preferable to keep quiet, praying she hadn't gotten herself into too tight a corner.

Back then, her name had already been recorded into the Organization's computer.

All that was left to do was make contact.

Eliane's uncle got one last letter from his niece, letting him know she was leaving for Mexico, where she'd taken a job as a pediatric nurse for a charity organization.

She was, of course, in no way ignorant of the true nature of the task she was being handed. Eliane started off by undergoing military training for six months.

At the end of that time, the first children arrived.

Most gazes stuck furtively to the group going around between the tables. The two men who served as escorts had stayed close to the door, leaving the young woman to show Meyrek and Novak around.

Eliane pointed to a small boy with curly hair and prominent cheekbones. He must have been around ten. He got up from his seat. The other children, at an order, began eating quietly. Their disciplined behavior would have made the strictest English boarding schools green with envy. Meyrek loomed over the child.

"What's your name?" he asked.

"He only speaks Portuguese," noted Eliane. "They start language lessons next week. His name is Jorge."

Meyrek's eyes flashed.

"I asked you for a weapons handling demonstration. You could have at least pointed out a kid I can understand."

"I actually think Jorge makes for a great example," retorted Eliane in a neutral tone of voice. "Our task is made all the harder by where most of these kids are from. Watch him."

She led little Jorge to a partly free table. Along the way, she borrowed a rifle off one of the guards. She set it before the child and clapped her hands.

In a few seconds, Jorge had stripped it, all its parts arranged on the oilcloth.

"Every one of these children shows the same skill. We only put the oldest of them through weapons training."

She gently lay her hand on the little boy's shoulder.

"He's starting to be able to aim," she stated proudly, "and he can reassemble the rifle with blindfolded."

"Very good," asserted Meyrek. "Get that one to reassemble it."

He pointed to a very skinny child seating at the same table, and who was trying to focus on his soup while throwing them furtive glances.

"He just got here," protested Eliane. "He hasn't been through a single class yet."

For a moment, she stared the colonel down. Her glare was fulminating.

"I can pick at least thirty other boys, if you'd like. And a few girls. Several of them speak English."

"That won't be necessary," retorted Meyrek. "We're not here to see a circus act."

He stepped away towards the conference table. Instantly, the officers stood up straight from their seats.

"These children are not in uniform," Meyrek stated dryly. "Their hair is long and likely full of fleas. And what's more..."

Meyrek grabbed a plate and sniffed at its scent.

"...what's more, they're too well fed."

Eliane approached him, Novak on her heels.

"Colonel..."

"Captain Khouri, I suggest you and I meet in your office in a few minutes."

He gestured for the officers to sit. Eliane Khouri stiffened. Meyrek turned to look at the room.

"I was given to understand that your mission was to prepare young children for uncompromising military training. I'm surprised to find myself attending a youth club meeting, though I'll admit it's not without its charm. The song was nice, and their efforts touching. Novak, who's charged with the stewardship of this place?"

"Lieutenant Roberts, colonel."

A rather elderly man stood up as soon as he heard his name. He was practically bald and bore the signs of numerous fights. He peered worriedly at his superior officer.

"Tell me, lieutenant, how much fuel do you intend to use to heat up the dorms this winter?"

"About a thousand gallons a week, colonel."

"And what kind of field trips have you scheduled for their vacations?"

The lieutenant's face froze in a stupefied rictus.

"I… I don't understand, colonel."

"You don't understand," thundered Meyrek. "We buy children to put them through the hardest disciplinary training there is, to teach them complete obedience towards their leaders. We're trying to make them into infallible combat tools, in keeping with the new generations of enemies.

"And here you are, a handful of experienced soldiers, seated around a table, staring moon-eyed at a rabble of brats kept in the cushiest comfort. You've planned for the temperature to be kept at sixty-eight degrees no matter the season, for a food provisions budget that's bigger than the training ammo one, for workout clothes, for civvies, for… Novak!"

Meyrek held out his hand towards the captain, who rushed to hand him a folder he'd been holding tight under his arm. Meyrek opened it.

"I see here eight TV sets with DVD players. A projector. Four thousand books! Movies!"

Meyrek snapped the file shut. A heavy, complete silence had descended on the room, as though in a single moment two hundred children had frozen down to the breath in their lungs.

"I'll skip over the school supplies, and I'll trust you as far as the movie catalog. Lieutenant, your report is illuminating. I fear these children's presence may have softened you somewhat."

He turned towards Eliane.

"Unless I should put that down to the women… Captain, do they show educational movies in the Beqaa Valley training camps? Or do the children there still learn how to count in dead Jews?"

Silence ensued. Eliane watched the colonel partly in question and partly in animosity. Still ramrod straight, the lieutenant was keeping his gaze down, his face clouded with worry. Meyrek took a step towards Novak.

"The lieutenant will come with us to the base this evening. See to it that he gets replaced. Take care of everything. Captain Khouri will accompany me to her quarters."

Novak straightened into a regulation salute.

Most children had barely dug into their dinner. None dared look towards the group of officers anymore. Still, few of them understood English.

At the girls' table, a blonde-haired child was sobbing softly.

Much like the colonel's room, the quarters occupied by Eliane Khouri were minimalist in comfort. An office adorned with metal furniture, separated from a minuscule bedroom and water closet by a narrow partition.

When she'd accepted her job, Eliane had opted for a spartan life, and her only concession to whimsy was to always wear feminine underwear beneath her military uniforms. Her civvies were stored in the sole suitcase she had brought from France. Stuck to the wall by her bed, a postcard from Beirut maybe helped her to fall asleep.

From her window, she could watch the children during their courtyard exercises. Through a set of bars.

"All the reports concerning the past four weeks' activity were forwarded to you yesterday," noted Eliane as she opened the door to her office to let Meyrek through. "I have nothing here, outside of the children's medical records. Nothing about where they're from, outside of their names and ages."

"I need no other information," stated the colonel. "Merely a private talk with you."

Eliane stepped around her worktable. The phone could only be used to communicate with the main base. In a gesture that wasn't soldierly in the slightest, she gracefully placed her hand on the wooden ledge.

"Your nails are short, and unvarnished," indicated Meyrek.

"No kidding, colonel."

"Your answer is no way to talk to a superior officer."

Eliane's hand crept away from the desk. She straightened her spine.

"I'm just surprised you'd take note of that kind of thing."

"I notice all things," he spat dryly. "Now, strip."

Eliane didn't move. Nothing about her even hinted that she'd heard him. Meyrek stepped in close.

"I don't have a lot of time," he hissed through his teeth. "Not enough to persuade you, even less so to seduce you. In case you hadn't understood me, I asked you to take off your clothes."

"Are you carrying out an investigation into the physical health of the female personnel on base, or is this merely routine?"

Meyrek was so close to Eliane he could rub against her. He seized her face and slid a bloodthirsty smile a couple inches from her lips.

"Take it that way. I'm responsible for both bases, and you're in charge of the children. Any breach of discipline must be signaled in a report. In no time at all, those reports reach me. And above me, there's nothing. If you're dissatisfied with the treatment I'm subjecting you to, there's nothing stopping you from filing a report. Do you understand what kind of game we're playing?"

Eliane took a step back.

"I understand, colonel. You're not addressing me as a woman, but as a member of the military under your command."

She began unbuttoning her BDU shirt.

"As a soldier, I follow orders scrupulously, but as a woman, don't expect me to show the slightest enthusiasm. I can't fake it."

Her breasts sprang from the coarse fabric. Two firm, proud globes. Eliane loosened her hair, which fell in dark waves over her bare shoulders. Unselfconsciously, she slid her pants down and unlaced her boots.

"Keep your panties on," went Meyrek, voice rough. "And turn around to face the desk."

Eliane complied. Her body was tanned and slender, made of whipcord muscles. Her back turned, she closed her eyes and angrily tightened her lips. Behind her, Meyrek was still. After a few moments, she turned her face in his direction.

"Lovely body," uttered Meyrek cynically. "Congratulations. You take great care of yourself."

He adjusted the knot on his tie and sat down in a chair.

"Did you think I would rape you, captain Khouri?"

Colonel Meyrek's face had hardened into an impenetrable expression. Only a very light spot of color on his cheeks could have betrayed a semblance of emotion. Eliane turned around, looked straight into his eyes.

"No," hissed Meyrek, "think again; I'm not crazy. I can appreciate the obedience of a good soldier. Even if it's a woman. You can sit down. I still have a couple of minutes to talk."

Eliane stepped away from the desk, sat in the chair, and crossed her legs. Her bush cast a shadow through her tiny white panties. In a burst of defiance, she held back from crossing her arms to hide her chest.

"Here we are, face to face, like civilized people in a tearoom," taunted Meyrek ironically. "You're not getting dressed?"

"You didn't give me the order to, colonel."

Meyrek burst into laughter.

"Excellent. Your mind is sharp as a tack. And here you are, offended because I'm not using your body. Do you believe me impotent?"

Eliane did not reply.

"I could have taken you, upright, on the floor, dragged you into your bedroom, abused you until I'd heard you scream! The only thing stopping me is the respect I have for the uniform you wear and the officer's rank I gave you."

"I no longer have a uniform," uttered Eliane slyly. "Yet there's nothing making you humiliate me the way you are."

"Does my language shock you? You're in the army, captain Khouri. Whatever the country, the nation, or the homeland. In the army, nothing is obscene. Nothing is clean. It's all much easier."

Eliane picked up her shirt and summarily put it on.

"Pardon me, I don't know where you're going with this."

"What do you find obscene," whispered Meyrek. "Sex, or your own parents gutted before your eyes?"

Eliane shivered and closed her eyes.

"An army has no limits," Meyrek went on in an even voice. "It's given the ultimate right: the right to kill. But to kill according to certain rules. Here, we have no rules. Do you follow me better now, captain?"

Eliane nodded, her body tense. She lit a cigarette.

"I entrusted the children to you," Meyrek went on. "I want you to make them into an army. Most of these kids were starving to death when the Organization bought them. There's still millions of them, all over the world, who could join us, rather than go begging in Western Europe.

"In a couple of weeks, you taught them to eat with a fork and to field strip a gun. Congratulations!

"In six months, I want them capable of slitting each other's throats for a crust of bread. I want their killer instincts sharpened, honed; I want them able to massacre at an order."

"Why didn't you pick a man, if you have such little faith?" spat Eliane.

"But I do have faith, captain. I have faith in my ability to prevent you from making mistakes. And you have something I value: hate."

"You think you know everything about me, don't you, colonel?"

Eliane loosened her face into a beguiling smile that her eyes remained detached from. She slowly uncrossed her legs and crushed her cigarette.

"There's a side to me that you're going to be surprised to discover."

Eliane got up, her shirt flapping against her sides. She got close to Meyrek and displayed her stomach level with his chest, legs straddling his thighs. Her skin gave of a musky scent, the fruit of a natural blending, intrinsically heady but lacking in sophistication.

The colonel abruptly straightened up. For a moment, Eliane saw panic in his gaze. He quickly pulled himself together and ground out,

"I'm ordering you to get dressed, right now. Do you have any idea what your attitude could cost you?"

Eliane watched him frankly. His forehead was moist and his lips white.

"Two thousand men driven mad by frustration," Meyrek suddenly shrieked. "And you, tied to four pegs, on the ground, legs spread. An endless chain of animals desperate to sample your flesh! Can you imagine what your body would look like after even a hundred assaults? The last in line would only have your body to slake his lust."

Meyrek felt fear overcome the young woman. He quieted down and went on in a softer voice:

"You have two hundred kids to train up. Make me an army!"

Eliane realized he was gone when she heard the door slam.

Chapter 11

Dawn filtered slowly through the room, crisscrossing the floor through the bars. Two enormous flies buzzed. The window was open. An already tepid breeze stirred the dust, millions of dully glinting particles suspended.

Theo opened his eyes.

The first thing he felt was a stretch about his shoulders. He shifted and found he was still dressed. His descent to reality was instantaneous. His night had been dreamless, and the muffled thumps against a metal panel, the dim roars of engines, the indistinct, aggressive invectives from outside all heralded a presence that would be looming over him in the minutes to come.

The base was awake. Mechanically, he massaged his sore muscles, numb physically but his mind awfully clear.

"Don't think. Whatever you do, don't let the memories stream in. Focus on the little things."

He got up, rubbed his hand across his bristly cheeks and his scalp. He was stunned not to feel the curls of his hair slide between his fingers.

'My laces are untied. There's a fly in the room. No, two flies. What's the lifespan of a fly? A day? Two? Why am I contemplating this crap?'

He opened his mouth, and his eyes widened. Gaze fixed unblinking on the bars of the cell. The pain had come back and was buffeting him like never before. It was no longer this surreal feeling, this numbing half-lethargy, this backdrop of wrenching suffering dominated by a stronger urge, a buried will to survive.

"There are two flies in my room. There's a hole in the window..."

The hurt was raw, acid, like an open wound that you're aware of without feeling it before the nerves react. One that suddenly takes over the body by its presence, sends out distress signals, bands around the heart and the mind, forces all thoughts towards it.

Three days that his existence had come at an impasse in so absurd a way that his logical reasoning couldn't manage to fight it off, unable to find an anchor in any of his past experiences.

146

Of course, there were the others. And Fate. Words devoid of meaning today, words to which he could only react with the selfish frankness of a "why me?" or "why them?". Bombs shredding neighborhoods, diseases, accidents tearing families apart forever, the only thing real and possible about them was the dimension the media attached to them, a taste of ash and superficial sadness, a feeling digested by distance as though caused by the imaginations of Others.

He remained frozen, trying to use motionlessness to tamp down on the waves of physical pain that swept over him.

And the memories.

Katia! That singular moment when he'd seen her appear, greyish-pink and mysterious, from his wife's straining body. The doctor's features, taut with concentration, a nurse's encouraging smile, and Juliette's nails embedded in the palm of his hand.

Farther back. Juliette letting him know, timid and emotional, that, maybe, in a few months… Hold on, I'm not sure yet, I'm waiting on the result!

He'd covered her in all the protection he could give, dedicating the bulk of his thoughts to the event that was to magnify their union, sometimes deliberately, oftentimes juvenile, clueless as to a future mother's abilities to protect herself.

"Don't get up on that chair! …Good God, I can still change a bulb. …No, leave it, let me do it." The bulb falls and breaks. Juliette protests, ending in a laugh and holding her stomach with one hand, her stomach that was already no longer just hers.

Her laugh again, and her hoarse voice the moment he takes her despite it all, despite the months and the presence of a life in progress. "Do you really think we still can?"

It was too late to turn back the tide of images. Theo could feel her scent. Warm, intoxicating, hair washed with apple blossom, generic soap ("This one's just as good as any other!"), thrilling womanly body, maddening scent of desire, reassuring odor of routine. He felt the touch of her flesh, his muscles hurt from clasping her, his body nestled against hers, a strand of hair irritating his eye, blowing it away while grumbling in a fake irritated tone.

And now? Keep going despite it all? Guard his own life in the hopes of some imagined revenge?

Shouldn't he start by self-destructing to avenge them? He who had truly caused their disappearance. But his own death was not enough, not compared to theirs. And besides, there was that survival instinct. Despicable. Traitorous. That gene, locked fast since the dawn of time, that prevents man from taking his own life, even in the grips of the worst torment.

All that remained for him to do was to resign himself, knowing that what he had to endure might end up making him pay, slowly, as the months went on, with his only hope undoubtedly to one day forget.

It was only fitting. In his new thought process, there was no other reason for the camp to exist outside his own penance, and, amid the questions he still asked himself, this leap was the solution to the mystery of the base. The fact that colonel Meyrek's Organization existed, like an affront to mankind and its freedom, no longer mattered.

Slowly, he closed his mouth again, taking stock of his position, arms alongside his body, like a soldier at parade rest. His eyes caught a shadow on the wall.

Fifteen years had slid away in an instant, and here he was, a mere conscript, a teenager rejecting the obligations he hadn't been able to extricate himself from despite all his attempts, completely powerless…

Completely powerless? No. Just like fifteen years before, he was in possession of his ability to aim true, which had seemed so trifling all through his civilian life, despite that it had already shielded him, had already prevented his being sent to the front with his unit, his being killed or declared MIA like his brother in misery – what was his name again? – had enabled him to survive, to go through this present day that he couldn't comprehend.

Through a strange play of light, the shadow took the shape of the colonel's face and cast him back to the present. He was going to pay for them, yes! But not just him.

Meyrek had decided to train him. He was choosing, here and now, to accept.

And the pain dulled.

His creased shirt gave off a strong stench of sweat. It was then he remembered that endless run. The walls of the dorms on his left, then the mess in front of him, the sun dipping below the horizon, the perimeter wall, a grey and impenetrable border, the garage. Slowly. Inaccessibly. Then the walls of the dorms once more.

The ochre dust drifting into his lungs. The sergeant's cries. The garage. The last red flickers. Second lap. His legs, heavy like his blood had turned to quicksilver, and that he needed to lift, one after the other, never fast enough, never far enough. Four laps. Nighttime. Six more laps. Five. His lungs ablaze. His wrists in shreds.

Then the ground, so close, the dust sullying his face, not sparing his eyes. The sergeant pulling him up, pushing him with all his might. His heart reaching a hundred and sixty beats per minute. The walls of the dorms. The mess… And then that unbelievable feeling, beyond his physical limits, that certainty that he could surpass himself, the rest of the run taking place in a surreal universe, upright then on his knees, his muscles oxygen-starved.

Garroni had stepped in close, a sort of respect in his eyes, and had said to him,

"Don't just lie there, you did your twelve laps. Up. Get moving."

He'd sliced through the bindings around his wrists and had crouched down next to him.

"Twelve laps. Twelve plus five? How many? How many? Add. Twelve plus five."

"Seven… teen," had muttered Theo, his saliva turned to foam.

"Seventeen minus eleven multiplied by three. Come on, Collin, add. Your brain cells have never been richer in oxygen. Your glands are pumping you full of endorphin. You're riding the best kind of high. Add."

"Eighteen," whispered Theo. "Eigh… teen."

"Now, get up and walk. All the way to your barracks. You mustn't eat tonight. Go sleep."

Several men surrounded him, throwing him pitiless glances; maybe they'd learned to cover up their feelings. Quickly, following an order from Garroni, they'd scattered.

Staggering, Theo had reached his dorm; he'd collapsed into a deep sleep.

"Outside, Collin! It's oh-five-hundred. You slept more than everyone else put together. Five minutes to wash up and ten minutes to have breakfast."

The sergeant face split into a wide smile.

"Man, do you look like crap. Don't look at yourself too much while you're shaving, it's gonna give you nightmares. The privy is at the end of the hall to the right. Change your socks, you're gonna be doing some more running."

Theo joined him in the doorframe. The two flies had settled at the corner of the window and were coupling in a sunbeam.

"I've gotta coddle you," said Garroni, "or else you're gonna cock up your toes on me. Five minutes, so haul ass."

Men were running down the hallway, some of them in fatigues, others in smallclothes.

They swore at each other in different languages, shoved at one another, a panicked determination contained in the act.

The showers were freezing, as was the water from the sinks. There was no foam, the men would cut themselves to shave faster. Nude, they jostled, their sex shriveled. No-one paid him any mind. Garroni gave him a shove and let out a fresh growl to round out the effect.

"Enough lollygagging, guys! Last one in the shower gets squeegee duty before chow."

Theo noticed a shift in his intonation. Garroni had imperceptibly softened the condescending tartness of his barks as he addressed his men. The order, for that matter, had no other result but an indistinctly muttered acquiescence from the soldiers.

As soon as he'd turned his back, a red-haired colossus tore into two Asians sharing the same shower.

"All right, you clowns, that's enough. You've been splashing around in there for an hour!"

"We get a minute each," retorted the younger one, unflappable. "For two, that's two minutes."

"Give them a break, Lochlan," cut in one of the soldiers in the process of shaving. "They pull this on you every morning, and you still haven't figured out they're yanking your chain."

The redhead shrugged his shoulders and rushed towards a free spot. Through the stream of water making him shiver, he noticed Theo a couple steps away. The latter looked petrified.

"Yo, new guy! You planning on staying dressed? You should, actually. Your utilities stink so bad I can smell you from here."

Wordlessly, Theo removed his top and untied the laces on his boots. The American's words had drawn attention towards him from the other men. The elder Asian guy stepped out of the shower and wrapped a towel around his hips without taking his eyes off him.

"You're pretty skinny," the redhead went on, head leaned back, eyes closed under the water stream. "Which section you in from?"

Theo finished getting undressed before replying.

"None. I came to camp yesterday."

"He's the guy who was running," interjected a swarthy, youngish boy who'd foregone the showers and was washing his feet in the sink. "Right?" he said to Theo. "You're the one Garroni tied up before giving you twelve rides on the merry-go-round?"

The redhead got out of the shower in turn and stepped in front of the two Asians, who'd both stopped to stare intently at Theo.

"Clear off, Slopehead! Lemme get a look at the new guy."

He propped himself before Theo.

"What's your name?"

"Collin."

"What are you doing here? You a volunteer?"

Theo shrugged his shoulders without raising his head. A remnant of the propriety of a man little used to community life had him hesitating before taking off his briefs. He realized he was being ridiculous, tore off his underwear in an abrupt motion, and hurtled himself under the shower that the ginger giant had freed.

His muscles clenched under the frigid bite of the water stream.

"No way does he look like a volunteer," snickered that same Lochlan. "Hey, Collin! What are you doing in the elite section?"

Garroni's return left the question hanging. The sergeant swept his gaze over the bathroom and addressed each one of his men.

"Juan, a shower doesn't mean a footbath. Huang, Tran, clear off. You, too, Lochlan! You slow asses, the rest of the section is already in the mess hall. Salinas, you're staying behind with the squeegee."

He took a couple steps into the shower room.

"Now, listen closely. Collin here joined your section without training. He's a special case. You don't talk to him, you don't give him a hand. You don't make him part of your lives before you get the authorization to. Is that understood! The first guy who gets it in his head to be a smartass returns to his original section for eight days. You get me?"

The threat had the intended effect on the soldiers, who instantly looked away from Theo and left the privy one by one, grumbling all the while.

Lochlan was the last one out, and he stopped level with the sergeant.

"What's "special" supposed to mean?"

"It means you don't ask any questions and you take a hike. Collin, we're going back to your cell. One minute left to get dressed."

Spurred by an old habit, Theo reached out behind him, feeling out for a tap. There was none.

Outside, it was the same old circus. Shouting from the officers, fatigues being assigned, frenzied running from panicked men. Orders rang out, and column after column of soldiers streamed out from the multiple dorms.

The coffee was light. The bread, hard. The butter gave off a pungent whiff.

Armed, fresh and sturdy, their uniforms pressed, the guards wandered between the rows of tables, designating soldiers at random, who didn't have the time to finish their frugal repast and rushed outside, mouths full, reappearing in a window frame carrying a shovel, a pipe, a broom, or pulling a cart, sweat already beading on their foreheads.

It was oh-five-thirty.

Two shots rang out. Then two others.

Theo started.

In a few seconds, the mess hall emptied out. The latecomers didn't reach their tables and did about-turns, stomachs empty. In less time than it takes a magician to turn a red handkerchief into a white dove, the rows lined up.

The sky shed its grey color and adorned itself in mauve. Silence blanketed the camp once more. Meyrek and Novak appeared.

"Section chiefs, make ready to call the roll!"

"Section one: present, forty-seven; absent, none."

"Section two: present, fifty-two; absent, none."

"Section three: present, forty-nine; absent, one. Infirmary."

In a matter of minutes, the forty sections had called the roll. Six men were absent in all. Two had died, the day before, during training. Three were sick, and one badly injured. Theo's section was only made up of twenty-eight men, who all responded present to sergeant Garroni's call.

Novak unfolded a computer printout before his eyes. The noncom at his side handed him a megaphone.

"Odd sections, up to twenty-one, artificial lake. Even sections, all the way through twenty, urban warfare. Remaining sections, desert march; combat load: thirty kilos."

A half-dozen all-terrain vehicles arranged themselves in a half-circle before the courtyard entrance.

The men on fatigue detail loaded the weapons on board in seconds, then the supervising officers climbed aboard. Several megaphones appeared in the noncoms' hands and the camp anthem began to ring out, mechanically at first, then picked up in a crescendo of deep vocalizations by the troops spreading out in long phalanxes.

Their movements flowed with a ballet-like precision. No jostling, no rushing, contrasting strangely with the frenzy these same men had displayed just moments earlier over a bowl of colored water.

Garroni and his men marked time. They saw Novak climb on board of a Land Rover equipped with a sophisticated transmission system and disappear behind the troops. The colonel alone was left in the middle of the courtyard, a light machine gun strapped across his body, his gaze adrift towards the blue mountains.

He turned his face toward the group, and, despite the distance, Theo felt the weight of his gaze on him like a brand. Meyrek turned his back and moved away. Garroni called the halt. Twenty-eight boots snapped as one.

Right step.

The elite section had drifted into small groups. According to their specializations, they moved towards the practice ranges, the shooting stands, or the conference room. The biggest group had found itself issued sophisticated weapons, light sniper rifles mounted with scopes, and, as the ammunition was being handed out, the sergeant had pulled Theo aside.

"You see this dozen guys? We're trusting them. We're giving them bullets – and believe you me, they're not blanks. No chance they're turning them against us. All of them volunteers.

"That gets them some advantages, too. Not like the two thousand schmucks you saw filing out of here. It's all up to you. You say yes, I'll call the colonel in and we'll join them at the range…"

He bared his gums in a beguiling smile. Theo noticed that a bit of bread had gotten stuck in the space between two teeth, a blackened detritus that emphasized the sergeant's rather unappealing grimace.

"I won't shoot," whispered Theo, gaze level with his mouth.

The sergeant spat on the ground.

"All right! Turn around, then, so I can tie you up."

The courtyard was deserted, now, with the exception of the guards keeping watch by the gates, some three hundred yards away.

Docile, Theo allowed his wrists to be tied behind his back. The sergeant raised his eyes to the sky. There were a few cloudy trails there, translucent and immobile, the perfect alignment of which wasn't disrupted by a single puff of air.

"Hell of a day!" noted the sergeant. "One hell of a nasty day, stuffy and scorching, just like we've been getting for the past couple weeks. Your first dozen laps are gonna seem like a walk in the park compared to the next ones, when the sun is gonna be nice and high."

He lifted his shoulders.

"This was your choice…"

Nothing seemed able to change the atmosphere inside Webster's. In a few days, the rainy weather had given way to more spring-like conditions, a slight, persistent wind having swept the last layers of fog from the streets of Washington D.C.

In the light of day, the traces of rust that spattered the pub sign almost seemed to be in defiance of the modernity of the street that it was nestled in, thumbing its nose at the passing of time. Avi was waiting for Beck in the same spot, a glass in front of him, and greeted him with a welcoming smile, immediately signaling the bartender for a second beer.

"I'm not here for a drink," Beck uttered dryly.

Haim's smile tensed for a split second; then, as though in challenge, he raised his glass and drank down a big gulp, leaving a strip of foam behind on his upper lip and wiping it with a swipe of his tongue.

"All right, then let's get down to business. You didn't call me just to have a courtesy call, I imagine?"

The same clamor as last time rose from the back room, and Beck diverted his attention there for a few moments, wondering whether those were the same players. The bartender, indifferent, put the glass he'd picked up back where he'd gotten it from.

"I'm afraid I don't come bearing good news only," said Beck.

"Would that be bad news for me, or for you?" retorted the Mossad agent, a glint in his eyes that was simultaneously impish and worried.

"As far as your sometime agent goes, I believe we can make something happen. Technically, he carried out industrial espionage. Since no-one pressed any charges, there's no serious reason for the FBI to bring this to trial. Otherwise it would mean implicating the E.C. Tronics subsidiary into weapons contracts. We greased the wheels a bit and got a provisional parole agreement. He could be yours in a month or two…"

"That would be the good news," said Haim. "What's the bad news?"

"That's all I've got for you. No-one at the agency has heard of your op."

The Mossad agent slowly nodded his head, his lips pinched in an ironic expression.

Beck had laid out all his rejoinders since that late-night meeting, at the end of which it had been decided to give them as much of a runaround as possible before opening the door to other negotiations, providing no information on White Cells. A discreet top-level call between Washington and Tel Aviv had even gone on for several minutes, insinuations flying back and forth without anyone being able to actually find out what it was that Israel knew.

Beck had found himself charged with an impossible mission: getting the identity of the mole while giving nothing back in return. Vincent White was that nothing.

He was surprised to hear Haim pronounce, in an almost bemused tone,

"The democratic body and its immune system… The lymphocytes of civilization… White cells versus terror cells… Come on, Howard, please; your leaders are capable of a naivety that's always dumbfounded us. How could you even imagine I'd believe you?"

A cloud of sadness descended over the smile that briefly lit up his furrowed mien. Haim had an ageless face, the look of a man used to the worst kinds of visions, that of a soul who harbors no illusions about either the world or his fellow man, and Beck, stunned by what he'd just heard, couldn't help the frisson of admiration he felt towards the man.

"Don't you think it's time to put all our cards on the table?" the Israeli went on. "What should really have you aflutter isn't what I know, it's how I know it."

"At this level," stammered Beck, bested, "it's above my paygrade."

"I'm not so sure, Howard. I rather think you should listen to me. Make your decision after."

The Israeli went on without giving Beck the time to think.

"The rumor has been going around for two years at least, and you know agency rumors just as well as I do; we take them for what they're worth, which is smoke that doesn't necessarily signal there's fire. But it was when we uncovered your mole that we got our confirmation.

"I was in Tel Aviv, and I swear to you I have never seen a storm like that in all my career. Our greatest dream and our worst nightmare were coming true at the same time. Uncle Sam was finally opening his eyes! Only to go and spit out a time bomb..."

Reaching out a nimble hand, Haim gripped Beck's arm as he made to get up.

"Don't go. I'm not here to insult your government, or to pass judgement on its decisions. We've got something of a saying, back home, that if your president sneezes, it's our prime minister who catches the cold. And this, Howard, is a cold I don't want to catch."

"You know as well as I do that I'm not authorized to tell you more," ground out Beck. "Between you and me, I was sickened by what I found out, but that's not gonna change a thing. And the fact that your agency knows as much as it does only adds to the danger, which is something I'm gonna have to notify my chain of command of asap. Let me go!"

Beck freed himself roughly. The barman cast an intrigued gaze in his direction, only to immediately resume his duties. Haim leapt at the opportunity.

"The threat of our time is information. The Islamists have become experts at manipulating the media. They make themselves out to be victims before the whole world, and half your citizens have ended up buying into the idea that Israel is the one responsible for the current situation.

"As though it was us behind 9/11, behind the attacks in London, in Madrid... And why not behind the extermination of baby seals?

"An eye for an eye and a tooth for a tooth; you've got part of the answer. But imagine the impact this weapon could have in the hands of our enemies! Anti-democratic commandos created to safeguard democracy: the very founding principle of our civilization would be called into question if that information was tossed to the baying hounds of the media.

"Well, now they know. And believe you me, they're waiting for just the right time to detonate their bomb!"

"What's the connection between this alleged op and your OptroNex sting? We are laying all our cards on the table, aren't we?"

Haim shrunk in on himself, like a turtle that cautiously edges its head back into its shell.

"Unfortunately, our current discussion framework is not informal enough."

"In that case, I don't see what use this conversation could possibly be…"

"Because we're in the same boat! Your mole, I've been granted the authorization to give them to you without getting anything in exchange!"

Haim pierced Beck with his gaze. He was no longer smiling. His face was expressionless. Thousands of years of baseless persecutions were suddenly weighing down his figure, frozen in an attack stance, as though about to leap.

"That's a new one…" whispered Beck.

"Not as new as all that, Howard. Come now, relax. Officially, you're handing Vincent White over to us, a man for whom we have no use. That way, no-one loses face.

"In exchange, we put ourselves at your disposal. White Cells is as much our concern as it is yours. The information was not supposed to reach its first target, so, here…"

The Mossad agent pulled several items out of his pocket, sliding them across the tabletop. A newspaper clipping, a folded photograph, and a thumb drive.

"The weather is bad around London these days," he whispered.

The large article headline read:

"Tragic accident on Dover cliffs. Saudi businessman, his bodyguard, and two diplomats lose lives after driver loses control over vehicle"

"The thumb drive is yours, of course. The information it contains is largely financial. The makings of a business plan… Someone needs a lot of money to expand the system. As for the mole…"

Beck unfolded the photo with a trembling hand.

So it was: behind his trifocal glasses, Feldman looked like a mole.

Theo collapsed on the seventh lap. The air was so dry that each breath in burned his mucous membranes. Opening his mouth – he'd given it a try several times – only made things worse for him. Within a few strides, he lost all feeling in his tongue and palate. The temperature had only climbed a couple degrees so far. The sergeant stepped in close to him with a flask and sprinkled water on his face.

"Up. You've got five laps left."

Lying on his side on the ground, Theo had curled up his legs in a nominal defensive position. He'd scraped his cheekbone lightly on a rock, and a trickle of blood followed the contour of his face, slid down his cheek, and pooled into the corner of his lips.

"I can't," he breathed.

He panted for a few moments before going on.

"My lungs… no air…"

"Yes, you can!" roared Garroni, leaning over him. "They've all been here. You'll see that you can do it!"

Nipping all protests in the bud, he grabbed him by the collar and lifted him up off the ground. Theo wasn't heavy, and the sergeant's powerful muscles only met with minimal resistance. Not giving him any time to struggle, he set off at a small stride, not letting go. Theo had to move along, his breath wheezing.

"You can run," Garroni was screaming. "You will run. Run, you sonofabitch! Run. Come on!"

He sped up. His strides got longer. Half carried, half dragged, Theo dug deep for his last strength, his muscles bunched, and managed the hectic movements needed to keep the pace. The sergeant's fist, clenched close to his neck, occasionally, inadvertently, struck his chin.

Deep down inside, a voice kept on repeating, *'This is your choice. You're paying the price!'* And, bizarrely, this thought was helping him endure, unfold his joints for yet another yard, another lap of the courtyard.

Near the conference rooms, a nondescript building that a part of the section had disappeared into, a motionless figure had appeared.

Theo wouldn't have noticed a group a thousand man strong. He therefore didn't see his Vietnamese spectator. However, just like in the privy before Theo had gotten in the shower, Huang kept his gaze riveted on him intently, his eyelids squinted to the point that they might have seemed shut.

A string of vibrations streamed from the depths of his chest, all aimed in one direction. Huang was focusing his energy, a silent supporter of the Frenchman he only knew by name. He didn't even know why he was doing it, consumed simply with helping him, with being part of his efforts.

"Run," the sergeant kept bellowing. "That's what you're here for. You run or you die. Run."

The Vietnamese man's heartbeat had sped up. His breathing had begun panting out. He kept count of the number of times that he'd seen the two men pass before him.

Theo covered his final five laps before Garroni let him go. He walked a few yards, determined to remain standing, face soaked with sweat, blowing air out like a steam valve. And lost consciousness.

Huang opened his eyes again. He waited for Garroni to lean over Theo, put his ear to his chest, and unbutton his fatigues. He then went back the way he came.

Night took over the base in one fell swoop, a quirk of mountain areas amplified by the latitude of the Sierra Madre. The sun blazed fiercely before disappearing behind the Pacificward peaks, then dusk faded into a limpid darkness in less than a quarter of an hour.

At the height of summer, life on camp took on the pace of the sun calendar, lights out scheduled two hours after the bulk of the troops had dinner, with the exception of nighttime maneuvers. For over a week now, night training had been sparse, the officers in charge of planning having decided to take advantage of the intense heat and subject the men to endurance trials.

It was out of the question to experiment with the soldiers' stamina at the cost of their physical condition, and the acceptable fatality rate, established

156

by the colonel in advance, accounted for a big safety margin. Meyrek's theory went as follows: "There's no room for rebellion in the mind of an exhausted man. Pushed beyond exhaustion, he'll find new strength to save his life."

And his daily unease came from the potential for rebellion among the "semi-volunteers," an elegant turn of phrase coined in reference to nearly thirty percent of the force, enrolled through coercive means ranging from blackmail to the commutation of prison sentences and the use of force. The task wasn't an easy one, despite nearly limitless financial backing from the Organization and strategic support from Tamazula.

Meyrek had objected, back when he'd taken over his duties, and he'd attempted to convince Feldman and Ellen Cheston of the effectiveness of an army made up entirely of professionals, even at substantially reduced numbers.

In counter, he'd been served with the Organization's prospective design, which mapped out the existence of the army over several decades and could hardly have cared less about a horde of mercenaries…

We will be operating as cells, Colonel, never forget that…

These were the thoughts the colonel was mulling over as he made his way towards the base's computer center that night. A secluded outbuilding watched over by a sentry post that only a few officers and noncoms had access to.

Novak was escorting him, as quiet as he usually was, but relaxed. For the first time, the report on the men's morale seemed rather positive, and the rivalry challenge set up after dividing the sections in two opposite sides had shown its worth once more during mock combat. The even sections crowed over having defeated the odd sections, while the latter were already nurturing the thought of a rematch.

Little by little, despite it all, they were becoming soldiers.

The two officers crossed paths with a patrol. Meyrek scanned them with a quick, critical glance, found nothing to say, and returned to his initial thoughts.

When he'd arrived eight months earlier, the first camp had been nothing more than a jumble of aimless mercenaries and adrift soldiers, none of whom grasped the purpose of the base, and all the less so their own involvement. The "semi-volunteers" were on their third bid for escape, attempts carried out in waves, barely caught at the last minute by unmotivated staff who picked off one or two of them with a rifle every time so as to set an example.

Training was as run of the mill as could be: forced marches, hand-to-hand combat, weapons handling and shooting drills, endurance training, CBRN exercises, explosives and landmine clearance; then poker in the evening at dusk, brawls among the rank and file. It was then that Meyrek had recalled the pose that "Marylin" had struck in that Manhattan parking garage, and the irony weighing down her voice.

"Wait until you see your army!"

He'd had to haphazardly put together a new training regimen, motivate the mercenaries through meetings during which he'd orated himself, and – the Organization be damned – hand out raises, despite their pay already being three times what the best armed forces in the world could boast.

It had been necessary for him to spend over fifteen days poring over the reports, identifying his men, rooting out their individual motivations, and above all put a system of merciless punishments into place, one meant to strike a blow to the imagination and terror in the heart.

One first goal checked off: uniting the men through fear.

Next, he had needed to build. He had on his hands close to two thousand aimless men, and not only did most of them have no idea for what purpose they had been yanked from their previous existence, but to top it off they had found themselves subject to a training regimen bordering on amateurish.

The base had quickly expanded. Over the course of eight weeks, several new buildings had been erected, the constructions rudimentary but sturdy. They'd been built with sweat rather than cutting edge technology, the base only owning two Caterpillars and zero cranes. Fortunately, however, it had plenty of former masons, electricians, and carpenters in its ranks.

Innovation had also been important to him, and he'd decided to replicate real combat conditions in a restrained space. Off base, he'd had a "Tex-Mex"-style far west town built from pasteboard, taking his inspiration from movie sets. There, the men learned to deal with street ambushes, freeing hostages in urban settings, camouflage, infiltration, the works. All of it far from prying eyes, under skies partly covered by the meshes of giant nets.

At the edges of one of the cliffs overlooking the *rio*, an artificial lake had been dug out, filled with water pumped from an underground river. After two months of relentless work, the base could move its military training to the active phase.

By then used to working all together, the men had naturally found themselves grouped into sections, and a handful of quite cruel examples being made had cured them of their breakout plans.

Meyrek hadn't rested on the laurels of that first victory. He'd handed all the men's files to the camp computer experts and had asked them to sort through the millions of ensuing data files in order to filter out the most capable, the least intractable, the most experienced. This was how the elite sections had been born.

Under the guidance of Garroni and the supervision of captain Novak, the best one of those sections had, as a matter of course, come under the colonel's direct orders.

The two officers walked past the computing center guard post, briefly returning the salute from the men on duty but not slowing their pace. Novak pulled out a smart card and inserted it into the electronic lock while placing his face in the scope of the retina scanner. The armored door instantly slid open.

The premises, roughly a thousand square feet in all, housed a handful of computer engineers, volunteers recruited from among E.C. Tronics employees, and a server center. In its memory they stored, among other things, all the information concerning the base and its men, provisions, munitions, flows of funds, statistical tools, and the scant encrypted documents exchanged between the base and the Organization's outside structures.

The computer center also served another function. A mission that was of vital importance to the base. It housed the center that detected satellite sweeps and the countermeasure system enabling the interception of observation satellite transmissions, and the modification of their contents in real time.

All traces of activity, be they visual, thermal, or radiographic, were systematically erased. Deleted, the hot car exhaust trails. Gone, the training sections' thermal signature. Vanished, the tire treads and footprints.

The base was invisible, the system even masking the satellite dishes that made up its own transmission/reception device. By trading the real signature for a pristine, uninhabited, quasi-desert landscape, the jamming gave the eye in the sky a forged perception of what was on the ground. It was the centerpiece of the furtiveness device deployed by the highlands base. A component to which Theo Collin had contributed massively without knowing it.

For safety reasons, only an on-call technician remained inside the center after nightfall, their power coming from an oil-fired electric powerplant built outside the base. In the event of a power outage, the inverters took over and the server automatically saved all data before shutting down. Use of the powerplant was restricted to the satellite transmission interception system exclusively.

Meyrek made his way to the officer in charge, a lieutenant. In a less abrasive tone than usual, he asked,

"Has the weekly report been stored to memory?"

"No, colonel. We waited for you, as you instructed."

Meyrek nodded approvingly.

"Let's step into your office."

The tranquil atmosphere dominating the inside of the center was surprising after a day spent amid the turmoil on base. Although each of the technicians was overworked, things ran harmoniously. The dull hum of the hard drives added to this meditative ambience, and the lights from the screens were almost merry in their blinking.

As soon as you crossed the secure threshold, you found yourself a thousand miles away from the Sierra Madre, from its steep slopes, its rocky drops, and the fever that had burrowed its way inside two thousand men for months now. It was a leap into the future and the present all at once. The HVAC system kept the temperature at a constant 68 degrees no matter the weather.

The lieutenant's office was isolated from the main room by a soundproofing sheet. As soon as Novak closed the door, the computer engineers turned back to their workstations.

"Have you pulled the Collin file for me?" asked Meyrek.

The lieutenant grabbed a manila folder and held it out.

The colonel accepted it without appearing interested.

"I want him officially assigned to your team. From now on, you'll personally see to it that his name is regularly on the rosters."

"Consider it done, colonel. Although I don't understand why Collin doesn't join us. His information sheet does put him on the civilian side?"

Meyrek didn't respond. In his mind's eye, he replayed the moment when pure chance had made him see Theo's name pop up on the E.C.Tronics international staff lists he was consulting. A note had flagged him as a potential recruit for the computer center, while a subfolder placed him in the restricted category of software developers authorized for military projects.

In fifteen years, Meyrek had been unable to forget the frustration he'd felt the day that teenager had gotten out from under his thumb, stupidly breaking his leg during a training exercise.

At first he'd thought it a coincidence, but then he'd faced facts. The creator of the Enterprise 17 application, the man whose file was brimming with praise, was none other than the sickly young hyper-gifted faker that he'd sworn to himself he would turn into a true soldier over the course of a conflict that had come to a premature end.

Despite the processing power of the New York computer, nothing in Theo's file even hinted at the amazing ability that he'd revealed one rainy afternoon, his hands on an old FAMAS rifle that only the grunts used, the outstanding feature of which was that it shot straight.

Meyrek was thus the only one who knew. And destiny did not smile down on you like that without a reason.

The colonel had immediately requested Theo's presence on camp, and he had found himself constrained to ask for Tamazula's help. The Mexican had been introduced to him as one of the Organization's master keys. An incredibly wealthy man whose connections were sometimes shady yet indispensable to his duties as a recruiting agent. A man who moreover owned the immense lands on which the camps were built, and who was capable of seeing to their protection, much as he did for several more or less legal networks across Mexico and Southern California.

Ellen Cheston had questioned his motives in vain. He may have been the author of a piece of software that had been adapted to indirectly serve the camp, Collin did not fit the profile. Why him?

"Because he's French, like me."

Meyrek had remained intractable: the fate of this training camp, the future of this private army, had been placed in his hands. He meant to see his mission through his way. That Theo Collin had started a family and built a whole life over the past fifteen years had no bearing on anything. Natural sharpshooters were maybe one in a hundred thousand, and very few of those displayed Collin's aptitude. Meyrek wanted his prize toy. The new circumstances surrounding Theo's life simply made things more complicated. Simplifying them was Tamazula's problem.

"Are you unable to send me a man if I request him of you?"

"There is nothing we're unable to do!" had snapped Ellen Cheston.

Now, Collin was here. Collapsed in the infirmary after running and running some more, up until nightfall. Tomorrow, he would take part in other, more

160

strenuous exercises, ones that would push him to his physical limits; and soon, he would shoot again. That, Meyrek had sworn to himself.

Still faced with the lieutenant's questioning, insistent look, the colonel gave him a short answer.

"For the time being, Collin has proven to be recalcitrant. He needs to be trained up…"

The sounds produced by the small instrument would have pulled cries from the slightest music lover. But there were no real music fans around the tall redhead. The men used their feet, their hands, their belts or helmets to slap out a rhythm that approached the plaintive wails of the harmonica.

Making some noise. That was all. Tough break for the recruits who were already asleep. They'd stepped far enough away from their own barracks that they wouldn't disturb those of their teammates who were too tired to take part in their little party. The perimeter wall, which Lochlan was leaning on, extended out from the building housing the even sections. Every window had closed when they'd gone out, despite the heat.

A third of the section was there. Night owls buzzing with energy who couldn't bear their state of inaction and wore themselves out training during the day.

First there was Lochlan, with Irish roots, so sun sensitive that his skin turned as red as his hair after an hour under its glare. Wounded in Afghanistan after jumping sixty feet down from a burning helicopter, his fall had been broken by vegetation, and he'd gotten away with a broken scapula and tibia.

The latter he had set in the field before dragging himself along the twelve clicks that separated him from one of the patrols from his own company. An eight-day trek through a Taliban-infested Panjshir Province, delirious with fever. His teammates had already declared him missing when he'd sprung out, screaming as though the hounds of hell were chasing him, reeking, madness in his gaze.

By some miracle, his leg was saved by the camp surgeon. He'd been unable to step back into civilian life, despite his disability pension and the Purple Heart he'd earned through his injury, and he'd enlisted as a mercenary in Columbia, then run off, only to one day find himself seated in a bar, sipping at scotch after scotch next to a Mexican who seemed awfully interested in his story…

There was the mysterious Vietnamese duo, inseparable, with serious eyes but cheerful faces. Unparalleled when it came to natural traps, strangler vines, spiked bamboo trunks. Since the defeat of South Vietnam when they were still children, they'd thought of themselves as stateless. They'd volunteered in the South Korean army and had unfailingly found themselves on the front line in the DMZ, the boundary zone between Seoul and Pyongyang.

The two had often come across each other while on duty, frantic eye riveted to the sighting reticle, taking aim at the sentries opposite them, in the hopes of being able to have it out with the reds in the North, to finally exorcize the curse of their native Vietnam there on that foreign soil. An eye for an eye, a territory for a territory. They dreamed they'd get to play the rematch to a game they hadn't been able to play.

The way they'd been recruited remained a mystery. The only thing anyone knew was that they'd spontaneously volunteered at the Organization. Their mystical side gave the other recruits goosebumps, and they avoided any quarrels with them.

There was also Marcos, his tongue tied on a secret that had still spread through the camp like wildfire. A former paratrooper trainer, he was suspected of having caused his wife's death, and still insisted he'd fallen prey to a conspiracy that he and his two children were supposedly the focus of.

Some of his teammates believed that he'd completely made up the children, but not one of them would have put their lives on the line in an attempt to challenge him. Marcos had found himself with a new chance on his hands when the Organization had recruited him, like the Foreign Legion back in the day, but that hadn't granted him oblivion.

He had become inseparable from Salinas, a young Peruvian who boasted that he'd trekked across half of Latin America on foot. Only those closest to him knew of his other claims to fame: murdering at least five men – the sixth being in a permanent coma – during a bar fight somewhere around Sao Paolo.

It had all started when the color of his hair – a neon green – had been the butt of some jokes. Salinas had been getting ready to cross the Amazon region just for the hell of it. He'd gotten it into his head to hunt for new medicinal plants and make his fortune after he tested them on himself.

But that was neither the time nor the place to make fun of his personal grooming. Salinas had spent a year trekking in a bid to wean himself off of some of his heroin addiction, but even more so in tribute to Teresa, who'd died of an overdose while he'd been prepping a syringe. Before becoming a junkie, he'd learned to survive in the streets, by fist and by knife.

Then there was Juan, the most sensitive of them all, baby-faced, widowed just like Marcos, enlisted in his country's Navy when we was fourteen, then turned mercenary in Nicaragua, settled down for a few short months he'd spent with a young woman in his village, then volunteering on base after he lost her.

One morning, he had simply found himself all alone in his bed, a hastily written goodbye note pinned to the center of his shirt where it was draped over the back of a chair. Juan wasn't even sure he'd recognized her handwriting. The police had arrested him two days later, after he'd blown up half his building trying to rid himself of his memory of her, down to every place where they'd made love.

Also there was Will, a black man whose hulking figure could have cast a shadow over half of them at once. Despite the racket, he dozed while reclining at the bottom of some stairs, his head propped into a hand as big as a carpet beater.

Several others still. Matthew, a former trainer with the Delta Force, thrown out of Fort Bragg for indiscipline. Tall, a volunteer in Iraq, adrenaline junkie, discharged from the Marines for cruelty towards the prisoners. Brucker, a Belgian, a former bodyguard to several African heads of state, involved in the disappearance of a small briefcase full of diamonds, though nothing was ever proven. Welsch – the Australian, first world recordholder for skydiving on a motorcycle.

Men without a past, or whose pasts were buried deep in their own memories, who'd let themselves be seduced by the promise of triple pay, acts of valor, glory, rehabilitation, and who came together one night a week like a gaggle of teenagers sneaking out.

All contact with the outside world was prohibited. No mobile phone network, no TVs, and their radios were regularly confiscated during searches. Sure, some of them had kept a CD or MP3 player. But opportunities to unwind were few and far between, and it wasn't like the guys on guard duty were gonna turn them in. Too glad the rumpus was keeping them awake.

As for the NCOs, they had their instructions: on Friday nights, the elite section was entitled to a few drops of alcohol and, within reason, free run of the inside of the base.

A bottle of tequila split twelve ways didn't stand much of a chance to get them even in the vicinity of tipsy. If the two Vietnamese guys didn't drink, Lochlan for his part could put it away like a champ, and with no ill effects on his overall metabolism.

At Lochlan's feet there lay a supine figure, deliciously stretched out in a replete position. From ten yards out, you could have sworn it was the body of a woman. It was all there. The long legs with their rounded thighs, the stirring roundness of hips and stomach, two firm globes jutting out proudly, a half-open mouth, a silky fall of hair…

The legs were spread in a lewd display, all the more so since the body was bare and that, routinely, Juan rounded out a musical phrase by quickly pistoning his stretched index finger deep inside the orifice on offer, vocalizing an emphatic, "Pum! Pum!"

That night, that was the thing to celebrate. The magnificent body reclining among the soldiers was not of flesh and blood, but plastic. An inflatable doll that Juan had stolen from the section 4 chief, and which must have cost the noncom a pretty penny, given the perfect quality of its reproduction.

Their latest score. They'd bet it at poker later, before returning it to its owner, not necessarily in a pristine condition.

Each Friday, the elite section threw themselves into a "blitz commando," a term they used to designate the sophomoric pranks that usually targeted the "lesser" sections.

They'd already infiltrated the "odd" dorms and swapped around all their boots the night before a forced march. They'd ransacked the guard post – without any of the men on duty realizing it – and dropped off the "liberated" weapons, unloading them first, smack in the middle of dorm five. A quick investigation had revealed that the section five grunts were perfectly incapable of giving their section chief the slip; the guards, even less so.

They had abducted two grunts from the maintenance section, without waking their teammates, and had tied the wretches in the middle of the cemetery, a barren strip of dirt north of the base where they buried the slain runaways as well as the unfortunate victims of their dangerous training exercises…

Every Friday was a call to innovate, then to celebrate their accomplishment in the noisiest way possible.

Lochlan ended his tune on a note that strangely resembled the dying siren of a US squad car, and a mere twitch of his wrist let him lap up the last few drops of tequila.

"Who's got the cards?" he asked, belting out the final word.

The men looked at each other, questioning.

"Goddamn it! Nobody thought to grab them? Well tough luck then, fellas. I get the first ride."

"You're certain her owner has not caught any bugs?" whispered Juan.

The big redhead had reached a possessive hand towards the plastic girl's shoulder. He froze with it still in the air.

"What bugs?"

"I don't know," said Juan in the same tone of voice, his accent thick. "Herpes, for example. The noncom is a Yankee, like you."

The two Vietnamese guys giggled, aped by Salinas's hearty laughter. Looking sheepish, Lochlan tried to reassure himself.

"At any rate, you can't catch germs off plastic. And how do you know I don't already have herpes ? Or chlamydia, or why not AIDS?… I'm riding her first!"

Juan grabbed the empty bottle off the ground and upended it sadly.

"If you've got something, we all caught it already. We all drank from this bottle."

"I may not be a doctor," Marcos broke in, "but I agree with Lochlan. These diseases, you don't catch them off objects. Just asses that aren't clean."

The men grew rowdy, thrilled to have an excellent topic of conversation to share in, and it only took a few minutes for everyone to learn just about everything there was to know on their teammates' sex life and disease history.

Then Lochlan once again complained about the lack of alcohol and the mean trick Garroni had pulled, quaffing a third of their bottle tonight.

Just then, Huang stood up. Looking intimidated, he clumsily made his way towards the Irishman and produced a metal flask from a pocket of his fatigues.

"I always have this on me," he said with a stiff little smile. "But I don't drink."

Lochlan roared and promptly reached out an arm. The Vietnamese man stepped back to safeguard the flask.

"On one condition," he said. "Tonight, the one who most needs it is not among us. I propose for us to drink this in his honor."

He paused for a beat, then, mangling the sounds, revealed the identity of the man he was thinking of.

"Collin."

"The hell's he talking about?" grumbled the Irishman. "The scrawny Frenchy from the showers? The special case? Gimme that bottle so I can drink to my health and to the bitch they modeled this beauty off of…"

164

He took a step towards the Vietnamese man, ready to grab the object of his desire by strength, if need be.

"Easy," interceded Juan. "That's his. Among ourselves, there is no stealing."

"I for one agree," said Marcos. "Let's drink to the survival of this… Collin. Whatever his story is, whatever twist of fate threw him in this mess."

All the men agreed. They'd seen Collin run, they'd seen him fall and get back up again, face off with Garroni, resist the colonel's pressuring him, even if no-one understood what Meyrek expected from him.

"He's not gonna last," grumbled the Irishman. "Go on, give that bottle over. I'll drink to whoever you want me to if you haven't watered your whisky down."

Huang tossed the flask towards him. Lochlan peered at it attentively. It was a luxury item made out of engraved silver, ultra-slim and beveled. The cap was kind of thistle-shaped. He unscrewed it and held the flask out to make his toast.

"First off, what's your deal with that guy?"

"You agreed to the deal," protested Huang.

"O.K., O.K.!" The Irishman gave in after a brief glance at his teammates' faces. "Here's to the poor sucker in the sickbay. May he long draw all attention to him, so Garroni can give the rest of us a break."

He drained half the flask in one swallow, burped, wiped his mouth, and held it out to Juan. Everyone in turn uttered a toast, never saying Theo's name. But there was a significance to this ritual. Despite Lochlan's protests – a front, his teammates thought – the section would now have their gazes turned towards the new recruit. They couldn't do much to help him (and actually had no intention of doing so), but they were ready to take him into the fold as soon as his term in isolation was up. Provided he lived until then.

'Shape he's in and the treatment they're putting him through, no way!' thought the Irishman as he sucked up the last drop.

The mood had soured. Drinking to the survival of their mysterious teammate had suddenly reminded them how precarious their own situation was. The elite section! Mercenaries! Words they reveled in, trying to use pride to dampen their fear.

They had been spared the "lesser sections," and they took pride in how they'd thus escaped the most humiliating of tasks, the daily indoctrination, the endurance training. But the voluntarist fire that had driven some of them, the fierce zeal that had brought the true volunteers together, the longing for heroic actions that had led the less militant, all that had long become extinguished.

The question "Who are we fighting? What's our primary objective?" hadn't gotten a straight answer out of any of the officers. Only evasive phrases, definitions that could just as easily have applied to a rough three quarters of the rogue states.

Certain recruits, in addition to their military training, were learning Arabic or Farsi. But the section they were in focused on weaponry and ambushes. Nothing too intellectual. That was more than all right with them.

The base was a training camp. It was organized into sections. These sections would be divided into cells.

Great! They were training… That was earning them triple pay. And four years from now, when it came time to reenlist, provided they survived, they'd all be rich enough to get back to individual lives that would make the highlands base look like nothing more than a blip, ultimately.

One by one, the soldiers got up, suddenly mindful of the late hour and the amount of energy they'd have to use up the following day. They broke up into small groups and wordlessly headed off towards their common dorm.

The great winners of this sudden turn towards depression were without a doubt the odd sections, which were finally going to be able to get some rest.

Lochlan, the last one to go, grabbed the abandoned doll by an ankle and dragged it on the ground behind him like some kind of Neanderthal tableau. The girl had deflated somewhat and its foot was twisting oddly in his hand.

He ended up abandoning it in disgust right in the middle of the courtyard.

Right on the spot where the flag should have flown.

"I won't tie your hands this morning," said Garroni. "You're gonna run your twelve laps a free man. Breathe. Clear your mind. Focus on your muscles and your breath. Don't count the laps. Focus inward to be in control of your body, then step outside of yourself to take stock of it. Give it a try."

Theo made his way to the outer edge of the courtyard, dragging his leg. Garroni caught up to him.

"Hand me your shirt."

Theo stripped down to the waist and handed his uniform shirt to the sergeant. Garroni feigned grabbing the clothing, squared up his stance, and suddenly swung a mean fist into Theo's stomach. He bent double, the breath knocked out of him.

"Lesson one! Always be on your toes, even around a superior officer."

He lifted Theo's head up and sought out his gaze. The pain had his eyes misted over with tears.

"Lesson two! Show enthusiasm for your training."

Garroni tossed the top at Theo's feet and shot him a wink. He called out to one of his men, put him on watch, and headed into the first building alongside his section. Theo slowly straightened up and walked. The pain was getting better with each step. He started to run, keeping his steps small.

"As a free man…" the sergeant had said.

He felt the air rush into his lungs, saw the sun peek above the mountains. His feet were stirring up the dust as rhythmically as a metronome. He made it through his first lap without even realizing it. His lungs started burning in the middle of the third lap. He coughed, panted, his throat on fire; then, slowly, very slowly, he felt that exhilaration he'd already gone through the previous days filling him up with a sort of serenity.

The fat was melting off him, his body temperature was rising, the toxins in his body were being flushed. His blood beat out a pulse in his temples. Ramrod straight in the middle of the courtyard, the soldier watched him imperturbably.

This time, Theo didn't collapse, didn't drag himself along. He slowed down his pace, stumbled, pushed his body on, picked his breathing and his run back up.

His facial features were tense with fatigue, but his muscles were alive, gaining in shape. He lost count of his laps, lost track of time. His thoughts had left his body behind, far away, in communion with the universe.

At that moment, the tense thread of balled-up pain that tied him to Katia and to Juliette morphed into a vibrating string, for a short trip beyond matter. The waves of adrenaline flooding his heart and his brain were leading him into a dreamlike state, transcending suffering, abolishing grief, turning his soul into an empty shell. After all, nothing was real…

"That's it, you've done your twelve laps."

Beads of sweat were blinding Theo. Astonished, he came to an abrupt stop. His lungs were burning, his breath short, wheezing. The pain in his bronchi crept up over his neck, overwhelming his thyroid and slamming against his eardrums.

"Twelve?" he panted.

"Walk," the man went on. "Don't stop. Walk and swing your arms."

He obeyed. In a matter of minutes, his breathing returned more or less to normal. His heartbeat dropped below one-twenty.

This was his twentieth day of forced training. He was taking it as a first victory.

From the window to his room, Meyrek had followed Theo's run from the start. Fascinated, he had started betting against himself. *Seven laps; seven laps and he'll collapse like yesterday.'* He'd counted out the seven. Then had upped the stakes to eight. Ten. Theo had finished his run.

At first the colonel was vexed, but then he decided to take pride in that. Theo would bend, he would become one of his men, the best of them. Carrying out that transformation was on him.

'One day,' thought the colonel, *'one day, Collin's going to thank me.'*

And he truly believed that.

Ten minutes to regain his breath. He was then led to a weight room, where an officer in a tracksuit walked him through a series of exercises on a bunch of complex machinery.

He spent two hours handling light weights that felt like unmovable tons.

He was granted a frugal meal. Plenty of water. A half hour's rest. Then still more laps of the courtyard, so many he couldn't count them anymore.

His disconnect from the outside world had become the only thing guaranteeing his survival. In his worst moments, a flash of superstition led him to wonder if he hadn't crossed some kind of barrier between life and death, if he wasn't simply in hell, someplace far worse than that described by Dante, whose seven circles overlapped momentarily in a cursed place, somewhere in northern Mexico.

The sun disappeared in a splatter of blood and dust. Death roamed a picture-postcard landscape. Here, between the barbed wire, the watchtowers, the dorm buildings crowding soldiers of fortune together, life lost all meaning, time looped around, and man was robbed of his most basic choices, with but one exception: giving up.

Beyond the pain, deep in the rift within his soul, Theo felt himself draw on a new strength, a strength born of his rage towards this choice he'd refused.

His day over, he was once again locked inside his cell.

This time, he did go to the trouble of undressing, and he collapsed onto his bed, mind empty, body worn. He slept a dreamless sleep.

The door flew open with a bang like an explosion.

"Up, chucklehead. Five minutes to get dressed."

His stomach heaved. Garroni was standing in the doorframe, looking tired, his eyes mean. Outside, it was pitch black.

"What time is it?" Theo couldn't hold back the question.

"What, are you kidding me," bellowed the sergeant. "You think this is the Ritz? Get your ass up. The colonel has a special training in store for you, and I'm tasked with watching your ass."

Theo dragged himself out of the room. The camp lights were still out. Electronic alarm systems, much more effective than searchlights, prevented escapes.

"Come on, you're gonna have a blast. It's exciting, especially by night."

Garroni pushed him down the hallway. Outside, two men were waiting, looking terrified. They were handcuffed to one-another.

"They fooled around during training," commented Garroni. "Don't try to talk to them, they're Mexicans and the only English they understand is orders. They're going to be taking part in your little vigil."

A soldier joined them at the guard post and wordlessly escorted them outside the camp.

They followed the wall for a few yards, then delved into the shrubbery. It must have been three in the morning, four at the latest. There wasn't a single speck of light yet that heralded the oncoming dawn, and their walk was lit by the beam of a flashlight held by the second soldier.

Their trek was brief.

The ground quickly became gravelly, and their progression was no longer hindered by the vegetation. Soon, the wan light revealed an indistinct mass several yards high and a dozen wide, like an earth hillock. Garroni stopped them.

"Here we are," he said. "Sisyphus's hill. One of the colonel's inventions."

Theo widened his eyes, trying to understand. There was nothing worrying about the heap of earth – or whatever it was made of – at the heart of such a rugged terrain. Garroni's words, however, made it sound menacing. Theo felt a knot of apprehension choke him.

"Nice name, isn't it?" Garroni went on.

The Mexicans were looking at the hill in horror, foreheads bathed in sweat. The sergeant stepped closer to Theo.

"The colonel is a poet," he said without the slightest pretense of irony. "A poet and a cultured man. He came up with this exercise in tribute to a movie: *The Hill.*

"It's the story of a British army prison in which a bunch of mavericks were ordered to build a sand hill under the desert sun. We're building ours from rocks.

"He told us that, in a Greek myth, a god condemned Sisyphus to an eternity pushing a boulder up a mountain, only to have it roll back down each time he reached the peak. That's what gave him the idea for the name."

He turned to the soldier.

"Have them take off their boots."

The order was repeated in Spanish. The two Mexicans obeyed, atremble.

"You get to keep yours on this once," the sergeant told Theo. "Now here's what adds a little spice to this exercise: this whole entire area is crawling with snakes. Every time you lift a stone, there's a chance you might come across a nest. That'll do the nerves some good."

He lit a cigarette and sat down on a rock, next to the soldier. The latter placed his rifle over his knees, looking cynical, and lashed out an order.

"Go play nice with your little friends," said Garroni. "And try not to worry. If you get bitten, we've got a whole minute to open up your arm and suck the poison out."

He pulled out a second flashlight from his fatigues.

"This one's for you. So's I can have you clear in my sights."

Cautiously, as though he was touching the most precious and fragile of objects, Theo lifted a first rock. The flashlight barely managed to light his way, and it was as though he was plunging his hands into a dark pit. In a few seconds he was covered in sweat. The rock was heavy. He propped it against his stomach and walked to the hill.

"To the top," cried Garroni. "Climb up and set it down right at the top."

On bare feet, still handcuffed together, the two Mexicans were already climbing the other face of the hill.

Unable to prop himself on his hands, Theo had to get on his knees and push his way up with his elbows. From the first climb, he gouged himself, despite the thickness of his fatigues, and felt blood run down his legs. The rocks were jagged and sharp like glass.

He placed the stone down and straightened up.

"What's the use?" he cried to Garroni. He got a burst of laughter in response.

"None. None at all. The colonel is a poet. I told you already."

In under an hour, Theo's hands, knees, and elbows were gouged raw. Bit by bit, his anxiety gave way to fear, and he left all caution to the side as he lifted the rocks, pushing his arms forward, the muscles in his back straining painfully. His movements were tracked by the flashlight, he second beam of light accompanying the two Mexicans. At times, one of them would moan, feet undoubtedly shredded by a jutting rock. Dawn seemed destined to never come, and the sergeant had said, "Until first light."

Next, little by little, Theo felt a new emotion come over him. That rage he'd been feeling lately swelled in his gut, progressively replacing all the other types of suffering. This rage was everywhere: in his hands, in his lungs. It made him want to yell, and his movements turned jerky, robotic.

The rage was heightened by the memory of Katia and Juliette that he had tried to bury as deep inside as he could, for fear of losing his mind. But every time he reached the peak of the hill, their image filled up the darkness, as all-encompassing by now as the panting around him, the pull in his muscles, the sharp tip of the invisible knife that pierced his throat, his heart, his mind.

It was absurd. Beyond absurd. There was something ridiculous, almost laughable, about their rigmarole. One rock, another. Just as heavy, just as sharp. They were overcome by the despair of the cotton fields, the fear of firedamp in the coal mines, surrounded by withered shrubs as though in a Gehenna without flames.

Garroni and the other soldier were laughing at some joke, just a couple yards away. Maybe at a run, with the element of surprise, if he had enough strength to lift a rock above his head…

An inhuman wail put an end to his thoughts. He heard shouts in Spanish. One of the Mexicans was frantically bashing at the ground with a rock; collapsed on the ground, his teammate writhed convulsively, clutching his leg with his free hand.

Instinctively, Theo moved towards them.

"Stay where you are," ordered Garroni. "Keep going with your exercise!"

In a couple of leaps, Theo had reached the two terrified men. That same moment, he realized it was daybreak at last. A sinister rattling sound made him tremble, and a silver flash wriggled on the ground before vanishing between two rocks.

"Snake," the Mexican was howling. "Snake!"

"Step back," choked out the sergeant, running towards them.

He grabbed Theo by the collar of his fatigues and yanked him backwards. The soldier reached them, pulled the slide back on his semi-automatic. Down on the ground, the wretch rubbed convulsively at his calf, eyes widened in fear.

"*No quiero morir. No quiero morir!*"

His leg was swelling already, the skin taking on an awful color. Theo returned to the fray. The sergeant intercepted him and smacked him with a hand as big as a paddle.

"I told you to step off. Get back to your rocks."

With a desperate gesture, half stunned by the hit, Theo seized the sergeant's arm.

"He's been bitten," he yelled. "He's gonna die."

The soldier snickered. There was a machete hanging off his thigh that the sergeant grabbed hold of.

"You wanna help him?" gritted out Garroni. "Fine. Go ahead, then." He held the machete out to Theo.

"Go on, go ahead. Cut off his leg."

Theo hesitated, stomach twisting. The Mexican was begging him with his gaze.

"Your choice," snapped Garroni in an icy voice. "You either cut off his leg, put a bullet in his head, or let him die like this."

Theo furiously grabbed the machete. He let himself drop to his knees.

"Ladies and gentlemen, our President!"

Close to two thousand people stood up as Gregory Cheston entered to an enthusiastic clamor that immediately gave way to applause. The main room of the Stephens Convention Center, not far from O'Hare airport in Chicago, seemed all the more crowded since the marketing board of E.C.Tronics had had huge tables covered in white tablecloths brought in. Atop them stood over thirty huge screens, set up to broadcast the entirety of the quarterly talk that would take place following the huge multinational's earnings report.

Six strategically placed cameras were already taking turns providing the best possible angles of the 27 members of the board of directors. Those same images, relayed by satellite, would be watched simultaneously by 150.000 representatives of E.C.Tronics's small shareholders in some thirty American cities and eleven stock exchanges in Europe and Asia.

For their part, the 2000 participants in Chicago made up the main stockholders, and they were split between billionaires in evening dress and highly successful stockbrokers. Every quarter, at Cheston's whim, a different city was picked to host the customary report, at the end of which E.C.Tronics's stocks generally soared.

The electronics giant and its 400 subsidiaries were a safe bet. Happy traders saw Cheston as a genius. His detractors put his success down to a blend of lucky opportunism and a complete lack of scruples.

Howard Beck, for his part, was curious to see the man from this close up. From over on the stage, where Cheston had helped himself to the microphone to greet his guests with a customary quip, he thought him to be a whole lot bigger than he seemed in news clippings and other CIA archive photos.

Beck had rubbed shoulders with enough high-ranking people in his life to be able to recognize that special aura that the greats of this world exude, the one that imparts a unique stature on them and makes them capable of intimidating with a mere smiling glance.

Seated in the third row, Beck was patiently waiting for the first break, during which he'd secured a ten-minute interview with the man himself. When the time came, which he would be notified of by the company's chief marketing officer, he'd need to walk a tightrope, the only type of play that his higher-ups had approved: a soft approach under the cover of anonymity, using an identity borrowed from the FBI.

Here in the US, Beck wasn't on his turf: all he could do was collect information that had previously been filtered through the Bureau. Unless he temporarily changed hats, an exercise the Agency had become an expert at, to the great displeasure of its alter ego.

The MC must have been one heck of a patriot, or at the very least familiar with the emotional effect that the national anthem would have on the attendees, because the majestic notes of the Star Spangled Banner filled the loudspeakers, intoned by a choir that was briefly unveiled by a curtain opening immediately following the introduction. On instinct, Beck brought his hand to his heart, as did almost the entirety of the participants.

When the anthem died down, the MC invited the room to consult the documents placed before everyone, while Cheston made his excuses, promising to come back for the end, at least unless one of the decisions adopted during the meeting would be his dismissal.

Bursts of laughter.

Keeping a casual eye the backstage door, where he would soon be hailed from, Beck spent a few minutes attempting to parse the astronomical numbers being brandished in the report.

E.C.Tronics directly employed 147.000 people around the world. Its subsidiaries employed a further 420.000 blue- and white-collar workers, to say nothing of their intricate executive spiderweb. The R&D department alone boasted six Nobel prizes and spent more per year than the biggest pharma lab in the world. Cheston's personal net worth, sixth in the world, was estimated to rival the combined GDPs of Poland and Romania…

These numbers brought back to Beck's mind the other rundown, the one printed out from the thumb drive Haim had handed him, the one that never should have seen the outside of Cheston's electronic safe. The one that nevertheless had nearly made it into enemy hands. A nightmare. The "White Cells" presentation, laid out like a business plan, as the Mossad agent had emphasized, indicated a 15-million-dollar daily expenditure, which amounted to a half a billion a month, six billion dollars a year.

No slush fund in the world could cover that kind of money. And that was the most worrying and sobering part. What were these tallies doing making the rounds in the Arab corners of the high finance world? For what possible reason could a freelancer of Feldman's caliber go and betray his main employers?

As to the latter point, the director of the CIA was being beyond circumspect. An internal investigation conducted interdepartmentally had estimated that probability to be quasi astronomical. Feldman had never had access to the slightest crumb of intel concerning Operation Buridan. If he was the mole they were looking for, that entailed a hair-raising network of collusions inside the Agency. Just thinking about it turned Beck's blood to ice.

For the time being, therefore, Feldman had simply been placed under the tightest and most unobtrusive surveillance possible. They needed to at least find out the real raison why he was in London before reaching any other conclusions.

A tall, lanky guy wearing red-framed glasses stepped in front of Beck's table. "It's time, sir, if you'd care to follow me."

Within a few moments they'd reached an adjoining conference room by way of a maze of corridors as wide as avenues. Gregory Cheston was conferring with three people there, among them a woman, and he asked them all to leave as soon as he saw Beck come in.

"I've got ten minutes," he said dryly, shaking his hand.

"I know," replied Beck. "Your chief protocol officer let me know."

His retort put the semblance of a smile on Cheston's face.

"You wanted to talk about my assistant. I'm not the President… But let's cut to the chase, Mister Beck. What does the FBI want with me?"

The room housed long conference tables set up in a horseshoe pattern and surrounded by thirty chairs. Ramrod straight, looking as rigid as any career soldier, Cheston didn't hint at any desire to sit down.

Quickly, Beck went over the official purpose for his visit. Obviously, he wasn't the one under investigation, but rather his main right-hand man, Feldman. Cheston's features hardened progressively into a suspicious expression. He cut Beck off in the middle of a phrase.

"I'm not sure how Feldman's allegedly illegal private stock trading has anything to do with me. I think you've reached the end of your ten minutes…"

Cheston was already moving to lead him out of the room, but Beck had kept his ace in the hole for the end.

"Even if some of those transactions appear to involve your own daughter?"

Before any investigation into people this high up, the questions they'd be asked were carefully written up by a CIA profiler. As far as Feldman went, what mattered most was finding out the amount of trust that Cheston placed in him, knowing that the former enjoyed a special status as much in the eyes of the Agency as in the business world.

Twenty years of dubious dealings and services rendered out of personal interest had given him an immunity against any direct hit. But if he was involved in the leaks, it was imperative to isolate him from the upper echelons of E.C. Tronics immediately. Cheston's psych profile revealed a single chink: his painful affection for his daughter Ellen, who suffered from an incurable genetic disease.

"I would just like to know if you were in the loop as to the various trips that your right hand took abroad," ventured Beck. "A permanent contact appears to have been established between him and your daughter. According to our initial report, Feldman broke several rules involving illicit international wire transfers, unsanctioned support to failing companies, and cash transports, in contravention of antiterrorism laws…"

Always follow the money to the source,' recalled Beck, who was settling for dropping hints about some of the methods described in the White Cells report. Cheston let silence reign for a beat.

"You're well aware that your weapons dealings are very sensitive in nature," continued Beck. "For the time being, this is a routine investigation. But as soon as your name, and what's more your daughter's, showed up on the preliminary reports, I was tasked with reaching out to get your cooperation."

"All right. What exactly is it you want to know?"

Beck pulled a notepad out from his jacket pocket. Inside, there was a catalog of all of Feldman's trips over the past two years. A very close cooperation between the CIA and its European counterparts had enabled them to fill in certain blanks, despite his frequent identity changes.

"You've gotta imagine I don't keep tracks of the comings and goings of everyone I work with," the president of E.C.Tronics rejoined dryly.

"Certainly. But maybe you could recall some trips to London and Paris? Or at least the most recent ones?"

"I'd need to ask my assistant…"

"Please, Mister Cheston, we're not interested in the kind of information that your assistant would be in possession of. Only the immediate relationship between you, your daughter, and…"

The door was suddenly opened by the man with the red-framed glasses, who uttered his announcement like a well-oiled machine.

"The ten minutes are up, Sir. Should I show in your next appointment?"

Beck sighed. He should have known that Cheston's appointments weren't just being timed, but also scheduled by his assistant.

"Could you at least take a look at this list," he said, tearing the page out of his notebook. "If something were to come back to you…"

"I'll be sure to give you a call!" concluded Cheston, grabbing the piece of paper.

Beck briefly shook his hand and thanked him before starting to make his way towards the corridor.

"Just one last little thing…" he said, turning back.

"Go ahead. But hurry!"

Beck doubled back.

"You've got a smudge of makeup just there, on your shoulder. Your chief protocol officer didn't even notice."

With a nimble gesture, he brushed off Cheston's jacket. The man flinched back as if he'd been bitten by a snake.

"Don't ever do that again!" he growled. "Jonathan, Mister Beck will be leaving the conference. See him to his car."

No sooner had Beck, escorted by the man with the red-framed glasses, stepped over the threshold that Cheston slipped off his jacket and dialed an internal extension.

"Get me a fresh suit right now," he demanded.

He began to pat down his coat along every seam, then quickly gave up. He knew enough about alphabet agency tactics to know that this FBI guy had planted a miniature bug on him just before leaving. But he also knew he'd have a hard time finding it without the appropriate tools. The pressing thing was getting rid of his jacket.

With a rapid gaze, Cheston scanned the list that Beck had handed to him, then he folded it and put it in his wallet.

The advantage of the elite section dorms was that they only housed a small number of beds. With six or eight beds to a room, the men had grown accustomed to the night-time quirks and noises from their roommates. They lived together in a forced intimacy that was becoming less annoying with each passing month, particularly since the pecking order had been established from the start, and a sort of tacit respect for the natural hierarchy in play prevented all clashes.

Each dorm had its own rules. No leader. No squabbles for privileges. Their regimen had been deliberately toned down by Meyrek, who'd seen that as the means to favor his first internal combat section. These men were either professional soldiers or gifted with the kinds of abilities that had granted them the honor of joining the elite unit, the first combat cell.

Their sleep was troubled, more often than not. After a hard day's training that sometimes pushed them to their very limits, they plunged into a semi-conscious state, their fine-honed senses on alert, ready to leap into action at the slightest unusual sound. Most of them were up before the first flush of dawn, already antsy from inactivity, their strengths back up after a scant few hours of such superficial rest.

The Vietnamese man opened his eyes. He turned his head towards the empty bed next to his and sought his brother out with his gaze. A wheezy, uneven snoring came from the gigantic bulk of the Mexican asleep on his back next to the door. He sat up on the scratchy sheets and made out a figure backlit by the window frame.

It was morning. Soon the dorm would be overtaken by a frenzy of activity, the prelude to a new day filled with pressure and anguish. He spoke in a whisper, taking care to be mindful of his teammates' final moments of rest.

"Huang?"

"They took him to the hill," the reedy figure replied in the same tone, not turning around.

The Vietnamese man slipped to the foot of the bed and joined his brother. They were the same size, but their physical makeup was different. The elder, Huang, was slim and bony. His clean-shaven face was made up of prominent features, with very elongated eyes and a wide, smooth forehead. Tran was stocky. If not for his almond-shaped eyes and his high cheekbones, he could have passed for a westerner, so white was his skin and so unrepresentative his facial features.

"The Frenchman? How do you know?"

"I've been awake for hours. Garroni took him in the middle of the night."

Tran was used to his brother's mysterious attitudes. It was tradition in the family to respect and obey the first-born, but Tran would have naturally followed Huang's lead even if fate had brought them to life in a different order.

Huang looked at things differently from the way most men did. A philosophy buff, he spent his few off-duty hours reading his favorite writer, Huỳnh Phú Sổ, a violently anti-communist thinker and the founder of the Phật Đạo Hòa Hảo secret society, whose members were the first to take up arms against the French forces occupying his country and against Japan. Legend claimed the rebel philosopher had been infirm until the age of 20 and his initiation by a Buddhist priest, at which time he'd been granted powers such as foresight.

More than once had Huang guided their paths in surprising directions that had, in time, proven to be both wise and prescient. The two Vietnamese men were fighters, warriors, mercenaries. But it was Huang alone who chose the fights and the sides that they came to join.

Their family tie was a secret they'd shared with no-one since their third brother had died during torture, after refusing to disclose the movements that an exfil team they were part of was making in North Korean territory. In another world, in another conflict. "No nation is still worth fighting for," Huang had said at the time they'd enlisted at the base. As always, Tran had acquiesced.

Since, he had been a sad witness to Huang's long, solitary retreats, from which his brother emerged with a worried frown and a lost gaze.

They no longer fought. They were relearning how to fight. And the rules being set in place did not seem to sit right with the small Vietnamese man, who watched mutely as their leaders used very distinctive means to create an army.

"Little brother," he had once avowed at the end of a long stretch of contemplation, "any man has the right to make a mistake at least once in his life. The important thing is not to get the timing of that mistake wrong. And I got it very wrong!"

And then the Frenchman had come, a few days earlier. And Huang's eyes had flickered back to life. The man looked nothing like a soldier, not even like a fighter at that.

In the elite section, grunts were treated just as deferentially as the veterans. That was one of the rules. No taking on the attitude prevalent in prison settings. Keeping a sliver of humanity by refusing to let the group run roughshod. They'd gotten ready to welcome him, to help him clear the hurdle.

But the Frenchman had been placed in isolation. Locked inside an individual cell, almost as though they'd feared that his presence would disrupt the balance that the section was in.

"If that man survives," Huang had said, "maybe I didn't get things entirely wrong."

He'd refused to disclose more, despite his brother's insistent questions.

Huang abruptly turned around. An excited flame glowed in his eyes.

"They're coming back," he said. "They're coming back from the hill. Let's go watch."

Docilely, Tran followed his brother across the dorm. The Mexican had stopped snoring and was starting to toss and turn in his bed. Tran didn't ask how Huang had been aware of the sergeant's return. He knew full well that the window didn't overlook the courtyard and that there was no way he could have heard their footsteps outside.

They opened the door leading to the hallway and waited. By tacit mutual agreement, they kept silent for a few moments.

At first, Tran thought that the Frenchman was dead. His fatigues were covered in blood and his immobile body hanged piteously from the arms of the sergeant who was holding him up by his armpits with no apparent effort. His head was lolling forward and his frame looked as fragile as a child's.

A couple of steps behind them, a soldier was following them carelessly, a smeared machete tapping at his hips.

The sergeant reached them. He barked out an order for them to reenter their dorm. It was then that the Frenchman lifted his face. He was alive. His body, at least, was alive. His gaze was utterly expressionless, and his eyes were cloudy, like a wounded animal.

Tran turned towards his brother. It shocked him to see a satisfied smile on his face.

Eliane shoved the magazine into her Uzi in one emphatic motion. It wasn't her first time using this weapon. The small Israeli-made submachine gun barely weighed more than a handgun, and its size was such that it looked like a toy. Incredibly efficient, however, capable of filling its target with a spray of twenty or so nine-millimeter bullets in a few seconds without jamming. She was more comfortable with it than the heavy Kalashnikov. A slight shake of her head declined the helmet the noncom was handing her.

Fifteen yards out, several empty bottles had been aligned on the parapet. Eliane took in a deep breath, held it in, and, her left arm held along her body, pointed the short barrel towards the bottles. Two short bursts. The glass splintered into shards. Over on the ledge, there were only a few chips of glass left.

Without changing her body's position, she turned her face and the gun towards a paper target on her right. She emptied out the clip in one squeeze. Ten holes framed the circle in the middle. The shot wasn't perfect, but then the weapon had a reputation for being imprecise. It wasn't for nothing that the Tsahal had taken it off their official weapons roster a few years ago now.

"How many have we got?" she asked.

The noncom checked a list.

"We received two crates last week, with the MP5's. There's twelve in all."

"Very well. I'm keeping this one."

She slid the strap of the Uzi onto her shoulder and released the mag. The NCO handed her a box of ammo. Eliane stepped away, reloading the magazine she'd just used as she went.

There were two sections coming back from training. The children were standing still in the courtyard, listening to orders from a training officer. The young woman slid her gaze over the faces of the small uniform-clad urchins.

Their eyes seemed huge, propped in the middle of their angular features. Tiredness sank their cheeks and, despite the glow imparted by daily workouts out in nature, most of them didn't look particularly fresh. They were standing scrupulously straight, a piece of wood carved into the shape of a rifle on their shoulder. The officer noticed Eliane's presence and barked out,

"Attention!"

The children, thirty of them in all, obeyed with impeccable alacrity. Thirty rifles were propped upright in a smack of boot heels. Eliane held back a shiver.

"At ease!" she uttered mechanically.

She walked past the two groups. Behind her, the officer announced the end of the day's training.

"Section three, section five, dismissed!"

Eliane headed into the surveillance building and made her way towards the conference room. The space could fit several dozen officers and was used for weekly meetings and for orientation when they got new staff.

Several tables had been pushed together in the middle, with documents and operational maps piled up on them. Two soldiers in shirtsleeves, jackets folded over the back of a chair, were leaning over a printout representing the base and its surroundings. They stood to attention as Eliane approached.

"Where are we at?" she asked.

"Done," one of the soldiers said proudly. "Just a couple minutes ago. The reproduction is very accurate."

He showed Eliane the map. The area had been digitized on a major scale, and the camp buildings were represented on it down to the slightest detail. Eliane nodded her satisfaction.

"The photos taken from the chopper were very useful. The local area maps weren't accurate enough."

"Print out four or five copies," ordered Eliane. "I want one in my office and one in the mess hall. From now on, each section will have assigned training areas. We'll make a joint decision as to what sector each group gets."

She set the Uzi down and pulled up a chair.

'At least,' she thought as she sat, *'we won't be planning ops blind anymore.'*

She'd been working on a new organizational chart for a few days now, and she intended to apply some of her own methods to the way the base was set up. For a start, the supervisory staff was prone to a complacency that had only been getting worse. The training program didn't include them, and the men were lacking in exercise, despite taking part in the children's drills. There were several months to go before they moved on to a more active phase. She was going to find something for them to do.

Eliane dedicated herself to perusing the map.

She was just finishing taking notes when she was interrupted by the appearance of a soldier from the guard post, who saluted her summarily. He stayed in the doorway and said gruffly,

"We've had a call from the even sections, captain. They've got an injury."

Eliane quickly got up.

"Did you alert the infirmary?" she asked in a tense voice.

The soldier nodded.

"The lieutenant tasked me with letting you know. It sounds serious."

Eliane watched the small group make its way towards the camp through the shrubbery. At her side, the two nurses were smoking a cigarette, looking bored.

"There they are," she said. "Get moving. Go get him."

They hoisted the stretcher off the ground and, dragging their feet, headed towards the children. Eliane signaled for the noncom who'd supervised the maneuver to follow her to her quarters. He came in on her heels, closed the door, and stepped closer to the desk, looking uncomfortable.

"I never gave the order for a live firing exercise," the young woman stated coldly. "Who authorized you to bring an M2 into play during the assault course?"

"It was scheduled for today. The kids were supposed to go through their first trial by fire."

The NCO's tone was cheeky. Eliane got on his nerves, and it was bad enough having to do a job taking orders from a woman… The decision had come from on high for a change. He pulled out a sheet of paper.

"Here's the order, captain. It was handed out last night." The document bore colonel Meyrek's signature. It was stamped *"Confidential and Restricted."*

"A child just got crippled for life," retorted Eliane, her lips a tight line. "No orders of this kind should be carried out without keeping me apprised. I would have had safety measures put into place."

"It was an order from the colonel," the noncom repeated flatly. "It's my duty to obey the highest-ranking officer."

He avoided the young woman's gaze, shuffling from foot to foot, in a rush to be done.

"Get outta here," she ordered. "I'll see to this."

The NCO saluted and complied. Grabbing the phone, Eliane unleashed her anger as soon as she had Meyrek at the other end of the line.

"You gave the order for a training exercise without letting me know. A child is seriously injured. Why?"

"If the order did not reach you, it must mean there's a failing in your organization."

"My organization? How does a day planner get handed out to my subordinates without notifying me? Who sent it out?"

"*I did.* Intentionally. I wish I'd been wrong, but I can see your men will leap at the first opportunity to act without your agreement."

"You ordered a trial by fire for ten-year-olds just to put my authority to the test?" Eliane choked out. "That's insane!"

"Captain Khouri, you forget who you're talking to."

"A child panicked," the young woman screamed into the receiver. "His leg was drilled by bullets."

"Warning you wouldn't have made a difference."

"I would have picked out the kids. Some of them are better trained than others. This test was ridiculous. Obviously every man here will give priority to your orders…"

"What is it exactly that triggered your outrage, captain? That injured child or the slight to your authority?"

Eliane nervously rooted around for a cigarette. She found a butt at the bottom of her ashtray and lit it.

"The issue here isn't my outrage, but your actions…"

"In that case, file a report with me. You're not in charge of a summer camp, but a training camp. I've already warned you. If your men throw themselves on a machine gun and let loose shooting children, that means they need to see some action.

"These are extremely well-trained mercenaries who live and breathe the chain of command, even if their commanding officer is a woman. See to it that you maintain a military feel to your camp and this kind of incident won't happen again."

Eliane was about to raise an objection by retorting that that was exactly what she'd been planning on doing. Meyrek hang up on her, leaving her to stew in her anger and frustration.

"There's been injuries?" asked Novak, who'd been there for the conversation.

"A child," replied the colonel. "Badly hit, sounds like. Got Khouri in a tailspin."

"If I may, sir," continued Novak, "I never could figure out why you entrusted the command of the second camp to a woman. Don't you think it's time to replace her, or assign a higher-ranking officer to supervise her?"

Meyrek was staring vacantly forward, as though he hadn't heard the question. He'd ditched his BDUs and slipped on his glasses. Free from his ceremonial duties, he looked the part of a man in his fifties who had never granted himself a moment's rest.

Excepting for when he needed to read, he preferred the strain of having to make out objects over conceding to the first weaknesses brought on by age. His time poring over reports was the only occasion for him to unwind, and he was duty-bound to share it with the officer closest to him.

Meyrek felt no friendship towards Novak, no more so than for any of the officers who had ever been in his command throughout his career. He merely saw in him a capacity to inflict the same level of cruelty as him. In that respect, Novak was his equal, and that made him a potential danger.

"No," he responded. "I don't want to replace her. She's the only thing making the second camp feel even slightly human, and children cannot be treated like adults."

Novak watched the colonel without letting any of his amazement show. This was the first time he'd heard Meyrek reveal any semblance of compassion. Like the other officers read in for strategic reasons, the creation of the second camp had initially stirred moral objections inside him, quickly dispelled by the worry engendered by the inefficiency of this machinery. The "White Cells" concept was based on faithfully cloning the tactics that the enemy resorted to.

But if Hezbollah's Shia militias, like the Iranian army and certain Palestinian factions, had no scruples about recruiting children, which were generally seen as an insignificant, replaceable resource, their fight was religious in nature and their recruits steeped in fanaticism from the earliest age.

The quandary that was proving impossible to solve, according to those same officers, was how to use the same methods without paving the way through brainwashing. The best training in the world wasn't enough to make up for coercively implanted faith, and if Iranian children had been able to run across Iraqi minefields, the key to heaven around their necks, it was because they wholeheartedly believed in the afterlife promised to them by the Mullahs.

As for Novak, he still didn't understand what the point of the second camp was. But he was an officer first. And even a mercenary abides by discipline.

"These kids have no families, no attachments," continued Meyrek, as though in response to a silent question from his subordinate. "They can't get their heads around what's happening to them. I can't leave them in the hands of the recruits. They'd make minced meat out of them. Today's experiment proved that."

"As long as Khouri remains in command of the second camp, it's under my control. And, more importantly, the most children possible will stay alive. Eliane Khouri is a soldier with maternal instincts. That's exactly what I wanted."

Novak had no answer to that.

"When the time comes," Meyrek went on, "those two hundred kids will follow her blindly. And her own men will keep her in check. On my orders."

Garroni looked at his watch with a grumble. After a day like this one, he still needed to wait around until it was two in the morning so he could be sure that he'd be waking that bastard up during first sleep!

He decided that a short fifteen minutes wouldn't really count as disobeying the orders he'd been given, pulled on his BDU jacket, grabbed his standard issue sidearm and his flashlight. Moments later, he was exiting his building and stepping down the hallway of his section's barracks.

'A solid, booted kick to his metal bedframe,' he thought as he unlocked Theo's door, *'and the flashlight beaming right in his eyes…'*

It didn't bring him any particular satisfaction to subject him to this kind of treatment in the middle of the night, but orders were orders. And besides, all Collin had to do was give in. That would spare them both these forced sleepless episodes.

However, the only one to get a surprise was the sergeant himself. Completely awake, Theo was seated on the edge of his bed and looking at him calmly, already dressed.

'This son of a bitch,' thought Garroni.

"Well then," he asked, "the hill or the range?"

"The hill," replied Theo.

Chapter 12

The black man was gigantic. His name was Will Bordez. Born to an African-American father and a Mexican mother, he boasted a nimble, sculpted body, muscles long and bulging, his chest alone accounting for the volumetric equivalent of the trunk of a small car.

His skin as dark as that of the Malian tribes his father's forebears had hailed from, he had inherited his mother's almost Inca features, beneath a large forehead hanging over a gaze brimming with mischief. No-one on base had ever had the guts to give him a hard time.

While on patrol, he plastered blanks all over himself, crisscrossing them across his chest like a Mexican revolutionary. He carried the 50 cal and its tripod all by himself. Over a hundred and twenty pounds that he moved with all the dexterity of a juggler and all the efficiency of a bulldozer.

As soon as he'd been recruited, he'd been assigned to the elite section, under Garroni's command. He constantly displayed a placid, happy-go-lucky air that only hinted at one side of his true nature.

Will was the very picture of kindness, as is usually the case for men capable of unleashing that kind of strength. Pushed to his limits, however, he could prove to be unbelievably fierce. His ebullient disposition had earned him several months in a Mexican prison after he murdered – massacred, more like – two men in a bar with his bare hands.

Witnesses had claimed that he'd acted in self-defense. A credible statement, considering he'd only been passing through the small border town that his mother had been born in, following seven years with the Marines and a refusal to reenlist.

The judge had only sentenced him to ten years, since the bodies had been found with switchblades in their possession.

Ten years was still a long time to bear, and Tamazula's men, always on the lookout for recruits of his caliber, had pulled him out by getting him to sign on for a two-year commitment with the base. Will, then, was satisfied. The volunteers' pay was three times what a Marine of his rank would earn.

He was now perfectly content with camp life. All he wanted was to fight, run in the mountain air, keep perfecting his shooting, do close-combat drills, or plant explosives. And he carried the 50 cal. Which earned him the admiration of his superior officers as well as the men in his section.

He had been taught to ask no questions; therefore, the objectives of this mercenary army were of no interest to him. And besides, truth be told, anything was better than Guanajuato prison. Life was easy. His teammates, too. For him, this was a new family.

What had piqued his interest lately was the presence of this quiet and tormented Frenchman who was isolated from the rest of the group and treated as an absolute pariah. The man only took part in the most punishing maneuvers, and in camp life only when they were on fatigues.

'Yo, man. One case. Not my problem,' thought Will. Had to be some recalcitrant who'd avoided a heavy sentence.

There were rumors about him flying around. Claiming him to be some kind of sharpshooter. The colonel had supposedly swore he'd get him to buckle because he was obstinately refusing to grab a rifle...

Looking at him, Will didn't get how this little Frenchie had the guts to stand up to Meyrek. Those first few days, he wouldn't have put his money on him. Collin did not physically look like a soldier, despite his shaved head, bisected by a long and recent scar. Several nights now, he'd been dragged off to the Sisyphus hill, a diabolical, punitive exercise that the colonel had come up with.

But he was resisting miraculously, almost like there was some kind of supernatural fire driving him.

Some of the men who'd gone through the hill punishment with him reported back that Collin lifted the stones up without fear, with delight even, as though he was expecting some deliverance.

Twice a day, Collin would run alone, and his figure had become a familiar sight by now. They saw him after reveille, his boots stirring the dust in the courtyard with the even pace of an elite athlete at practice.

'If the colonel wants to break him, he hasn't found the right way yet,' Will said to himself. *'This dude don't give a damn about his trials.'*

True enough, a handful of months had lent staggering proportions to Theo's body. His shoulders had widened; a network of long muscles was taking shape across his torso and legs. With all that running, his chest cavity was starting to expand, and there was no longer anything scrawny about his build. Tanned and framed by short, thick hair, his face was defined by rugged features; his desperate gaze had surpassed all human illusion.

Ultimately, maybe Collin had earned the budding legend surrounding him. He was said to be in possession of a secret that was awkward for the Organization. He was said to be an elite shooter. If it was the latter, if there was truth to that rumor, he could become a combatant who was worthy of his section.

Will Bordez was certainly intrigued by what they had in store for this little soldier.

Four months after Theo had come to the camp, Meyrek felt he was ready for a second interview. Up until then, Garroni alone had conveyed his orders; he had been subject to no direct pressure.

That morning, for the first time, Garroni did not burst into his bedroom prison. Used to these sudden wakeup calls, Theo had gotten into the habit of preempting him by a few minutes, to spare himself the annoyance. He waited.

The first sounds of the men getting ready for training gave him the confirmation that he'd gotten up at the usual time. He got up and propped his face against the door. It was winter, there wouldn't be light out for several more hours. However, the lights in his bedroom weren't on yet. Through the peephole, he could see the hallway teeming with men, all in uniform already. He pushed hard against the door; it was still locked. There was something unusual afoot.

Theo slipped on his BDUs, grabbed his bedspread and made his bed tightly, then sat on the edge of it.

Ever since he'd arrived at the camp, he'd lost all track of time.

Unlike prisoners who kept track of the days still left for them to get through, he hadn't fashioned himself a calendar. Some crossed X's into the wall with a pocketknife or a fork; others amassed small pebbles. Theo had no date, no hope that he could cling to.

Yanked from his bed every morning, and sometimes in the middle of the night, by the sergeant, he hadn't, from that point on, had any other concerns except the continued survival of this body they were shaping for him. A succession of exercises filled up his entire day, leaving him exhausted long after nightfall.

For him, that was a blessing. His one chance of escaping the insanity that – he could feel it – his thoughts would drag him into if he let himself go.

He had discovered the joy of letting his strength flood through him when he ran. He impatiently waited, every day, for the moment when his foot would tread on the courtyard ground, freeing him from the first fears overcoming him, dispelling the image of his lost family, of his shattered life.

Living!

He remembered that first night at the hill, the terrified look in the young Mexican's eyes; he'd had no hope if he didn't sacrifice his leg. Theo had then, in one second and for all eternity, let go of every last one of his civilized instincts. He'd let the man have it, clumsily, furiously, fighting to save this life that he had no claim over and that some wise guy had placed in his hands.

The venom had been quicker. Or maybe the pain. Unless the very idea of the sacrifice he'd just accepted hadn't stripped him of any will to survive.

The young man had died in Theo's arms, just when the latter had thought he'd managed to save him.

He had since gone looking for those moments of physical terror, delighted in all the times that Garroni had pulled him from his sleep to drag him over to the hill and put him through that life and death trial, him and others. Theo had ascribed a symbolism to the Sisyphus hill that he abandoned himself to with a morbid passion.

184

Sacrificing power to consciousness. Moving away from the ground by lifting rocks. Climbing, rising towards the heavens, step by step, in the penetrating darkness.

Every rock was a new victory. He had very quickly learned not to fear the unknown into which he plunged his arms. All he had to do was keep the snakes away with the power of his thoughts, to deny they were there. And the rocks became harmless pebbles that he was carrying to build a tower of his own.

And so, at the top of the hill, he became a free man once more. He thumbed his nose at the guards, whose master he became, for one brief moment…

The noises died down. Then the building went completely quiet. The men were in the mess.

The four gunshots of the call rang out a few minutes later. The cries of the men falling in reached his ears, muffled by the thickness of the walls.

Theo waited anxiously for the door to open at last. For someone to come save him from his own presence, so he could run and escape.

The call ended. The troops scattered. He was being left alone! Theo instantly understood that his torturers had concocted the most sophisticated torment yet. He'd accepted the bullying, the fatigues, the most exhausting exercises without complaining.

A hundred times had Garroni suggested he join his group, live among his section, and take advantage of all its benefits, or even go work at the base's computer center, something that would have enabled him to regain something of his former life. All he had to do, to make that happen, was grab hold of a rifle, aim it at a target, and prove to the officers that colonel Meyrek hadn't made a mistake.

A hundred times had Theo declined.

In the end, they'd understood that the rigid strictures of his existence were giving him a rush, and that he couldn't have cared less about the paltry advantages they had to offer him.

And so, to make him give in, they were leaving him to his own devices, a prisoner to his own thoughts.

'No!' he howled inwardly. 'No. I don't want to think. About anything. Ever. Especially not about them.'

He threw himself backwards onto his bed. The grey walls of his cell were the enclosures of his existence. Inaction: the one thing he couldn't bear. They were going to abandon him like this. He needed to run, he needed his body to hurt, he needed his muscles to cord, again and again, until his thoughts were obliterated.

Theo rolled off his bed. He let himself drop to the ground. Face on the floor, he looked for ways to work his body. Yes. It was obvious. They hadn't beaten him yet. Theo corded his muscles and he started a series of pull-ups, stomach down.

'Even if you leave me alone,' he thought, 'you won't get me. You'll have to tie me down. As long as I'm able to move, I'll find a way… I'll find a way…'

He counted out thirty pull-ups. Huffed. Then got up and walked to the door. Three steps separated him from it. He turned back, walked towards the window. Five steps.

'I can run,' he raged. *'In a circle. If I focus hard enough on the number of steps.'*

He reached the door again at a trot, did an about-turn when he grazed against it. Sped up the pace. Five steps. About-turn. Five steps. He hurtled his shoulder against the door, turned, struck the wall at the window. That way, he wouldn't lose his momentum.

'One, two, three, four, five. I have all the room I need.'

Closing his eyes, he vanished the walls. The floor of his cell became solid ground, the ceiling a blue sky, the bars on his window a perimeter wall. The perimeter wall disappeared in turn. And the camp itself. He was in a field and he ran in a straight line, a stallion looking for his herd, master of his own destiny.

Five steps. Five steps that added up and became a hundred yards, a mile, a league. Theo threw himself to the floor, began a new series of pull-ups. His body was sweating again.

He took a deep breath of the fresh air outside, his window wide open. Then the night shifted to grey and he heard the first of the birdsong. He sat on the edge of his bed, out of breath.

He was hungry.

'Better still,' he thought. *'They're going to leave me without food or water. Until I crack. Hungry and alone. Garroni will wait a few days, then he'll show up with a steaming plate in one hand and a rifle in the other. "Shoot. Shoot and you'll get food. If not, we'll let you die."'*

He tried to picture how long he'd be able to hold out without food. Bit by bit, he would undoubtedly succumb to an irreversible madness. What use would they have for him then? Was the colonel so determined to break his will that he was ready to sacrifice him whole after investing so much in him?

That made no sense. But did Meyrek have any sense outside of his wish for power? Theo placed his face between his hands, overtaken by a new wave of dread.

'What gives me the right to still care about my fate?'

He sat motionless. His thoughts, given free rein, went digging through memories. His wife's face emerged, vague and imprecise like an old photo. Then sharper, like in his dreams.

They were in Chihuahua, in that hotel room where they'd made love for the last time. Tamazula was opening the door and stepping towards them in slow motion. He had Katia by the hand, and he was smiling: "Your plane is taking off in an hour. There's barely enough time to catch it. My car is waiting downstairs. We'll drop you off at the airport."

Juliette seemed happy: "See, the nightmare is over. I knew Mister Tamazula was a good man. We're headed back to Paris."

He held his hand out to her and snaked his arm around her neck. Tamazula's face twisted into a rictus then and he let out a shriek. Juliette's eyes were two black hollows. Her breath reeked. Theo's hands were sinking into the rotting flesh of her shoulders. He released his hands to shield his face from her grip, taking strips of flesh along as he moved…

186

He woke up with a start. Sunlight was flooding into his cell. His legs were touching the ground, but his chest was stretched out on its side on the bed. The snick of a lock made him straighten up; the door opened to reveal Garroni.

"Well now, chucklehead. Glad you got a lie-in? It's nine o'clock. Bet that's a surprise, eh?"

The sergeant entered the room, leaving the door open behind him.

"But you're already dressed," he noted. "A few weeks' training and you've already gotten into a soldier's habits! I have a surprise for you."

An Asian guy appeared behind Garroni, someone Theo recognized as being a part of the elite section. He was holding a platter covered with aluminum foil.

"Breakfast in bed, Collin. Even the officers aren't treated to that. Colonel's orders."

"I don't want any," spat Theo.

"Oh, but wait. There's no strings attached. It's free, you can gobble up your fill, there's no obligation."

Theo threw the sergeant a suspicious look, then extended it to the Asian and to the platter. Tran was staring at him intently. He bunched up the aluminum and placed the spread next to him on the bed. There was a cup brimming with steaming, decidedly dark coffee, a plateful of sliced bread, a pot of honey, and some butter. Tran bowed his head imperceptibly and took his leave.

"Why?" asked Theo.

"Eat. You can ask your questions after."

He hesitated some more, then grabbed the coffee and drank it down in long draughts that burned his tongue. He devoured the sandwiches. This wasn't the usual tasteless bread, but an eggy, golden sort of dough that he'd forgotten the taste and even existence of.

In a scant few minutes, he finished his meal. Standing against the wall, Garroni watched him eat, face devoid of expression.

Theo set the platter on the ground.

"The colonel is going to pay you a visit," said Garroni. "He's very happy with your training; he wanted to reward you with several hours' rest."

"I don't need his rewards," Theo retorted dryly.

"Come now," went Garroni. "Take life as it comes. You've got a full stomach, you've gotten some rest. Goes to show you, life could be sweet for you once more."

"Oh yeah, and how's that?"

Garroni shrugged his shoulders.

"Today, I'm not asking anything of you. The colonel will come see you in a couple hours. That gives you the time to catch a bit more sleep."

He closed the door behind him and vanished down the hallway.

The colonel slid silently inside his cell. Theo had dozed off, but his instincts warned him of a foreign presence at his side. He leapt off the bed in one move.

"Stay seated," said Meyrek.

He swept a gaze over the room.

"Not too comfortable," he noted. "But after a day spent training, all you need is a bed."

"Have you come to bring my wife and daughter back to life?"

Meyrek watched him without responding.

"…If not, there's no need for you to be here," Theo went on. "I have nothing to say to you, nothing to give you. Your men are seeing to me; spare me your presence, at least."

Meyrek stepped closer to the window. The most unfettered landscape in the world stretched out beyond the bars.

"You're still blaming me for their deaths," he said in an utterly bland voice. "You're refusing to admit it was an accident. It could have happened anywhere in France, while you were driving. But it happened right when you lost control of yourself, when you gave in to panic. You take me for a maniac, don't you?"

He gave Theo his back, contemplating the vista offered by the mountain peaks melting into the wintry mist. His standard issue sidearm was swinging from his hip. Three feet, if that, stood between the two men. Theo stiffened. A plain strap fastened with a snap secured the gun. All he needed was a split second. One leap, one coordinated gesture…

The colonel turned around. He caught Theo's gaze and smiled.

"That would be too easy," he said, laying a hand on his holster. "You want it?"

Discouraged, Theo lightly shook his head, and blew out the breath he'd been holding.

"Collin, I need you," the colonel went on. "And I've decided to explain what I expect from you. You have the right to know why you're here and what we're planning."

"I know what you're planning," retorted Theo. "I'm not interested in the way you intend to use me."

"That so?" went Meyrek. "What exactly do you know about the base? The things you pieced together from Tamazula's obscure revelations? The slight information I've been able to give you, coupled with the things you've seen every day and some fragments of conversation here and there.

"What conclusions have you reached? Do you know our true purpose, our objectives, the end goal of all this? Look at me, Collin, and listen carefully…"

"You're the one who's going to listen to me," broke in Theo in a choked voice. "Even if you gave me back my freedom, my life, right this second, that wouldn't bring either my wife or my daughter back to life. You can keep your confidences."

"You're right. Nothing is going to bring them back to life. Not what I'm going to disclose to you, not your hatred, not your tenacious resistance. However, the things I'm offering you may manage to replace what you've lost…

"Everything you've ever dreamed of, your fantasies and your dreams of power, can become a reality. Where are your urbanite stresses and worries

188

today? In a matter of weeks, Collin – a drop in the bucket of your existence! – you've become a new man. A soldier!"

Theo clenched his fists as tight as he could.

"And you, Meyrek, are sick. Fit for the asylum."

The colonel went on as though he hadn't heard him.

"Your wife, your daughter? Nothing would have happened to them if you'd shown the slightest hint you'd be cooperating after you met the Mexican. But you ran. Like a coward.

"Do you think I'd have run the risk of disclosing everything to you while you were still in a position to turn us in?"

He suddenly cut himself off and trailed a worried gaze over the room.

"Good God! This room reeks!"

"Where do you think I take a leak at night, out the window?"

Meyrek crossed the minuscule cell and pounded on the door.

"I've made up my mind to talk to you, and you will listen to me one way or another. But there's nothing keeping us in here."

Theo took the wheel of the SUV. Seated to his right, the colonel snapped his gun out of its holster just as the vehicle started forward, and, in a sharp motion, slid a magazine in. The base seemed deserted. Several guards were positioned near the weapons locker, the computer center, and the garage. Motionless.

The Humvee crossed the yard and sped past two guard posts before passing the main gate. The officer on watch signaled for them to slow down, briefly examined the inside of the vehicle, and smartly snapped into an obsequious salute.

"I'll be gone for a few hours," said Meyrek.

"Is everything all right, colonel?" asked the officer, concerned about Theo's presence in the SUV.

"All clear," replied Meyrek. And he signaled for Theo to move forward.

Theo focused all his attention on veering the Humvee as it jolted across the rocky terrain. The landscape was a curious mixture of tropical greenery and arid sprawl, rocks, and prairie grass. Here and there, the path – though it would have more aptly been named a trail – vanished, broken by fallen masses of rocks caused by the recent rain. Candelabra cactuses bearing almost human shapes occasionally clustered together in motionless herds.

"I like this plateau," noted Meyrek. "We're lost in the middle of an area the size of Italy, barely populated by a couple thousand Indians. Must be among the poorest people in the world. Have you ever heard of the Tarahumaras?"

Theo was vaguely aware of this tribe, this people rather, who were famous for cultivating a hallucinogenic mushroom that they consumed during their religious rituals.

"Peyote is more of a cactus than a mushroom," Meyrek went on. "Only their witch doctors are allowed to use it. But the Tarahumaras are also the fastest runners in the world. They say they hunt hares barehanded and race faster than their prey.

"The air in these areas is very rich in oxygen. Didn't you find it funny, that you were suddenly able to run – you?"

Theo barely avoided a deeper rut, one that would have undoubtedly flipped them over. He fishtailed across a dozen feet before he regained control of the vehicle.

"We're almost there," said Meyrek. "Someplace we can talk in peace. Here, pull over right there."

He'd pointed to a bank overlooking the trail, over on their right. Over on the other side, the plateau seemed to descend, only to disappear abruptly, bisected by a crack they couldn't guess the depth of from inside the car.

"Here's how this is going to play out," said Meyrek. "You're going to listen without interrupting, and you won't try to get away. If you try to run, I'll put a bullet in your leg. It hurts like a mother, but you'll be able to start training again in a month.

"There's beer and sandwiches in the back. Help yourself. We can stay in the car, take a seat with our legs hanging over the ledge, at the edge of the ravine, or settle in on the other side of the embankment, with a magnificent view of the huge camouflage netting that covers the pasteboard town."

"The what?"

"A full-scale urban setting intended for simulation drills. What's your pick?"

Theo lifted his shoulders.

"We can stay here."

"Very well!"

Meyrek pulled his gun from its holster once more and placed it on his knees, his hand carelessly brushing against the grip.

"This whole entire plateau is ours," he began. "It has no name, and it was bought from the Mexican government six years ago under the cover of "scientific testing." We're at an altitude of nearly four thousand feet.

"The unique thing about this plateau is that it's cut off from the rest of the world by a ravine a thousand feet deep. At its bottom, there's a *rio*. We're close to that side now. The other access point is cut off by a desert area stretching across dozens of miles. We don't own that, but who would want to?

"That's where the deserters usually try to take off. The chopper finds them in a few hours. It's the only area where even the Tarahumaras have never lived. And that concludes our geography lesson."

"That also concludes our dissuasion lesson."

The colonel adopted a mocking air.

"Not really. Dissuade you from what? Running? Where would you go, Collin?"

A strangely multicolored bird had landed on the hood of the car, letting out sounds that were more croaks than chirps.

"An army with no flag, no name, no nation… That must seem like a paradox to you?" Meyrek went on. "A man becoming a mercenary must seem kind of insane to you… And yet."

190

He raised his sidearm, aimed at the bird, eyes squinted, arm stretched out, elbow locked, then he turned the barrel to peer inside, before suddenly shoving the gun in the holster.

Theo opened the car door, persuaded the colonel was about to grab his gun again, but the latter did nothing. He let himself drop to the ground and moved a couple steps towards the ledge. A slight wind stirred the sparse, dry shrubs. The sky was a washed-out blue. *Walk. Just walk…*

"Just look out for the snakes," called Meyrek.

"The snakes?" Theo grimaced. "You kidding? They're old buddies, by now."

"Collin!"

Meyrek took a leap out of the SUV. He caught up to him in a couple steps and grabbed him by the arm.

"I know you hate me. I know, given the slightest opportunity, you'd be capable of sacrificing your life simply to have the satisfaction of killing me. Am I right?"

"Your gift for psychology astounds me." Theo snickered.

"Pure hatred, the kind that would drive you to suicide, doesn't that ring a particular bell?" The colonel yanked off his cap, baring a head as smooth as the back of his hand. He wiped a few beads of sweat with the back of his sleeve.

"Do you know what motivated Japanese kamikaze? Their families were taken hostage. Their tanks only just had enough fuel to get them to their targets. But at the last moment, right as they were bearing down on their targets, it wasn't fear for their families, and it wasn't an awareness of this absurd fate that sent them careening into American ships.

"It was hate! A towering, senseless hatred, the result of years of brainwashing that made their God-Emperor the sole target of their worship."

"And where are you in this picture?" Theo didn't let up on the irony.

"Enemy and Emperor at once," retorted Meyrek without batting an eye. "And who even could have guessed that another civilization would adopt the same MO? The kamikaze launched themselves at military targets. In some way, they were admirable…

"But imagine the level of hatred, of destructive rage, of ignorance that you need to reach in order to wrap yourself up in explosives and go blow yourself up in the middle of a marketplace or in a club filled with kids."

The colonel pinned Theo's gaze with his own.

"Do you hate me to that extent?" he asked. "I don't believe you do."

Theo held his gaze.

"You are a military target, *colonel.* You're not a bus filled with women and children."

"That's not even the question anymore." Meyrek sighed. "Your level of hatred is that of a good soldier. Despite everything we've been putting you through, you've remained civilized. Isn't that thrilling?"

Theo watched the colonel for a few moments. This man embodied everything he'd ever hated. Violence. Brigading. Brutal, unjust force. He was directly responsible for the deaths of his wife and daughter, and for his absurd, agony-filled, desperate fate.

And yet, despite himself, he probed that grey area he felt lurking in the very depths of his soul. Did he hate him to literal death? Something inside him snapped instantly shut, refusing to answer. He was left with that question, frustrated and surprised.

"I'm French, just like you," Meyrek went on. "That doesn't mean much here, does it? I enlisted young, driven by sheer patriotism – don't make that face, I'm being serious!

"I believed in the greatness not just of France, but of the West as well. I was proud of our civilization. By enlisting, I was becoming a defender of the free world… So disillusioning!"

He sighed; his gaze went unfocussed.

"The Suez Crisis, in 1956, my own CO was there. An Arab dictator under Soviet protection took it upon himself to nationalize one of the masterpieces of Western engineering.

"The operation they devised was going to return the canal to us in under a week. And then there went Nasser, off mewling to the Russians, and in a few days our victory turned into a fiasco. Our first defeat after the war…

"Pay attention to all the nationalist or separatist movements throughout the Arab world. Behind them, virulent, insidious, omnipresent, Islamism and its propaganda machinery, ready to get us to believe in the validity of these organizations, while every "freed" country plunges back into obscurantism…

"For decades, Lebanon has been the site of Christian massacres, exploited by the PLO fedayeen, while an Islamist neo-Nazi movement took root in the shadows and then became more and more powerful.

"And now look at the European attitudes towards Hezbollah! Behold the deer-in-headlights fear that our world shows in the face of the outrageous statements made by the Iranian president!

"On one hand, you've got oil in the hands of dictators, and whole peoples howling out their suffering and their hatred of the West; while on the other hand, the leaders of our countries grovel like bitches in heat for a few drops of gas!"

Meyrek's forehead had become covered in sweat. Each of his phrases had been emphasized by his right fist hammering into the open palm of his left hand.

"The army, the guarantor of our institutions, has lost in advance so long as it's accountable to politicians," finished Meyrek. "That's why I joined this unit!"

Theo shook his head, his expression blank, worn out inside. How do you fully hate a man who talks to you, who tries to persuade you? He wanted to run, to tear off out of there and get as far away as he could from the colonel's voice and the fascinated feeling it seemed to be sparking inside him.

That was it: Meyrek was hypnotizing him. He was playing both parts of the good cop-bad cop bit, switching between characters to gradually weaken him. Theo struggled against the beginnings of an idea. In a world taken over by absurdity, why not behave absurdly? What if he gave in, right now? What if he just up and became the colonel's pet?

After all, what was there left of him, of the man he used to be? By obliterating his family, the Organization had uprooted him, ripped him from his foundations. What was there left of his personality, inside this bulging, muscled body that wasn't even his own anymore? He gave himself a stinging mental slap.

"This unit? You mean this sorry bunch of screwballs? And you'll make them into what? The phantom army of democracy?"

Smiling, Meyrek shook his head.

"Cells," he replied. "Independent, they'll be a force to be reckoned with. All it took was a handful of properly motivated men to change the course of history, on September eleventh.

"Terror cells are dormant cancers. But oncologists have long understood that the best way to fight an internal threat is to give the body's immune system a boost. Cells versus cells. We're not the disease, Collin, we're the cure!"

Very high up in the sky, a jet was drawing a white line as straight as a ruler, its edge fanning into a plume.

"We went from Hitler to Stalin and from Stalin to Khomeini," Meyrek went on, firing up suddenly… "And the threat is still there! Kim Jong Il? Ahmadinejad? Bin Laden? Imad Mughniya? How many assholes get let loose and granted political asylum they make their own and still get to do what they want after?

"They're part of the deal, untouchable, and they're able to steer their way through both worlds. A few years of sponsored killings, then a smattering of politics to buy themselves some respectability, and they'll even end up getting the Nobel Peace Prize, like Arafat. What a travesty!

"They've opened war on us. A merciless, borderless, completely clandestine war, one that can strike anywhere, at any time, provided it gets them some media coverage. They consider every individual, whether civilian or military, to be an enemy. And our governments can't counter it in any way other than through a legal system that's hobbled by a whole web of humanitarian laws that these fanatics shield themselves behind and use to grow.

"In a war of this nature, this kind of asymmetrical war, our only hope is to create a force that's similar to theirs. An army of outcasts… And it's this army, Collin, that's in the process of being born. Right here."

He swept a wide gesture over the landscape, then pierced Theo with a deep, sharp gaze. The latter tried in vain to make out a spark of madness in those dark orbs made pinpricks by the light.

"Do you see, now? Do you see why, if somebody like let's say Ahmadinejad was our primary target, I'd need a sharpshooter that wouldn't show up in the records of any secret agencies! And a French sharpshooter, what's more!"

Looking disgusted, Theo shook his head.

"You're no better than them," he breathed through gritted teeth.

"Come on, Collin," snickered the colonel, "you yourself are better than a lame line like that."

Theo suddenly felt hugely weary. His own rebellion was worth about as much as parlor talk. And besides, what could he do, relying on himself in the middle of a landslide-wrecked desert, far removed from any civilization, aside from sticking to making jibes about an insane project? Even if he managed to grab the colonel's weapon, to neutralize him, he'd never make it to a town, a police station, an embassy, a newspaper office where he might reveal this terrifying secret.

'Was it even a secret?' Theo asked himself, stunned to feel so little outrage. Meyrek was right about one thing. On base, he had learned to care about his own survival. His survival ahead of everything. The world could give itself up to any and all forms of injustice and destruction. Nothing new there. He'd already paid that price.

Swiftly, the colonel changed tack. He grabbed Theo by the shoulder and used all his strength to pull his face close to his own.

"I haven't driven you out here to persuade you," he said in a tone of voice that was no longer even in the neighborhood of affable. "I've been patiently waiting these last six months, and I'm under no delusions! But look down there, and look closely: that's your new training ground."

As suddenly as he'd seized him, he let go of Theo and reached the Humvee in one sprightly step. From inside, he grabbed a radio receiver and adjusted the channels, not taking his eyes off Theo.

"Garroni? Ready your men. Showtime!"

On the other side of the slope, a gigantic camouflage net, some fifty feet high, scored the azure skies, supported by pillars resembling electricity poles. The sight was impressive, soaring from nowhere like a movie set crisscrossed with lights and shadows, in the middle of a clearing leveled by bulldozers and zeal.

In a couple strides, the two men found themselves on an unpaved street lined with buildings put up hastily and without a thought for authenticity. There was a hotel – complete with fake windows and fake pool; a movie theater with the register painted right on the wood paneling; a barber shop; a couple homes; two storefronts; one bar that even a drunkard wouldn't have thought a mirage. Each set piece was made up like a hideout and a snare at the same time.

All of a sudden, Theo found himself surrounded by several men wearing BDUs. He instantly recognized Garroni's section. The man in question came down the middle of the street in turn and stepped in front of Meyrek with a smart salute.

"My men have their orders, colonel."

"Very good. I'm entrusting Collin to you."

He turned to him, looking amused.

"Now this is the final phase of your training. A life for a life. We're going to find out just how much you care about yours…" Then, to Garroni, "I'm headed back to the embankment; see to it there's no stray bullets in this sector."

"Well, Collin," growled Garroni with a mocking laugh, "feeling rested? I hope you'll like this new game."

Theo curled in on himself, wracked by a shiver. The faces around him were as tense as they were closed off. The mercenaries were looking at him like he was a strange animal, all devoid of compassion. The barrels of their weapons were pointing towards the ground, in that nonchalant way typical to hunters.

"This town setting is an arena," explained Garroni. "Usually, the sections face off in two or more opposing sides. It's the exercise we call "urban guerilla." Obviously, the weapons are loaded with blanks."

Garroni signaled two of his men. They stepped away and disappeared around the corner from the bar, which stood opposite a bridal boutique.

"Today," Garroni went on, "the exercise is gonna go a little differently. First off, only two men are gonna be facing off. And guess who that second one will be, Collin?"

A grimace split the sergeant's face. The soldiers reappeared from inside the bar, dragging a giant of a black man whose wrists were handcuffed together.

Garroni turned their way.

"Meet your opponent: Will Bordez. An excellent member of the elite section, up until yesterday. This moron tried to break out tonight, and he was caught behind the wheel of a 4WD he'd just hotwired.

"On the base, any and all escape attempts are punishable by death. But, thanks to you, he's been given a second chance."

Garroni stepped close enough to Theo for his breath to wash over him. He lowered his voice and went on in a menacing tone:

"The colonel wants you shooting, and this is the last time he'll be providing an opportunity for you. We'll be handing Will there a .50-cal, his very favorite weapon, along with a sixty-round mag, of which every fifth round will be a tracer.

"His one shot at getting out alive is if he nails you. He's been promised that his death sentence will be commuted to a month in the SHU if he took on this duel. He's incredibly well trained, he's twice your size, and he's only got one thing in mind: to kill you so he can live!"

He stepped back, grabbed a rifle that one of his men was holding out for him, and handed it to Theo.

"And here's your slingshot, David," he said mockingly. "Heckler & Koch PSG1 with 7.62 NATO rounds. Ya see, we're not messing with you.

"One bullet only, but this weapon is incredibly accurate. Your one shot is to carry out his death sentence. In other words: take him down before he takes you down."

Theo grabbed the rifle, trembling with rage. Garroni and his men departed, leaving the town in small clusters. Two of them uncuffed Bordez and handed him the terrifying machine gun, a slightly old-fashioned piece of hardware that nevertheless still brightened the days of many a Central American *guerrilleros*.

"One more thing," cried Garroni without turning around. "My men will be posted at every one of the town's exit points , and their orders will be to shoot whichever one of you tries to escape. You have thirty seconds to find cover, Collin!"

The town emptied out before the echo of his last phrase died down. Stood in the middle of the street like a very old tree, which he could have almost rivaled in size, Will watched Theo. He was holding his .50-cal like a toy, whereas Theo felt encumbered by the sixteen pounds of his own rifle. The giant's BDUs were covered in dust, and he'd opted for a jungle camo look, soot smears on his cheekbones enhancing the menacing look of him.

Theo stepped close to him.

"I don't want to kill you," he began.

"Yo, man! You heard the sergeant," bellowed the giant in a voice every bit as imposing as his stature. "Take cover, or I'll plug your ass right now." To underscore his words, he tore a burst of gunfire through the air, uncaring of a couple wasted bullets.

The staccato of the machine gun yielded the desired effect. Theo hurtled himself to the ground, rolled over like during training, and got up six feet from the first fake building, which he darted into by crashing through the door.

'A couple seconds' rest,' he thought, heart beating hard enough to burst. *He can only reach me by skirting around me. He'd be too sweet a target if he took the same path I did.'*

He raised his eyes to the roof of the frontage, the back of which was nothing more than a stack of wooden planks, and found a bell tower.

'And I'm in a church, to boot. Just the place to die.'

He picked up a large rock off the ground and threw it as far as he could towards the right, towards the thickets walling off the fake church gardens, then he crawled as quietly as possible towards the next set piece over on his left.

The noise of the rock falling in the shrubbery earned the sinister whistle of spraying gunfire in response. Instantly, the bush got decapitated. Theo reached the second set building. A sort of hacienda with a Spanish-style patio and balcony, the latter of which had a ladder hanging off it.

He suddenly stood up, scaled the wooden rungs in three strides, then grabbed the ladder and lifted it off the ground to leave it lying on the balcony. He tried to center himself.

'He needs to run out of ammo. For every burst, he uses up about eight to twelve rounds. If I keep giving him targets, I'm emptying his clip in five or six turns.

'And then what? Do you kill him in cold blood as soon as he's in range, or do you take him prisoner? What are you playing at? Meyrek has him convicted either way.

'Tomorrow, he'll come up with a new arena, a new challenge, again and again, always with your life as the only stakes.

'I don't want to kill him,' howled Theo inside his own mind, to drown out that voice that was telling him the truth.

He made out Will's figure three yards down. The black giant had caught on to the ruse and was now looking for him in the right direction. If he lifted his gaze, he'd undoubtedly make him out, and would be able to hit him through the balcony floorboards.

Theo straightened up, staking his agility against the bulk of the machine gun. He crossed the balcony at a run, leapt once he reached the edge, and found himself hanging off the front of the second building. Will hefted the .50-cal, aimed, fired right as his body was hanging in mid-air, missing his lower legs by a scant inch. He shot a second time at the piece Theo had been

196

hanging off of, but he had already let himself drop to the ground and was crossing the street to take shelter inside the hotel.

'One bullet. I've only got one bullet in this gun.'

Taking advantage of the time bought to him by the detours that Will took so as not to cross the street without a cover, he crouched low behind the hotel desk to take in his weapon. The breech was oiled. He'd never seen this kind of weapon before.

Four feet long. No tripod. Adjustable parts, to enhance comfort and precision while shooting. Without a doubt the sniper rifle of choice of US SWAT troops, or maybe special units of the German police. Scarily accurate, even from hundreds of yards out.

Of course! Just one bullet. Now or never as far as opportunities to find out if he still had his gift. All of one chance, or his body, shredded by bullets the size of his forefinger, would be rotting away somewhere in the Sierra Madre, without anyone ever knowing what the Collin family had come to…

That thought suddenly transformed his instinctive fear into rage. Katia and Juliette only lived on through him, and he owed it to them to survive. At least for them… only for them…

'Good grief! You gonna make up your mind or what. This guy won't pull any punches.'

Theo did not have the time to answer himself. Rustling alerted him to Will's presence, dangerously close by.

Cautiously, he extricated himself from his improvised hidey-hole and exited the hotel through the front door. No danger of the black giant waiting for him in the street. The bar that Will had been pulled out from a few minutes earlier with his hands handcuffed together seemed like the right place for him to grant himself another couple moments' respite.

'Respite, Theo? To do what?

'Shut up!'

He straightened up and crossed the street with all the speed he was capable of, his stomach churning, his back muscles tense, expecting to be mowed down by bullets at any moment, making him out a fraction of a second too late.

He'd taken shelter inside the garage, trying to get around the final hiding spot where he'd placed Theo. The .50-cal bullets shrieked as they tore through the air, crashed against a billboard boasting the pure flavor of Corona beer, sending it splintering, its shards piercing through the front of the bar with a crash of broken glass.

'Three times. Three times he's shot. He must have used up half his mag.

'Meaningless. One bullet is all it takes to blow your brains out or spill your guts onto the ground.'

He looked around and felt despair overcome him. He'd pictured a true inside of a bar, with tables, chairs, a bar top, and most especially a mirror where he'd be able to watch the street while staying hidden.

The place was empty. Just a few torn posters on the walls to create an ambiance. He needed to get out of there and fast. He heard a click behind him and quivered. Not bothering to turn around, he leapt towards the window, his forearm held out, breaking the glass and hurling himself outside in one and the same move.

Right then, a dozen bullets whistled a streak over his head. He landed on his shoulder, rifle gripped tight in both hands, and rolled forward. Will appeared in the doorway. Theo got up before there was time for him to shoulder the heavy implement once more. A burst of gunfire sprayed the dust a couple inches away from Theo. A second burst followed behind him, tracing his path through the ground.

The window of the bridal boutique was shattered, the torn mannequins flew apart, littering the street with their macabre debris. Theo darted around the corner of the place. He only had the time to cross the street once more, out of breath.

Will reappeared in the entryway of the bar, right behind him.

'The garage. I've gotta be able to hide inside the garage…'

He took a quick peek inside. Empty, just like the bar. Four wood panels painted in an imitation decor. As luck would have it, Will, weighed down by his .50-cal, was not as fast as Theo, despite his strength.

He sped past the garage, rushed in the adjoining alleyway, went around the faux building, and came to a stop before a thornbush hedge. The alleyway was a dead end.

Damn the scrapes! He tried to dive into the bush.

"Stop!"

A rifle pointed at his chest.

"You've stepped beyond the town limit," whispered one of Garroni's men. "Turn back."

Theo turned back. Will was gaining ground, cutting him off from the mouth of the alley. Over on his left, the back of a set piece bristling with nails. He'd need to climb that. Every other way out was blocked. Will noticed him and roared.

Theo sprang towards the palisade, tried to grab a crossbeam, missed, and got his hand impaled. His blood spurted out, sticky, as pain radiated through his arm up to his elbow. Will was only forty yards out. He squared up his legs, calm as could be, placed his machine gun into position, and started shooting once more.

The projectile stream lifted the rocks a couple yards from Theo, slowly edging towards him, bullet by bullet, a red flash briefly brightening the line of fire. Theo turned his gaze toward the bushes: the man hadn't moved, intently watching the scene.

The front was too high. His injured hand was a handicap. No way out! Theo hurled himself to the side, narrowly avoiding the deadly spray that had come level with him, shouldered his rifle, breath seizing.

He blinked his eyes. The black giant's figure seemed to be looming closer, far closer, just like those targets during training, so long ago…

'Shoot, damn it. Shoot. Now. Shoot!'

His finger squeezed the trigger, calmly, slowly. The machine gun bullets were carving a new furrow in his direction. Theo barely felt the shot go off. Forty yards out, a jolt. The .50-cal lifted up vertically, shooting towards the skies of the Sierra Madre, then quieted down. Like an imploding building, Will crumpled backward, his body still contorted from the impact of the bullet that had just struck him.

Then he collapsed.

The scene hadn't lasted three seconds.

Theo looked at his hands, struck dumb. The rifle. The prone body. The soldier still watching him like a circus spectator. He yelled, threw the weapon far as he could, and dropped to his knees.

Silence.

A clamor surged suddenly from the bush to his right, followed by applause. The tumult grew, spreading like an echo, and one by one the soldiers came out of the thickets, the bushes, the boulders behind which they'd taken cover. Theo raised his head, gaze crackling with hatred. At the end of the alleyway, Garroni was approaching his direction. The men had gathered together to cheer him.

'If only I had another bullet, just one other bullet!

'For Garroni? For Meyrek? Or for yourself?'

Then, as though in a dream, he saw the sergeant lean over Will's body, and the man stirred. The giant propped himself up on an elbow, then sat up. Garroni touched his chest.

'I only injured him,' thought Theo in relief.

But Will used one hand to support himself, got up with a stagger, and began applauding as well, to Theo's overwhelming surprise, coming in closer.

"Hey, yo! You gotta slap me five right here, *hijo de maricón!*"

"Right to the heart," cried Garroni. "You put a bullet right through his heart."

Teeth bared in a wide smile, Will ran at Theo, unsnapped his BDU jacket, and uncovered the Kevlar vest that had just saved him from a certain death. He reached him, leaned over him, grabbed him bodily, and lifted him off the ground.

All the men in the section surrounded them, shouting out their joy as though he'd just carried out the most accomplished act of valor.

This was their victory, their way of supporting Theo in spite of him, and especially in spite of Garroni, in spite of Meyrek.

Juan was delivering hard, rapid slaps to Lochlan's shoulder. Huang, stood farther back, was silently nodding his head near Tran, who had picked up the PSG1 and was taking the weapon in with an appreciative gaze. Marcos and Salinas were shouting in Garroni's ear.

"*Eres mi carnal, ahora!*" said Will.

And he kissed him full on the mouth.

Chapter 13

The Learjet 60 belonging to E.C. Tronics landed at La Guardia a good five minutes early. Gregory Cheston immediately made his way out and sighed upon catching sight of the limo already waiting for him at the bottom of the stairs. With sprightly steps, he sidled around the vehicle, outpacing his driver, opened the door, and slid into the backseat.

"Don't apologize, just drive."

He pushed a button and closed the partition.

"Did you have a good trip?" asked Ellen blandly.

"Forty-five minutes do not a trip make. Thank you for coming to welcome me home."

The limousine veered around a security vehicle, slid onto the company car lane, and got on the bypass in seconds. Traffic was heavy around the terminal, but there was a chance they'd avoid the biggest standstills before the Queens Midtown Tunnel.

Cheston settled back in is seat, saddened despite himself by his daughter's presence. He had no idea how Ellen had caught wind of his visit to Washington, but experience had taught him that she had frighteningly easy ways to attain this kind of information. Numerous times in the past, Ellen had taken an unhealthy glee in popping up in her father's life at the most unexpected times. He watched her briefly and instantly caught the change.

"You look tense," whispered Cheston, voice laden with a sort of tenderness. "You sure you're OK?"

"Let's not start playing daddy-daughter time," jeered Ellen instantly. "I imagine you're going to see Feldman…"

Cheston held out a hand, then pulled back. She shot him a brief gaze before shrugging her shoulders.

"I went back to Mount Sinai. They gave me some injections. But I'm having more and more trouble moving my legs and my left arm."

It was as though an ice-cold hand had settled onto Cheston's heart. The disease was progressing. Very soon, his daughter would be fully paralyzed, her joints stiffened by their own chaotic growth.

200

He'd have liked to question her further, but he knew Ellen. Ever since White Cells had come into being, she'd been keeping their relationship strictly professional. In a certain way, he'd wanted it that way. At least, by bringing her in on his project, he'd managed to keep a certain amount of closeness between them.

"And you, did you get a visit too?" she went on, deliberately changing the subject.

Cheston confirmed he had.

"He's no amateur, however there's no trace of him anywhere in the FBI."

"I know. But that doesn't surprise me. He must be a member of a special unit, maybe operating jointly with the IRS."

"No, this whole business doesn't feel like an audit. Or maybe…"

"CIA?" ventured Ellen.

"If that's the case, I'll find out."

A yellow cab had slid close to the limo, and the driver was trying to see through the tinted glass and make out who was inside. The sky was overcast. A greyish drizzle was magnifying the sensation of filth that clung to the borough of Queens like an incurable disease. In the middle of several blocks of colorful, uneven houses, a huge white mosque stood out for a brief moment in the rear window frame.

"They asked me about you," Cheston went on. "But it's Feldman that they care about the most."

"Indirectly, they're after you."

Cheston pushed a button embedded into his armrest. A panel slid out of the console inlaid with precious wood set before him, revealing a miniature desk bearing a computer and some sophisticated electronic hardware. He grabbed a detector from its charger stand and turned it on before gently scanning it along his daughter's body, then his own. At last, propping himself onto one arm, one knee to the floor, he wrapped up his scan by extending it to the cab, not skipping the smallest nook.

"We're clean," he said with a sigh. "I was convinced that Beck guy slipped a bug on me, but I haven't found one anywhere. Apparently, he spared you, too."

A kind of a giggle left Ellen's throat. Cheston couldn't stop himself from closing his eyes. He'd have liked to plug his ears, too. His daughter's laugh was even more repellent to him than her physical appearance.

"At least," she said, "he didn't have the temerity to come near me."

Beck had needed to solve a logistical puzzle that was as ridiculous as it was highly critical. How could an unmarked van be left parked in a strictly residential area for several days, where no vehicle was authorized to idle for more than an hour? For a brief second, he even considered causing a gas leak in an adjoining building, but the presence of a repair van for over 24 hours would have ended up raising red flags.

Once again, the CIA technical services had come up with the solution. A relay transmitter. In the middle of the night, a deliberate surge to a streetlight had led to a limited blackout along a small section of the avenue. Immediately, a CIA team in maintenance worker disguises had rushed to the scene, using a sky lift to install the incredibly powerful relay adjacent to the bulb, roughly level with a certain second story window offering a magnificent view over Central Park.

Just across from Feldman's living room.

The man had long turned his luxury apartment in a veritable bunker. No-one gained access to it with the exception of his handpicked staff, and the case was too time-sensitive to put together a sting operation.

Beck was thus left to rely on the technical prowess of the "James Bond" department, the name derisively bestowed on the CIA's R&D offices, who frequently produced some of the most sophisticated, but likewise some of the most outlandish gadgets. The relay had enabled them to leave the surveillance truck three blocks down, in an area where it wouldn't draw any attention.

"In complete breach of a half-dozen laws!" Beck's boss had pointed out while he authorized the operation. *"If anyone were to find out that the Agency was spying on American soil, many a head will roll."*

"Mine first!" admitted Beck.

Uncomfortably settled inside the surveillance van ever since he'd been notified of Cheston's arrival, he was currently mulling over some other issues.

"And you're certain, positive, that this will work?"

"About as well as Castro's cigar!" retorted the technician, who was seated in front of a control panel worthy of NASA missions. "If it goes belly up, it won't be because of us."

Beck shrugged his shoulders. He didn't get it.

"Castro…" persisted the man, whose laughing eyes betrayed a persistent ability to see the fun side of life. "Sixty-one. The Cuban revolution. It's recent history.

"We were asked to find a way to get rid of said dictator. My own department head – who retired several years ago now – came up with an exploding cigar. Undetectable. It worked like a dream.

"Only, no agent managed to get close enough to Castro. The only thing the Agency could get working was the Bay of Pigs disaster…"

"Don't worry about it," uttered Beck coldly. "I approached the target myself. I'm only wondering how you can hide a microphone inside a piece of paper."

Delighted, the tech guy set his headphones down. Plainly, he'd been eager for the opportunity to reveal his secrets. His plump physique also revealed a lack of exercise that would, in a matter of years, put him on the path of dangerous obesity, earned through vast amounts of fast food gobbled in the sedentary confinement of a multitude of vans like the one they were in now.

"There's no bug hidden in the paper! It's the paper itself that works as a transmitter. Here, lemme walk you through it."

From inside an ultra-slim drawer, he extracted a notebook page similar to the one Beck had handed Cheston a couple days earlier, and he held it out before the lights inside the van.

"See the watermark? Looks like a logo. It's actually an electronic circuit made out of silica gel, a matter that our service has perfected. The gel is conductive, even after it's dried, but it contains no metallic residue. It's undetectable.

"The paper around it acts as a vibrating membrane. Obviously, the sound will be distorted, indiscernible, almost inaudible, but that's where I come in."

The technician turned back to face the screens, where several component diagrams were displayed.

"Before handing you the transmitter mic, we tested it, we analyzed it, and we calculated and digitized its distortions. When the sound reaches us, it's going to resemble some kind of animal growling against a crinkling paper background.

"But as soon as I pass it through my filters, it'll feel like you're standing in the same room as them, seated comfortably in their chair. There's only the scent and taste of cognac that I can't replicate."

"And where does the power come from? Don't you need power to send out a signal?"

A beaming smile splitting his face, the tech guy held his hand out to Beck.

"Touch me. Feel the heat of my hand? Pull back a bit. Still feel it?

"Our bodies are electrical powerplants. It's all about knowing how to harness that energy. As long as your target keeps that piece of paper inside his pocket, the bug will be dormant. But as soon as he holds it between his fingers, it'll be like he stuck a battery to it. That's where Castro's cigar conundrum comes in…"

"Meaning?"

"For it to blow up in his face, we still needed him to light it up and smoke it."

His stays in the Middle East had left Feldman with a marked taste for Oriental art, the styles of which he'd been able to distill and combine into an interior decoration that was simultaneously luxurious, overly busy, and nevertheless harmonious.

The living room, which also served as his office, was lined with light wall hangings with inlaid furniture pieces niched between them, over a sea of Persian rugs in pastel tones. The light inside was given off by a multitude of small cast iron cages set on the furniture or hanging from the ceiling at different heights.

Inside a display case, a collection of daggers with curved blades was showcased by a sophisticated lighting system filtered through multicolored veils. The few paintings hanging on the walls depicted dromedary caravans, veiled women, or desert landscapes.

Simultaneously a museum and Ali Baba's cave, the vast room, with its softened depths, was suggestive of a miniature palace whose *mashrabiya* could have opened onto a palm-lined oasis had the windows not, in actuality, been overlooking Central Park.

In the middle of this bulky yet delicate clutter, it had been arduous in the extreme for Ellen Cheston to navigate her electric wheelchair. As soon as the young woman and her father had arrived, Feldman had dismissed his butler, who was also his bodyguard on occasion, as well as his maid. Foregoing the usual pleasantries, Cheston had dived right into the reasons for his visit.

"I have no idea what triggered this investigation, but I'm certain they couldn't care less about our transfers of funds; that's just false pretenses."

"But I conducted myself with the utmost caution…" protested Feldman, looking troubled. "You know me, Gregory…"

"That's just it. That's what I don't get!"

"The questions had more to do with your travels than with the amounts of money involved," added Ellen. "My father got in touch with the FBI, and they vouchsafed that he was not the object of any ongoing investigation."

Sprawled across silk cushions, Feldman looked like a pasha, despite the western cut of his suit, and his attitude was at complete odds with Gregory Cheston's, who sat stiffly as per usual. He went to the trouble of taking off his glasses and polishing them slowly before replying.

"It's a trap, that's more or less a given. There's no reason for the FBI to go digging through your business, or mine for that matter. As for the IRS, they tend to employ much more frontal methods."

"More frontal…"

Cheston opened his jacket to delve his hand inside in search of his wallet.

"… I have several questions of my own to ask you. And I hope I'll get the answers I need before leaving this place… this… capharnaum! You know I hate wasting a trip, Feldman!"

There was nothing threatening about the tone of Gregory Cheston's voice. Years spent heading his own business empire had taught him to modulate his voice no matter the circumstance. By his reckoning, only the weak needed to raise their voices in order to assert their authority. He opened up his wallet and extracted the torn notebook page that Beck had handed him.

"This here is a list of all your trips. It contains your travels within the US, but also your trips to Europe…"

 Feldman held out a hand, but Cheston kept hold of the piece of paper, not even unfolding it.

"You injure me," murmured Feldman.

Cheston slid a quick peek towards his daughter, who had inched her wheelchair forward with a push of her joystick. He handed her the list.

"I'm injuring you? You yanking my chain?!"

"Not in the least. I am saddened that you would describe my inner sanctum as a capharnaum. I had no idea that fine art left you cold, Gregory…"

"This is it! I'm getting something."

The tech guy suddenly brought his hand up to his headphones, then swiveled towards his monitors to fiddle with his filters and his equalizers.

At first, the sound was nothing more than a fizzle, quickly drowned out by crackling and whistling like those from an old crystal radio. For several moments, things sounded like the old resistance transmissions during World War Two; then, little by little, the sound turned clearer, and a still unidentifiable voice permeated the space inside the van.

"… I had no… prevent… inform…"

Howard Beck instinctively leaned closer to the computer screen, as though he could have gazed through it and inside Feldman's living room.

"Can't we get anything better?"

"Hold on… lemme figure out the right dose… Someone's unfolding the piece of paper. I hope there's a whole bunch of writing on there. You better pray your target isn't done with the paper right away."

Cheston's voice suddenly emerged from the speakers, as clear as a recording.

"I can't make sense of all these stays in London. But more importantly, what did you do to draw attention to yourself?"

Beck's heart was pounding. He practically heard Feldman's sigh.

"I should have known, should have been more cautious when I learned of the accident."

"What accident?"

This time, the voice was female, and even clearer than the two men's. Beck felt hope surge inside him. She must have been the one holding the paper. Ellen Cheston was motion-impaired, she'd have a harder time setting the piece of paper down, and it seemed obvious that she'd keep hold of it until someone else took it from her. He felt his heart soar in admiration for the inventiveness displayed by the Agency's tech engineers.

"A few months ago," Feldman was explaining, *"my contact fell victim to a… complication. His car was found at the bottom of a cliff, close to Dover. He and his three bodyguards were dead. The vehicle burned. The police found nothing that would point to anything other than a mere accident. It roused my suspicions, but…"*

"But you kept up your trips," cut in Cheston. *"After returning from London, you went to Mexico. That same month, you pop up in Riyadh, then Bahrain…"*

Feldman's voice, usually so unctuous, altered in a flash.

"Then Tel Aviv, after a layover in France since there are no direct flights! So what? That's not the issue, Gregory. You know it as well as I do.

"You may have one of the biggest fortunes on the planet, you still need my various networks to covertly move the billions of dollars that you need to finance your project. The question remains: who are they, and what do they know? Who is trying to wield this fine-tooth comb?"

"You didn't answer my question," said Cheston. *"Now I need to know who your contacts are."*

"That is entirely out of the question."

"It is, however, a necessity. I'm not going to keep forging ahead blindly, not if one of your blunders has put us in danger."

"Blunders?" Feldman snickered. *"I have been facilitating interests like yours for twenty years now. Do you truly believe that I still fall prey to blunders? If anything has transpired, and we are hardly yet sure of that, there is absolutely no way that it came from me."*

"Feldman" – Ellen's voice – *"my father put his complete trust in you to find the additional funds we need. Who have you been trying to sell White Cells to?"*

Silence. Then, as though mollified, Feldman's voice once more.

"I did what you asked me to do, and you were right about one thing. Your experimental project has been blowing through all the projections and emptied out all your slush funds.

"Without outside money, you'll never be able to maintain the additional camps being built. You know I was against that, Gregory. We've argued over the matter often enough…"

"Whose?" broke in Cheston.

"Who else but the Saudis? I look for money where money there is!"

A crinkle followed by a piercing whistle forced the tech guy to rip the headphones from his ears. He turned towards Beck, a pained expression on his face.

"She must have gotten pissed off and bunched up the paper before dropping it. There's nothing else I can do."

Beck kept on gazing blankly ahead. He was ashen.

The lights blinked a first time. The children rushed to their beds and pulled the blankets down over their chilled little chests. At night, temperatures fell below fifty degrees.

The soldier on guard duty slowly made his way along the corridor separating the rows of beds, gaze scanning over the face of each child, their hands placed on the edge of the coarse canvas sheets.

The hygiene instructions were most strict. In the beginning, the children who had forgotten – or forgone – washing before going to bed had been locked in the freezing shower room until dawn.

At random, the night guard lifted a blanket and checked the state of the occupant's feet. Cleanliness had quickly become part of these children's daily habits, despite that most of them – little *peones* from too-large families, orphans, fugitives from overcrowded countries – had never been around bathrooms, or even running water.

His final inspection completed in silence, the soldier closed the dorm door behind him and turned the key once. He made his way to his own room, within hearing distance of the children, locked himself in in turn, and slumped down onto his cot with a bottle of mezcal and an old *People* magazine that was half confetti from being leafed through so much.

Eliane waited for the printer to spit out the last page of the report she'd just typed out. Typing was not normally part of her duties, and she could have contented herself with handing her rough drafts to her aide de camp. But, strangely enough, this represented her time to unwind. The opportunity to get back to some of her activities from when she was young.

206

She grabbed the sheaves, settled comfortably into her rough armchair, and rechecked the final corrections. It was getting late. Eliane could feel her eyelids getting heavy and a sweet and welcome languor overcome her. She wouldn't be remiss in granting herself a small couple hours' rest, even fully dressed, before her final inspection of the dorms…

It started off as a murmur that no-one seemed to hear. In the dark, noise carried far, and it paid off to be careful. The whispering picked back up, more distinct.

"Shush, be quiet," retorted a reedy voice. "I heard you."

"So, shall we go? Now?"

"Five more minutes."

A little shape slid outside the blankets, made its way to the neighboring bed on hands and knees.

"Are we waking Rosa?" insisted the barefooted little boy.

"She's not sleeping," retorted his buddy, still bundled up between his sheets. "Five more minutes, I said."

"Well I'm going to see Rosa."

"Fine, go then. But be careful."

The moon was waning. The stars appeared so close, in this area so remote from all pollution, that they swaddled all shapes in a fluorescent blanket, like thousands of fireflies. The child crossed the huge dorm, still on hands and knees, to reach the girls' section, separated by a screen.

"Rosa? You sleeping?"

"That you, Luis?"

"When do we go? I'm hungry!"

"Where is Rafael?"

"He says five more minutes. You ready?"

Eyes used to this magical half-shadow, Luis could make out the young girl's features, the white sparkle of her teeth and her impish smile. She folded down her blanket, revealing a tracksuit clinging to her teenaged curves.

"You sleep like this?" went Luis, amazed.

"No, dummy. Only tonight."

A second figure sidled up behind Luis. He got a light tap to his shoulder.

"At least put on your socks," said Rafael. "You'll be cold."

"I have socks," offered Rosa, joining the two boys. "No need to go back to your bed."

She pulled a pair of woolen socks from her bedside table and handed them to Luis. He put them on without a word.

"Do you have the key?" asked Rosa next.

"Don't worry," replied Rafael proudly, patting the pocket of his own tracksuit. "It hasn't left this spot since I pinched it from the guard last night."

"It's a *bolada* he hasn't noticed yet," commented Luis.

"Let's go," said Rosa.

Crawling along, hearts pounding, the three children covered the several yards that separated them from the dorm exit.

"Come on, open it," said Luis impatiently.

"Just a second. Look first, see if the guard isn't on the other side."

Luis stepped up on tippy-toe.

"I can't; it's too high!"

"Let me," said Rosa in an amused but quivering voice. She was a good head taller than the two boys.

"The coast is clear," she stated.

"How can we be sure he isn't hiding behind the wall," asked Luis anxiously.

"We can't be sure, but why would he do that? He doesn't suspect a thing."

Rafael pushed the key into the lock. He took one last look towards the sleeping dorm before turning it once. Two seconds later, the door was open. The three children slipped inside the windowless hallway, and Rafael carefully pulled it shut behind them.

It was almost completely dark.

Rosa leaned over the two boys and whispered in their ear:

"Not one more sound now, not one more word, and we'll hold each-other's hands so we don't get lost. The guard's room is just next door."

"Door's closed," responded Rafael in the same tone of voice. "He must be sleeping."

"You never know," went Rosa. "Quiet, now!"

Like three little ghosts, they snaked through the gloomy tunnel, holding their breaths, their socks rubbing against the concrete with a noise like a night rodent.

The staircase leading them to the exit was only made up of a few steps. As luck had it, there was no guard posted at the building entrance. Hearts pounding, they found themselves out in the open, inside the central courtyard, separated from their target by a twenty-yard stretch of earth.

All the lights were out, but they could see like it was daylight. Luis stepped fully into the courtyard. Rosa nimbly held him back by his sleeve.

"Are you crazy? You forget what they taught us. Don't make a move in the light. We're going to get caught."

Docilely, Luis followed behind his two friends. Luckily, their clothes were dark. They were unnoticeable, so skilled had they become at the art of sneaking around.

"There, that's it," said Rafael.

"The mess!" sighed Luis ecstatically.

"The door is locked, but there is a window at the back that leads right into the kitchen. It's for the smell."

Rosa let out a giggle. Luis clapped his hands in excitement. The sound of boots, still far off, made them freeze.

"Face down," breathed Rosa.

The ground was arid and dusty. Rafael risked a peek over his shoulder. Two soldiers were coming their way, chatting all the while.

"Quick, to the window. They can't see us yet."

They crawled, like they did during training, their movements perfectly in sync, and they vanished around the corner of the building just as the two guards were coming level with it. The children stayed frozen, ears out for the sound of the steps moving farther out.

"We don't have much time," whispered Rosa. "If they ever found our beds empty…"

"The window's open. Let's go."

"It's too high, what do we do?"

"Rafael," ordered Rosa, "get on your knees. Luis and I will climb on your shoulders. Then, we'll pull you up."

"Esta bien," said Rafael.

Their climb occurred without a hitch, and, breathless with nerves, they found themselves inside the "cave" of their dreams: the kitchen! Instantly, Luis hurled himself at a casserole and reemerged with his hands dripping with gravy, which he licked off delightedly.

"Not that," grumbled Rafael. "That's nasty. The real food is in the pantry, behind the cabinets with the pans."

Rosa rushed over first, lithe and graceful, and came to an abrupt stop. She couldn't bite back a disappointed noise.

"It's padlocked! Rafael, it's padlocked!"

"Let me see," said Rafael, gently pushing her aside.

A deadbolt as big as his hand irretrievably cut off their access to the treasures. He rattled the handle, to no avail. The door didn't budge a smidge.

"I'm hungry," said Luis, on the verge of tears.

"Hijo de puta," swore Rafael. "Where's the freezer?"

He looked all around and let out another cry of rage. The cold storage was locked up every bit as tight. They could take all night and still be nowhere close to unlocking them.

"Here," called out Rosa. "I found something."

The two boys made their way to her, trembling with impatience. On her knees behind one of the huge ovens, she was pulling on burlap sacks.

"That's potatoes," uttered Rafael disdainfully. "We're not here for potatoes."

"Hold on," said Rosa. She opened a second sack. "Look, apples!" Before Rafael could hold him back, Luis dipped his hands inside the bag and pulled out two dark red fruit that he delightedly sank his teeth into.

"Oh well," went Rosa. "That's all we could find. Let's fill up our pockets and head back."

"Shut up!" spat Rafael suddenly, voice worried. "I heard a noise."

The three children crouched down once more, keeping an ear out. The kitchens now no longer seemed like a paradise of plenty.

Seen from the ground up, the ovens were gigantic, big enough to fit all three of them inside, like in all those fairytales that their parents had never read to them. Every last nook could hide a monster, a bloodthirsty animal come to steal a meager morsel, just like them.

Stored on their racks, the kitchen knives were so many threatening weapons, the handles of which wouldn't fit in their tiny, exercise-blistered hands. Rosa huddled in closer to Rafael, and Luis sniffled fearfully.

"Let's bolt," said Rafael.

The neon lights all blinked on at once, flashing a glare into the huge room. A key in the lock. The door opened wide.

In a same panicked movement, the children stood up, relinquishing their apples and their sangfroid. Two guards as big as ogres shot them an astonished glance, then rushed their way.

"Freeze!" barked the first of them. Already, Rafael had reached the window and was trying to slip outside. The man nearly slid across the floor, caught himself on the edge of a stove, and practically dove onto the small group. He gripped Rafael's ankle and yanked him in. The second guard came to back him up and barred the children's way. Rafael ceased resisting and was tossed to the ground. Luis was crying bitter tears.

"What do we have here? Three little thieves gone AWOL?"

"How'd they managed to get out?"

"Oh, but I know the girl. Look. It's Rosa. And the big kid, that's Rafael. You, show yourself."

He gripped Luis's arm as he tried to hide behind his friend, and he pulled him as hard as he could. The boy let out a cry.

"You know this one?"

"No, but I've seen him around. What's your name?"

"Luis," the child sobbed.

The guards looked at one-another with a snicker. They seemed gigantic, burly muscles covered with bristling hair, rifles to their shoulders. Their hands looked like pairs of fuzzy tarantulas, and one of them sported a gash from the bridge of the nose to the corner of the lips. Rosa slid a protective arm around Luis's shoulder and pulled him to her.

"Three little thieves just for us," said gash-face with a grimace, laughing harder than ever.

"We were hungry," ventured Rafael in a firm voice. "Luis was on duty tonight, and he didn't even get anything to eat when he sat down at the table."

"What do we do?" asked gash-face, ignoring his interruption. "They need to be taught a lesson. Any ideas?"

The children didn't catch sight of his wink.

"How about we lock them up in an oven, to see what temperature they start to cook?"

"Unless we smear them in jam and bury them behind the toolshed. I saw an anthill around there this afternoon."

"You don't have the right to punish us yourselves," protested Rosa, not taken in. "We only took two apples."

"She's right," said the guard, looking bored. "I vote we toss them in the *rio*. That'll spare us a whole bunch of awkward questions."

"Great idea," affirmed gash-face. "At least that way we'll be sure they won't do it again."

There was a roguish glint in his eyes.

"Three big sneaks try to escape," he went on in a playful tone of voice. "They slip between the surveillance posts, but they go the wrong way in the

210

night. They get lost, and a rock fall drags them to the edge of the cliff. Their bodies break on the rocks…"

Luis let out a cry. The guard pulled him from Rosa's arms and slapped his hand over his mouth. The child's face disappeared altogether behind his fingers. Rosa moaned.

"Why would you hurt us? Assign us chores. We could shine your shoes every morning. Clean your clothes, your toilets, tidy up your rooms…"

Gash-face seemed to give it some thought.

"No, that won't cut it… Unless…"

"Unless?" asked the second guard.

"Go turn off the lights. No need to wake the whole base."

He turned back to Rosa.

"Would you be willing to make a small sacrifice for your friends?"

Trembling, Rosa agreed with a nod of her head. Gash-face was staring intently at the two mounds that her developing breasts pushed into the fabric of her shirt. Instinctively, she pulled her chest in. The neon lights went out.

"You got the key to the pantry?" gash-face asked his accomplice.

"It's on the ring."

"Come over here, you two."

He harshly grabbed Rosa and Rafael by the shoulder, sinking his fingers beneath the collarbone, into the softest and most painful part of the muscle. The second guard seized Luis by the hair.

"If any one of you screams, I'll put his eyes out before tossing him from the cliff. Got that?"

The storeroom door opened to reveal its treasures. Crates full of provisions were stacked up against the walls, all the way to the ceiling. Bags brimming with fruits and vegetables formed a pile at the bottom of a stack of cans. Eyes wide, the children looked in disgust at the mounds of food, their appetite gone. With one shove, they were hurtled inside.

"We can turn the lights on, won't nobody see a thing."

Gash-face grabbed hold of Rafael, squeezed his neck, and began to cruelly bash his head against a wooden crate.

"Now you listen to me good. You and your little friends here are going to shut your mouths. We want to have ourselves a little fun, and if things go right, we'll let you live. We might even slide your little escapade under the rug. You feel me?"

Eyes bulging out of his head, Rafael made a gesture that might have been taken for an agreement. The second guard let out a satisfied grunt.

"Go 'head. I'll watch them."

Gash-face let Rafael go and backhanded him to lend weight to his words. He grabbed Rosa by the collar of her track top and pushed her towards the end of the storeroom, close to the vegetable sacks. In an abrupt movement, he yanked her backwards and pulled roughly on her shirt, tearing it from top to bottom. Rosa let out a cry and crossed her arms to cover her breasts.

The man hurled himself to his knees beside her and violently pulled her arms apart. He rolled himself on top of her to crush her under the weight of his body and he sought out her mouth, biting at her to force her lips open. With both hands, he grabbed the elastic waistband of her pants.

The young girl tried to struggle, she moaned, her vision hazy with tears. Gash-face leapt to the side to avoid getting struck by her knee, yanked all the harder on her waistband, making it give way, tore away her track bottoms and her cotton underwear. Using one hand, he managed to immobilize her, while with the other he delved between her thighs.

At the other end of the pantry, the second guard took in every second of the show, all while keeping watch on the two boys out of the corner of his eye. Powerless and mute, Rafael and Luis could not tear their gazes away from their friend.

Eliane woke up with a start, her forehead covered in sweat. As they did all too often, her dreams had taken her far from Mexico, to her homeland, Lebanon.

She was walking around her parents' garden as a little girl; the sun was shining and the air was fragrant with the scents of jasmine and orange blossom. Her father was calling out to her from the porch and she was running to him, happy to see him again like after a long time away. He was beckoning her inside and stepping away to let her through.

Eliane was opening her eyes wide to get used to the darkness from the closed shutters, taking a step inside, and turning towards her father. The entryway was empty. A huge feeling of anguish would come over her then. She was no longer willing to look inside the room, but something compelled her to it. She would then lower her gaze, and find her father's body on the floor, prone in a pool of his blood, throat slit from one side to the other, holding her younger sister by the hand while her little belly…

Eliane got up in search of a glass of water. Her watch showed it was one in the morning. She'd left her desk lamp on and had stretched out on the bed fully dressed, having only taken her boots off.

She had fled her village, empty of all its Christian inhabitants, then Beirut, then Lebanon. She had left her uncle's home, departed from France, knowing the memory of that night would never leave her, merely hoping that her exhausted body would occasionally grant her the respite of a dreamless night. And the nightmares had grown farther apart, had turned less accurate, blending her current life and her memories from Lebanon… But tonight, her ghosts had come back full force.

Eliane found the bottle of sparkling water set on the ground by her chair. She brought it up to her mouth and drank long draughts, her face tipped backward, her eyes closed.

Fully awake, now, she recalled she'd gone to sleep before doing her rounds, hesitated for a moment, then slipped her feet into her boots. Before stepping outside, she grabbed her Uzi.

The air was chilly and invigorating. She passed the guard post overlooking the officers' quarters and returned the salute of the two soldiers on duty.

"Nothing to report?"

"All clear, captain. The patrols left an hour ago. They shouldn't be long now."

"No-one reported AWOL?"

"Not a one, captain."

"Thank you. Have a good shift."

She grabbed a flashlight from its spot on the wall and moved away towards the main courtyard. She wasn't obligated to do her rounds, but she liked these nighttime walks, the singular sight of the stars, and that feeling of safety she'd been feeling since her arrival at the base. The tap of the Uzi against her hips added to her reassurance.

Even if she was sometimes overcome with doubt, her solitary walks had the ability to reconcile her with her own morals, bringing her a kind of peace. The world around her was a microcosm of civilization, albeit harsher, more warlike, almost inhuman. Peripheral to all establishes rules.

But there was a goal she still believed in. She felt confusedly as though she was in the right place. She had learned discipline. Long before arriving here and now. Each day that went by removed her farther from her initial thoughts of revenge. Gone were the days of political meetings and ferocious discussions till dawn, between two drinks, in a haze of cigarette smoke.

She wasn't entertaining any delusions about what would come of the agitation on base. The air was altogether very pure, as it must have been when the world was created. And nothing truly evil could come into being so far from civilization. At the very least, she hoped, not as long as she was involved.

She made her jaunty way around the first barracks, the beam from her flashlight trailing carelessly along the hard ground. On the second floor, a stream of light pierced through the half-shut curtains in the guard's room.

For a moment, Eliane thought about paying him a visit, rifling through the attendance book, and making sure none of the children had any issues during their sleep. The previous week, a flu epidemic had torn through the second barracks, occupying every bed in the infirmary and setting back training for an entire section.

Some of the children had had alarmingly high fevers, declining all food for several days, and spasmodically spewing out the few bites of vegetables and broth that the nurse had managed to press on them.

'No, we're certainly not at summer camp,' she repeated to herself, recalling the colonel's words.

But this was a truly beautiful night, and despite the late hour, the mist that usually rose up from the *rio* around dawn seemed to be sparing the clarity of the air for a change.

She gave up on the visit with the guard and allowed her steps to lead her towards the second building. She'd skirt around the outside of the base, keeping along the surrounding wall, and would then make her way back towards her bedroom through the central yard.

She was surprised not to have come across the soldiers out on patrol. But it was a very big base.

Gash-faced slumped to the side with a grunt. Rosa's small body was shaking with tremors. He pushed her back, as if in disgust.

"Hurry it up," he told his accomplice. "We're gonna need to clock out at the post."

"Hey, yo!" grumbled the other man. "You got to take your time. Why don't you go watch the kids."

The mercenary gave a hard pinch to the tip of one of the young girl's breasts, pulled up his pants as he stood up, and grabbed a juice box from on top of a crate.

"Hurry it up anyway."

Luis and Rafael were huddled tightly together in the corner of the pantry, close to the door.

"So," said the guard, "how'd you like the show?"

His accomplice had already thrown himself atop Rosa and was trying to flip her over. With an energy born from despair, the young girl swung out her arms and her legs, slipping through his hands like an animal. The man grabbed her by the hair and pulled her towards him, tearing a cry from her throat.

"Stop struggling," he growled, "or I really am gonna hurt you."

He threw her face forward, partially smothering her between the vegetable sacks. With one hand, he secured her wrists behind her back, and with the other, he started unbuttoning his pants.

Gash-face finished his juice box, crushed it between his fingers, and threw it down on the ground. He picked up his rifle from between two crates and leaned over the two boys.

"Now," he said, "I need to make sure you never get it into your heads to tattle about our little party."

He unbuckled his belt then, gripped the buckle in his hand, and took one step towards the two teary-eyed kids.

Eliane was slowly making her way up the alley that bordered the courtyard terreplein. She strode past the infirmary, past the mess, and kept going diagonally, decided this time she'd inspect the dorms before heading off to sleep.

Getting to the center of the courtyard, she dithered, recalling that four children were still abed in the infirmary. There hadn't been time for her to inquire about their health since the day before, and it would be easy to go over their records alone. She wouldn't need to wake the nurse on call up for so small a reason.

Eliane backtracked. As she walked past the mess, she mechanically swung her flashlight beam over the wall of the building, took another couple of steps forward, then froze. Something irregular had just caught her attention. She swept the front of the mess in the opposite direction, paused the beam on the heavy double doors. No question about it, it was cracked open. Maybe the patrol was doing sweeps inside?

She suddenly found it strange that she hadn't crossed paths with the two men during her rounds, when she'd covered the entire length of the camp. The only explanation for that was that they'd returned to the guard post, in which case they'd forgotten to lock up the mess behind them.

She took the keycard out of her pocket, promising herself she'd bring this to the attention of their CO the next morning. Just as she was locking the doors, she had the thought that the two men might very well still be inside. She'd skirted around most of the buildings, and if by some chance the patrol had walked parallel to her, their paths could have crossed without catching sight of each other.

To set her mind at ease, she slipped inside the mess hall, just to make sure. The chairs were set neatly on the tables, legs up, casting distorted images on the walls in the glow of the flashlight. The immense building was empty. No, if the guards had swept the place, they had clearly made their way back to the post already.

She moved between the tables, stopped level with the third row, then made her way back to the door with determined steps.

'The infirmary, a visit to the dorms, and to bed,' she told herself.

The following day was promising to be long and exhausting. Even if she didn't always shadow the sections during training, planning out maneuvers and more to the point setting up a security system was taking up the bulk of her time…

The double doors opened once more to show sky studded with stars and the lights from the guard post a hundred yards out. Eliane found herself outside and slid the key in the lock before pulling the door behind her.

A sort of a muffled cry, like a yelp coming up through a well, stopped her in her tracks. She pricked up her ears, uncertain as to where the call had originated from. Some animal outside the camp, she thought. Some owl species let out an almost human-sounding cry that was enough to turn the blood to ice. But her instincts told her this was no bird. One of the children? The infirmary was too far away, the barracks even more so. No, the cry stemmed from elsewhere.

"The kitchens. I didn't check the kitchens…"

Heart hammering, she pushed against the door, keeping an ear out for a new cry. But there was nothing outside the silence, sliced by the cadence of her steps on the well-waxed flagstones. She switched off her flashlight, slid the safety off her SMG, and waited a few moments for her eyes to get used to the dark.

'Just like in my dream,' she said to herself. And she quickly shoved that thought away. On the tips of her toes, she crossed the mess hall, pushed on the rubber double doors leading to the kitchens, and slid herself against the wall.

She froze, all senses on high alert. No doubt about it, there was someone moaning not more than a couple yards away from her, but through a wall, or… a door. There was something going on in the pantry.

For a second, she thought about calling for backup. But the feel of the submachine gun set her mind at ease once again. This could only be her own men, or maybe a stunt by some of the children. She made her way past the cold storage and noticed light coming from underneath the pantry door.

She made out cries, laughter, and… some kind of hits striking a bag. With a decisive gesture, she turned the doorknob and pulled the door in, her Uzi pointing inside.

Gash-face turned around abruptly, his face frozen in an animalistic grin. At his feet, Rafael and Luis were trying in vain to shield themselves with both hands, curled up like caged animals.

In an instant, Eliane made sense of the scene. At the other end of the storeroom, the second guard was pumping his bare buttocks, too busy working over his prey to notice the young woman's ill-timed arrival. She felt rage wash over her.

"Hey," cried gash-face to his accomplice. "Stop that! We've got company."

The man turned around, his visage caught in a grimace of pleasure. Slowly, the look on his face gave way to surprise. He leapt swiftly off Rosa and tried clumsily to restore his modesty. The young girl collapsed onto the sacks, breath panting, and folded her legs in on herself in a final attempt at decency.

"What are you doing here?" uttered Eliane, voice trembling in indignation.

She was holding her SMG at hip level, the barrel pointed at gash-face's stomach.

"We can explain, captain…" began the man, a beguiling expression in his eyes.

"Like hell," shrieked Eliane. "You, over there, come stand next to your accomplice so you're both in my sight."

She jerked the barrel up threateningly and kept speaking in an even harder, borderline histrionic voice.

"What the hell are you doing with these kids, out in the middle of the night? You're on patrol."

"They're thieves," began the second guard, stepping closer to Eliane. "They snuck out and we've been teaching them a lesson."

"A lesson? Beating twelve-year-old kids with a belt. And the girl? You been teaching her a lesson too? You have any idea what this is gonna get you?"

"Listen, captain," went on gash-face in a gruffer voice. "Sure, we had us a bit of fun. But we didn't mean no harm. Besides, these kids' days are counted. You know it as well as I do…"

"One month in the hole on the main base," broke in Eliane. "I will personally see to it that the colonel awards you the harshest penalty."

Gash-face's mien twisted in anger. He tightened his fist around his belt, all his muscles tense.

"You're not gonna shove us in the hole for this," said his accomplice. "The kids were out here stealing food. They escaped their dorms and we don't even know how. We're not gonna take the rap for them!"

"Hand me your weapons," said Eliane dryly.

The two men shared an incredulous gaze. Rafael took advantage of their inattention to rush towards Rosa. The little girl was hiccupping, her breaths short. He tried to cover her with the shreds of her tracksuit and put a tender arm around her shoulders. Emboldened by a brief, friendly look from Eliane, Luis joined him and began to comfort Rosa in a low voice.

"Look, captain," said gash-face in a rough voice, "you can take care of the kids if you want. After all, that's your job. Now us, we're soldiers. Not nannies. We're gonna head back to the guard post and forget about this whole thing sharpish, sound good?"

"Your weapons," repeated Eliane stonily.

The mercenary lifted his shoulders, readjusted the strap of his rifle, and took a step towards the young woman.

"You gonna let us through now?"

As her sole response, Eliane lowered the barrel of her gun, aimed for the man's thigh, and fired a short burst. There was a lag before the stupefied mercenary felt the pain pierce through him. He tried to grab hold of his leg, lost his balance, and collapsed with a shriek.

"Look what this bitch did to me!"

"Your weapons…" repeated Eliane with the patient tone of a schoolteacher talking to her students.

The second guard rushed to hand her his rifle, looking staggered. He leaned over his injured accomplice and tried to slide the strap off his shoulder. Gash-face seized his wrist and violently shoved him away, grimacing from the pain brought on by his move.

"No way you're listening to this bitch. We're soldiers, damn it! Drag me out of here!"

Eliane racked the slide of her SMG and pointed the short barrel between the prone man's legs.

"If I shoot a second time, you won't ever, ever, even think about feeling like raping a kid."

"Come on, man, don't be an idiot; hand her your weapon."

The second guard had taken on an almost begging tone of voice. He knew that the game was over, and there was nothing scary about a stay at the first base, after all. He looked at the children and merely felt regret that he'd been interrupted a second too soon. At least the other bastard had gotten his fun in. And he'd be doing his month in the hole in the infirmary for sure. A little more than a month, he corrected himself, taking in the state of his leg.

Gash-face groaned and spewed a few more invectives at Eliane. Without any support from his accomplice, he couldn't take any chances. He grudgingly freed his arm from the strap and threw the rifle in the general vicinity of the door. Rosa and the two boys raised admiring faces towards Eliane. From up close, the young woman could have seen the affection in those miens.

"You did what?" choked out Meyrek.

He waited for Eliane to finish explaining, the phone pinned to his ear while he mechanically sectioned the fish he'd been served for breakfast, freshly caught from the *rio*.

"Locking those two soldiers up at the base is out of the question," he responded dryly. "I don't want any of the rank and file from the second camp coming into contact with mine. Only a handful of officers know about the children. If the news were to spread, I could have serious issues with my soldiers."

Eliane tried to object. Meyrek instantly talked over her.

"You're welcome to either establish your own punitive system or wipe the slate clean. After all, the kids did nab the key to their barracks.

"Your role is to maintain order among the recruits, not the volunteers. Next time, they might get it in their heads to steal the key to the weapons stock. That would really put you in hot water."

He listened to Eliane's arguments with half an ear. As far as he was concerned, this interview was over.

Two all-terrain personnel carriers brushed by his window, stirring up clouds of dust. Through the tarp covering the trucks, the curtains of which were pulled down, he made out rows of men in fatigues. *'The lakeside maneuvers,'* he thought to himself. Inside the speaker, the young woman's voice had broken off.

Meyrek followed the convoy with his eyes until it disappeared around the perimeter wall. A Humvee slowed down when it reached the guard post and followed the trail of the trucks, bouncing along the base's poorly paved drives.

"Lock them in the infirmary and have the children make their meals," said the colonel after a silent stretch. "After the kids have pissed in their coffee a half dozen time, they'll learn their lesson."

The fish on his plate was starting to grow cold, and Eliane's tenacity was starting to rankle. There were so many things she was incapable of understanding. Would she have felt this thrill at the mere sight of a few sand-colored vehicles? No, undoubtedly not.

Two of his men had caught a couple children in the act. They'd cut loose and had pushed the envelope a bit. Meyrek knew how long and boring patrols could get, and could imagine the mercenaries' state of mind after six months without leave.

The pay was good! Better than you got from any army in the world. But money was not enough to tide men over for indeterminate lengths of time. And the young woman hadn't hesitated in callously taking her shots. To avenge a teenage girl's virginity! One injured, two soldiers in the brig: captain Khouri was taking ill-advised risks.

"Fine," he said in closing. "I'll send captain Novak over to assess your men. That'll provide you with some official support. But next time, leave your safety on. Or do a better job locking up your kids."

He hung up. What a meandering path the life of this young Lebanese woman had taken, leading her to run the world's least charitable orphanage. Meyrek was seriously starting to hope that he hadn't made an error in judgement…

He swiveled his chair a quarter turn, crossed his legs atop his desk, and mechanically swallowed a few fish morsels, keeping watch on the guards bustling around the gate. The flesh was cold.

"This your first time at the lake?"

The bumps were rattling the men from one uncomfortable position to another, while certain ruts hurled them painfully together.

Old blankets had been thrown onto narrow metal benches, a scant few inches wide, so as to spare the fatigues from rips. Twelve men were seated face forward on either side of the truck, a rifle propped between their legs. The tarp fluttered open at the whims of the wind, and clouds of dust fluttered through inside.

The rumble of the engine, coupled with the slap of the tarps and the hiss of the air streaming over the chassis, muffled all possible conversations. Most of the soldiers were keeping silent, their muscles tensed to keep a semblance of balance, their gazes unfocused. At the deep end of the truck, crowded up against the cab, the two Vietnamese guys screamed jokes at each other while slapping their thigs, under the disapproving glare of a South American who was irate that he couldn't understand anything they were saying.

"Yo, *carnal*? This your first time at the lake?" repeated Will, leaning closer to Collin's ear.

Theo had been left with the worst seat, between the tailgate and the spare wheel. He nodded his head without raising his gaze to the black giant. Even seated, Will was a good head taller than him.

"It's my third time," he yelled to be heard over the noise from the truck. "Ain't nobody like this. Two people have died already. 'S a bitch of a day!"

Theo nodded. Through the opening in the tarp, he distractedly watched the hurtling of the second personnel carrier and, each time there was a gap, he tried to make out the passengers in the Land Rover at the rear of the convoy. He was holding onto the bench with his right hand, his rifle gripped tight between his knees, his other hand, still in pain despite being scarred over, resting on his thigh.

"How come you never talk?" persisted Will. "We ask you questions and you answer, your answer's no. What, you got no other words? You been with us three weeks already, and nobody knows you."

"I've grown disused to it," responded Theo laconically.

The truck swerved suddenly and the men in the left row found themselves thrown into the teammates across from them in an explosion of swearing and laughter. Will was holding on tightly to the chain securing the spare wheel. He shot his free arm out in front of Theo and kept him from landing on his neighbor's knees.

"Thanks."

"Hey, *de nada carnal!*" Will grimaced. "Next time, you'll save my life."

Theo turned suddenly towards the giant, his face shrouded in anger.

"Don't look at me like that," shouted Will to drown out the groan of the gearbox. "It's just an expression at the camp."

From his seat in front of Theo, Juan unveiled teeth yellowed by nicotine, flashing an appreciative smile. He leaned forward.

"Hey Will, you heard about the black guy who fell in love with a female gorilla?"

The giant looked at his huge fingers as if seeing them for the first time. "Naw, but I've heard about the black sausage stuffing a mestizo ass raw."

"Stop bullshitting. You're always first in line to call yourself a nigger…"

"Yo, man, 's aight. Let's hear it. If I don't like it, I'll tell you mine."

Juan swept an impish gaze over each occupant of the APC, drawing it out. "This black dude, he goes on vacation in the jungle, back home in Africa…"

"I was born in San Diego," grumbled Will, not taking his eyes off his huge fingers that he kept fidgeting.

"… and he comes face to face with a gorilla. A female, there's no words to describe…"

Hands shaping curves along his body, cracking up, Juan described the dream figure of a creature overflowing with charms.

"After a week of banging in the forest, he takes her to the airport to bring her home. Only, the customs guys don't let her through. No wild animals on the plane, them's the rules. The black guy, the gorilla, they can't stop crying… You with me, Will?"

A new rut, this one deeper, hurled most of the men towards the back of the truck. Juan carried on as though nothing happened.

"But then our black buddy gets an idea. He goes into a supermarket and buys out their entire makeup aisle, plus a little pink dress, a wig, tights, razorblades…

"The next day, after he's shaved the gorilla from head to toe, he puts the tutu on it, puts the wig on it too, adds a bit of makeup. His heart swells: shorty is smokin'!

"So he rushes to the airport, and this time they let him through. The plane takes off while he and the gorilla are sitting together comfortably and holding hands. That's when the head steward starts making his rounds. He freezes when he comes level with the black dude…"

Juan choked. Will curled the two fingers either side of the middle one, which he brandished while pulling a face.

"…Then the steward rushes over to the captain, and that's when he starts bitching: "Damn it, captain, every time I see a gorgeous Italian honey, she's hooking up with a black guy!""

The giant got up to smack Juan with a slap that would have uprooted a tree. The other section members had lost it, their guffaws booming back and forth like explosions underneath the tarp. Theo couldn't bite back a brief smile before he delved back into his contemplation of their route.

"Your joke is some racist shit," bellowed Will, snickering despite himself. "Hey-yo, man! Ain't no Italian woulda let you off this lightly, you hear me."

The truck driver, comfortably seated behind the wheel, thought it funny to hit the brakes hard, and he threw a delighted glance through the back window of his cab to look at the result of his little prank.

Most of the men had careened into a heap at the front of the truck bed, swearing in a cosmopolitan tangle of languages that would have greatly thickened a slang dictionary. Once again, Will held Theo back.

"Next time, I'll save your life…" uttered Theo to the black giant.

For his part, the driver was already unlatching the tailgate and signaling the men to drop down to the ground. Juan shouted "Go!" and leapt down with a hand pinching his nose.

"…But the first time, I shot you," Theo went on. And he jumped in turn.

"Hey, *carnal!* Take it easy," yelled Will, his gigantic body emerging from the back. He held on to the tarp, swung his legs outward, and reached Theo in one leap.

"I agreed to the exercise," he pleaded, laying a hand on his shoulder. "The only risk I was in was if you were gonna aim for my head. But the sergeant swore to me that you'd shoot center mass."

In a sudden movement, Theo shook off his hold.

"And if I'd missed?"

"Oh, no. I knew you'd aim true. The colonel guaranteed it!"

"That man's word is enough for you to risk your life?"

Will smiled at his astonished attitude.

"I'm a soldier, *carnal*. My first duty is to trust my leaders!"

The second truck had parked right up to the first and was now unloading its cargo of men. Garroni and two NCOs leapt out of the Land Rover. Theo couldn't explain it even to himself, but he was disappointed not to see Meyrek. Before the supervising officers reached them, the thirty-eight soldiers lined up in a single row.

"And that really sits right with you?" persisted Theo.

"Dude, you have no idea," replied Will kindly. "Out here, nobody defies the colonel. Except for the volunteers, sometimes. And even then! It's over the small stuff: what time they get chow, or the leave schedule.

"But never the other recruits. Those guys flap their gums the first day. They refuse to eat, to fall in line. And so Novak selects a couple of them at random. You catch that old rust bucket behind the mess?"

Theo recalled having noticed a rusted old shell dominating a small courtyard close to the swill drainage pipe. It looked like such a natural part of the setting that he'd never questioned it. Nor asked himself why anyone had expended the effort of dragging it all the way there.

"That was another one of the colonel's ideas," went on Will in a lower voice, keeping watch over the noncoms out of the corner of his eye. "To make an example of them, the designated men get locked in the car. The doors get fastened with chains and they're left to stew out in the sun, no food. Just a bit of water to survive.

"Around noon, the inside of the car is like an oven. And they can't move. The windows are covered up with metal sheets, except for one to let the air and the whiff of rot flow in.

"To say nothing of the fact they're forced to shit their pants. After twenty-four hours, you can hear them begging, night and day. You getting the picture here?"

Theo was horrified.

"Not really…"

"When I saw you that first time, I often looked out towards that car, confident I'd see you in there. But every morning, as we were heading out to train, you were in the middle of the courtyard, doing your running…"

Will beamed out a wide smile that showed all his teeth.

"The colonel knows what he's doing!"

"That's for sure," gritted out Theo. "And you, do you know who you're fighting for?"

Across the horizon, the mountains taunted them with their spectacular presence. As though all of nature had rallied to make them grow aware of their misfortune.

The landscape combined the contrast of a thirsty vegetation, combatting a drought that gained ground in patches, with the immutable hugeness of the fatal crests making up those inaccessible peaks. From the depths of the gorge rose plumes of bluish mist, wrapping all shapes in an ethereal light. An ephemeral yet eternal painting that you keep engraved in the deepest corner of your soul.

Their footsteps stirred up a garnet dust, fine like a powder. Overcome by the serenity of the place, the men had slowed their pace, almost fearful of committing a sacrilege by disrupting the silence. Even the birds had gone quiet. For a moment, they had forgotten the colors of their uniforms, and even so far as the rifle propped like an antenna over their shoulders, the butt slapping the small of their back with each step.

Garroni barked. It was like a sudden awakening. Muscles tensed, backs straightened, stogies struck the ground firmly, and the section broke into a run.

"Naptime's over," shouted the sergeant, already at the top of the hill. "Move it, ladies! Get to climbing! Faster!"

In a tight formation, the men were practically jostling each other, their breathing short. Will was first to reach the sergeant, Theo on his heels.

"Faster!" yelled Garroni. "Faster! The other side, no stopping."

Once again, the men saw the huge camouflage netting score the sky. The artificial lake dug into the limestone glittered from in the middle of a large plateau decorated with candelabra cactuses. The incongruity of its existence attested to the presence of human life.

The banks were made out of cement, ruler-straight like the edges of a pool. It had taken weeks of work and two bulldozers to dig it. The pumps drew water from an underground river that streamed out as a waterfall a couple hundred yards away and fed the *rio* at the bottom of the canyon.

The men tore down the steep incline, their rifles pitched up above their heads. They crossed the plateau without regaining their breaths and hurled themselves into the lake, two at a time, one hand holding their weapon above the surface. The water was cold like a Norwegian fjord, and their clothes hampered their movements. The crossing seemed endless. They came out on steady feet onto the other bank – barely a hundred and fifty yards out – where the noncoms were already waiting for them. Dry.

Fatigues clinging to their skin, boots sloshing water, the soldiers fell back into line, trembling from an otherwise lukewarm breeze. The hill obstructed the mountains.

"An excellent exercise to get into shape," proclaimed the sergeant as he stepped around his men at a tranquil pace. "You've come in contact with the water. Your rifles are dry. And now you're freezing your balls off."

Chest held high, he scanned their faces with a carefully calculated gaze, acting the noncom without even realizing it, an almost laughable artifice to him.

"The next phase," he went on in a louder voice, "is trickier and a lot more dangerous. But we have not dug a lake into this goddamn mountain for you to splash around in swimming trunks. The new guys would be wise to perk up their ears."

He looked all around him to make sure they were all listening attentively.

"This training exercise comes to us from the French. Now, no laughing! The Frenchies aren't all surrender monkeys!

"In Paris, GIGN divers train in the Seine river, and they slip in under the barges while holding their breaths. It takes a good minute for a boat of that type to cross over its own length, and as soon as the diver has gone under the hull, there's nothing for him to do but wait to be clear.

"If he panics and tries to resurface too soon, he's in danger of getting knocked on the head by the boat or torn to shreds by the propellers… Catch my drift?"

Most of the soldiers had already gone through this exercise and were only distractedly following Garroni's explanations. Theo and a few others were listening intently, uneasy already.

"Since we lacked the room for a barge," the sergeant went on, "we just took over the concept. At the bottom of the lake, we set up a moving platform weighted with cement. It's ninety feet long and twelve feet wide. At the bottom, we dug in a cage.

"One by one, each of you will dive and get in there. The platform moves. As soon as it's displaced by three feet, it blocks the entrance and won't free it until its ninety feet have been cleared. Between the top of the cage and the platform, there's only enough room to move at a crawl.

"The snag, however, is that the bottom of our "barge" is spiked with very sharp rebar. The propeller, if you will. To move the slab forward, two men pull ropes tied to it from the bank. Depending on their strength, it takes them between sixty and eighty seconds to free the diver.

"Is that understood? Once inside the cage, you stick to the bottom and you hold your breath for the time it takes to see the light of day. Do not panic. If you try to get out before the exercise is over, you're in danger of getting caught in the propeller."

"Will he shut up already so we can get this over with!" whispered the soldier closest to Theo.

"These French guys are sickos," said another.

"Not all of them. We've just got the worst one on our hands!"

"Meyrek, that son of a bitch!"

"You know, what I'd like to see is Meyrek and Garroni buck naked in their goddamn cage, and for me to get to pull on that barge! I'd take my sweet time, that's for sure. Damned if I wouldn't need an hour to free up their goddamn hole."

The soldiers were murmuring almost without moving their lips. Their whispers could hardly be heard more than a yard out. But Theo read a latent revolt in them that went beyond the typical rancor of the rank and file towards their COs.

His name, whispered twice, yanked him from his thoughts. Several rows ahead of him, Will was trying to get his attention. By then, Garroni had already picked a "volunteer" and was walking him to the edge. Two soldiers were untying the rigging of the invisible platform and checking its range of motion.

"Collin," repeated Will, face turned to one side without seeing him. "Listen up. At the bottom of the cage, you get nothing to anchor yourself to. You have to paddle the whole time to make sure you don't float up, and if your ass gets too high you get hooked on the rebar. You hearin' me?"

"Crystal," retorted Theo in the same tone of voice.

"Soon as you hit the bottom, look for a big rock and grab it before throwing yourself into the hole. That'll keep you from needing to paddle and wasting your breath. No-one's gonna see a thing."

Several men caught the advice and shot Will thankful looks. The first diver went into the water. As one, every man there stepped closer to the bank.

Theo was among the last ones to be designated, as the sun was already beginning its descent. His fatigues were dry by the time he got in the water, and the cold sank into him a second time. Before he dove, he shot a quick glance towards the two men tasked with pulling on the "barge."

Another moral of the exercise: during a maneuver, trust your teammates. He felt a wave of reassurance wash over him upon seeing Will at the end of the rope, along with one of the Vietnamese guys. His last vision on dry land was an encouraging grimace from the giant. Lungs filled with air, he plunged down.

The lake wasn't very deep. Barely twelve feet. He shallowly swam the distance separating him from the pit and resurfaced straight up. The underwater world surrounding him was every bit as fake as that making up a swimming pool. He took a second deep breath of air, signaled with one hand, and dove back under.

In a couple strokes, he reached the cage. He checked that the previous divers had left a rock on the bottom and slipped in, letting a few bubbles out. There was just enough room in there for a grown man to crouch.

Theo felt his heartbeat speed up. Fortunately, the rock was heavy enough, and he could be sparing with his movements as well as his oxygen. Above him, the "barge" started moving immediately, slowly. So slowly. He pictured Will, out on the bank, and the Vietnamese guy, muscles bulging with effort, pushing off the loose earth, heels looking for a hold.

In a matter of seconds, the pit was plunged into darkness. Theo started to count. Vague reflections drew arabesque designs on the pool walls, but there was no reference point for tracking the passage of the platform. The water was stagnant in the cage. The "barge" might as well have been motionless.

Theo let a bit of air out of his lungs. Twenty seconds. The platform should have conducted a third of its trek. He'd watched the maneuver thirty times from the bank, holding his breath to practice for the exercise. It had seemed like a short time, then. But he hadn't been shut into this liquid tomb, spikes barring all exit, a wood and concrete mass crawling above his head.

Forty seconds. If the rope were to break now, after all these back-and-forths…

No. The iron bars were only dangerous in motion. If the platform came to a stop, all he'd need to do was slide between the spikes and resurface. But how would he know?

His heart sped up and his lungs started to burn. Sixty seconds out on the bank did not require the same amount of effort. He'd needed to dive, use up his oxygen to reach the bottom. How much longer could he still hold out?

He counted to fifty. Fifty-five. Soon, he should be seeing the light of day. Will was the strongest man there. He could pull the barge all on his own. Just a few more seconds. Theo let out another few bubbles. Sixty-five. Above him, still dark. His temples were starting to throb painfully, and his ears were blocked.

As soon as he'd see light, he'd kick off and shoot towards the surface. Seventy-five. His lungs were close to bursting. Eighty. Theo felt panic overcome him: Will had forsaken him. Never had it taken the platform so long. Ninety. He needed out. Red spots swam before his eyes. Right now. Damn the rebar. Better to die in shreds than to suffocate.

Theo let go of the stone. For a moment, he remained afloat at the same level, then he slowly rose. Ninety-five. A ray of light the width of a hand. Theo struck the platform with his forehead, grabbed the edge, and jerked himself from the pit. He curled up his legs and gave a violent heave towards the surface. His head surged from the water like a buoy and he breathed in an endless gulp of air, coughing all the while.

He breathed out, breathed in again, trying to regulate his breathing. Beneath him, the barge had finished its route, clearing the cage. *'Two seconds off!'* thought Theo.

"I'm sorry, *carnal*," apologized Will. "As soon as you went under, Garroni had me replaced with the second Viet guy. That dude has no bulk. I thought for sure you were gonna be stuck down there."

There was nothing to dry off with, and Theo was trembling head to toe like a leaf.

"This is where I die," he grouched as his teeth rattled. "Of pneumonia."

Garroni had shot him a mocking look as he'd been clambering up the bank, and had instantly busied himself with getting the platform back to its starting position. Twenty-odd men were helping with the maneuver from the other side.

"You want my jacket?" offered Will. "It's almost dry."

"No. I've got a better idea."

Theo winked at the giant, quickly unbuttoned his fatigues, slid his pants down, took off his underpants, and rolled around on the ground.

"The earth is warm," he said before bursting into laughter.

Will looked at him like he'd gone crazy. He then let out a groan and his face lit up. Caked in dust, Theo's body looked like an animal's. He stripped down and hurled himself to the ground in turn.

"Goddamn, that feels good!"

The two men rolled around in the dust while letting out cries of joy. Like puppies after being forced to take a bath. Two yards out, seated on some sort of embankment, Lochlan the Irishman kept throwing an alarmed look their way. Juan, who was pacing around with mincing steps, delivering harsh slaps to his sides, stopped horsing around. Marcos and Salinas were lying on the ground; they sat up, jaws dropping in the same grimace. One by one, each one of the soldiers not taking part in the maneuver got overcome by a laughing fit.

Fatigue jackets and pants piled up on the ground. In a handful of seconds, twenty stark-naked soldiers found themselves covered in dust and dry grass, howling out their happiness at still being alive, on dry land, burrowing into the ground to sprinkle sand and gravel on themselves like waves on a beachfront.

For a few moments, there was nothing more on this side of the plateau, a few yards out from the concrete bank, than a gang of punch-drunk savages.

Nearby, a pile of abandoned rifles.

The change had been palpable.

Whereas the overall organizational framework of the base was similar to that prevalent at grunt, Marine, or Legionnaire training camps, life for Garroni's section was similar to that of actual officers in those same military branches.

If there were bars on the windows to their barracks, their doors nevertheless remained unlocked at night, and they could make their way to a small room set up in the same building, where they could play cards or watch a movie.

They were never on fatigues. Their food was varied and served on plates, the epitome of comfort compared to the two thousand soldiers who needed to stand in line at chow time, a mess tin in hand.

The only thing missing for them was the freedom to communicate with the outside world. And women. They were allowed no contact with the female personnel, as quasi nonexistent as it was.

Theo got no satisfaction from his sudden promotion. He'd held a gun and fired upon a man. But against his will. And he was on tenterhooks waiting for the moment when Meyrek would require a second demonstration of his talent, knowing that the result of this new faceoff would end with him in his cell and the undoubted resumption of his nighttime walks to the outskirts of the "hill."

In the interim, he was trying to make the most of all the daily improvements he was suddenly subject to. Without necessarily getting invested, nor becoming part of their community.

If Meyrek was an adept of the old carrot and stick method, he would soon find himself disappointed. Theo was psychologically ready for new trials.

The days had gone by, and Theo had become an integral part of the section despite himself. The training his group was subject to was comparable to the one undergone by special forces. Pitiless and exhilarating.

Neither Meyrek nor Garroni had tried to take him to the shooting range again. As a matter of fact, the colonel hadn't even visited him again. Apparently, he was contenting himself with this partial victory for now. The demonstration had been made: after fifteen years, the young Frenchman hadn't lost his gift.

So much the better! Theo wasn't admitting defeat. He'd fired that gun in self-defense. Not as a spectator sport.

He had no idea, however, of the impact his body's transformation had had on his personality. And his teammates respected him as much for his tenacity and his refusal to be part of their lives as they did for his unyielding attitude towards them.

He was giving off a new vibe: rage has become strength. And there was a hard, dangerous glint in his eyes that shielded him from the jibes and bad pranks that defined communal living. In a matter of months, Theo had learned to only depend on himself.

But, for the first time, that second when he'd been meant to hurl himself into the frozen water of the lake, he'd felt that sense of reassurance and safety when he'd seen Will's giant figure out on the bank.

That evening, he sought, as per his usual, an isolated seat at one of the mess tables. One of the privileges enjoyed by the section was the right to dine at the same time as the officers, before the bulk of the troops could invade the building.

No sooner had he set his plate down that Will moved towards him. Authoritatively, the black giant settled in at his side. Theo didn't raise his head. Not sparing the giant a glance, he dug into his meal.

"You know," Will told him, "one of these days Meyrek would have found a way to get you to crack. This way, I'm the one who forced you to shoot. Not him."

He held his huge hand out to him.

"You see the crux of the game, *carnal?* You're the winner here."

Theo hesitated, then slowly moved his hand to the giant's. The food, though bland and too spicy, still seemed outstanding.

Chapter 14

Ellen Cheston was in pain. A week ago now, the joint of her left hip had stiffened, and every single move she made caused shooting pains that sometimes tore outright moans from her. As her old family doctor, now deceased, had predicted, her acromegaly had evolved once again, in her thirties.

The disease was a secondary manifestation of a rare cancer of the pituitary gland, programmed into her genes by radiation during the Des Moines incident. Hypertrophic, the gland occasionally gave her neuralgia beyond endurance, and secreted growth hormone in a completely chaotic way. Weakened, Ellen was inoperable, and nothing save the excision of her pituitary gland might have saved her from an inevitable short-term end.

First, the abnormal growth of her joints would leave her completely paralyzed, and then she would die, either from cardiac arrest or by suffocating. There was nothing modern medicine could do for her, and the research financed by her father had only managed to delay the progress of the disease, without truly bringing any hope. It would undoubtedly take at least two more decades to find a cure. But who would want to live twenty more years in her state?

Ellen occupied a world all her own, a world of illusions and built up resentments. Of her childhood, she only had memories of nannies and tutors who had come and gone like so many nurses at a sickbed. Fearful of exposing her to looks from other children, Gregory Cheston had isolated her, believing he was compensating for something as indispensable as human contact through the obsequiousness of a horde of servants, and he had put together an artificial world made all the more flamboyant by his vast fortune.

But how do you enjoy pretty dresses, jewelry, or even 260-foot yachts when you're a monster? Nothing had been able to make the suffering child smile, nor the cynical and irascible teen she'd become before making her way into adulthood like someone hurling themselves into darkness.

Well beyond her physical appearance, there was something more insidious troubling Ellen, something eating away at her soul: as surely as she'd hated every human being shoved into her path since her earliest childhood, she hated her father. There was an additional facet to her loathing for him. After all, was he not effectively responsible for her state? By granting her life, he had created a monster.

The fact that he might be suffering as much as she was, that he'd never sought to remarry, and that she was his only weakness, the focus of all his attention and all his remorse, had long stopped factoring into anything. He himself was often unable to look at her! That was something she would never forgive him for.

She was a sideshow character.

Ellen sometimes wondered whether her father hadn't set up the huge organization they were co-running with the sole intent of bringing her closer to him. Obviously the thought only skimmed the surface of her mind, for only someone who didn't know Gregory Cheston at all would imagine him capable of turning the whole planet on its head, putting the entirety of civilization in danger even, in order to earn himself some scraps of affection. Her father was a monolith. If he had dedicated his life to a cause, it was his own power in a world that he felt getting away from him to the point of wanting to remake it from its foundations.

"White Cells"… Settled in front of her mirror, Ellen snickered. He could have just as well called his project "Monocytes," "Leucocytes," or "Granulocytes." Her own system had never been able to produce any of those cells in ample enough amounts to fight off this disease and the toll it took, which she was right this moment contemplating.

Ellen would long wonder what had been her father's true motives when he'd made her the offer to take part in creating the Organization and to manage several of its elements. Had he once again wanted to make up for his shortcomings? Or was it a way for him to share his power with his sole heir?

…A monster.

After having spent several minutes gazing at herself to the point of nausea, Ellen revved the engine of her electric wheelchair to go back to the huge, Spartan room she used as an office. Just like every morning, she started off by decoding the reports she had coming in from the base. That was one of the conditions she'd set her father: if he wanted her involved, she would have sole stewardship of the high plateau.

With the exception of herself and a few handpicked executives, who else knew the exact location of the training camp? Isolated, camouflaged, protected by the local mafia as the result of a deal that her father had been able to strike with one of the most powerful Mexican cartel bosses, the camp was as nonexistent as a ghost town. An outright challenge for even the most well-informed secret agencies. The protection network that had been put into place stretched the bounds of imagination, and Ellen felt proud to have taken part in its conception.

As for the annex camp…

Seventeen percent of a budget she had the privilege of administering as she saw fit had enabled her to push the bounds of experimentation far beyond her father's megalomaniacal excesses. All she'd needed to do was stir up interest, and she'd garnered both attention and immediate assistance from that Tamazula that Gregory only talked about contemptuously, all too readily forgetting that he'd been the one to recruit him.

Just one power transcended all others…

Or at the very least, that was the principle according to which Ellen's father had consented to surrounding himself with individuals who were indispensable to the underbelly of the world, men like Tamazula, Feldman, and so many others. Hadn't the CIA, during the war, gone so far as to recruit the worst of Sicilian criminals in order to ensure an Allied victory in Italy?

The threat to the free world was today much stronger than it had been during Nazism, and Gregory Cheston's daughter, for whom the world freedom held no meaning at all, knew what alliances to secure in turn to get her victory.

Replicating the enemy's methods and holding a mirror up to him: that was the secret to the Apocalypse!

The report. Meyrek would send her encrypted information, and it took her decryption software a couple seconds to reconstitute the message that a powerful algorithm had scrambled.

Ellen treated herself to a small cigar, which she lit up before beginning her reading.

According to estimates, the base was meant to enter its operational phase towards the end of the following trimester. The most recent report described an elite unit comprising forty perfectly trained, combat ready men. The bulk of the troops was made up of eight hundred men. Five hundred reservists would take a few additional weeks of training before they had the necessary physical condition.

Lastly, and this was the hurdle, nearly six hundred men were classed as being "limited in ability, recalcitrant, or uncontrollable." Considering Meyrek's disciplinary methods, this didn't leave out much hope as to their future as soldiers.

"What do you intend to do with them?" Ellen had asked during their last talk, three days earlier.

"Send them back home," had retorted Meyrek ambiguously.

"Are you being serious?"

"No. Two hundred of them will remain on base as permanent staff. I've already spotted cooks, hairdressers, a few electricians, and I'm training up nurses. As for the others, I'll need a few extra months, but I'll make something of them."

The provisional outcome, then, was a unit some one thousand, three hundred men strong, equipped with the latest in weaponry and tac gear, same as the most efficient units in all modern armies.

The sections were divided according to specializations and objectives, and were subdivided in turn into groups numbering a handful of men each. *The cells.* A quarter of them was already operational.

Pretty encouraging, considering the origins of most of those men. Already, the base was no longer a training camp, but the command center of a new army. *Assassin cells.*

230

The time had come to test Meyrek's efficiency. Ellen savored the moment as she once again called the Colonel on his secure line.

"Tamazula has run into some trouble with one of his associates. He has stopped transporting certain merchandise that he had exclusive rights to, and is trying to launch his own business.

"The guy has barricaded himself inside his villa in Oaxaca, two hundred and fifty miles south of Mexico City. He's guarded by thirty or so men, and the hacienda is protected electronically. Tamazula asked me when we could be ready."

She relished the brief silence that followed her statement. The colonel's voice grumbled at the other end.

"We're not going to send our men out to get involved in a gang war!"

"Calm down. My father has his reasons for approving the operation. Tamazula managed to find the right arguments to persuade him... And most of your soldiers haven't been through a trial by fire, yet. It's the perfect opportunity to conduct training in a real setting. Trust me, Tamazula is doing us a big favor."

"And if he makes a habit of it?"

"Things have been established clearly. One time only, chalked up to an experiment, and meant to lend him a hand. After all, there would be no base without his protection.

"But don't worry. Your men won't be turning into guns for hire for a Mexican gang. Our objectives are different... Even in Oaxaca."

Ellen didn't need to see the colonel's face to picture the tense line that slashed his forehead when he was confronted with a dilemma. She particularly liked the idea of getting him to cross yet another one of his very particular moral boundaries. Meyrek had his own take on good and evil: he placed all military action that occurred under his command firmly in the former category.

"So what you're asking me is to risk the lives of my men to deal with a small-time local hoodlum? Essentially, you want me joining in with drug trafficking..."

"Essentially," snickered Ellen. "Come now, colonel, it's not that hard. Might as well break yourselves in with small-time criminals. You'll get your shot at the real baddies when you're ready!"

Months spent in a cell had changed Vincent White physically. A lot of his hair, still black as raven's wings a few months ago, had turned grey, while the top of his head was showing signs of an oncoming baldness that was aging him by several years. He held himself stooped, his muscles flabby.

The spirited engineer looked all the weaker since an allergy, undoubtedly caused by nervous stress, had left reddish marks on his forehead and upper lip. The orange prisoner's uniform only highlighted his wan features, and it was at a hobble, with his feet cuffed together, that he dragged himself over to the table where Howard Beck was waiting for him.

"I don't understand. Who are you?"

The gleam that should have been dancing in the Italian's light eyes seemed dimmed forever. Beck moved a hand out towards him, out of pure reflex, then drew it back.

"My name isn't going to mean anything to you at all. Let's just say I'm a friend, and I'm here to help you."

"A friend…" White mustered the strength to snicker. "I've had a lot of friends these past few months. Nobody really ended up helping me."

Two guards were stood behind the wire mesh door. They'd gotten instructions to let the interview go on for as long as the visitor wanted it to.

"White, listen carefully. I'm only here to ask you a few questions. But a deal has already been reached between the FBI, the district attorney, and a… certain foreign government. If everything goes well, you'll be outta here in less than a month."

"If everything goes well…?" A hint of liveliness seemed to suddenly come over White. "Meaning? And why a deal? I didn't even have the right to see a lawyer."

"It's the new procedure when it comes to the war on terror. I'm not saying I agree with it, but placing you in incommunicado detention was completely legal. However, it can't go on any longer. And that's something of a problem."

White chortled.

"I'll bet it's a problem! I get arrested for industrial espionage. My lawyer's gonna swallow his briefcase with all the paperwork in it when he learns I've been placed in secret detention due to Homeland Security regulations."

"That's right!" uttered Beck. "And we wouldn't want a lawyer dying of asphyxiation on our conscience."

White froze. Elbows propped on the table, he peered at Beck from underneath his lashes, clearly wondering if his visitor was being serious or facetious.

"It won't take you long to get the picture, White. Here's the deal. Your arrest happened by the book. You underwent the standard questioning. You enjoyed all the rights guaranteed to you by the Constitution. Are we on the same page so far?"

Vincent White was keeping his eyes squinted, as though the weak light from the neon fixtures overhead was bothering him.

"Now, do you have any idea what was on the thumb drive you had in your possession when you were arrested?"

"I've already answered that question a thousand times. I didn't do this for money. Only for…"

"Rebecca Bruhl? You only did this for Rebecca Bruhl… That's OK, White. It took you a long time before giving up her name, and that's to your credit. She was already long gone by the time you ended up making your confession."

Vincent looked relieved. Beck noticed that a hint of color had come back to his cheeks.

"I only have one last question to ask you, and then, if you would consent to the proceedings, all you'll need to do is wait a few days for your release."

"Go ahead! It won't cost you anything to ask."

"Your work gave us access to a significant volume of technical and logistical information. Among the data that your… friend asked you to copy, is there anything in particular that caught your eye?

"You're a top-level engineer… You've got to have a gut feeling about what's important and what isn't…"

"The umbrella!" whispered White.

"I beg your pardon?"

"The umbrella. That's what we call the satellite imagery jamming program. The algorithm was developed by one of the group's French computer experts. What Rebecca was most interested in was knowing the number of systems being set up, and what their ultimate purpose was."

Beck caught on instantly. Dozens of spy satellites, eighty percent of which belonged to the US, swept the slightest recess of the Earth's surface twenty-four-seven. This surveillance required the processing of millions of data points, and the slightest movement of troops that was out of the norm, the slightest anomaly, would trigger alerts at all intelligence levels in quite a number of countries.

The training camp being financed by Cheston had to be somewhere in North America, and its location was an element that neither the Mossad nor the CIA's action department could be in possession of. It was something that specifically vouchsafed for the proper running of the operation, its founding principle. No surprise that the Mossad had tried at all costs to get its hands on that information as soon as they caught wind of the existence of White Cells.

"One last thing," shot Beck. "The deal explicitly stipulates that you won't be able to stay on American soil once you're out of prison."

White didn't look surprised.

"So you're giving me my freedom in exchange for my keeping quiet… and taking off?"

"Better than that. A new life. But I'm not the one giving it to you."

The blade was getting dangerously close to his throat. The Guatemalan's hand was yanking his forehead back, revealing his jugular and priming it for a fatal slash. His opponent's knee was shoved into the small of his back. Theo grabbed hold of the hand holding the weapon, let himself drop, and tumbled forward, upsetting the Guatemalan's balance in one move and sending him flying over his head to land on his back.

Without letting go of his wrist, he shot back upright, bending one leg to keep his balance, and brushed the side of his hand against the prone man's neck.

"Technically, Marcos, you're dead."

Garroni threw them an appreciative glance and scribbled some points in his notebook. He signaled the next group, who replaced Theo and his opponent on the mat.

"I didn't cut you?" asked Marcos.

"No, but it was a close call. These damn knives are razor-sharp."

Theo stepped away from the practice mat and joined Will by the showers. The black giant had filled up an old plastic bottle with water and was drinking it in huge gulps.

"Damn, man, you're improving," complimented Will once Theo got within reach. "Marcos has six months of training on you."

Theo's response was a shrug before he hurled himself under the spray of the showers. His face reappeared, grimacing from the blast of the water stream.

"Six months? You sure? Are you still able to keep track?"

"And how! I even know the number of days you've spent here so far."

"Well keep that to yourself then!"

An angry outburst arose from the mat, followed by cursing and shouting. One of the men was holding his jaw with one hand and gesturing with the other, shaking his fist at his opponent.

"There goes another dude getting himself sliced open. Amateurs should never be allowed to play with weapons."

Theo held his breath before abruptly turning the hot water faucet, then he forced himself to stay under the burning hot water for a few seconds. He repeated the maneuver, and this time he endured a full, chilled minute under the icy bite of the spray.

Over half the section was still gesticulating around the tatami. In a handful of months, at a rate of three classes a week, most of the men had become martial arts experts. Granted, they lacked anything resembling style. But the mixture of close combat and tae kwan do they'd been taught on the fly had focused on efficiency over acrobatics. Out on the mat, some of them were heavy, ungainly, but their slightest gestures had been honed into a fearsome weapon. They were being taught to kill, not entertain.

Will tossed a towel at Theo, who immediately wrapped it around his waist, trembling, skin reddened by the burning hot stream.

The forced encounter between the two men dated back over three months now, and they'd been inseparable since; their growing friendship was starting to be the only balm to soothe Theo's gaping wounds. The mixture of English and Spanish that comprised the lingo of SoCal gangs sometimes proved incomprehensible, but the two of them took great pleasure in communicating in a jargon that by now included some French slang words.

"Chief, we're headed back to barracks!"

Garroni barely spared Will a glance. Legs apart, hunched in on himself, he was hopping around the mat, closely taking in the combatants' moves. Theo and the black giant stepped out into the blisteringly hot air to head back to their quarters.

"You hear about the Oaxaca mission?" asked Will.

"Yeah, I heard. They're gonna send out twenty men, so five of them will come from our section."

"For that *puerco* Tamazula. At least if they were putting together a strike to smoke his ass. Nobody's been named yet?"

234

"Not as far as I know. But I trust Meyrek to already have people in mind for it. We'll get briefed the day before takeoff."

"You think we'll be in, me and you?"

"No clue. What difference does it make?"

The black giant came closer to him and gave his shoulder a meaty shove.

"Yo, *carnal*! You're not thinking of spending the rest of your days on this damn base! Oaxaca is in the south of Mexico. Me, I've spent two months looking at nothing but the sergeant's mug and these mountains. I'm even more sick of the mountains than of him! In Oaxaca, we'd see us some *chicas*."

Will stretched his full lips in a hungry smile. He brought both hands up to his chest as though to hold up two imaginary breasts.

"*Chicas*," he persisted. "With boobs to here. *Madre mia.* How long's it been since you last seen a *mamacita*?"

Theo opened the barracks door. Three men were playing cards. They grumbled as soon as they felt the wave of hot air he'd just let in. The air conditioning had the same effect on him that the Scottish shower from a few minutes earlier had had.

"Cause you think they'd let us get near any? I can see it now, your little tourist jaunt. Chopper to Chihuahua, private plane to Mexico City, then a twenty-four hour drive down to Oaxaca in a personnel carrier. All heavily guarded, and double the food rations the day before the op, if all goes well. Next, trip right back home."

"And what if we took it?"

"Took what?"

"The *cargo bello*. The midnight express. C'mon, man. We hijack the plane and take off for Belize."

"Stop talking bullshit. We'd get shot down by the Mexican army before we've cleared the Sierra Madre. Besides, who'd you even want to take hostage? The pilot? Tamazula does as he pleases in this country."

"So we take off with the truck and we hide out until they forget all about us…"

"Oh yeah? Where? Acapulco, in some tourist-filled luxury resort?"

"*Hijo de puta, carnal*! You gonna spend the rest of your life training here and waiting for them to ship you out to the front, not knowing who for or why?"

Theo let himself drop down on his bed. The barracks smelled of cold tobacco, dry heat, sweat. He took the water bottle resting on his shelf and took a few deep draughts.

"I thought you were the one who volunteered," he went, acidly.

"Volunteer, my ass. Ten years in the joint or two years in the force. That was the only choice I had."

"So you've only got one year left to endure."

"Don't tell me you've turned *estúpido*. As soon as I stepped through the gates and on base, I understood I caught me a life sentence. You think they'll be letting us walk someday? With everything we know. After what they did to your wife and your little girl. To Marcos's kids. To Juan's wife?"

Theo turned suddenly, his throat tight.

"What'd they do to Marcos and Juan?"

Will shrugged his shoulders.

"I'm not too sure about Juan. He's a former merc who decided to hang up his boots. Tamazula's men came to pay him a visit one day and made him an offer. He'd have accepted it, but he didn't want to be away from his woman. They'd only just gotten married, see.

"A couple days later, she gets run over while she's out biking. I don't know the full story. Anyway, when the guys came to see him a second time, he went with them. That's what they call a volunteer over here."

"What about Marcos?"

"Marcos, now he's told us all his story about a hundred times. This one night, he goes home, same time as usual. Finds his wife in bed with this huge guy. She's screeching, she's struggling.

"Marcos, man, he's a pro with a knife. And it just so happens, there was a knife out on the table. He goes for the guy, and he misses.

"The other guy grabs the knife, and – cool as a cucumber, looks him right in the eye – buries the blade in his wife's stomach. Then he gets up and he goes, "Damn, man, you just killed your wife. I was out here paying her a visit and you just killed her right in front of me."

"Ain't nobody bought Marcos's story in court. Gave him ten years, just like me, and his kids got shipped out to an orphanage."

"He may have made that whole story up."

"Maybe. But his parents went looking for them kids. They ain't ever find the orphanage that they were supposedly sent to."

Theo felt his heart speed up.

"You mean to say that Administration officials never gave them the address of the institution?"

"Sure they did. But they didn't have no visitation rights. Since Marcos's dad had a cousin on the force, he tried to find out how they were doing. Well, they weren't on any of their lists.

"So the grandparents went before the judge again, try and get some explanations. They were told the kids had been transferred out to another orphanage.

"The next day, the cousin gets transferred to the other side of the country. Since then, Marcos has been out here, and of course he can't have any updates.

"What's going on with you? You've gone all pale!"

"There's other cases, others like Marcos and Juan?"

"I don't know. They're it as far as our section. But there's two thousand men here, and at least two other elite sections out there that we never have any contact with."

Theo felt like a wave of dizziness come over him. He emptied out what was left in the water bottle on his face.

"You sure you're OK?"

"I'm all right," said Theo with a sigh. "You got a smoke?"

"Hey, take it easy. We're running in an hour. You'll be all out of breath."

Theo lit the cigarette and greedily took a puff. He let the smoke filter into his lungs and slowly blew it out through the nose.

"What does Marcos think?"

"He says Tamazula's men stole his kids and sold them off. There's a lot of child trafficking going on in Guatemala and Belize. For rich people who can't adopt…"

"And if they haven't sold them off?"

"What are you thinking? What else would they have done with them? You're thinking about your own kid, right. But she's dead. She died with your wife. You yourself told me that you saw them in the car."

"I saw a car burn," spat Theo. "There was fire everywhere. The hood was up. I couldn't make out anything inside."

"But they were in there. You know they were. You felt it. Marcos, he got his kids taken from him alive."

"Why would they do that to him? It's him they wanted. Not the kids."

"I told you. Tamazula has his fingers in a whole lot of trafficking pies. He plays recruit for the camp and he takes a commission in the process. With a bonus when he can swing it."

Theo got up, lost in thought.

"I'm going to talk to Marcos."

Howard Beck had been simmering since this morning and the confidential, top level meeting that had enabled him, for the first time, to come face to face with the boss himself.

Richard B. Willis, latest acting director, a successor of Roscoe H. Hillenkoetter and Allen Welsh Dulles, whose black and white portraits had captured their inscrutable stares within frames hung on the wall behind him, had summoned him for this ten-minute one-on-one, something unprecedented in his career.

Ten minutes that had been enough to call into question an entire lifetime of service to his country and to the intelligence community.

"Do you have any idea the number of regulations you violated during the course of your investigation?"

Richard Willis's scathing voice still sounded out inside Howard's head every bit as clearly as if the director of the CIA had been seated right next to him, inside the car tearing down the speedway that crossed Arlington and would soon take him to downtown D.C.

"Unauthorized wiretapping cost a president his term. Agency operatives ended up in prison for impersonating federal agents on US soil. For the love of God, Beck, what on Earth possessed you to submit a detailed report outlining those very same activities?"

The eight pages Howard had typed up, including a wiretap summary regarding the Chestons and Feldman, were fanned out on the surface of a pristine desk. Frozen in time for eternity, Dulles and Hillenkoetter still weren't smiling.

"Sir, my investigation into the mole led me to…"

"Your investigation? What investigation are you talking about? Are you even remotely aware of the Agency's separation principles?"

After a moment's hesitant pause, dedicated to sizing him up, Willis had contented himself with opening the safe built into the bookcase behind him, and then holding out a folder only a few sheets thick. The flap was stamped "Top Secret," the highest of the three classification levels that defined a document's confidentiality status.

"Concerning the hypothesis of a leak having led to the loss of two agents during Operation Buridan"

"This isn't how this thing should end," had sighed Willis. "But I want to wrap this whole thing up, now!"

Alarmed, Beck had jumped from the introduction straight to the conclusion. Even now, behind the wheel of his car, while the tombs of heroes fallen for their country sped past his right-hand window in orderly rows of white crosses stretching almost to infinity, he was going white with rage upon recalling what he'd read.

"Agents Glamore and Shirton were unaware that their true mission was to be discovered and to feed the enemy false intelligence that had been established to be true during their debrief. The special training they underwent should have enabled them to withstand physical and mental pressure long enough that they retained the credibility of their cover.

"The intelligence meant to be leaked essentially constituted a fake network of operatives working on the Iranian nuclear program and purportedly in the United States' pocket. Once out in the open, this list was to ensure the protection of the legitimate, established network, some of the elements of which were starting to be the focus of closer surveillance…"

"To withstand physical and mental pressure, Sir?"

Beck had lifted his eyes from the report, horrified by what he'd just read.

"Obviously, your department was meant to be in the dark. That's the very foundation of our operating principles. Eleven vitally important informants owe their lives to this two-pronged operation, while a host of first-rate technicians who are loyal to their government and true to their faith have been put through the mill by the Iranian secret services.

"We'd been planning on buying back our men or getting them in an exchange after this ordeal. Not like it would have been the first time…"

"And you let us go on believing…"

"Separation principle." Willis was famous for repeating the same thing several times, as though that in itself was the whole explanation. He'd gone straight on. "I had no way of knowing that a small-time Mossad agent would get in touch with you and offer you his services for another operation of a different level of importance that we're running.

"Feldman, a mole? Did the absurdity of that statement not strike you where you stood?"

"That same separation principle did not authorize me to form an opinion on an outside agent, Sir."

"Well consider yourself illuminated! And as for you report…"

In a fluid motion, Willis had torn it in two before tossing the strips into the incinerator at his feet.

"…It obviously never existed."

"Sir, if I may… Whatever Gregory Cheston's political backing, and whatever logistical support he may be granted here, this recording proves that he decided to go entirely too far. The very concept of a parallel army would have a hard time getting a pass in the media or in Congress, but if Cheston intends to replicate the experiment…"

The CIA director's glare was spearing into Beck's eyes, ablaze like a knife heated in embers.

"You're a patriot, aren't you, Howard? That is what your psych profile says. That means you have to know there's more than one way to die for your country…"

An icy trickle down Beck's back.

"…The intelligence that you gained access to is of such vital importance that we will be taking no risks if it were to turn out that your moral conscience won out over that indispensable patriotism.

"And so I'm going to ask you, right this morning, to have a session with the psychiatrist on this level, and to quickly undergo a lie detector test. In the event you were to decline these two tests…"

"I have nothing to hide!" had spat Beck before withdrawing.

He was choking with rage.

The first white houses of the D.C. suburb began replacing the funereal Arlington landscape. At this time of the year, nature was lush, thick bushes and trees of all shapes and sizes attempting to spread out by inching their branches between the gaps in the safety fences lining the Whitehurst Freeway.

Beck had cleared both those tests with flying colors. Yes, he was a genuine patriot. No, he would never betray his country, nor would he ever betray the western democratic powers. No, he would never reveal any secrets to *anyone not read in or lacking clearance.* Yes, it was his intention to unquestioningly pursue the missions entrusted to him, of which his primary assignment had just been communicated to him by the director himself: make certain that the separation principle was in place.

Your right hand must not know what your left hand is doing!

Eleven Iranian traitors, acquired from the West, had survived thanks to the sacrifice of the two agents he'd known for years, one of whom was married with two kids. The picture evidence of their agony was proliferating on the net across sites geared towards fans of sadistic highs.

Faced with the Islamist threat, the West was losing its grip. Handing over control of a defense system, however efficient it might be, to corporate bosses was tantamount to leaving gang leaders in charge of their neighborhood's safety. Wouldn't changing up the command structure have been more worthwhile? Showing a firmer hand. Getting it through the enemy's skull that there was nothing that the West wouldn't do, too?

Wouldn't it be more efficient to conduct outright interventions against rogue states, rather than resorting to obsolete institutions like the United Nations, or waiting for absolution from a Europe that was timorous by nature and bogged down in official principles meant to camouflage its leaders' cowardice?

Confronted with a determined and zealous enemy, the free world was unable to offer up any bigger a resistance than procrastination and sermonizing. It was history repeating itself, the eternal cycle of incomprehension on the part of men who clearly never learned anything.

That was how the Roman Empire, the first shining jewel of Civilization, had plummeted from repeated assaults from the barbarian hordes, making way for a thousand years of darkness. Giants were, by definition, possessed of feet of clay, and decadence lurked in wait of the victors straight away.

Mind teeming with more or less depressing ideas, Howard parked his vehicle at the top of the small incline that 16th street rose in before the corner of Church Street. He walked a few minutes to make sure no-one had followed him, then he stopped at a Starbucks to get a clearer view of his outside surroundings while sipping on an orange juice.

Mind set at ease, and persuaded that his successfully passing that morning's trials had pushed back the storm, he doubled back until he reached a small Episcopalian church that had been on his way. Once outside the front steps, he acted hesitant, then, like a sinner yearning for redemption, he resolutely entered the small wooden building topped by a white cross.

Beck wasn't any more an Episcopalian than he was a Catholic. If he looked back at his parents and his grandparents, he could have certainly defined himself as an Adventist. But today was not a day for worrying about the labels he'd stick to a faith he felt he had in short supply.

Up in the third row, he recognized the stocky figure of the man he was there to meet. Seated before a stylized Christ whose gaze bore all the world's suffering, a kneeling Haim had forgotten to take off his hat.

"You certainly took your time," whispered the Mossad agent as Howard sat down next to him.

"This is a church, Haim! Take off that hat at once."

The Israeli shot him a quick, amazed glance before complying.

"Force of habit," he demurred. "In synagogues, we keep our heads covered."

"Yeah, well, Christians pray with their heads bared!"

"And Muslims take off their shoes before prostrating themselves," sighed Haim. "As though any of this posturing has even the slightest effect on Man's fate.|

"It does… That of leading us to hate one another and tear each other apart."

Haim set one foot in front of him to sit up and take a seat.

"Phew, a few more minutes in that position and I would no longer have felt my legs…"

Beck kept a long gaze on his counterpart, still hesitating. As he'd walked into the church, his anger had vaporized all at once, making room for a nauseated feeling that now drove him to doubt. Haim had to have at least fifteen years on him. He was an old hand in the secret agent game. He'd known more existential crises than Beck himself would ever go through.

The CIA had so often placed itself in a bad light that Beck sometimes wondered why his job still held any appeal for him, and where his loyalty towards the Agency even came from. But when he'd called Haim, as soon as he'd cleared both tests, hadn't he quite literally broken his fresh oath?

No, he would never disclose these secrets to anyone who was not read in and authorized. He hadn't lied. Matter of fact, the polygraph would have instantly outed him had he not, in good faith, held the Mossad agent as being part of those both in the know and authorized.

Haim had proved that more than once. He knew more than Beck himself did.

"These past few days have to have been rough," uttered the Israeli, not shifting his gaze from straight ahead.

"For a lot of people," sighed Beck.

"Go on, then. Make the most of this place of sanctuary…"

"…to unburden my conscience?"

Howard snickered.

"Forgive me, Haim, but outside a professional setting, you wouldn't make a great confessor."

"Why's that?" The Mossad agent smiled, adopting a playfully upset look. "Because I'm Jewish? You invented confession, and we invented psychoanalysis; I'd say that makes us even, hmm?"

"Haim…"

Howard's voice had grown faint. The two men were alone in a small church dominated by a mingled smell of incense and wax polish. Only a few candles dotted around Christ's feet added their flickering light to the dwindling daylight filtered in by the stained-glass windows with their abstract designs.

"…what do you want to know about White Cells that you don't already?"

"Just about everything."

"And what would you be willing to give me in exchange?"

"Just about as much."

"Without knowing where the camps are situated, nothing we might find out would really lead to anything. That is what you're looking for, isn't it? Why?"

"There are several ways to bring insanity to an end. The best way is by controlling it."

Howard sighed. His heart was doing somersaults inside his chest. He knew that, a moment from now, there would be no going back, and the thought was making him feel something close to panic. Haim went on, his tone as philosophical as it was mysterious.

"It takes a lot of shadows to create darkness, but the mere light from one candle is enough to lift them away."

"We're not talking about exchanging intel this time."

"We don't only sell secrets," said Haim. "What's more, those secrets would be worthless if they didn't lead us to taking radical action."

Beck briefly nodded his agreement. The two men understood each other.

He began by revealing the miscalculation committed by Mossad when they'd pointed to Feldman as the mole in Operation Buridan. That was the one and only piece of intel concerning Buridan that Beck took the liberty to relay. Then he talked about Cheston.

The two men were still discussing the multibillionaire when the dark of night crept into the little church.

As Theo had thought, the men were selected on the eve of the op. He wasn't among them. Will, Marcos, the two Vietnamese guys, and an Australian mercenary who lived isolated from the group had made the cut. Novak had been designated section chief, and he spent several hours in the breakroom with his men to walk them through the action plan.

For the first time since the infamous duel, Meyrek had approached Theo not long after the list had come out. He'd joined him in the weight room right as Theo was wrapping up a set of reps. As ever, he enjoyed the element of surprise.

"You're not bound for Oaxaca, did that come as a shock?"

Theo sat up on the workout bench and let go the chest expander.

"I'm sick with disappointment."

Meyrek didn't follow up.

"Your condition is improving by the day. You've been doing a great job."

"You here to measure my biceps, *colonel*?"

"I'm here to explain why you're not getting shipped out with the team."

"Easy to grasp; it was to spare me the temptation... But that's a chance you'll have to take someday. Else you'll have done all this for nothing!"

Meyrek let out a noise that was meant to sound like a laugh.

"Guess again. I lose no sleep over your escape. After this kind of training, I'm not about to send you out to slaughter a couple of mobsters. You're worth more than that."

"I haven't fired another shot," taunted Theo.

"I never asked you to. And if you'd declined, I'd have been forced to send you back to your cell. Start the cycle all over again. A waste of time. Two more months and you'll be ready."

"For what? A trek to the Middle East to trigger world war three?"

The colonel set his boot down on the horizontal ledge an inch or so from Theo. His regulation boots were shined to perfection, as was his wont, and his BDUs were pin-straight and neat. For a moment, Theo wondered what he might look like in civvies.

"You know what, Collin, I do believe I hold you in some esteem. You're a pretty straightforward guy. That's a rarity in these parts. And I believe you'll like the objectives that I'll be setting for you. That day, you'll be asking me for a weapon, and you'll go train like you're possessed, for fear of missing your target."

He stepped away from the workout bench and gave a parting shot before leaving the room.

"In the meantime, take care of your physical shape. Keep working on that bulk, soldier!"

Theo grabbed a barbell off the ground. Staring straight at the hallway down which Meyrek had vanished, he lifted the bar level with his hips and, with a last show of effort, brought it above his head with a rage-filled howl.

Will was laboring over his pack. The travel orders entailed a brief list of apparel and equipment that he needed to stuff into his kit. His bed was strewn with his military effects.

"Get shipped out three days," he was grumbling. "We're off for three days and they're making us bring two combat gear kits. Not to mention the civvies."

"Don't forget your tux," kidded Theo. "Just in case you meet some *chicas.*"

Will grimaced out a smile and paired it with a lewd gesture.

"Got my machine gun for the *chicas,* man. It's been locked and loaded for a year."

Three beds down, Marcos was calmly folding his own clothes. The two Vietnamese men were ready to go, and they were amply gesticulating their commentary of the plan of attack, packs of cigarettes set up in a half circle on the floor to represent the Oaxaca villa. Close to the farthest window, the Ozzie was already asleep.

Theo watched Marcos's tormented face. His talk with the Guatemalan had been a disappointment. He seemed convinced that his parents hadn't taken their search in the right direction, and he held out hope that he'd find his kids once his contract with base was fulfilled. Theo hadn't wanted to shatter his illusions, nor to share Will's observations. He nonetheless had the feeling that the young Central-American man had reached the same conclusions and just wouldn't admit it to himself.

Will broke into his thoughts.

"Yo, man, lend a brother a hand. I can't fit this here second pair of boots."

"Hang them off the strap," suggested Theo. "Your dogs are too huge."

The former marine lifted his shoulders and followed the proffered advice.

"Pity you're not coming with us. We could have had us some fun."

With the exception of Theo and the team members being shipped out, the dorm was empty. The rest of the section had put together a lottery in the break room. They were playing for cigarettes, rations, and the pages of some porn mag left behind by an NCO.

"Don't act up," fretted Theo. "Novak's gonna be on the lookout. You won't stand a chance."

Will hopped onto the bed. His head was nearly brushing against the ceiling. He grabbed his pack by the strap and, swinging it like a club, violently struck the wall. He dropped the rucksack, seized a broom, and brandished it horizontally in imitation of his favorite weapon.

His commentary rang out with all the frenzy of a sportscast.

"Will takes the villa. He smokes all the guards. There's bodies flying out the windows, piling up in the hallway, in the stairwell, then he knocks out his teammates, takes out his captain, hotwires the truck…"

He threw himself face down onto the bed, his pack between his legs.

"…and he storms the best whorehouse in Mexico."

The Vietnamese guys had broken off and were shooting them apprehensive glances, worried they'd missed a new game. Marcos was used to the giant's eccentric nature. He paid them no mind. Out of breath, Will flipped around on his back, then pinned Theo with a serious look.

"*Carnal*, the day I get out of here, you're coming with me. Just this once, I'll only let loose on them lowlifes in Oaxaca."

Theo didn't respond. Will got rid of his pack, sending it flying to the ground, and signaled him closer.

"One day, we're gonna get sent off on a mission, you and me. Thousands of miles off this base. They'll drop us into the street, weapons hot, fake I.D.'s in our pockets, maybe even fake faces slapped on. We'll take care of their goddamn mission and we'll disappear. Pfft… All we need is guts."

"Guts…" whispered Theo.

"What's to stop you from dreaming?"

Theo shook his head. His thoughts strayed towards his past life once more. His memories were like a stranger's. His wife and daughter lived on in his memories like some distant nostalgia. The time barrier seemed impenetrable. How could he explain it to his friend that you needed to still feel alive in order to dream?

"Will," he replied softly. "The day you wanna leave, don't wait for me. Take every precaution and go to ground. Don't even try to reveal our existence. The Organization is powerful. They don't take any chances. And we don't know whose support they enjoy."

"Hey, *carnal*, you take me for some kinda *maricón*? I don't give a shit about the base, about the world, 'bout morals and none of that crap! When I'm really, truly done with playing soldiers, I look out for me first."

He stabbed a decisive finger towards Theo.

"And I'm taking you with me. We can start a new life, in a new country. Start a business, buy us some *chicas*. One day, you might even start a new family…"

"This isn't a prison camp, Will. We don't have allies waiting to give us a hero's welcome on the other side of the border. We'll spend the rest of our lives waiting for them to find us. Someday, we'll break. We'll go spill our guts to the first police station on our way. And the next day, they'll be there."

The former marine's face twisted into an enraged expression. His voice turned almost threatening. His mouth dragged out an elongation of his favorite phrase.

"Yoooo, man! Guess the colonel's right, then. One month ago, you were the one all gung-ho about leaving! You turning into them, is that it?

"Everyone else here, they either volunteers or they got their balls cut off when they got here. You think I'm playing, saying that? There's two thousand heads of cattle out there. Right at the start, some American guy tried to escape. Fleisher. I knew him well, he wanted to leave with me. Only, at the time, I was kinda feeling it here.

"Meyrek let him die in the desert. The only thing he brought back was his *cojones* in a plastic bag, and he hung that at the mess entrance. So the men turned into cattle, like it was their balls swinging from that plastic bag.

"Two or three groups still tried to make a run for it. And Meyrek used them as targets on the shooting range. Me, that shit made me laugh. Only had eighteen months left in this place. And then I figured it out."

Theo shot him a questioning look. Will went on in a calmer tone of voice.

"For a long time, I thought the base was a refuge for convicts like me."

"This army isn't affiliated with any country; it's not the foreign legion."

"Damn it!" rumbled the black giant. "I don't want to spend the rest of my days here. So what if I have to live hidden away for a couple centuries. And you, after what they did to you…"

"You wouldn't understand," mumbled Theo.

How could Will have understood that he had unfinished business in this camp. Theo had never talked about his first meeting with Meyrek, nor about the man's obsession with making a soldier out of him. That was so many years ago now!

Ever since the disappearance of the only two beings who could give his life any meaning, he'd run the gamut of emotional stages engendered by the death of a loved one. From denial and disbelief and through anger, there was one that he hadn't wallowed in for more than a second: acceptance.

"An escapee is not a free man. As long as Meyrek runs this camp, there won't be any other choice."

"So what Huang says is true, then."

Theo turned to face the two Vietnamese men. They'd gone back to their combat plan and no longer paid the two men any mind.

"I had no idea Huang had taken an interest in me."

Will adopted a mysterious tone of voice.

"The two gooks over there, they crazy. I mean it, *carnal…* Back in their country, they belonged to some sect or something like that. Two weeks after the duel, he came to see me. "Take care of your new friend," he told me. "He's not like the others. *He has the third eye.*""

Theo couldn't hold back a laugh.

"Viets don't belong to any sects. They're Buddhist; that's a religion."

Will sat up straighter.

"Yo, Huang, get over here a sec. Tell me again what you said to me. That thing about the eye in the middle of the forehead…"

Interrupted from his preparations, the eldest of the two Vietnamese men went to Theo and Will. It was the first time Theo was taking an interest in this man, someone so subdued as to almost be forgotten. In a polite, almost obsequious tone, Huang spoke to Will.

"Do you believe he's ready to hear me?"

"*La puta madre!* I'm not the Buddhist here… Tell him…"

The Vietnamese man turned to Theo, his mien suddenly grave.

"What do you feel when you shoot a gun?"

"It makes me sick to my stomach!"

"No!" Huang shook his head. "How do you see your target? With your eyes, or from within?"

"With my eyes, of course. Anybody can do it with enough solid training…"

"Yeah, but you have no training, *carnal*!" interrupted Will.

"It's called having a gift. Some people are good at math, others play Chopin at the age of six…"

The Vietnamese man placed his hand on Theo's arm. His eyelids were set so closely together that his eyes nearly seemed closed.

"No… That's not it. You think you see the target, but the moment you take your shot, it comes alive in here… and in here."

He pressed his fingers onto Theo's chest, and then his forehead.

"Something like that, yeah," admitted Theo.

"Everything has a meaning, even here," the Vietnamese man went on mysteriously. "You were not sent here at random…"

Will snickered.

"Sent? By who? To do what?"

Huang lifted his shoulders.

"We will know once he has passed his tests."

He was already getting ready to go back to his brother, his plan, his buildings made out of cigarette packs. Theo caught him by the arm.

"What's all that about? What tests?"

"Do you really want to know?"

"You've said too much already, or not enough actually…"

"Very well. Will told you I belonged to a sect…"

"You heard us?" said the former marine, astonished. "From that far out?"

"You're a Buddhist," continued Theo without getting derailed by his friend. "That's not a sect."

"A Buddhist… and something else. But you wouldn't understand…"

"You can still try to explain it to me. Does it have something to do with that book you tote around everywhere?"

The Vietnamese man let out a modest smile. Blushing was a near thing.

"*Oracles and Prayers*, by Huỳnh Phú Sổ," he whispered tenderly. "He's a thinker from my region."

"Where were you born, Huang?"

"In the Mekong River Delta, in Hòa Hảo. The same town as him…"

"So then, do you want to tell me what's in this book that might have something to do with me?"

Huang acquiesced, still hesitant, then told the story of Huỳnh Phú Sổ, the

246

scrawny and nearly lame man who had reincarnated in himself after receiving the Buddhist teachings of an unusual minister, Bửu Sơn Kỳ Hương.

"That means "Strange Fragrance from the Precious Mountain"."

"Strange fragrance? That's a little like you," ragged Will immediately. Theo shot him a dark glare. Huang paid him no mind.

"Everything is a symbol, a parable, bearings for our lives so long as we understand the language of our sages," he went on in that same high-pitched, monotonous voice. "Huỳnh Phú Sổ taught us that every man is in charge of his own destiny inside a world of illusions. He was a farmer, and a warrior. He and all his disciples became living Buddhas…

"But that's not something you can really understand. There are about two million of us in Vietnam…"

"I'm with you… this is fascinating," broke in Theo. "But what does this Huỳnh Phú Sổ have to do with me?"

"He received the signs… All his possessions were taken from him… Then he accepted his training at the same time as his initiation.

"He was infirm; he became a warrior, the prophet of a new religion. He would have ended up inside the asylum where they locked him had ne not managed to persuade and convert his jailers.

"He founded the Phật Giáo Hòa Hảo. Buddhism without temples…"

"All right. I'm assuming this religion happens to be your own…"

"According to our doctrine, everyone must undertake their Great Work at the end of four trials connected to the elements, which are air, earth…"

"…Water and fire," added Theo. "Like with the Freemasons."

Huang shook his head, admitting to his ignorance, before stubbornly plowing on, like a litany.

The air that you breathe and that enabled you to run, to resist. The earth and its dangers, the rocks and the snakes that you have survived… The water that helped you be reborn… The man that you did not kill… It all comes together… You are here to achieve the Great Work…"

"It's missing…" Theo broke off, taken aback.

"Yes, it's missing the fire," summed up Huang before stepping away from the two men.

Will was shaking his big head hard enough to tear it off his own shoulders.

"Hijo de puta Madre de Dios! That is some serious, intense goddamn crap!"

Chapter 15

Gregory Cheston was distractedly following the progress of the rescuers out in the middle of the rubble of what had, up until a few hours ago, been one of the biggest nightclubs in Djakarta. The CNN news cams were broadcasting the latest updates on the situation every fifteen minutes. Every time, the same images paraded on the screen, of smoking ruins spattered with blood, of emergency lights intermittently flashing onto the haggard faces of the few survivors, of the convoys of stretchers carting out motionless bodies torn asunder by the violence of the blast.

Camera flashes popped when the chief of the local police moved towards the reporters to give a statement. The death toll was staggering. Nearly two hundred victims, the great majority of whom were Western tourists. So far, no-one had claimed responsibility for the attack, but the Indonesian authorities had good reason to believe that they would uncover conclusive clues in the coming hours, because, he said, "in this type of attack, the first hours of the investigation are critical. No leads should be ruled out."

Around the scene of the massacre, journalists bustled, eager to get a scoop, and it was a race to see who'd photograph the best angle, who'd reveal the most evocative look, who'd immortalize the most touching expression, who would record a historic phrase.

The newscaster specified that, since 1960, the number of terror victims had been assessed to total around twenty-six thousand people. In a bid to flesh out a fuller overview of how the threat had risen, he added that in the interval spanning from January 2001 to December 2007 alone, over fourteen thousand people had been affected by terrorist activity – meaning a one hundred and fifty percent increase in a five year period over the preceding forty years.

Cheston pushed a button on the remote and the image vanished. His brother's favorite expression was never far from his thoughts.

"In the ten years to come, terrorism will spread around the world the way crime did during the Prohibition. And governments will be have no other solutions outside of negotiations and counting their dead!"

Words that he had thought extreme, paranoid, but that had, sadly enough, proven to be premonitory. World war three was indeed underway, wholly outside the rules, and not one person could expect to escape it.

Cheston spared a rage-filled thought for his own illusions, his humanitarian ambitions. Memories of World War One had hung over his childhood, and his own father had died in 1943, seven years after he was born, during the American intervention in Europe.

He himself had distinguished himself in combat with the highest honors, having even been awarded the Purple Heart, during the first phase of the war in Vietnam. Back from the war, his mother's second husband had bequeathed him a small radio factory. Cheston had suddenly found himself a calling.

Thanks to the scholarships handed out by the U.S. Army and his uncommonly keen mind, he'd been able to earn himself a spot inside the ivied halls of M.I.T. During his studies, his stepfather managed the factory. Gregory would often return to see him, always with more cutting-edge and audacious ideas.

His infallible instinct had enabled him to anticipate the makings of a scientific revolution that would overturn the very foundations of society. The electron was the basis of the "thinking machine," that device that would relieve humanity of its basest tasks, allow it to communicate instantly, and find new means of feeding itself, and perhaps one day introduce it to other worlds...

Cheston had personally kept up with the declassified work of Alan Turing and other pioneers, and he consulted all of the available documentation having to do with the enormous computing units of the time.

His first company, renamed C.G.E. (Cheston General Electronics) after his step-father had passed, had immediately undergone a bout of unprecedented growth, and the small radio factory had gone on to manufacture first transistors, and ultimately specialized components and equipment, turning into an outright empire that provided over a hundred and twenty thousand jobs...

From radio transistors he had rapidly moved into the design and manufacture of much more sophisticated materials: high-power electrical switches such as thyratrons. Then came ignitron, then krytron – one of the key pieces in certain detonator models used in nuclear weapons. In this way, he was essentially positioning his company at the center of two key sectors of the American industry: nuclear power and weapons manufacturing.

His researchers had perfected a revolutionary electronic alarm system developed for nuclear power plants. Unfortunately, mistakes can happen to anyone, and so too can maintenance errors, and as fate would have it that failing had caught his own alert system out right at the moment when Cheston himself was visiting the new Des Moines power plant, accompanied by his wife.

His five-month pregnant wife...

Ellen had been born. Victoria had left him for a retirement home that she had never set foot out of.

C.G.E. had not survived the wave of panic brought on by the incident. Nor the astronomical compensatory damages demanded by the families of the

Des Moines victims. Even less so to the depressive episode that had claimed Gregory Cheston for many long months…

Still, Gregory was not a man to succumb to irredeemable despondency. Virtually ruined, abandoned, left in charge of a small child that even seasoned nurses flinched back at the sight of, he had quickly recovered his determination and he had found new things to strive for once more.

E.C.Tronics. Built in 1980. E for Ellen, C for Cheston. He was going to force his daughter's name on the whole world. His daughter, whose intelligence was a constant source of surprise, despite how hard even he found it to look at her.

Through twenty years of unremitting work, of innovations, of almost premonitory instincts, he had reconquered his own empire, left his competition in the dust, innovated in all areas, diversified his activities and progressively phased out the hardware to move into the software side of things, built subsidiaries, outposts throughout the world, forged partnerships with the heavyweights in the domain of microprocessors and operating systems for microcomputers.

It was not the lure of profit that drove him forward, but he nevertheless wanted to go fast, to live life to the beat of a world that was seeing its very sense of time changed by the way technology was evolving.

He wanted to bear witness to the birth of this better world… And for that, he was trying to speed up its arrival.

But, inside his mind, a better world presupposed a free world above all else. And his humanitarian calling had channeled itself into one purpose as he'd grown older: defense.

Needless to say, the terrorists responsible for suicide bombings, ephemeral stars to a televised show taking advantage of the framework of the free world in order to try and paralyze it before annihilating it, were not part of this future that he believed in.

The expenses incurred by the U.S. Army amounted to the same budget allocated to defense by the next twenty most powerful nations in the world. According to all logic, nothing should have stood in America's way. Nevertheless, it was fumbling in Iraq, floundering in Afghanistan, had bumbled in Vietnam, always weakened by those same principles that it was its duty to defend, once it was faced with an enemy that suffered no principles.

And his inability to act was making his blood boil. Him, the founder of the White Cells project, who even six months earlier had been dreaming of responding eye for eye and tooth for tooth to the inhuman actions on the part of these degenerates, even if it took overturning governments and taking hostage entire territories, provided that meant saving innocent lives.

For a few weeks now, Gregory Cheston had been having the confused feeling that the operation was getting away from him. A training camp could at best provide a dozen truly operational cells. Its complete independence was the only thing that could guarantee success, and that was why no government agency was to know the location of the camps.

So then, what was the reason for this investigation? Who was this free electron who kept digging despite the pressure he was applying at the most strategic levels? What would become of the operation as a whole if, one day, he would need to face the media or explain himself before Congress? What use would have been all this money, all this energy, the pain and suffering of all these men who had consented in advance to making the sacrifice that a head of state, commander in chief of his army, would be called to make: the sacrifice of the few for the good of the many?

In a world fallen prey to mindless violence, could he still afford himself the luxury of a moral compass that ran contrary to brute force, sole guarantee of survival?

It was a dilemma that Cheston, the type of man who didn't shy away from drastic decisions, had long resolved. But he was currently pushing back against constraints that were holding him back every day, and thereby delaying the parade that he – and he alone – had pictured. Certain shadow alliances that he had sworn allegiance to were weighing him down, and the emotional side that he'd gotten involved was beginning to turn detrimental to him.

From up on the 47th floor of the E.C.Tronics tower, where he'd taken the liberty to convert the top two floors into his main apartment, a conservatory, and a helipad, Cheston contemplated Manhattan and its bustling streets as they stretched on at his feet.

He was loath to make the decisions that now needed making.

Garroni was circling around his men with all the elegance of a dog sniffing a lamppost. He doled out a few nudges, let out a few growls. The ritual was a show in tedium.

"Special section, thirty-three present. Five men on mission. No absences."

Meyrek was not present for the roll call. His aide de camp folded the attendance sheet back up, saluted, and ordered the men into formation.

Half the men had been on a training exercise in the hills for two days now. Survival and ambush. The attending sections, mostly made up of "reservists," gathered together in several columns. An SUV loaded up with ammunition crates joined the weapons truck next to the guard post.

It was six o'clock.

Garroni called his men to rest.

"Today, you will once again be joining in and supervising the sections out on training. In groups of five. Weapons and live ammo will be handed out to you. So no messing around. Since Will is not among us, three of you will inherit the .50-cal."

He got a few laughs in response.

"And now for news from the front. The mission in Oaxaca was a complete success."

If Garroni was expecting some applause, he got nothing for his troubles. The men were looking every which way. Some of them shrugged their shoulders marginally. The sergeant gave the order to break ranks. The training exercises would pick back up after a couple minutes' rest.

"Collin, no walk for you this time. The colonel wants to see you."

Theo sighed. His teammates shot him baleful looks. Meyrek never summoned the rank and file. This was the first time he was having him called in while other soldiers were present.

"Collin! Have a seat. Coffee?"

The tone was warm. There gleamed a cheerful light in Meyrek's eyes, as if he were honestly glad to have Theo there. He was seated at his desk, behind a pile of folders, a computer screen, and a basket full of cactus-green tropical fruit that were rutted like little moons.

"They're *cherimoya*, the epicurean's fruit," said Meyrek, noting his gaze. "You can help yourself. They're delicious, but full of seeds."

Theo shook his head. He stepped closer to the desk but remained standing.

"Did anyone die in Oaxaca?"

"You've already heard? Garroni couldn't help himself from taking. An easy victory. You didn't know the victim, he was in section 5. Seriously, no coffee?"

Theo shook his head.

"I'm wondering if you're more detestable as a civilized man or as a single-minded soldier."

Meyrek grabbed one of the fruit and sank his teeth into the flesh.

"It's still your dream to shoot me, isn't it? At least it's made you put your heart into your training…"

He poured out a cup of coffee and held it out to him.

"Drink up, and hate me as a civilized man. For once, our interests are aligned."

Theo dithered. He ended up pulling up a chair and grabbing the cup of coffee. As always, the colonel would see his thought through. It would be pointless to offer him any resistance.

"We have a serious problem, Collin…" began Meyrek.

"In that case," interrupted Theo, his tone of voice ironic, "you could have found a better confidant to go to."

"Not necessarily. There's an infallible rule that states, the enemy of my enemy is my friend… In our particular case, it may seem paradoxical…"

Meyrek set down the fruit to drink a few mouthfuls of coffee. He was looking for the right words, buying himself some time, clearly taking delight in this little game of cat and mouse.

"I'm not going to attempt to rouse your…patriotism," he said at last. "Your training has come to an end… and you're going to be able to make yourself useful."

Theo was more intrigued than he wanted to appear. The office window was closed, but the noise from the section's training session was filtering in through the glass. Knowing that Will was out there, so close, hearing the shouts from training, for a second it all had an unexpected effect on him.

He felt safe. The mere realization nauseated him. The coffee was warm, very strong. He twisted the cup between his fingers, waiting for the colonel to finally go on.

"Our efforts have almost come to a head, Collin. You'll soon get back to the outside world."

Theo couldn't bite back a chortle.

"That was almost believable. Like you're going to let me roam free when all I need to do is reveal the existence of your camp to bring everything crashing down?"

Meyrek abruptly set his cup down.

"We're training freedom fighters, Collin. They deserve to be defended! Even by you."

"You're training assassins."

"Assassins, terrorists, combatants… Whatever. We're on the brink of success, of triumph. Look at yourself, at what you've become. Thousands of men, all every bit as well trained, will soon be ready for combat at last, with no constraints, no risk of getting tossed in jail for a stray bullet, for some collateral damage, for not abiding by some rule of engagement…"

"Those kinds of armies already exist. In Africa. Is that your ideal, a rabid horde?"

"It all depends on the ultimate goal… of what we're fighting for!"

Meyrek took a beat before turning his computer screen around towards Theo. The slightly blurry picture showed two men on a busy street, and appeared taken without their knowledge. The doughy traits of the smaller man, the forehead lined with furrows, the eyes sheltered by glasses so thick they masked all expression, they all made him easy to spot from a mile away.

"Joseph Feldman," uttered Meyrek. "I'm sure that face rings a bell…"

Feldman!… A name that brought back painful and distant memories. Nicolas Serry's office. Theo could still picture the man's placid, indifferent, almost bored look from a little more than a year before.

A year? Time clearly didn't pass the same way for everybody. That day, Theo had needed to make a decision. What an error in judgment! Feldman had taken his whole life from him by dangling before him the prospect of a little money, a bit of prestige, some adventure. The man had acted like a technocrat on a recruiting mission, and he'd sent them all to this hell, him, his wife, and his daughter, without batting an eye.

"Obviously," ground out Meyrek, "who could forget him? I'm liking the fire that just came to life in your eyes, Collin."

Theo kept quiet. He only wanted one thing: to get up, leave this cramped room that smelled like death, get back to his section, forget. Or even, yeah, rather than forgetting, suddenly throwing himself at Meyrek, overturning that desk, and digging the edge of it into the colonel's throat, slowly, relentlessly; a few seconds of terror and suffering for every month he'd endured… And yet, he didn't move.

"I may have wanted to have you here at the camp," continued the colonel as though he'd read his mind, "but what happened to your family is less my fault than it is this man's, and maybe even less my fault than it's yours…"

This time, Theo couldn't hold back. He propelled himself out of his chair and, in the same motion, set his coffee cup down on the colonel's desk, splattering several folders. He felt his fists clench convulsively. His hatred made his skin crawl, his rage had him seeing red. Meyrek had injected him with this burning acid now flowing through his veins, not giving him a moment's rest. He was the cause of all his suffering, but if he wouldn't shut his mouth, let him just be spared his hypocrisy. Any moment now, he was going to take action… Grab the corner of the desk…

"Where would that get you?" The colonel's icy voice was at odds with his bemused smile. "Come on, Collin, let's stop wasting our time. Why don't you take a good look at the two men in the picture instead, especially that second one, the one you've never seen before. Imprint their faces into your memory, I will soon have a mission for you…"

The sound that burst from Theo's throat was as much a curse as it was the cry of a wounded animal. Tears sprang to his eyes.

"You're nothing but a perverted son of a bitch!"

He felt his legs straighten, his hands reach out, he stepped around the desk, Meyrek was only feet away, still sitting, still smiling.

"Good… that's good! That's what I call a soldier's reflexes. Now pull yourself together, man, I'm not done yet."

Reaching out a nimble finger, the colonel pushed a button on the keyboard. The picture of the two men vanished, leaving the screen black. A video stream started buffering up.

"We'll get back to those two in a second, but for now… watch!"

Despite himself, although he was within an inch of grabbing the colonel by the collar of his BDU jacket, Theo turned his gaze towards the screen, where another image had just taken shape.

For the endless length of a split second, he thought he was dreaming. The world around him ceased to exist, and so too did the noises coming in from outside. The shockwave boomed forward from the deepest pit of his stomach and out to the farthest edge of each of his fingertips, while his heart, his every internal organ, liquefied. His knees started trembling, so hard he thought his legs wouldn't hold him up anymore; and, at the same time, he stopped giving a damn about his body, about himself, about his presence in this place, about the colonel and his bloodthirsty smile floating around the room like Alice's Cheshire cat.

The little girl on the screen, she wasn't smiling. She was wearing some kind of grey T-shirt, and her hair was cut short… It couldn't be her, her being there flew in the face of all logical sense, of everything he'd believed for over a year. And yet, she'd grown. At that age, it couldn't be called "gotten older," older would come far later. Because there was a later. Even a second ago, Theo would have still given his life just to see her picture.

From the surface of the computer screen, looking surprised, unhappy, his daughter Katia was looking at him without seeing him.

The image vanished instantly, and the colonel stood up suddenly to support a Theo who had just begun to collapse.

"Accidents aren't necessarily all deadly…" he whispered in his ear. "Get back to your seat, I'm sure you'll be hanging on my every word now."

Eliane still couldn't figure out the colonel's game, or even his motives. She took Katia by the hand and kindly asked her to get off the chair where the little girl had settled in before the camera.

"That's it? What do I do know?"

"Head back to your section. It's OK, we only took your picture."

She stepped out of the room at the same time as Katia, who took off at a run, and was glad to be breathing the dry plateau air a few moments later.

An entire section of kids passed in front of her, moving at a march. There were twenty of them, and there were already some who wore the uniform with pride. God, but it was easy to mold human beings at that age! The children's numbers swelled each day. Orphans, for the most part. Soon there would be over two hundred of them.

The works carried out a few months earlier had resulted in the construction of more modern barracks, units where the children could now live in halfway decent conditions. As a result of several incidents, and just as many confrontations with Meyrek, Eliane had managed to negotiate for more leniency in the way she supervised. The children made the most of it. There are many different ways of fashioning little soldiers. Terror is one of them, but by her very nature, a woman will more readily choose compassion.

"Mejicanos, Americanos!"

Soon, Eliane's task in this camp would be accomplished. Her contract, which she'd extended, would take her someplace else, someplace far; she didn't yet know where. At least, she mused as she watched the kids trot by, she'll have given them a chance. Her mission as a soldier was very far removed from what she'd pictured when she'd allowed herself to be recruited by the Organization, so many months before…

"Mejicanos, Americanos…"

…But she had no reason to look down on the task she'd carried out. Without her, these children's lives would have been a thousand times worse. Without her, the *combat orphanage* – as Meyrek sometimes called it – would still have existed, but under what conditions?

"Mejicanos, Americanos…"

Eliane had moved ahead of the little section that, still marching, was making its way around the main building. She made an abrupt about-turn and came to stand before the noncom in charge of training. Instantly, the children stopped, snapping their feet together.

"Captain?"

"What's that cadence song?"

Eliane had to raise her head to look at the man, who had nearly a foot on her.

"You're the one who asked us to change it," defended the NCO with a shrug. "We're teaching them in whose name they'll have to fight…"

"For Mexico and America… Is that what you're drilling into their heads?"

"It's a way to create their identity." The man smiled. "I've seen that being done, where you're from."

"Where I'm from? Tell them to stand at ease!"

Eliane signaled the noncom to step away with her.

"It is in Lebanon that they train children to fight," the man went on as soon as they'd gone far enough away. "I watched a documentary about that. They march in a cadence while shouting Allah… Allah!"

"I don't give a damn what you've watched," retorted Eliane dryly. "These kids look ridiculous… We're trying to train them, not radicalize them."

"Oh, are we?" The noncom granted himself the liberty of a contemptuous smile. "With no country and no religion, how are you gonna make soldiers out of them?"

Without waiting for a response or for permission, he did an about-turn and joined the small troop, who immediately picked up their pace once more.

Most of the time, mission orders were handed out verbally. It was part of the "necessary confidentiality" surrounding CIA field ops. Beck was therefore surprised to find a roadmap issued from the highest level – the director himself – placed on the tray on his desk. He knew the contents of the letter before he even opened it, so he wasn't surprised by the marking in the header. The reaction from up top hadn't been long in coming.

He was being sent to Iraq.

But Beck could peruse the mission order all he liked, it contained no details. He didn't know what corps he was being posted to, what unit to go before, what his transit route was, he didn't even know the day of his departure. That, however, was new. A bit like leaving the ins and outs of an operation at his discretion; not at all the Agency's style. He picked up his phone and got Paul Murphy on the line in an instant.

"You're leaving," stated Murphy immediately.

"Thanks, I can read. Since when do orders no longer come dated?"

Silence. Then…

"I think you should have gone over the rest of your inbox before you dialed me up. You're being given fifteen days leave…"

A knot tightened in Howard's throat. A pile of memos was indeed hiding a second letter addressed to him, this time issuing from Murphy's department. So that was what the Agency had in store for him… A forced vacation.

"I was going to come down and tell you," continued Murphy, "but you got in ahead of me. It's a rare thing to find you at the Agency this early in the morning."

"You find me here even earlier when I pass the night," gritted out Beck.

He knew his boss wouldn't be long in hanging up. His mind dialed it up a notch. Ever since he'd begun his own investigation into Cheston and his entourage, the scrutiny his actions were subject to, discreet though it was, must have been thorough. But this order was the first sign that a net was tightening.

One of his meetings must have triggered an alert. In this Beck could fully recognize his employers' methods, which could rarely boast a feather-light touch. He and Haim had seen each other twice, but they were both professionals, and he was sure no-one had followed them.

Had it been his attempt to approach Feldman three days earlier, despite the formal interdiction to pursue his investigation? A peculiar meeting, for that matter. A scant few seconds long, during which time he'd only just managed to catch a panicked flinch from the man before he vanished without answering any of his questions.

Something wasn't in running order, however. If his initiatives were an irritant, he should have been transferred out immediately...

"I hope you'll really make the most of this leave time." Murphy was already wrapping it up. "You need this..."

"Hold on..."

Beck was beginning to cotton on.

"Where am I supposed to spend it?"

There wasn't the slightest trace of irony in Paul Murphy's voice when he said, just before hanging up,

"There's a whole bunch of travel agencies that put together excellent trips. Exploration and adventure strike me to be your style, am I right? Not quite the Club Med!"

For several minutes, Beck stood motionless in his office. If the narrow, partitioned spaces that field agents were entitled to could even be called offices. By pursuing his investigation, all Beck had done was follow his instincts, and there were only a few elements missing now. One of them being the capital... But as far as that one went, he'd have to put himself fully in Haim's hands, hoping that the Israeli had it in him to keep his promises.

On the whole, he had a grasp on the bare bones of what he saw as one of the worst deviancies of a panicking civilization. Still, aping the enemy's sacrificial rites to induce in him a terror that mirrored his own fantasies was hardly a new strategy. History was rife with harrowing anecdotes involving civilized explorers compelled to devour the liver of a native in order to make himself respected and survive. Roman centurions behaving more fiercely than the barbarians. Combatants deploying the same torture methods as the enemy in the name of civilization.

Terrorizing. That was the heart of the matter. Inducing that panicked fear in the enemy, to the point that it paralyzed him down to his marrow.

Beck felt the deepest contempt for the methods that the Islamists resorted to, their manipulation of the masses in their thrall, their cynicism and the religious brainwashing they'd become unquestioned masters of, to the point of concocting the principle of suicide out of hatred, rather than despair.

But, pushed to the breaking point, how far would Cheston's strategists be capable of going? Organize terror attacks? That angle was out of the question. According to the information he'd gathered, the framework created by the shadow organization had the makings of an army, a well-ordered one for all its relentlessness.

These men were trained to kill on command, and they were guaranteed not to incur any punishment, no matter what their target might be. But no officer would ever be crazy enough to have them set off a bomb in the middle of a crowd.

No, Cheston's organization was sure to be aiming for the heads. It took a lot of supplies, a lot of men, and ruthless logistics to carry out the assassination of a head of state, a religious leader, or the head of a gang.

Instilling terror into the architects of terror… As in the days of the Old Man on the Mountain, of the Alamut fortress, of that Hasan-i Sabbah whose legend he'd discovered so long ago now, on that day when fate had decided to spare his life.

Just like the head of the Assassins, Bin Laden had made himself invulnerable by falling back into the mountains in Afghanistan, in the same way that their invisible nature was the only thing that guaranteed the ongoing existence of these shadow armies concocted by the West.

It was at this point in Beck's thoughts that his interoffice line rang. He balked at taking the call, knowing that it couldn't be the bearer of any good news, considering he was officially on vacation as of an hour ago. His dithering didn't catch up to his force of habit.

It took a few beats for Beck to place the grating and incredibly unfeminine voice at the other end of the line once the operator, after making a few terse apologies, had patched him through to Ellen Cheston.

Theo came to a stop before the entrance to the building, looking lost, his vision blurry. His rage had first given way to despondency, then to a wild, boundless, unprecedented hope, of the kind he'd never felt in his life.

That gnawing, numbing sadness he'd been dragging along, the way a schmatte gets dragged around to protect from the cold, it had torn loose in an instant and opened his wound raw once more, without him being able to tell pain apart from joy, hatred from relief, love from fear.

For several minutes, he had drifted to the edge of reason, in that irrational no man's land where the mind is overcome and survives only to break free, to run off forever. But he could close his eyes all he wanted, the picture was still there; it wasn't a dream. Katia had survived. Katia was alive. Katia needed him.

Katia was love, she was life, she was his child. In the same way a frozen limb becomes excruciatingly painful once it gets warm, Theo's soul had come back to life, raw and open. Out of its coma. Torched like a third-degree burn.

Meyrek had picked his moment, the end of his training. Now, he had him for good.

And, strangely, Theo was no longer capable of feeling hatred towards him. His heart was no longer in it. His child's future once again depended on him. Let him accept his missions, and he could see her again. Let him carry them out successfully, and she would soon be by his side, safe. It was a promise, he had to believe that. All he needed to do was keep quiet, keep that secret to himself. *Katia had survived.*

The occurrence was so far beyond his understanding that, for a moment, Theo hadn't even dared hope for another miracle. The questions, however, poured in; painful, nonsensical sometimes. Where was his daughter? What ordeals had she endured? How had she lived through that whole entire year, a small, confused ten-year-old girl? What had happened to her mother?

Inside of Theo's chest, a howl, the sharp tip of a knife, the terrible misery of a stabbed heart that keeps on beating.

One of them survived. The other did not. Consider yourself lucky, Collin. What do we fight for if not for our children!

Above it all, happiness turning to anguish. And the entire world around him, caught in a cloud of dust, beneath a surreal sky, running in slow motion.

Two sections were walking in cadence one after the other along the perimeter wall. Combat outfits, haversack on one shoulder, rifle slung across the chest. Their shirts stuck to their skin. In an hour, the heat would become unbearable.

He watched them move farther to the south. The computing center and the garage. He wiped at his forehead, adjusted the brim of his cap, and took one step into the courtyard.

Garroni headed him off.

"AR or precision rifle? M16 or M99?"

He'd furtively slid in behind him. Theo didn't go to the trouble of turning around. The sergeant stepped around his body to bring himself face to face with him against the light.

"What would you rather start off with?"

"Sleep. I'm going to head back to the dorms and spend the day in bed."

"The colonel told me you might want to train."

"I don't need to."

Garroni squared up his stance, fists planted on his hips. His head was bare and his shorn hair was sticking to his scalp.

"Finally figured it out, then? It only took you a year. And now you think you're invulnerable because Meyrek entrusted you with a mission…"

Theo shrugged his shoulders and stepped away.

"You're still under my command," gritted out the sergeant.

"Tomorrow," went Theo, making an evasive gesture.

"That's right. Live it up. As much as you can. In two days, the section is off into the desert for survival training. And you're coming with them."

"I couldn't give a crap about your training, Garroni."

"Sergeant Garroni!" yelled the noncom.

"What's to say you know how to hold a weapon? Come show me. I'll take you on at the stand. Pick your caliber."

Theo came to a stop in the middle of the courtyard. The two sections were coming back their way, stepping along the eastern buildings, punctuating the left step with a common cry of,

"One… one… one!"

"Go on then, you little shit, pick! Two hundred yards out. What's your weapon?"

Theo stepped in closer to the sergeant, smiled at him like he was going to reply, then abruptly loosened all his muscles and leapt, fist first. He made contact smack in the middle of his face and felt the cartilage of his nose give way under his phalanges.

"This one," he retorted.

He went back on his way with a spring in his step. Taken aback, Garroni, brought a hand p to his face and looked incredulously at the sight of his own blood.

The men were ordered to halt. Thirty-odd faces turned towards the middle of the yard.

"Everything all right, sergeant?"

"Get back to your training," shrieked Garroni. He rushed towards Theo and grabbed him right as he was stepping into the building. He tried to throw the weight of his entire body into shoving him against the wall. Theo feinted. He struck the door.

"You're going to pay for that," he whispered, his eyes crazed.

"Terrific idea. Go ahead, sergeant. Clean my clock."

Trembling with rage, he raised a deadly fist. With his right hand, he seized Theo by the collar, yanked him closer. His breath was coming out in pants. Theo watched him calmly, an amused smile on his lips. Slowly, Garroni loosened his hold. His arm fell back down along his body. His eyes were bloodshot.

"A lotta things can happen in the desert," he whispered, mouth misshapen in a rictus.

Theo waited for him to move away and entered the dorm. The sun behind him seemed to set the dried grass of the high plateau ablaze. Was that a trial by fire? Had he passed? *Katia, my girl, did I pass the test?*

Mount Sinai hospital, situated on Manhattan's Fifth Avenue, had the reputation of offering terminal-stage patients the best palliative care in the United States, and thereby in the whole world. There was an entire wing dedicated to this prestigious department, where only a few hundred privileged individuals, whose lifetime of labor had ensured they had top of the line insurance, had access.

It was a given that the best gerontologists on the East Coast would, at some point in their careers, be part of the incredibly brilliant and innovative team that embodied the pride and joy of the Hertzberg Institute, named after the founder of the program. From outside, only a few indicator panels enabled the passerby to distinguish the imposing building from the ones surrounding it.

Beck had no trouble finding his way along the endless meandering corridors with their heavy antiseptic odor and their naïve painted decorations, the result of a children's competition.

Much like five-star hotels, prestigious hospitals offered some of their of their guests the equivalent of a suite of rooms. Ellen Cheston was waiting for him in the most spacious and elegant of them all. An uniformed guard was posted in the entryway. Beck brandished his CIA card; no more call for him to hide. The man patted him down briefly and let him through.

Settled in a half-prone, half-seated position, chin supported by a strap, tubes coming out of both arms like the legs and sensilla of some disproportionate insect, "Marylin" seemed to be in tremendous pain. An elegant parlor couch had been set up facing the hospital bed. There weren't any flowers in the room. Gesturing with one hand, she signaled for Beck to take a seat.

"You got here fast, but I'm surprised that you waited for me to issue an invite before coming to see me. Feldman and my father were treated to more pomp than that…"

Gazing at her face, strangely beautiful despite its palor, perched atop a body tormented by nature, Beck couldn't stop himself from feeling pity. Ellen Cheston must have felt it, for she almost reflexively pulled up the edge of her sheet over to her neck, before unsnapping the chin strap that supported her head.

"You're standing before one of the richest and most powerful women in the world. Disturbing, isn't it? I'm assuming my file already goes into the details of my disease, so I'll spare you the topic.

"What you might not know is that its evolution has sped up over the past weeks. It was a given, but it's happening a little soon for my tastes."

Beck fidgeted on the couch, ill at ease. When he'd gotten that call from Ellen Cheston the day before, he'd asked himself whether to bring her flowers, since she was inviting him to visit her in her hospital room. He now regretted having foregone that.

"You're wondering why I called you specifically, when I'm in the state I'm in…"

"Miss Cheston…" Beck leaned lightly forward, his forearms nearly touching the chart hooked on the edge of the bed. "That's a question I'm not sure I want the answer to. You seem particularly dialed in, so I'm not going to insult you by letting you know that I've been taken off the investigation into your father's paramilitary activities."

"I know that…"

Ellen Cheston let out a kind of laugh, and was instantly overcome by a coughing fit. Worriedly, Beck got up to hand her a glass of water he grabbed off her side table. The young woman gestured her thanks.

"…Just as I've learned about your being placed on leave," she went on after she'd caught her breath. "How does that feel, a betrayal like that, after so many years spent in service to your Agency? Because you're not the kind of man who makes compromises, are you, and all the less so who compromises his principles?"

Beck nodded his head, his face impassive.

"I've especially learned to respect the greater goal, even if it flies in the face of my principles."

"Come now… I happen to think you're perfectly capable of putting two and two together. You get sidelined from an investigation that has a foregone result, you get put on leave, and the very same day, here you are brought into the very heart of the intrigue by a dying woman with nothing left to lose."

Beck kept silent. For a handful of moments, the beeping of the monitors was the only sound filling the vast room, which was isolated from the outside world by the horizontal slats of giant metallic blinds.

"I have to admit, you've made some waves," Ellen Cheston went on. "Your first cover, that of an FBI agent, had my father worried. As for Feldman, you need to know that we've already sent him back to Europe, a little bit because of you... I'm like you, Mister Beck, I'm speaking but I'm not telling you anything."

She sighed.

"Except perhaps one thing, in the end."

Ellen Cheston knew how to work a build-up, but she was interrupted by a fresh coughing fit.

"It's growing," she gritted out in a voice that sounded hollow, and terrible to hear. "Usually, cancer eats you from inside out, diminishes you. In my case, this hideous body keeps growing without a break. My chest cavity is growing in towards my lungs, and my joints have grown so much that every one of my bones looks like a club...

"Tomorrow, they're going to cut me open and remove almost a dozen ribs, just so I can keep breathing and living for a few more weeks, or a few more days. After which..."

"I'm sorry," whispered Beck.

"Come, I didn't have you come here to complain. Let's get back to the point."

"Does your father know about my visit?"

"In the abstract, perhaps. But as far as your being with me today, absolutely not. It's important to be able to maintain shadow areas, especially given that they're the mainstay of our business."

One of the phrases uttered by Haim came back to Howard's mind. "It takes a lot of shadows to create darkness, but the mere light of one candle is enough to lift them away." Were these the shadow areas that Ellen Cheston was alluding to?

"You've gotten a perfect grasp on the mechanism of our organization," she went on. "Ensuring the perfectly clandestine nature of our operation was my father's and his backers' first concern... And they've been getting worked up lately. But then, you'd know something about that."

The young woman suddenly turned crimson, holding back a new coughing fit. This time, she tried to sit up in order to grab her glass of water, but it slipped through her fingers and smashed against the floor, while her cardiac rhythm sent the monitors into a frenzy. The numbers on the displays began climbing higher with a dizzying speed, and for a moment Beck thought he'd have to press the emergency button to call in the nurses. But the episode stopped as abruptly as it had started.

"Sorry," went Ellen Cheston. "This isn't the kind of show I'd have wanted to put on for you..."

"I think you need to get some rest."

"Without disclosing the reason for your visit?" She grimaced out a smile. "You won't get me to believe that you'd be willing to give up this knowledge merely to spare my state of health. Down there, at the bottom of my nightstand…"

Beck shot her a questioning glance, then cottoned on. He nearly had to get on his knees to open the nightstand. He uncovered a bottle of whisky and two glasses.

"It calms me down," confided Ellen Cheston. "It's forbidden, of course, and completely incompatible with the junk they push through my veins. But I'd like to get through the end of our conversation without getting interrupted by that stupid cough."

Beck filled the two glasses halfway up and brought his up to his lips so as not to upset her. It was barely noon. As a rule, he waited for the end of the day before indulging in this ritual. The young woman drained hers in one gulp. Her voice had become astonishingly clear when she stared talking again.

"My father lives in constant worry of the camp being found. As for your agency's higher-ups and those rare politicians in the know, they live in a sort of constant terror…"

"The camp," cut in Beck, "or camps, Miss Cheston?"

"Let's not get ahead of ourselves. Let's talk about what is, not what may end up being. We've reached a phase where there's more and more pressure being exerted in order to grow the number of people aware of this location. The CIA wants to know, and not to know at the same time. Let's say it would like for someone to know…"

"But outside working hours!" cut in Beck.

Ellen Cheston showed her appreciation with a move of her head.

"My father obviously doesn't agree, but we don't share the same opinion on the matter. So then; are you ready?"

"I was given to understand that I was on vacation."

"Exactly. And you're dying to find out how our planes can get to the camp without being picked up by the radar network. I hope you're more of a south man than a north man, Mister Beck."

Ellen Cheston bestowed a smile on him that, for a fraction of a second, lit up her face and made her look happy.

"Because it's south that you're headed, aboard a gloriously comfortable jet, and I am sorry that you won't be able to bring your girlfriend along."

The summer had been particularly dry, and the first rainfall of the season wasn't expected for a few weeks yet. However, a few isolated clouds had strayed above the plateau a little after noon, bringing the training soldiers a few welcome moments of coolness.

Before they reached the camp, the mountains had disappeared beneath a blanket of black, electricity-laden cumulus clouds. Theo felt the splash of the first drop as he reached the mess. The clouds had formed an almost compact mass of dark and fluffy whirlwinds at rooftop level.

The base flew into a frenzy. The soldiers rushed outside, bearing tarps, buckets, shovels, to condemnations from the noncoms. Several Humvees crossed the main courtyard, bearing electrical pumps and hooded men sporting the hardened expressions of sappers in the course of duty.

Theo sped up, his clothes already soaking. A dump truck roared in out of nowhere and nearly ran him over. It skidded across several yards, its wagon full of sand. The driver rained curses down on him. In a matter of seconds, the shower had all the makings of a deluge. The moment Theo stepped through the door, a lightning bolt rent through the darkness, dangerously close.

"The chopper's gonna have a hard time making it back in."

Several men were already seated at the table. Theo grabbed a seat next to Juan, the Guatemalan he'd spoken a couple words to now and then.

"It won't be able to land tonight," he replied.

He grabbed the meat platter and served himself a generous helping. Juan was looking at him admiringly.

"Did you really plant your fist in Garroni's face?"

Theo lifted his shoulders in a shrug. His thoughts were adrift, away from here.

"There were thirty men who saw you," insisted Juan. "Word travels fast. Garroni claims it was an exercise. But we're not fooled…"

Theo lowered his chin in approval. He started in on his plate.

"How come you're not in the hole, then?"

Theo was getting ready to answer. Lochlan, the Irishman, had just sat down across from them. He leaned over his plate and said, looking mean,

"He's not going to the SHU anymore since he started kissing Meyrek's ass."

Juan watched Theo questioningly.

"Is it true what he says? Are you carving out your own little place, all for yourself like that?"

"Or maybe it's Meyrek carving out his," snickered Lochlan.

Theo kept his gaze adrift. If he'd had the stirrings of a plan during his year in training, even just the hope that he'd get his revenge one day, his one aim, consuming though vague as it had been, had crumbled upon Meyrek's revelation.

Since then, the hours trickled by, alike and monotonous, while the image of Katia occupied all his thoughts. All that was left for him to do was await his orders. Meyrek had made him into his puppet, and the worst of it was that he didn't give a damn. The last thing he wanted was to get himself dragged into a conflict between the members of his section.

"We're leaving for the desert the day after tomorrow," he whispered. "Garroni's hoping to get me out there."

The Irishman's expression changed in a flash. His sun allergy was common knowledge, and it earned him the worst kinds of jibes every time he tried to shade himself in the middle of a training exercise.

"What are we gonna do in the desert?"

"Survival training, three days."

264

"Not again!" grumbled Juan. "We had one of those not three months ago."

"Speak for yourself," went the Irishman. "Our buddy here doesn't even know what it's like. Isn't that right, Frenchie? You had your solo training there...?"

The mess hall door opened violently on a gust of wind. Instantly, sheets of water flooded a perimeter stretching out to the first tables. A soldier rushed over and shut it again. Thunder shook every window at once.

"Desert training?" snickered Juan. "More like flood survival."

"So," went on Lochlan, "Garroni's waiting for the next training exercise to give you a hiding? You broke his nose and he'd rather take care of that mano a mano, when all he has to do is say one word and you get locked inside the shell of the jalopy? And you expect us to believe that?"

Theo shook his head, indifferent.

"What's it matter?"

"Oh yeah? Lemme tell you. We've been locked inside this camp for months. We've been training. Some of us to death. And nobody's ever come tell us, "That's it! Next week, you'll be off smoking Pakis or Iranians or Koreans."

"Nah, camp's first op? Some sad little trek for a couple small-time drug dealers. But you, you get called in to see the colonel, and suddenly you can get away with anything.

"So I'm thinking, you've got answers. And I'd love to know where our asses will come under fire, and who from."

"I'm sorry" said Theo. "But I don't know any more than you do."

"Iran," growled the Irishman. "Iran is gonna be our first target!"

He swept a victorious gaze over the two men.

"I can't be wrong, right? That's why we're headed back into the desert."

Theo shook his head.

"I don't know."

"You do!" spat the Irishman in a menacing voice. "And you were ordered to keep it quiet. You're part of their gang. I caught on to it from the start, when you got here and you were kept aside. Special status, my ass!

"What did the colonel tell you this morning? Did he see you all cute and have his way with you? Did you two watch yourselves some porn together?"

Theo looked the Irishman right in the eye.

"He asked me to kill a man..."

He pushed his chair back and stood up from the table.

"...And I said yes."

The alarm bell rang at two o'clock in the morning. Most of them had been on alert since the storm had swept in and the trenches had been draining water across the base towards a river of mud. The fragile buildings weren't meant to withstand tropical rains of this magnitude. They needed to act fast. Make sure the flooding wouldn't weaken the foundations. The munitions store and the computer center were the most vulnerable spots.

The alarm rang a second time.

"Landslide!" shouted an NCO, shoving his head into the dorm. "The generators are getting swept away."

Theo hurled himself off his bed.

In a handful of seconds, all the men in the section found themselves in BDUs and pulling on rubber boots. The lights flickered.

"If we can find our way in the dark," said Juan ironically, "it's gonna be a hell of a mess."

The SUVs were swerving madly between the barracks. The garage had been emptied out, and a half-dozen trucks were filling the center of the courtyard. Here and there, the water was four inches deep.

"Never seen anything like this," whispered Juan.

A Humvee pulled up level with them, a floodlight mounted on. Garroni leapt to the ground.

"Five men with me! We're off to the secure area. Gotta lend the carpenters a hand."

The vehicle tore off, splashing out gushes of water. The headlights shone onto an almost unfathomable sheet of rain. They crossed the gaping-wide gateway to the secure military area without even realizing it.

"We lost a generator!" shouted Garroni to be heard over the roar of the engine. "Carried off by the mud. We've gotta secure the second one."

A column of floodlights mounted on just as many vehicles lit up the slope like a candle-lit procession.

"One of the guys got really bashed up," continued the sergeant. "The fuel tank collapsed on top of him."

They leapt out of the ATV. Three SUVs set up in a half-circle were lighting up the field of operations. A rocky outcropping had collapsed, triggering a mud- and rockslide. The stream had taken one of the walls of the plant, causing the flooring to sag. A huge generator had been torn from its metallic support structure, blast through a second wall, and had come to a rest in the middle of the muddy debris, its turbine asunder.

Several men were trying to prop up the ruins and shore up the second unit, which was listing perilously.

"Watch the cables!" howled the operations chief, a second lieutenant in charge of maintenance. "It's running full juice."

"Why won't they turn off the other machine?" asked Juan.

"Because of the computers," replied Theo.

"Unload the truck," ordered Garroni. "They need chucks."

They were up to their knees in mud. Five men were barely up to the task of dragging the beams. The ground was as slippery as a snowfield.

"Hurry it up. It's gonna collapse."

The lead man lost his grip and pitched into a rut, water washing over his entire body. The sudden excess weight taking him by surprise, Theo lost his balance, taking the rest of the bearers with him. The beam crashed down with a mighty splatter.

266

"Pick it up, faster! If that generator tips over, we're toast."

The five men got back up, caked in mud. They had no more purchase on the wood.

"We gotta grab another one!" shouted Theo.

They tore down the slope to the truck, yanked a second prop from the cargo. The rain seemed destined to never end. This time, they reached the ruined power station. The carpenter team took over. The strut got pushed upright against the generator and nestled into a hastily dug base.

"It's never gonna hold! We're making holes in the water."

"We gotta fill up that floor. Find some rocks, some planks, anything."

The generator swayed with a sinister crackle. Juan appeared animated by a sudden idea.

"The SUV!" he shouted. "We're gonna prop it up with the car."

Not waiting for Garroni's go-ahead, he rushed over to the vehicle and started the ignition. He began driving up the slope, wheels half sucked into the mud.

"Veer around that tree trunk," yelled Theo, hands cupped around his mouth. "Keep your gear low. Easy."

The grinding of the gearbox was agonizing. Yard by yard, the Humvee was coming closer to the power station.

"Move back!"

The wheels were spraying muddy gravel across several yards. Juan veered around the worst of the landslide, drove along the remainder of the foundations, steered the vehicle into the gaping wide hole. The tires found their purchase against the mass of rocks. The SUV climbed the ruins almost vertically, falling inside the building. With one last effort, Juan rammed the hood of the car under the flooring. At the very same moment, one of the beams gave way.

"The cables!" shouted Theo.

As it collapsed, the support strut took a section of wall down with it. The cables from the first generator came alive like writhing snakes. With a shower of sparks, they struck the Humvee, mowed Juan down. He seemed to flare into a blaze, his whole body shaking and jolting.

The cables started moving again in a cloud of ozone, flew to the overturned fuel tank. The entire power station caught ablaze. Several carpenters ran out howling, their bodies aflame. They rolled around in the mud. Two men collapsed, their faces charred.

With a final groan, the second turbine went offline. Theo had hurled himself to the ground right at the time of the explosion. He got back up and ran inside the plant. Garroni followed him in.

The flames were licking at the Humvee, inside which Juan's body was slumped like a puppet off its strings. The fuel had spread across the ground, flowing underneath the floor in long streams of blazing lava. The mud was fighting the fire already.

"The second generator is intact," shouted Garroni. He called out to the second lieutenant.

"He won't answer you," said Theo. "He was next to the tank when it all went up."

"We've gotta secure the second generator. The maintenance teams are sure to get it working again."

"The floor seems like it's holding, with the SUV in there. But there's no way the servers aren't down."

"How's that?" inquired the sergeant.

"The computers… The inverters won't hold for long."

He was getting ready to move away. After all, he'd done what he'd been able to, out of sheer compassion. But this wasn't his war. Garroni caught up to him, shouting.

"Get back here, Collin! Screw the computers. But there's the jamming system…"

"The jamming sys…?"

Theo froze to a stop, taken aback, just the time Garroni needed to catch up to him and grab him by the collar of his BDUs. Mud and soot caked his face like camouflage makeup, a nightmarish, apocalyptic vision of hell on earth.

"Don't play the fool! You know exactly what I'm talking about. The system only has one hour of autonomy built in. You know what's gonna happen next. And you find that funny, huh…?"

Theo was completely lost. The sergeant began to shake him with all his strength, his eyes crazed. He began to shout.

"No sonofabitch has ever raised his hand at me. Not ever!"

Raising a hand the size of a beater, he smacked him full strength. The storm and the death hanging in the air seemed to have cost him his reason.

"How 'bout I take care of you now, for good? Who'd know?"

Although slightly dazed, Theo abruptly dropped his whole weight down, taking Garroni with him as he fell. For several seconds, the two men rolled around on the ground, the sergeant reeling off a stream of insults and threats. Blows began raining down on Theo's face as, immobilized under the sergeant's weight, he became unable to feint them.

All of a sudden, Novak's figure loomed over them. There hadn't been enough time for the officer to pull on his uniform all the way. Soaking wet, his shirttails were hanging out of his fatigue pants. He was holding his service weapon and its holster in one hand. His order landed like a whip.

"Garroni, let him go."

Without a moment's pause, Novak rushed the two men and grabbed the sergeant by the shoulder, making him straighten up.

"You've got better and more pressing things to do. Sergeant! Take Collin to the center immediately. He'll know what needs to be done!"

Inside the hangar, the survivors were tackling the fire with buckets, while one technician climbed the control box. Two men were already trying to consolidate the floor. Garroni was trembling with rage. In the end, he acquiesced.

Face swollen, Theo took one last look at Juan's body.

They took a second Humvee. The camp was plunged into darkness. At the entrance of each building, the section chiefs were trying to assemble their men. There were orders flying around every which way, magnified by megaphones.

An auto-machine gun guarded the entrance to the weapons store. A patrol watched over the colonel's quarters. It was imperative to prevent certain recruits from turning the situation to their advantage.

Two men were guarding the access to the computer center, fingers poised on their submachine guns.

"I see light," exclaimed Garroni.

Theo leapt out of the vehicle. The building was secured with an electronic lock. The sergeant keyed a number into the panel.

"It's not working."

"Go to manual override."

"I don't have the key."

"Shoot the lock, the magnets will release."

Garroni buried three bullets into the panel. Together, they pushed the door open. A thick cloud of black smoke grabbed them right by the throat.

"Something's burning in there."

"The generator caused short-circuits all the way here. We've gotta uncouple the batteries and unplug the computers."

Garroni hesitated.

"Where's the technicians?"

"They're probably suffocating."

"I'll let the colonel know."

"We've gotta do this right now!" asserted Theo. "Those guys will die if we leave them in there."

"Well then go 'head," cried Garroni, a panicked look in his eyes. "Head into that oven."

He abandoned Theo right in the doorway and rushed over to the SUV.

"Take care of this goddamn mess yourself. You know your business. At least now you know why you're here!"

Theo didn't have the time to question the officer's last remark. He tore off a strip of his shirt, dipped it in a puddle of water, and wrapped it around his face. The smoke had filled the computer room and was streaming out through the secure door.

In a matter of moments, he understood the situation. The circuit breaker catching fire had melted the polystyrene insulation in the false ceiling. The material was nonflammable, but it gave off impressive amounts of smoke. The damage was minimal.

He looked around for the technicians and saw a body next to the control panel. The man seemed in shock. His right hand was burned up to the forearm. Theo leaned over him. He still had a pulse. He grabbed him by the armpits and dragged him outside. The technician had caught a bullet when the short-circuit had taken place, but he seemed out of danger.

He found a fire extinguisher next to the exit, spraying streams of dry ice onto the false ceiling and the broken circuit breaker. In a few seconds, the seeming conflagration was under control.

Theo got rid of his makeshift mask and tried to locate the batteries. The two rows of computer terminals were purring softly, all screens on, benefiting from the residual power off the inverters. He found a metal locker and moved a cartload of listings to free it.

Just when he made to open the locker, his gaze caught the title on the pile of printouts.

"Weapons and munitions supplies. Camp B."

Intrigued, he forgot all about the batteries, rapidly scanning the listings. The paperwork recounted the shipment of an impressive number of Kalashnikovs, as well as Heckler & Koch and Uzi submachine guns. Theo had never seen the slightest hint of that type of weapon on base. The second letter of the alphabet was an incontestable hint as to the existence of another camp. Heart hammering, he propped himself before a keyboard and typed up "Camp B" on the control screen.

> *Confidential. Input access code.*

Panicking, Theo looked around him. Computer guys sometimes kept their passwords jotted down in a notebook. He upended several drawers, rooted through folders. No use. He only had a few minutes before rescuers would get there.

Unless Garroni had taken advantage of things to…

Theo rushed outside. The man was still in the same position, head tilted back and supported by his shirt. His breath was whistling in and out. Theo gave him several slaps. The technician opened his eyes.

"The code. I've gotta uncouple the computers. What's the code?"

The man shook his head. Theo slid his arm beneath the back of his neck and leaned him forward. The technician coughed and let out a moan.

"My hand…"

"It's gonna be OK. It's a superficial wound."

He placed the man's injured hand on his thighs and covered it with the moistened shirt.

"The code. I need the code right now. The drives need saving."

"My hand," repeated the technician. "It's an AFR[13]… my prints…"

It was then Theo noticed the small box containing the biometric sensor, then examined the injured man's hand. It was one giant blister. There was no way for a palmprint lock to identify those mangled fingers.

The technician passed out once more. Theo laid him gently back and rushed towards the keyboard. He typed in several codes. The message "Input access code" flashed out and then appeared again.

Theo went back to the technician and dragged him to the palmprint lock. He gently freed the right hand from the blouse and placed it on the sensor. Excepting for a few moans on the part of the prone man, he got no reaction.

---

13   *Automatic Fingerprint Recognition System*: A biometrical fingerprint scanning system.

The message "Input access code" kept up its obstinate display.

That was when Theo caught sight of the make and model of the AFR system: made by CryptoQuest – a subsidiary of E.C.Tronics.

With a little bit of luck, Theo himself had contributed to the software conception. And if that was the case, he had to have done what he usually did and code in his own fingerprints inside a subfolder of the driver. Which was incredibly illegal, but could come in handy sometimes.

He went all for broke and placed his right hand on the designated space.

"Input access code"

Theo sighed. One of two things, then: either he hadn't been part of the software coding process, or the E.C.Tronics monitors had picked up his print within the code hierarchy and had simply erased it before putting the software up on the market, the way they did most of the time.

After all, coding these subroutines meant for personal use and their subsequent elimination was a little game that the programmers played with the monitoring and analysis personnel. A game of hide and seek where one party inserted, and the other party rooted out hidden files and other Trojans.

Coming up empty, Theo scanned the room around him. He knew the rescue team could be here any minute now, and there was nothing that could enable him to circumvent the safety device.

Once more, his gaze fell onto the technician passed out at his feet. Unconsciously, he was cradling his burned hand with his good left hand.

Wait, good?

Theo suddenly felt a mad hope. One out of every ten people is left-handed.

He gently grabbed the unconscious man by his collar, pulled him up by his armpits, and placed his left hand inside the scanner bed. He then let out a sigh of relief. This time, numbers blinked onto the screen, then an outline appeared. He moved the technician's body out of the way and returned to the keyboard. He navigated past "Weapons" and "Supervision" and selected "Personnel."

His breath was panting. Like a flash, a scene, a premonition, replayed in his memory. Hadn't his Vietnamese teammate, trained in that strange, insurgent religion, predicted that he would carry out an initiation after he went through a test of the four elements? Hadn't fire been the thing to lead him to this place, for a brief time putting him in complete command of the base's strategic nucleus?

The "Personnel" menu broke down into two categories: adults and children. Theo let out a moan. He selected "Children."

'They've got kids,' he thought. *'These assholes are training a child army!'*

The list appeared. Ordered by age and assigned activities. There were dozens of them. Theo scrolled down, mad with hope. The names were spinning around inside his head.

Girls, boys. South American, for the most part. Children from the favelas, orphans sold for a fistful of dollars, souls trafficked as weapons. He scrolled back, double-checked. The list went on. He paged down. Still more names. Still more children.

Theo suddenly felt his heart stop beating.

> *Collin*

His daughter's name was appended to his own. Dizzy with a reckless hope, terrified at the thought that what he was going through wasn't real, he selected Katia's file.

Two photos illustrated his daughter; one of them, in combat gear, brought tears to his eyes. Concise, the file indicated her entry date into the camp, an exact match to the date of the accident. The extreme confidential status that surrounded this "recruit" had rated a mention.

The child had her mother's huge eyes, even more beautiful than he remembered. Trembling, torn up inside at having to move on from that picture, Theo navigated to the adult section and typed in his wife's name.

> *Name not found*

He widened the search. Pitiless, the computer fed him the same result. Theo suddenly felt his rage rekindle. Spurred by a desire for revenge, he got the idea of typing up the command to have the server's memory bank reformatted. But, despite the storm and the camp-wide blackout, he didn't have the time to erase his tracks from the system. If Meyrek found out that he was involved in the slightest bit of sabotage, all hope that he might see his daughter again would be taken from him.

He had committed to securing the memory banks and safeguarding the machines. Now wasn't the time to get his revenge yet, especially since a plan, extremely vague though it was, had started taking shape inside his head. So he turned off the computers one by one.

All but one.

In that reddish half-darkness, the glare of its screen was as bright as a lighthouse in the night. Theo made a beeline for it.

Once more, the same inevitable words were blinking on the display.

> *Enter access code*

"Not again!" thundered Theo, thudding his hand onto the biometric scanner.

And, as though by magic, the screen went blue, displaying the message:

> *E.C.T…Viral print*

His heart leapt inside his chest. The message had appeared in French, and Theo knew that he had been the one to write it. Himself. In another time. In another place. They were the words that came up on his screen every day, when he turned on his office computer from deep inside his Paris E.C. Tronics office. "Viral print" was nothing other than a program he'd invented, the software called Enterprise 17.

They even kept the trace of my personal identifier. These shitheads can't even do a memory cleanup right.

Feeling a hint of pride, despite the dramatic stakes of the situation, Theo pushed the Enter key.

The interface was completely unfamiliar to him. He saw, but couldn't parse, a planispheric projection crisscrossed by a multitude of lines and wavy curves. Trajectories. Geographical coordinates.

Glowing points were moving along the lines, changing in real time. One of those points made it above the Gulf of Mexico just then. An alert rang out, and a red triangle appeared on the map, covering the point. The tip of the triangle seemed to point towards the location of the base. And up on the screen, the interface changed.

An endless data list scrolled by extremely quickly under Theo's dumbfounded gaze. In the upper left corner of the title bar, he managed to make out the only bit of constant text on the whole screen:

Enterprise 17 v 3.7

This time, it was the core of his program, several generations removed. The work that had led to his promotion within E.C.Tronics. The software that had, officially, never existed.

It only took him a few minutes inside the admin console to understand that his program had been modified to infiltrate thousands of personal computers all over the world, like a Trojan horse. A few more seconds, and he understood the purpose of it.

The system he was looking at was using an unfathomable amount of computing power to modify the data streams that linked civilian and military surveillance satellites to their relay stations and their control and imagery centers, no matter where they were from.

Even more so than the secret location of the base, even more so than the gigantic net that blanketed the Tex-Mex Town and the artificial lake, Theo's brainchild was singlehandedly ensuring the base's stealth.

An enormous amount of the harnessed computing power was necessary to crack the dynamic, 128-bit encryption keys securing the constant streams of information linking the satellites to their bases. Once the encryption was cracked, the software changed the code in real time, erasing the base off the mountain plateau by inserting fabricated data while it intercepted the data streaming down from the satellite.

The program acted like a robber who had recorded a video of a secure area and looped it back to the bank security monitors through the surveillance cameras before crossing said area. A classic heist movie trope.

In other words, the satellite imagery stations were unable to detect any sign of human activity in the area where the base was located. Or in any other…

It was child's play to locate the second camp on the map, only taking him a few moments. In possession of the coordinates that would enable him to find the place, Theo first began looking for the batteries, and rerouted all their power, as well as all the power from the other computers' inverters, to this workstation, in order to ensure Enterprise 17 stayed up and running.

He then keyed in several instructions, dissimulated inside an invisible admin file that it took him a few seconds to create. Since coming to the base, he'd lost all sense of time. The computer clock told him that it was Monday, and that it was twenty-three hundred hours here in Mexico.

'Let's go for Friday at the same time.'

After a moment's hesitation, Theo saved the final command, watching the responses as they came up on the screen. Then, heaving a sigh, he let go at last, submerged by a wave of emotion. This loosening up nearly proved fatal to his reason, for while he was mentally retracing his steps, a thousand scenarios suddenly stirred in his imagination, each more sordid and crueler than the last.

His little girl, his child, in fatigues, goose-stepping in the blazing heat, eyes forever dry from crying too much. Juliette trying to protect Katia. Or had the daughter been the one to defend her mother? Juliette, her clothes in tatters, curled in on herself while jeering men took turns raping her…

The rage he had inside bubbled over within him to the point of overwhelm. Then, just one word, one name, broke through his throat.

"Meyrek!"

His cry sounded out between the dead machines.

"Meyrek!"

He rushed out in the rain. No help was coming. As he'd suspected, Garroni had hoped he'd left him to die in the fire. The air filled his lungs. He grabbed a shovel from near the guard station. The soldiers watched him go by, astonished. The rainwater was mingling with his tears; the black traces from the fire made his face look insane.

Theo picked up his pace, brandishing the shovel at arm's length. The yard was huge. He needed to cross it. *One lap. Just one lap this time.* Nothing could protect the colonel. He crossed the path of a line of trucks, heard his name being called. The officers' building was still two hundred yards out. Familiar faces turned towards him. Let their bullets strike him! Even full of lead, he'd still have enough strength to reach Meyrek.

He was too late in noticing the gigantic mass rushing towards him. He turned away, tried to swing the shovel in self-defense. The man dove forward, grabbed him by the legs, and pinned him to the ground.

Theo struggled like he was possessed. The man came back towards him, shouting words he didn't understand. He tried to grab for the shovel again, crawling through the mud and twisting every which way to loosen the hold he was in.

"*Carnal!* It's me. Will."

His friend's name echoed inside his head. Will. He stiffened, lowered his eyes towards his opponent. His anger vanished all at once, at the same time that his reason returned to him.

"Will, let me go. I need to get to Meyrek."

"Hey, yo, *calmos, amigo.* Shut up. Come on out of the rain."

There were several soldiers surrounding them, looking curious and amused. Will helped him up. He'd reached him a few yards from the mess, between the rows of vehicles. He took him someplace isolated where it was dry.

"My daughter's alive," said Theo in a clipped voice. "Marcos's kids, too. There's a second camp. They're training kids there. That's their future army."

Will pinned him with a dismayed gaze.

"How do you know?"

"Meyrek… My daughter's alive, Will! He's using her against me. But I know where she is. I know the location of the second camp."

"Me too," uttered Will. "At least, I think."

Theo stiffened.

"What do you mean?"

"I think I can locate it. About thirty clicks out, in the south of the desert. We've just come from there. The chopper dropped us off on a private runway, and two of the base's SUVs picked us up. The wind was too strong to make the climb up to the plateau."

He watched Theo. His face was ashen.

"What makes you think it's the camp?"

"When the pilot said we couldn't cross the storm, Novak gave him the landing strip coordinates. He made a radio call. No sign of life on the ground.

"But as soon as we flew over the strip, the lights came on. The welcoming committee had on the same kinds of uniforms we do. The lights went back off as soon as we landed. Same as here."

Theo suddenly started shaking. Will lifted his head. His teeth were chattering.

"Yo, *carnal?*"

"My daughter is barely ten years old, Will. I thought I'd never see her face again. I'd forgotten what she looked like, I'd even forgotten her birthday. She lives in a military camp exactly like ours, and I almost didn't even recognize her. A camp where there's guards, and forced marches, and shooting and survival exercises."

"You're absolutely positive? Look me in the eye, *carnal…* You're not having a delusion?"

Will held Theo's gaze with his own. What he read there managed to convince him. For a moment, his features sagged, taking on a look of compassion and sadness the likes of which Theo had never seen him sport before.

"And your woman?" asked Will.

Theo hesitated; a stronger, crueler pain sliced at his insides. For the first time in months, a human sort of pain.

"I don't know, her name wasn't in the data."

Will grabbed him by the shoulders and brought him in close. A Mexican-style embrace, before stepping back and bumping fists with him in a classic salute. *My man.* Kindness and determination shone equally in his eyes. With, in their very depths, a tiny murderous spark.

"We'll go get her. You hear? We'll go get her. Her and all them kids. We're gonna get out of here."

"OK, you big lug." Theo smiled. "I'll leave you to tell Marcos."

The storm had eased off, and the downpour had turned into a drizzling rain that pattered almost joyfully against the truck covers, while the water level dropped in real time all over, barely reaching the bottoms of their shoes anymore.

The central courtyard was reduced to mud, but a stable, practicable mud. Weak and wavering, light streamed back through the barracks windows, prompting hurray's from the exhausted men who'd just gone through their first fight with nature itself and were already priding themselves on their victory.

Garroni's ATV crossed the camp, headed towards the computer center, and passed in front of the two men, whom the occupants didn't appear to recognize. Meyrek was seated in the back.

Theo's face hardened. A dangerous gleam had come to his eyes. He was back in control of himself.

"Yes, Will. We'll go get them. And I know exactly how!"

Chapter 16

The funeral ceremony took place just before the helicopter took off. The base had just lost men in the line of duty, and Meyrek insisted on upholding certain military traditions.

Juan and the lieutenant in charge of maintenance, an Englishman named Marlowe, were the first to be honored. Owing to their initiative, it had been possible to bring the second generator back up and running. A team of builders and electricians was already working on a new power station, somewhere more shielded.

The computer center had taken a big hit. And Meyrek could barely believe that the data, like the *umbrella*, had been saved thanks to Garroni, with Collin's assistance. From the two men's interrogation, it had come out that the sergeant had stuck to Theo like a burr.

The latter had finally been able to put his abilities to the service of the base; it was about time, to say the least. In a certain way, the colonel felt a sense of pride. A year's training, some carefully exerted pressure along emotional lines, and he could turn any given man into a loyal and disciplined fighting machine.

The mercenaries shot two salvoes, and every man on base held a few moments of silence.

The elite section was already in combat gear, desert camouflage and light helmets, one-pint flasks to the side. The order to break ranks sounded out. They rushed to the huge Sikorsky Sea Knight. The rotors whined. Twenty men had been picked. They piled up on the floor of the chopper. Garroni was the last to hop on board.

A minute later, the base was nothing more than a speck lost amid the vegetation.

The decor inside the Challenger 604 jet only partially hinted at the tastes of its owner, and it was lacking in any feminine touch. The four dark leather seats mounted facing the front of the cabin could pivot to create a conference area, or recline to yield four beds. They were separated from a small bedroom area by a space housing a lavatory outfitted for Ellen Cheston's disability.

A kitchen niched in behind a bar, a more conventional second lavatory unit, and an office space set up exclusively for communications and online connections rounded out the cabin. Extreme care had gone into picking out all the materials: cherry wood fixtures, partitions covered with darkened mirrors, plush and elegantly patterned carpets, indirect lighting.

Everything inside the plane was high-end, and its stunning performance matched its interior. It was capable of flying almost 4000 miles without stopping over, at speeds of 525 miles and a cruising altitude of 41 000 feet.

The CIA had a fleet of similar jets at its disposal, and Beck had made use of that more than once during his trips, but there wasn't a one among them that could hold a candle to Ellen's Challenger, either in terms of elegance or comfort. As she'd invited him aboard her plane, Gregory Cheston's daughter had let him know this was the first time she'd lent a stranger her plane. A veil of sadness had darkened her face as she'd mentioned, as though it had been necessary, that she wouldn't be coming with him.

A silent steward had been at Beck's disposal since they'd taken off. Courteous without being obsequious, he'd offered to prepare him a meal, something that Beck had declined with his thanks, preferring to set his sights on the twenty-year old Chivas that several bottles of adorned the bar.

The crew, made up of a pilot and a copilot, had greeted him with the same kind of circumspect respect. The plane had taken off from LaGuardia at twenty-hundred hours. The destination named on its flight plan was Mexico City.

Three hours after takeoff, Howard Beck still didn't know anything more than when he'd started. His whisky glass – his second, nearly empty – in his hand, he was beginning to feel himself drift off into a sleep that he instantly pulled himself from, instead asking the steward to make him some coffee.

"I would have thought you'd rather get some sleep," the man replied. "Miss Cheston never allows use of her bedroom, but your chair will be every bit as comfortable if you recline it."

Beck thanked him and let him know he wished to speak to the captain. Immediately, the steward picked up the receiver connecting the cabin to the cockpit. The captain joined them just moments later.

From his accent, Beck gleaned that he was Canadian. The man, in his fifties, looked very distinguished in his white uniform. With his flat stomach and wide shoulders, he could have played himself in any Hollywood production.

"Ellen Cheston didn't give me any clues as to the direction we're headed," shot Beck. "I was given to understand that Mexico City is our first layover?"

The pilot showed his agreement, looking inquisitive.

"Miss Cheston authorized me to disclose our final destination to you once we've taken off from Mexico City."

"In the same way I'm sure you'll disclose the procedure required to get there without revealing the location of the camp?"

Beck got a smile in response. The captain bobbed his head, visibly amused.

278

"It's not so much a procedure. Just a small intervention after we register the flight plan. And a pinch of piloting in extreme conditions… Was that everything you wanted to know, sir?"

He'd already straightened back up and was getting ready to head back into the cockpit when Beck hailed him.

"And where was it you learned to execute this extreme piloting? The army?"

The pilot shook his head, still looking every bit as amused.

"DEA, actually… We were nearly colleagues at one point, Mister Beck. Your agency was moving drugs to finance its black ops, and mine was trying to put a stop to it, not knowing who it was dealing with. It just so happens that ground-level pursuits in a twin-engine, 500 feet under radar coverage, are my specialty."

He was halfway inside the cockpit before he said his last words.

"Get some rest. It's gonna be a long flight. I bid you goodnight."

A warm wind blew over the arid ground and stirred the dry bushes between the boulders. The savannah stretched out as far as the eye could see. Its surface, however, barely covered a couple dozen miles, and there was no danger in crossing it in an SUV.

Encircled by the highland mountains, the desert spread was unusual in the area, a feature far more common to the very north of the country, near the border with the United States. It constituted an excellent training ground, and its proximity had been a deciding factor in picking the geographical location of the base.

The men leapt out of the helicopter and surrounded the sergeant.

"You're going to split up into four groups of five men. We're at the southern edge of the desert. Each group will have to make its way north along a different itinerary. North-west, north-north-west, north-east, north-north-east.

"You've got just enough water to last you one day. No food. Red ants and barbecued snake, for those of you who haven't tried it yet, is very nutritious. If you eat the head of a rattlesnake, empty out the glands first."

He tossed a bag to the ground.

"No compass, no firearms. One hunting knife for every group leader. It will take you two days to reach the dried out *rio* at the foot of the mountains you can see over there.

"Next, you're gonna have a good ten hours' climb. From there on, you'll need to keep an eye out for ambushes. The chopper will do flyovers on several occasions. As soon as you've spotted it, you'll have a few seconds to get to cover. We will shoot at anything that moves, and even if we're not aiming straight at you, bullets stray quickly.

"The soil is loose. You can dig trenches. Watch out for critters, most of them are venomous. If a teammate is wounded, take off your shirts, set them up in a line when the chopper arrives, and remain motionless nearby. We'll get the message.

"Now, on to the groups."

Huang took command of Theo's cell. It was made up of Marcos, Lochlan, whose scarlet face betrayed the agony he was already suffering, and Salinas, Marcos's Peruvian friend. Will got put in charge of the second group, assisted by Huang's brother. Their getting separated was a risk they'd taken into account, but one that complicated their plan. The two men shared a look, disappointed but every bit as determined, when Garroni issued his final instructions before getting back aboard the helicopter. The cells fanned out in their assigned directions. As luck would have it, Will's and Theo's itineraries were close to each other.

Barely two hours after the helicopter had taken off, it was already 113 degrees. From noon on, the feeling of suffocation overshadowed all other sensations, and each step became torment. In the complete, almost palpable quiet, rent sometimes by the cry of a vulture or eagle, the muffled sounds of their booted steps had a funereal quality, like something out of a procession.

The five men talked little, saved their saliva, barely moistened their lips, took care to save their water. The smallest drop would instantly turn to sweat, and they had to use the full force of their will to resist the itch to empty out their canisters.

At the bottom of the steep, rocky incline, the odd candelabra cactuses looked a sinister grey-green, and rarely came up taller than knee-high. A few wild grasses, brambles, and shrubs broke the monotony of a ground that was as furrowed as an old man's face, betraying the location of a former fossil shaft.

Toward the middle of the afternoon, Huang took care of their dinner by sinking his knife into a rattlesnake curled up at the foot of a rocky outcropping. With a launch like a carnival knife thrower's, he pinned the snake to the ground before beheading it, carving it up, then tying its scaly and still slimy skin around his neck. According to his terse explanation, it was a shield against the heat. Grilled immediately, the flesh got split five ways and placed in everyone's bags.

Marcos and Theo returned to their places at the back of the group, muscles already stiff from dehydration. Dead ahead, the mountains seemed never to be getting closer. Cracked, the ground occasionally reflected blinding flashes. Their eyes soon lost all sense of color. The sun was white, the sky golden, and the ground ochre.

Ever since Will's revelations about the existence of a second camp, one that housed his children, Marcos had withdrawn into a numb silence, paired with a robotic body language. Just like Theo before him, he swung between rage and despondency, in between euphoric highs.

Like each one of the camp's recruits, Marcos was capable of pitiless murder in his sleep. It had taken all of Will's strength to keep him from straying beyond the point of no return after he'd revealed the truth about his children. Marcos's teary-eyed conclusion had been as plain as it had been clear.

"When we're done, Meyrek is mine."

280

The two men hadn't said a word to each other since the helicopter had left. A few steps farther from them, a solitary figure, Huang was advancing with all the caution of a predator hunting for prey. Marcos broke the silence as they were skirting around the rugged perimeter of a sharp incline, the edge of which rose and splintered into a multitude of perilously edged ridges.

"And if none of the three follows us?"

It was a possibility that Will and Theo had considered from every angle. The section was tightly knit, the men respected each other, but their common goal remained the success of the military operations they'd been trained for. There were no idealists among them; only mercenaries. Excepting maybe one…

In a quick stride, Theo joined Huang. The scaly skin around his neck had stiffened and was beginning to give off a pestilential stench. The Vietnamese man was the only one there not sweating.

"Does that smelly thing really protect you from the heat?" asked Theo.

Huang lifted his scaly scarf to point to the back of his neck.

"This is where your body decides if you are hot or not. Reptile skin is as cold as their blood."

He looked unblinkingly at Theo. Some thirty yards out, Marcos had stepped closer to Salinas and begun talking to him, taking care to slow his pace so as to let Lochlan move farther away. The Vietnamese man took on a strange expression before backing up, suddenly leery.

"Wait, listen!"

"This is the time you pick?" Huang grimaced. "Here, in the middle of the desert? You don't have a chance."

A rocky ridge now separated them from the rest of the group. There wasn't enough time for Theo to persuade him. He barely knew the Vietnamese man, and he had no idea about what truly motivated him. One name came back to him. He decided to go for broke.

"Huỳnh Phú Sổ, Huang, tell me more about him."

"I should especially tell you about his fights. That's what you want to hear. Am I wrong?"

"A disabled man who becomes a warrior, after a long initiation, that's what stuck with me…"

"And you have gone through fire," acceded Huang in a thick, grave voice.

He brightened suddenly and started walking again.

"All that is nonsense. You heard your friend Will. I have to find something to do between two training sessions."

Theo grabbed him by the sleeve of his BDU. An ugly, dangerous glint slid across the Vietnamese man's gaze.

"Huang, they stole our children!"

"I don't understand what you mean."

"The Organization. Meyrek. They took my daughter, and Marcos's kids."

Within moments, Theo had told him everything he'd found out. The plan he'd cobbled together with Will. Marcos's collaboration. The necessity of finding that second camp, of putting an end to this absurdity. Of finding and freeing their children.

Now that they'd moved past the incline, they could once again see Marcos and Salinas, walking closely together despite the difficult, rugged terrain, far behind the Irishman.

"I don't know anything about your religion," ended Theo. "But I do remember that *strange fragrance from the precious mountain*. That sounds far too beautiful to really be nonsense."

"I'm a mercenary, Collin. I fight for whoever hires me."

"You're also the follower of a warrior philosophy. What is this *strange fragrance?*"

The Vietnamese man shook his head.

"An old story. It is not for Westerners."

"Then why did you take an interest in me? You and your brother both; I saw you two more than once, in the middle of the night, waiting for me to come back after the hill.

"What did you see in me, Huang? Consider it my initiation. If Marcos managed to talk Salinas round, it's three of us against you and the Irish guy."

"Huỳnh Phú Sổ fought for my people's freedom and spiritual elevation. Against the French colonizers, and then against communism."

"And that fragrance, Huang? That mountain? If that's what you believe in, explain it to me. You've already told me too much."

The Vietnamese man leaned down to tear at some dry grass that he brought up to his nose to sniff, eyes half-mast. Marcos and the Peruvian had stayed back once more. Very high up in the sky, prey birds were hovering in circles, not making a sound. The sun was casting long shadows across a ground that had shifted from white to ochre and from a dusty grey to a deep green. With a slow gesture, Huang freed his neck from the snake skin around it and held the scaly sheath out to Theo.

"The fragrance is the inspiration that pushes us to act for good, before the end of time. The Mountain… there are actually seven. It is from there that the Buddha must come down one day to bring us a new age of prosperity, after a long period of wars and misfortunes.

"You Westerners have something similar: the Apocalypse. Here, put this around your neck, it will stop you from losing all your water as sweat."

"Huang, you know Will is trying to talk your brother around."

This time, the Vietnamese man laughed heartily. It was as though this whole entire scene, Theo's near begging, had all been an act. Since the latter wasn't making any move to grab the snake skin, Huang placed it back around his own neck.

"Well, good luck to your giant friend if he didn't manage to be persuasive!"

"Huang!"

The man's eyes turned as black as a river during a starless night.

"The Apocalypse is right around the corner, Collin. It's what I have taken up arms to fight. But one of your philosophers said, "If you stare too hard at the abyss, the abyss will look at you right back."

282

"Even a mercenary has the right to judge the people who hire him. So, what's your plan?"

They made it to the edge of a narrow crevasse. Plagued by the drought, the ground had split open like a wound. The crack wound through the boulders.

Huang crouched, pushed off with his legs, and crossed over in one leap. Theo followed suit. He landed effortlessly across. Ten yards in front of them, Marcos and Salinas were waiting for them.

From the Mexican's satisfied expression, Theo understood there was one man left to persuade. The Irishman. They were now four against one.

The doctor finally let Gregory Cheston know that his daughter was awake and ready to talk to him. He continued in a respectful tone of voice, though one that lacked that annoying oiliness most people bestowed on the billionaire.

"Don't tire her out. If her heartbeat speeds up or her blood pressure gets high, I'll be forced to ask you to leave."

Cheston assented. He had already been informed that the surgery, although run of the mill, had been tricky, and that his daughter might suffer from complications.

"Not very predisposed to surgery. As though her body has an axe to grind with the whole world. We've truly done everything we could, but we aren't fully satisfied with the result…"

Ellen was lying in the half-darkness, immobilized by several straps, her chest cradled by a soft constraint, her lower body invisible beneath a structure shaped like a tent. An oxygen tube fed air through two cannulas inside her nostrils.

She had the waxen complexion and tormented mien of the seriously sick, and a heavy-hearted Gregory read a sentence within her nearly lifeless gaze that he dreaded finding.

"Hey!"

Cheston couldn't hold back a smile. It had been at least ten years since she'd greeted him so childishly.

"Hey!" he replied before taking a seat on the same sofa where Howard Beck had been seated not four days ago. Same as the CIA agent, he hadn't brought any flowers.

"The surgeon is happy with how the procedure went. You must already be having an easier time breathing."

"Surgeons are always happy with their work, up until their patient buys the farm right under their nose. Then, it's bad luck that's to blame… or the body being wheeled out of their OR."

Ellen had the sluggish voice typical of post-op patients. She was still under the effect of the anesthetic. She kept quiet for a few moments, giving her father the full brunt of her most intense stare.

"I was afraid I wouldn't wake up, that I wouldn't be able to talk to you one last time."

"Don't talk like that!"

The laugh she let out was as hoarse as ever, but it didn't cause any coughing fits.

"We sound like a melodrama. The dying daughter and the father who won't face facts. But look at the daughter, and look at the father!

"Well, in my opinion, you won't really feel like throwing a pity party anymore once I've told you everything… So listen."

She felt around for the remote that would enable her to change the position of the bed, and she elevated her back an inch or two. The dark circles under her eyes made her look wild, almost terrifying.

"We both know that nothing short of a miracle would enable me to live until I turn thirty, and I've prayed thousands of times for that miracle never to happen. But I guess there wasn't anybody up there to listen to me.

"So here we are. The end is near, and I can confess everything your little girl did against her father…"

"Ellen, it might be best if you lower that bed back down and get some rest. This is the drugs making you delirious. I can come back later."

"No. You won't be back, and you know it. That's why you're starting to panic. Look at the monitors."

Instinctively, Cheston took in the steady lines and diagrams taking shape on the screens.

"My heart isn't beating any faster, my blood pressure's steady," commented Ellen. "I'm conscious and perfectly lucid. To tell you the truth, I'm not even angry with you anymore."

"Why would you be?"

"Don't tell me it's a surprise. You never should have let me come into the world, even less so let me live once they found my disease."

Gregory Cheston was possessed of a special instinct, one that had enabled him to confront the worst kinds of situations. It was the ability to shut down any emotional response as soon as his brain got an alert. This ability to instantly turn into a block of ice came on in any circumstances, including when it involved his own daughter.

He'd already understood that this was a state of maximum alert. It was a moment of truth he'd been dreading without ever being able to put a finger on the source of his uneasiness. He just hadn't known – or hadn't wanted to admit it to himself – that Ellen felt such resentment against him.

"Your ambitions, your own race against the clock are what made me what I am today," Ellen went on. "A monster. A freakshow that no-one can look at without shuddering. *Acromegaly.* Even the name inspires terror.

"I was eight the first time I watched *Elephant Man.* You fired the nanny who brought me that movie, but I'm sure you don't even remember her. To get back at you, she gave it to me before she left.

"And I rewatched the movie hundreds of times, every evening that you weren't home. Up on the screen, that creature was what I was going to become. That was me."

"Ellen…"

"Let me finish. I know how much money you spent to fund research and find a medical solution, something to make up for the fact that I was inoperable. I know I shouldn't hate you. But I've learned something amazing: you can feel gratitude and hate all at the same time, especially towards your own father."

Over on the main screen, the number showing her heartrate had risen, while the diagrams on display started scrolling faster. Cheston was speechless.

"You were gone for almost my entire childhood, after you left awful instructions for the employees you put in charge of raising or taking care of me. Whatever you do, don't leave a mirror uncovered. Make sure no-one outside the team comes close to me.

"And then, when I turned twenty, you wanted to change the rules. Suddenly, the number of people taking care of me dropped. You gave me ways to move around, you opened the doors to life wide open. You allowed me to expose myself to the world, all because you were so desperate to convince yourself that I was normal.

"Until the day you set up that organization. White Cells. As if the idea could have been inspired by anything else other than my disease!"

Gregory Cheston stood up. His silence was usually the worst kind of response when he felt in the grips of an inextricable situation. The monitor displayed a bright 110. Twenty BPM more than when he'd stepped into the room.

"If you leave now, you won't know a thing," ground out Ellen. "You'll be asking how it happened for the rest of your life…"

"How what happened, Ellen?" said Cheston in a strangely calm voice.

"How all of your humanitarian plans, all your grand dreams, fell apart thanks to your own daughter…"

"Do you mean the initiatives you took while the camp was being built? Or your secret deals with Tamazula?"

Ellen's eyes conveyed a brief surprise. She nonetheless managed to smile.

"I know there are few things you miss. But it's not just Oaxaca. I didn't mind you being apprised of that operation. The budget overruns have always piqued your interest, but did you never wonder where that money was really going?"

Cheston had taken his seat once more. His gaze drifted slowly from his daughter to the monitors showing that she seemed to have stabilized.

"The op in Oaxaca served our interests, Ellen. Ours, not just your Mexican friend's. It enabled us to put Meyrek's work to the test, his reliability, but most of all his ability to run two operations at the same time, one of which is completely clandestine…"

This time, the surprise turned to stupefaction. The young woman tried to move her misshapen body from the straps holding it prisoner. That slight effort tore a moan from her, and sweat began to bead on her forehead.

"Unless you were alluding to that children's penal system you created using my own plans as inspiration?" Cheston went on. "Come now, don't tell me you truly believed you had such power at your disposal without my being informed of your slightest decision…"

"And you just let me at it…"

"Do you really want an explanation?"

"Coming from you… nothing should ever surprise me, ever."

"I gave you power, nothing more. Power that I could take from you at any moment. We shared an experience. We needed to be faster than the disease…"

"Are you sure you even know which one you're really fighting?"

Cheston's steel-grey gaze went unfocused.

"Now more than ever."

"So you know why I created that camp."

There was no need for Cheston to reply. No healthy, humane society would ever tolerate harm being done to children. He'd replicated the methods of a barbaric civilization in order to defend the values he believed in, but he had since become consumed by the ethical questions brought on by this mirror he was holding up.

Turning a blind eye to his daughter's excesses had been a way for him to delve down to the bottom of the abyss, all the more so since Ellen's questions were relevant. What disease had he really taken it upon himself to fight? His daughter had taken advantage of their complicity with his complete approval.

She had always been his one weakness. And it was in all consciousness that he had granted her the opportunity to get even with life. With other people and with him. Cheston had known for a long time that power had no limits in the shadow, even for someone who was dying, whose body was a tormented wreck.

"When I acted, it was in your name," continued Ellen in a voice that was growing weaker. "Soon the whole world will know it and turn against your lymphocytes, like a body growing a cancer."

"The whole world, Ellen?"

Cheston's voice was soft, as though he was discussing her disease and not politics, war, and, why not, the Apocalypse.

"Your support is on the brink of dropping you," ground out the young woman. "It didn't take much. I've only just provided that little assist. Government agencies don't like being taken for a ride, even when they've given their green light."

Having visibly exhausted the last of her energy, Ellen ended her phrase with a hiccup, then a sigh. The flicker of rage in her eyes had died down. All that was left now was an immense exhaustion, equally tinged with despair and relief.

"I wanted you to learn it… from me… Soon, the whole world will know…" she continued in a breath. "You'll stand alone… a man who will have to answer for his actions… for all his actions."

Cheston remained there a few more minutes before getting up. In the time it took him to step around the bed, Ellen had fallen asleep. He leaned down and dropped a kiss to her forehead, closing his eyes and squeezing his lids shut as tight as he could to catch his first tear in years.

"Goodbye, my girl."

He then left the room without turning back even once. According to the doctors' most optimistic estimates, and despite the success of the intervention, she only had weeks left to live. Barring some extraordinary treatment. Before making his escape from this luxury twilight home of a floor, Cheston signed a discharge requiring that she undergo no new surgery. Let them let her sleep, for as long as she'd like. And maybe forever.

Against all expectations, Lochlan had been the easiest man to talk around, while Huang and Marcos took turns scanning the horizon, worried they might see the chopper come back prematurely. The ebullient Irishman had built his own arguments against the camp, and even more so against Meyrek, after a much shorter enlistment than the others.

Lochlan had no past to atone for, real or otherwise; he was simply a mercenary, and only the promise of triple pay and glorious military exploits had gotten him to abandon the real army in exchange for a secret organization. Since then, quiet but observant, he'd soured.

"Eight months spent training, only to go toe to toe with a pansy-assed bunch of thugs… This camp is basically dropping the A-bomb on an ant hill!"

Salinas, for his part, had only given in due to his friendship with Marcos. The Peruvian had no children, nothing to rescue, if not an uncertain future that he thought he could build once he was freed from his commitment. His pay, saved up over the course of several years, enabled him to consider opening a shop once he got home. *Provided they let you leave, Salinas…* He was barely 24, and seven of those years had already been devoted to the army.

"I've seen what Meyrek does to escapees," the Peruvian had objected. "Nobody's ever managed to leave the base. There's this desert. The canyon. Before you've gone a hundred yards, the choppers find you. The men are scared. If they get asked to shoot a friend, they will."

"Well then, *coño*, think you could shoot me?"

Sworn at by his friend, the Peruvian had ultimately seen reason. No army in the world had ever turned out soldiers that were as well-trained as them. On the flipside, no army had managed to instill such a degree of demotivation.

The foremost principle of a soldier of fortune was believing in what he was doing, once he picked his side, even if he did it for the money. And besides, and this went for all of them, there were certain taboos that needed to never be broken. No matter the cause. They were all tired of living a life of complete secrecy, no longer having any idea what tomorrow would hold in store. And Theo had made them a promise they believed in…

During their frugal meal, Theo walked them through the plan he and Will had put together. The helicopter hadn't flown over them the whole day, which suggested a surprise visit as early as dawn. Temperatures had dropped with nightfall, and their clothes barely shielded them from the cold.

The dry shrubbery gave off plenty of smoke but very little heat. They squeezed in tightly together around the fire. Huang handed out the watch schedule. Before falling asleep, they drank half their ration. Whatever happened, they wouldn't need water beyond the second day.

Salinas roused them at the first flicker of dawn.

"The chopper."

Theo leapt up.

"Which way?"

"I can't see it yet, but you can hear it."

The five men pricked up their ears. The very distant rumble of a rotor reached them. The helicopter was looking for them.

"Huang, you're up."

The Vietnamese man got undressed in a hurry. They gathered shrubs together and stuffed them into his uniform. In mere seconds, his BDU pants and jacket looked like a puppet. They lay it face down and placed his helmet at the top.

From a few yards out, it was pretty convincing. Huang took off at a run, tore some more shrubs, and huddled down a good distance away, his body camouflaged like a bush.

The helicopter appeared from the west.

The men took off their shirts, placed them down like an arrow, and took one step back.

The blades stirred up clouds of dust and dry grass. Bushes tumbled and took flight. Theo threw a worried glance Huang's way. The Vietnamese man hadn't lost his camouflage. Garroni was standing in the cockpit frame, a megaphone in hand.

"What's going on?"

"Huang's hurt!" shouted Theo, hands cupped around his mouth. "He broke his leg yesterday. It got infected."

The sergeant ordered the pilot to land the bird. He hopped down and joined the group.

"You sorry bunch of maggots," he bellowed. "Send you on a pansy training exercise and you come back with an injury."

His face was burning with anger.

"Where is he?"

Theo pointed to the prone puppet. Cautiously, Garroni slid the safety off his submachine gun. He leaned over the "casualty."

"What the…"

The scene took place at the speed of lightning. Garroni got up, finger on the trigger. Theo sprang and violently hammered both his joined fists down on the back of his neck like a club. The sergeant staggered, sprayed the ground with bullets.

The American rushed him from the side, using his body like a battering ram, and threw him to the ground. Salinas hurled himself forward and held the submachine gun with his foot.

Barely shaking off his stupor, the helicopter pilot gunned it, but it was too late: Huang had already slid into the cabin. He pushed his knife against the soldier's jugular.

"You set this thing back down, or I'll wash these windows with your blood."

The chopper had lifted three feet off the ground. It touched down abruptly. Triumphantly, Huang pulled the pilot outside.

Down on the ground, Garroni had snapped out of it. Salinas had him pinned down with his own gun.

"What do you think you're doing?" screamed the sergeant. "Meyrek's never gonna let you get away."

Theo leaned over him.

"A lot of things can happen in the desert, sergeant. Remember?"

"Goddamn it, you've all lost your minds. This is Mexico. One call from the base and the whole of the police will be on your tails."

"There won't be a call from the base," retorted Theo in a glib tone of voice. "There's two days of training left. Plenty of time to sightsee until then."

"Oh, yes," snickered the sergeant. "If the chopper isn't back tonight, Meyrek will send out two sections to track us down."

"Perfect. That means we have all the time we need."

He turned towards the pilot.

"Have you ever landed at the second camp?"

Garroni sat up, eyes fiery.

"What second camp?"

"The one with the children. The one where they're holding my daughter and Marcos's kids."

The sergeant burst out laughing.

"You've gone crazy, Collin. The sun beat down on your head."

He turned towards Salinas and the American, mouth twisted in a rictus.

"Are you hearing this? His daughter died in a car crash. A year ago. He's lying to you. Salinas, hand me my gun. This man's crazy."

Salinas took a step towards the sergeant, barrel of the gun lowered.

"You enlisted, Salinas. Same as me. Pay's good. What's following him gonna get you? The second camp is a fairytale. He made it all up to drag you down with him.

"But, goddamn it! We've turned you into the best soldiers in the world. You have the most glorious missions in store."

"Like Oaxaca?" spat Lochlan.

Garroni got to his feet. He held his hand out to Salinas.

"Hand me back my gun and I'll forget all about this. I'll write it in my report that you gave me a hand against their rebellion. The colonel will be sure to reward you."

He stepped towards the Irishman, speaking in a rush.

"You never wanted to follow them, anyway. It's the sun. The thirst. You fell prey to temptation."

The burst of gunfire blasted apart the desert silence. Features tense, Lochlan kept his finger tight on the trigger. The submachine gun was jerking in his hands. Garroni bent double, an astonished expression on his face. The bullet impact sent him careening backwards. He tried to shield his abdomen. The bullets pierced his arms, his chest. He tried to shout; blood spewed from his mouth, muffling his cry. At last, he collapsed, fell to his knees.

His life had gone out before he'd hit the ground.

Salinas gave Lochlan a friendly nudge and spat at the sergeant's feet.

"The *maricón* almost had me convinced."

For a few moments, the entirety of the desert bore witness to the scene that had finally reached the point of no return. Whatever they did next, from then on the dice was cast, they'd picked their side.

The pilot was contemplating Garroni's body, his face expressionless. The Mexican turned the submachine gun on him.

"I asked you a question," ground out Theo. "Don't try to bullshit me. There is a second camp, he knew that as well as I do."

"If you kill me, none of you will make it out alive. Without me, you might as well strap that bird to your back and drag it to the border."

Huang swung his knife before the pilot's eyes.

"We don't plan on killing you," he said. "You can still take us there with just one eye, without a tongue, without your ears. Or you can remain whole and stop wasting our time."

"We don't need him," interjected the Irishman. "I know how to handle this thing."

Huge beads of sweat dotted the pilot's forehead; a look of terror clouded his gaze.

"I know where camp B is located," he said reluctantly. "I've landed there before."

The Mexico City layover didn't take more than an hour, just the time it took to refuel the jet and register a new flight plan, taken into account through a special procedure, as the aircraft captain had explained to Beck.

A hundred and thirty minutes later, they were flying over the Sierra Madre mountain range, which seemed to stretch out into endless, echoing peaks from the Trans-Mexican Volcanic belt on. The dark green shades etched in the rugged terrain revealed the old water streams that had crisscrossed a once lush region, one that was now ruled by drought.

That was when the Challenger executed a nosedive. Beck barely had time to get over the pressurization before the jet took on a twisted trajectory, hugging the ground dangerously close, and far below radar coverage, so as to follow the meanders of the narrow, steep-sided valleys.

For a few moments, Howard felt as though he'd been dropped into the high-speed pursuit scene of a blockbuster movie. But then the valley widened, and the flight became less jerky. The steward came to tell him that the captain wanted to see him in the cockpit.

"Sleep well, flight not too rough?"

The pilot was beaming. He looked like he was having a hell of a good time, while his tenser 2IC wasn't taking his eyes off his instruments.

290

"I'm gonna to let you in on a couple things. You see that dial? It's from the transponder, which is the device that enables radars to identify us thanks to a preestablished number.

"A few minutes ago, I cut it. In these parts, it's not unusual for a plane to disappear off the radar screens now and again. Now, look down there…"

Beck complied. Beneath a dazzling sun, the *rio* traced a cheery loop in the nearly red earth, with its patches of greenery. A brief flash caught his attention a good click out. The shiny, moving object soon took the shape of a small plane.

"That's a Cessna," explained the pilot. "Nowhere near as fast as our Challenger, but its cruising speeds can rival our approach speed. Now, one of its particular features is that it has the same transponder we do, bearing the same frequency I just cut a couple minutes ago."

The pilot was still smiling. Less than a second later, he'd overtaken the small plane, which pitched its wings in a show of gratitude.

"The minute it received our signal, it took off from a runway we had set up. As of a couple minutes ago, our identification tag has shown up on the radar screens in Chihuahua, 50 clicks from here.

"That's set their mind at ease as to what's happened to us, especially since the Cessna is going to land on a private airfield, which will also serve to wrap up our flight plan. We have the same registration, of course."

Beck couldn't stop himself from pulling a face. This was beyond child's play.

"Of course, this sort of thing only works in Mexico," finished the pilot. "Welcome to the land of organized disorder. Twenty bucks buys you a cop. Imagine what billions of dollars gets you!"

The winding flight continued for another half hour after Beck had gotten back to his seat. The steward soon asked him to fasten his seatbelt. The jet began flying more steadily so as to climb to an altitude of about sixty-five hundred feet and reach a high plateau area.

Apart from a few herds of bovines, not a living soul could be seen for miles around. The perfect setting, mused Beck, who was regretting how long he'd mentally tended to place the training camp up in the great Canadian north.

The unmistakable noise of the undercarriage lowering was accompanied by a brief judder. Through the window, Beck made out the equivalent of a movie set for the handful of minutes it took for the wheels to touch the ground. The Challenger reached the end of the runway before about-facing in a cloud of dust. Two men were waiting for them at the bottom of the plane.

"Colonel Meyrek," said the shorter of the two in a French accent, his voice loud to cover the whine of the engines shutting down. "Meet my number two, captain Novak."

Beck took in the makeup of the uniforms, close to regulation GI issue, with the exception of the epaulettes and rank identifiers. No Velcro to catch the name tag across the chest, either. *A shadow army*, he thought before he pulled himself together, recalling that was one of the nicknames bestowed on the CIA.

"Miss Cheston has asked me to take you on a tour of our base," continued Meyrek, leading him towards a Humvee parked a few yards from the plane. "I hope you're fully cognizant of what a privilege this is. It's the first time that an outsider to the Organization pays us a visit."

"I suppose she told you who I am…"

Meyrek settled in next to Novak, who had taken the driver's seat, while Beck slid into the back of the Humvee. The colonel burst out laughing.

"Oh, did she, Mister Beck! We know your Agency, your position, and we even know that you're on vacation… But what a funny place you've picked to get some rest in."

"My doctor recommended I get some dry mountain air," huffed Beck, deadpan.

"I have obviously not had the time to put together a welcoming committee for you. And I am sure you'll feel the lack of female personnel at our camp. But we have some very interesting features here, as you'll see."

The view that greeted Beck after several miles of gravel road was vaguely reminiscent of Iraq, close to the Syrian border. The area had been entirely cleared of trees. Gigantic tents had been set up to house a good hundred all-terrain vehicles. The first barracks looked like cubes that had been tossed next to each other in a haphazard order, depending on the layout of the terrain.

Like with every outpost, the hospital area spread out its prefab buildings in the middle of the military town, but without any way to identify them from a distance. Other, more spacious buildings, loomed over by gigantic antennas, towered over a sort of hollow dug out in the center of the plateau, and which seemed deserted at that early morning hour.

"The men are already out on training," explained Meyrek, as though he might have read his thoughts. "We're able to train up to 4000 soldiers, under the most extreme conditions. But, come…"

The colonel's quarters mirrored the sobriety of the individual whose French accent Beck had so quickly identified. Not one photo on the wall. Nothing at all except for the computer set on a desk that exemplified utilitarianism. No frames. Khaki-colored folding chairs. A spartan bed and a flatscreen TV connected to a DVD player. A handful of books on a shelf; among them, Beck managed to make out two titles from a distance: "The Fall of the Roman Empire" and "The Bronze Drums" by somebody Lartéguy.

Meyrek settled into an exaggeratedly stiff posture in order to make his announcement.

"Some of our methods will come as a surprise to you, but that is why you're here. There are, of course, certain things that I will be unable to show you…"

"Who do you take your orders from?" interrupted Beck.

"Miss Cheston, of course."

"She is your immediate superior in the chain of command?"

"You are aware of the principle governing our army. We don't apply the concept of a chain of command in the traditional way."

"So you're liable to get direct orders from higher up."

Meyrek's lips stretched in an enigmatic smile.

"That's one of the things you'll find out as we go. The visit has just started."

"And when are you planning on moving to the operational phase?"

"Whoa, whoa!" The colonel raised both hands in a bid for more patience. "You've only just got here. My aide de camp will get us something to drink, then we will tour the camp, and then I will answer some of your questions."

"Colonel Meyrek, I have to wonder if you've grasped the game we're playing here! Ellen Cheston has authorized me to come here after she was pressurized by my director, who in turn takes his orders directly from the President of the United States. Officially, I am on Paradise Island, wearing beach shorts, and sipping on a daiquiri.

"But as far as you, your camp, or all your men? Legally, you don't exist anymore than my mission here does. Except that I'm going home tomorrow, and my vacation pictures are gonna have to be goddamn convincing if you want to keep running your little Club Med. Take my word for it, we have no time to waste!"

The remote staccato of machine gun fire cut through the silence that had settled over the room. For a brief moment, the noise threw Beck back into distant memories, back to the time of his training, a few months before he was recruited by the CIA, and the different war zone missions he was on.

This time, the side he was investigating was supposed to be friendly, and that very thought, coupled with Meyrek's – *a French officer's* – presence, and the kind of condescension he was eyeballing him with, was just the thing to put him on edge. All the more so since he had no assurances as to the real purpose of his mission.

In response, the colonel clacked away at his computer keyboard.

"Fine, let's skip some steps. We've already entered the operational phase. Our way of doing things is more or less the same as what was used to bring you here. We use decoys.

"For example, for many on base, our men are supposed to have recently compromised themselves in the course of an operation aiding the local mafia."

Beck's unease mushroomed. The colonel was suddenly talking to him as though there needed to be no secrets between them. That was a complete one-eighty from his initial attitude, and Beck had not been read in on anything regarding any field op, especially one connected to the local *milieu*.

"To get back to the chain of command," continued Meyrek as he slowly turned the screen towards him, "here's the result of a direct order."

The huge title of a report was describing the loss of some men during the storming of a secure villa in Oaxaca that belonged to a drug kingpin. The name rang a vague bell for Beck. There was surely a surveillance file on Pedro Tamazula somewhere, but nothing specific was springing to mind just then.

"But here, we operate in odd and even sections. Your agency is certainly aware of the fact that Oaxaca is an insurrectionist region, fighting against the current government, which they consider too corrupt and pro-American."

The picture changed. Meyrek liked playing things up, and he enjoyed using visuals to aid his revelations, like a lecturer.

"So we used this operation, and the cover of the local mafia, to take care of a few regional issues, for practice."

A second report popped up on the screen, announcing the disappearance of a communist agitator, the president of a human rights organization that mainly focused on collecting funds to send to Iraq and the Palestinian territories.

"This," concluded Meyrek, "goes completely outside the bounds of our chain of command. Needless to say, Miss Cheston was not informed."

Beck could suddenly put a finger on his unease. What he'd just cottoned on to should have already been self-evident to him before he'd so much as set foot on the E.C. Tronics jet.

Strapped into the rescue harness, Marcos was scanning the desert, legs hanging in midair. Steered smooth and easy, the Sikorsky flew over the plain at very low altitude, heading along the first drop in the mountain range.

"There they are… nine o'clock!"

Theo relayed the message to the pilot. The patrol was still nothing more than a group of ants among the rocks. Marcos adjusted his binoculars.

"That's Will all right. They're trying to find cover."

"They have no way to know we already did it," noted Theo.

He ordered the pilot to fly over them, grabbed a signal flare from its hook in the cabin and shot it at the ground. The five men had already vanished.

An arc of purple smoke trailed behind the flare. Instantly, a cluster of bushes began to move. Will stood up and signaled by widely waving both arms. The black giant had over a head on everyone else. Even from this distance, his bulk was impressive.

"He did it," went Salinas enthusiastically.

Theo peeked over at Huang. The thought crossed his mind that his friend might have gotten some help. Settled deep in his seat, a rifle propped between his thighs, barrel pointed at the sky, the Vietnamese man appeared asleep.

Theo was the first one down. Salinas remained on board to watch the pilot.

"Way to go, *carnal!*" said Will, giving his friend a bear hug. His face was luminous with joy.

"Congratulations to you," retorted Theo. "You got them on our side."

"Them? Piece of cake. The Viet seemed like he was already in on it. All the others want is some glory. Ever since Oaxaca, half the section wants to escape. You shoulda seen the Ozzie, he was basically in tears when I told him about the kids. What do we do now?"

Theo's smile hardened.

"That all depends on the others."

The two groups had come together. Excitement shone in their eyes. Mercs. There were ten of them; they had one chopper, two guns, a rifle Theo had found in the cockpit, and Garroni's SMG only had three mags. Their deadliest weapon was the FN Mag bolted to the cockpit. It would take a good half-hour to dismount it.

Will turned their way.

"*Hombres*, we're all up the same shit creek, now. Even if we take out the pilot, we'll never be able to come up with a likely enough story to explain this whole mess. So there's two answers.

"If we head up north, we'll have just enough fuel to get us across the border, assuming we don't get shot down first. But we have not gotten ourselves through the best training any sonofabitch has ever dreamed of only so we can end our careers crying on the shoulder of some cop while trying to explain to him what clandestine unit we deserted from. OK, *carnales*?

"Over on the other side, there's two hundred kids who never hurt nobody. I don't know about you guys, but this is just the kind of situation that screams out serious mission to me…"

The Australian broke in.

"Don't waste your breath. Our minds are already made up."

"You see," puffed up the black giant as he turned to Theo. "There's nothing like a good speech. You two, dismount that machine gun for me."

"Your caliber of choice, Will." Marcos smiled.

Theo hopped into the cabin. Salinas wasn't taking his eyes off the pilot. With the bird motionless, the cockpit had turned into an oven. The smell of fuel, combined with the odor of heated plastic, was suffocating. Theo sat down in the copilot's seat.

"What's the landing procedure for camp B?"

"A scrambled radio call," muttered the pilot. "But they won't let anything set down without approval from the base."

"What's the nearest runway?"

"There's two landing sites. A platform for the shuttle, a few hundred yards from the camp, and a runway for planes, three clicks out on an open plateau. They're both under surveillance."

Theo grabbed a map and unfolded it across his knees.

"Show me where the camp is located."

The pilot traced a finger over a large grey area marked with encoded labels. He drew concentric circles and traced an imaginary line towards a difference in level represented as gradient shades of brown.

"That's the desert. The first plateau. The camp is over here, at an altitude of two thousand feet."

He underlined a mark drawn in wax pencil.

"Here's the runway. It's four thousand feet long. The helicopter site is over there, north of the camp."

"And the crisscrossed marker lines, here, what does that mean?"

"Those are the children's training areas. No-fly zones."

"They train out in the open?"

"I don't know. I'm just a pilot."

Just like for the first camp, the flyover ban had to be going hand in hand with two camouflages, one physical and the other electronical. The "umbrella" must really have required an enormous amount of power to be able to dupe satellites across this kind of a surface.

"How many men supervising?" Theo pursued his questioning.

"Forty-odd. Half of them take the kids training. The others keep the base running."

"That's not too bad," noted Salinas. "Four against one."

"You're forgetting the kids," retorted the pilot. "What do you think? That you'll be welcomed as rescuers? They've been trained to blind obedience for months.

"The base has brought in experts. Every day, they get shoved the same old crap down their throats." He chortled. "They'd shoot their own parents. What're you gonna do, Collin? End your kid if she doesn't want to be saved?"

Theo shrunk in on himself, throat tight. His months spent training had instilled new reflexes in him. Violence, something he'd so dreaded when he'd been younger, was now an integral part of his life.

Meyrek had taught him how to hate fiercely, how to kill on command, how to use his body every bit as much as his mind if he was put in a position to defend himself. He'd turned him into a soldier despite himself, for fun, for no other purpose but his own satisfaction. But he'd failed to do one thing. Emotionally, Theo determined that the colonel hadn't managed to touch his soul.

Aboard the *Consuela II*, Pedro Tamazula was gazing at Acapulco bay, lying right on the deck, his bare feet hanging over the ship's rail. His schooner did not display the ostentatious luxury of the big yachts, but the Mexican saw in it the tranquility of days gone by as well as a symbol of his own success. Indeed, had he not, just like the *Consuela,* elevated the nobility of his own aura above the mediocrity that ease and modernity encouraged?

He despised the *nouveau riche* – all too often forgetting that his own father only ran a small *cantina* in a Mexico City suburb – and the arrogance of their yachts. Yet his fortune would have enabled him to amass an entire fleet of them.

The season was in full swing. A half-league out, Acapulco's La Quebrada grew distorted against the crystal side of his nearly empty glass. When Tamazula let himself get lost in his daydreams, he had this involuntary move, close one eye and contemplate the world through a flute that he used like a telescope.

The two luxury hotels he could make out as silhouettes netted him enough per week to live on for several years. From this far out, the crystal glass surely couldn't catch sight of the shanty towns that gained a little bit more territory every day, inching their wretched borders forward up to the base of the most luxurious hotels. Tamazula had just purchased a casino. And was granting himself a well-earned day off.

Supine next to him, bare and golden like a bronze statue, an American lay dozing, a *gringa* with an unpronounceable name. She was an integral part of his latest acquisition, and certainly not among its least enticing fixtures. He'd spotted her as he'd been visiting the place.

296

Rorie was a craps dealer, and like the entirety of the casino's female staff, she sported curves that were barely concealed by the orange and black uniform designed specially to make the players lose their minds. When the time had come to sign the deal, Tamazula had pointed his forefinger her way through the one-way mirror in the office.

"Is there anything else you would care for, Mister Tamazula?" the casino manager had innocently inquired, fawning over his new boss.

She had her bush trimmed in a heart shape, very white teeth, hazel eyes, and an abiding life philosophy based around the value of the US dollar. *'In three years, she'll be too fat,'* mused Tamazula. *'Just perfect for marrying…'*

On the inside, he was jubilant. The schooner was pitching gently. It was truly a beautiful day. And his sense of humor, heavily tinged with cynicism as it was, delighted in the turn of events. The casino takeover was as it should be, he'd been working on it for months.

But the Oaxaca "strike"… What a circus act! Once more, he had benefited from the scruples, the hesitancies, the complexities of the American mentality. They created an armed force, then – worried about their motives, frightened at the thought of public condemnation – delayed bringing it into play, resisted its use. Like a boxer honing himself only to let himself get knocked out, arms useless at his sides, for fear of what his opponent's supporters might have to say!

The Oaxaca test had allowed him to carefully eliminate Ramon Estevez, a dangerous competitor. Without getting a single one of his men mixed up. And he'd even been thanked for his cooperation. Hadn't his information led to his own government and the CIA indirectly getting rid of a dangerous activist?

If all went according to plan, then in a few short months he would also have a small army of kids at his disposal, as well-trained as any soldiers, and trained to ferry the widest variety of merchandise for his benefit. Dealing with idealists really was a ball.

The young croupier flipped over like an enticing display of heads or tails and lay down on her stomach after gathering her hair into an updo.

Tamazula didn't hear the ringtone. One of his henchmen suddenly appeared before him, holding out his cell phone.

"Gregory?" the Mexican inquired in surprise. "I don't often get to hear you! How's your daughter?"

"Took a turn for the worst," dryly replied Cheston.

Reflexively, Tamazula sat up straight. The head of E.C. Tronics was not the sort of man whose voice you listened to while sprawled down on the floor, even when he couldn't see you.

"I'm sorry to hear that," he said, continuing to watch the bay through his glass. "But how did you find me?"

"Immaterial," retorted Cheston. "I simply wanted to be by your side, one way or another, when this took place."

"What are you talking about?"

"The mistakes I've made…"

Pedro Tamazula couldn't have heard the detonation, for the shooter was nearly two thousand yards away. The impact of the bullet, as it struck his chest dead center, projected him backwards, while his glass and cell phone dropped out of his hands.

The young dealer was surprised at first, thinking he'd gotten a dizzy spell; then she saw the widening brown puddle beneath her lover's chest and started screaming. The bodyguards were already rushing every which way like panicked rats, trying to pinpoint the origin of the shot, while one of them leaned over his boss's body to give him first aid. For naught.

Face tense, Theo kept his eyes on the vegetation, fruitlessly trying to make out the slightest sign of life. They'd just skirted around the camp, but they'd needed to trust the pilot as far as situating it. The camouflage was perfect. The runway alone, farther south, was indicative of a human presence, although the long strip of packed dirt seemed completely abandoned.

"Head farther out north!" shouted Theo to be heard over the noise of the blades. "No need to get us sighted."

"I warned you!" screamed the pilot. "There's no clear area. We won't find a wide enough clearing to land in."

Theo looked at the watch on the console. The time was one-fifteen. The sun was beaming down vertically. Despite the wind from the rotors, the air in the cabin had become unbreathable. Inside the cockpit, Will and the eight men were silent, their nerves on edge. Theo got an idea.

"Change course. We're heading back to the *rio*."

The pilot shrugged his shoulders.

"We can't set down on the bank. The bird's too wide."

"So be it. That's our only shot. We're gonna find an area that's less difficult somewhere."

The man lost his temper.

"This is crazy, you'll get us all killed."

"Just do as I say."

The helicopter flew a wide circle and moved away from the camp.

"Dial in on their frequency," ordered Theo. "I want to know if they're signaling our presence."

The pilot moved his hand towards the dials on the radio transceiver. Theo pulled his headset off.

"And don't get smart," he threatened.

The radio waves were silent. A thousand yards below, the mountain dipped, sloping gently down to the bed of the *rio*. The vegetation was as dense as a small jungle, with a complex mixture of thorn bushes, cactuses, and agave plants, sprinkled with colorful spots.

The helicopter followed the winding path of the river, looking for a less steep area. Mudslides had led to a multitude of pyramids being formed, their colors veering through shades of ochre and blue. Theo felt overcome by ruggedness of the landscape.

"That's where we'll land!"

He pointed his forefinger towards the *rio*. A bend had cleared a bank as sandy as a small peninsula skirted around by the turn.

"The chopper's too heavy," replied the pilot. "We'll sink."

"Screw the chopper. We've gotta land."

The embankment was wider than it had seemed from a high altitude. The chopper landed gently, inch by inch. The blades stirred up rushes of sand and countercurrent wavelets. Muscles tensed, the pilot managed to keep the helicopter balanced.

Theo let out a cry of joy.

"See that? No reason to get worked up. You did just fine."

Will poked his head into the cabin. His chest was wrapped up in cartridge belts. His gaze was feverish, and he was grimacing.

"We've gotta hurry. The camp is at least a three-hour walk."

He flicked a finger at the pilot.

"What do we do about that one?"

Theo pointed his gun at the radio transceiver and shot twice. The casing crackled.

"Tie him up in the back and yank the ignition wires out. I wanna be sure we find the bird here when we get back."

Lochlan took care of immobilizing the pilot, making sure his ties were sturdy. Before joining his teammates on the ground, he patted him kindly on the shoulder and told him,

"Thanks for the ride, buddy. You did better than I would have. Especially since I've never flown a chopper my whole life."

Chapter 17

The slope was steep. They'd come across some kind of a natural trail that cut through the vegetation. A rivulet trickled between the mounds of earth at their feet. The trail must have been the bed of some stream that fed into the *rio* at the bottom of the ravine. The trees' canopies tangled together above their heads, forming a protective dome pierced by a multitude of rays of light, like a magical, world-creating ambiance. Birds' cries punctuated their march, and rustling signaled the worried presence of the impenetrable forest's denizens.

They'd been on the move for over two hours, not saying a word, humidity sticking their shirts to their skin. The trail came to a stop at the foot of a horseshoe-shaped rocky promontory housing a mini waterfall. Will had taken point. He set the machine gun at his feet and let himself drop to the ground. Theo sat down next to him.

"Don't ask me to climb with this thing," grumbled the Mexican. "I can't even lift it up anymore."

"We won't climb," retorted Theo. "We'll go around the rock."

Marcos joined them and took a seat in turn. His features were drawn and his face shone with sweat.

"There's nothing to say we're moving in the right direction. We could be going around in circles in this forest for hours."

"We're climbing," insisted Theo. "The camp overlooks the gorge. While we're climbing, we're on the right track."

Will agreed.

"I looked at the location of the camp. If the pilot didn't jerk our chain, it should be somewhere above our heads, two or three clicks west."

Theo drew some water from between the rocks and splashed it on his face. He patted Will on the shoulder, then got up.

"Get somebody to take over, for the machine gun. Two guys can carry it."

Will stood up in turn.

"Yeah, right. Only thing that'll get us is losing them on the way."

The men had sat down at the edge of the stream, gazes blank, too exhausted to speak. Even in the shade, the heat was suffocating.

"Break's over," announced Will. "If we don't get a move on right now, we'll either fall asleep or drop dead right here."

They resumed their walk. Will consented to take off his cartridge belts and trotted forward, the machine gun at arm's length, as light as a child's toy in his arms.

They made their way around the rock and discovered a winding path in the middle of the vegetation. Steep but practicable. Theo stepped onto it, ensured the terrain was solid, and climbed out a few yards. He then returned to his teammates.

"If we grip the roots for leverage, we've gotta be able to make it through."

The climb took them almost half an hour. The rocks gave way under their feet, and the roots only gave them a fragile and uncertain leverage. Two of them tumbled several yards down the slope before finding a stronger hold and restarting their ascent, short of breath, muscles exhausted from the effort.

Six hundred yards down, beyond the forest, the *rio* was tracing elegant curves, glittering brilliantly.

At last, the trail widened down onto a softer slope. They could stand upright and move without needing their hands to climb. The temperature was already milder.

"The plateau!" breathed Theo.

The forest was looking familiar, almost welcoming. It was no longer the dense jungle that festooned the gorge, but instead a tangle of pine trees, thinned out by large open spaces. They gave themselves a few minutes' rest. Not far off, the water hurtled over the rocks with a clear, trickling sound.

Theo felt hunger gnaw at him. The snake they'd split the day before was nothing but a distant memory. Will's group hadn't been as lucky, and the ascent had sapped the last of their energy reserves. Theo swept a worried gaze over the men. Their faces all expressed the same determination, but the excited gleam in their eyes had dulled.

Will suddenly broke out laughing.

"We forgot two brigades out in the desert!"

The Australian was just done taking apart his arm and checking it was in working order. He raised his head and smiled.

"They must be looking out for that helicopter and throwing themselves on the ground every time a vulture flies overhead."

The picture of the two groups running around in the sun cheered them. They were going to reach the dried up *rio* at the foot of the high plateau and wait in vain for the bird to come take them back to the base.

"Persuading them would have been a risky play," noted Theo. "Pity. Some of them are sure to have joined in."

He crouched down and spread the aerial map down on the ground. The men gathered around him.

"Here's more or less the path we took over here," he explained, tracing a line with his finger. "We reached the plateau from the north, and according to the map, the base should be over on our right. Another hour's walk."

"Let's split up into patrols," suggested Will. "If we move forward in parallel lines, we've got a bigger chance to come across it."

Theo assented. They divvied up their weapons and handed out the itineraries. Theo joined Marcos and Huang. The other Vietnamese man took charge of a four-man patrol. Will gathered Salinas and the American with him. They established their rendezvous point at a forty-five minutes' walk, right below the gorge. Theo gave the starting signal. The men got up. Only the Irishman didn't move a muscle.

"You gonna haul ass," lambasted Will.

"We're headed to the front," retorted Lochlan, sounding nonchalant. "Before I risk my neck, I tend to want to know who I'm fighting for."

"What do you mean?"

The Irishman pointed his finger at Theo.

"Collin. There's one thing I want to get clear on. Meyrek gave him a mission. See, I'd like to be certain that we're working for ourselves and not for the colonel. Ask him."

Will stared him down in astonishment. He turned towards Theo.

"What mission?"

"We're not fighting for Meyrek," answered Theo firmly. "That was before I found out where my daughter is."

"What mission?" insisted Will in a hard voice.

"Shoot a man, someone with ties to Feldman, the guy who recruited me back in France. Is that explanation enough for you?"

The expression on Will's face didn't alter.

"What man? Why you?"

"I don't have the slightest idea. Meyrek has been fixated on me from the first time we met, which was years ago."

Will shook his head, looking nasty.

"What do you mean, years? What the hell are you telling me right now?"

Theo himself had always had a hard time understanding that obsession the colonel displayed towards him. He recounted the episode going back to his mandatory service, when he was a mere young insubordinate conscript whose rebellion had gotten him shipped out to the disciplinary battalion.

He'd barely escaped going to Iraq, and the only thing that had stayed with him from his meeting Meyrek had been that ridiculous nickname, so typical of what conscripts tend to saddle their superior officers with: *The Cannibal.*

Why was he such a gifted shot? That remained a mystery. But more to the point, it didn't explain the future colonel's unrelenting desire to train him up to the point of turning him into a war machine.

Without that absurd coincidence that had resulted in him working as a computer expert for the very outfit that was bankrolling Meyrek, the training camp, and the entire organization, he was more than likely never to have touched a weapon again his whole life. *Neither would he be leading a starving patrol in a search for his child,* who *just like him had been made victim of the most awful machination,* he thought, heart tight.

Will hesitated. He scrutinized Theo, who held his gaze. Then, a beaming smile broke out across his face.

"*Amigo,*" he said. "Your first mission on base, and you'll never know why." He grabbed the machine gun at his feet and swung it across his shoulders. "Let's go, *hijos de putas!*"

Beck had to admit he was surprised. The amount of technical expertise on base was in no way surprising, and neither was the quality of the weaponry and supplies. But the degree of training displayed by these two thousand men, who were trained like a professional army, would have made him feel admiring, had his principles not put him in a state of nausea.

For close to three hours, he'd been treated to a private parade, followed by a combat simulation, and all signs pointed to Cheston's first cells being good and ready. The men he'd come across all through his guided tour, conducted aboard an open-top Jeep that the colonel had made his aide drive, seemed proficient on every level.

Meyrek answered all his questions sparingly, somewhat distantly, with the exception of the occasional show of unhealthy pride. The Frenchman truly saw himself as a great soldier. Watching the rod in his spine and the vaguely sadistic gleam he'd been able to catch in his eye, Beck wondered why Cheston's Organization had picked a man like this.

But the multiethnic makeup of the soldier corps clued him in. Only France, back in the days of a military glory long gone by, had operated an army corps made up of nobodies, of pariahs, of gang-pressed recruits like in the filibuster days.

He remembered a Gary Cooper movie he'd watched as a child, one that had left him nostalgic for a long time: *Beau Geste.* It told the story of a man betrayed by love who enlists in the Foreign Legion and uncovers a heroic streak inside himself that culminates with the ultimate sacrifice. He questioned the colonel about the units he'd served with.

"Naval infantry followed by the *kepis blancs,*" answered Meyrek. "But I'm sure your agency has a comprehensive file on my career," he finished dryly.

That confirmed Beck's hunch. The colonel had indeed been part of the Legion. The hardest of all army corps, and the one that had an infamous legacy built on the back of some of its methods. Tortures, forced trainings that only complete exhaustion brought to a stop, humiliations. It wasn't hard for him to imagine the kind of training these men had been subjected to in order to bring them to this level of cohesion and professionalism. The only way to build an army without giving it an ideal is through fear.

On and off, the colonel kept looking at his watch, appearing worried. They arrived at a clearing, an area where the slightest hint of shrubbery, of succulents, of any plants, had been weeded out. A half-dozen BDU-clad men were waiting for them, silent, standing at attention in a perfect line, a Lapua Magnum Desert Camo rifle held close to the body.

"Look familiar?" asked Meyrek. "They're part of the *Accuracy* range; made in England, kitted out with Baush & Lomb 42 scopes. I would have preferred getting FR-F1's, which is what my first army used, but I can't complain.

"SWAT teams employ these, too, and my men have turned their use into a perfected art form. Would you care for a demonstration, Mister Beck?"

Howard silently gave his agreement. The more time went by, the more his unease grew. When he'd been on his way to the camp, he'd never pictured being on the receiving end of so many details concerning its running, nor be subject to his much attention. A parade, and a combat and shooting demonstration…? Meyrek looked to be having fun, whereas Beck was only hoping he'd be able to obtain some data, some numbers, some geographical coordinates. Meyrek issued a command and one of the shooters got into position.

"Our best man is out training right now," commented Meyrek. "He'll be back tomorrow. Until then, I'll walk you through our chain of command and the way we've divided our operation into cells. We've managed to train some twenty snipers, and each of them will be assigned to a section when the time comes."

One click out, a Jeep suddenly appeared, topped by a target, opaque armor plating bulking up its visible side. Face-down on the ground, the shooter began calibrating his *Accuracy.* There was a slight, satisfied smile on Meyrek's face.

"Wait!"

Beck put his hand on the colonel's arm.

"I think I've seen enough for today."

"Excuse me? Right when things are getting interesting? What would a unit like ours be without snipers?"

The blast surprised Beck. The shooter hadn't waited for his order. And Howard didn't need the binoculars Meyrek was holding out to know that the bullet had struck its target.

This was all so ridiculous. They were yanking his chain. The colonel wasn't even trying to impress him; it was as though everything he'd been going through since he'd gotten here was the result of some crude stage production. The colonel watched Beck and nodded his head with a knowing look.

"We'll spare you the rest, won't we?"

"My visit here wasn't arranged by Ellen Cheston," asserted Beck. "So why am I here?"

"Oh, you'll find out soon enough. You know, I'm just a commanding officer entrusted with a secret. I'm not the one who makes all the decisions."

Right then, a second Humvee appeared, a cloud of dust in close pursuit as it sped their way. Beck could make out Meyrek's aide de camp, captain Novak.

"Is there a problem?" asked the colonel.

Halfway between the two vehicles, Novak was waiting for his boss to join him. Meyrek hopped down from the Jeep, listened, then gave an order before returning to his seat at Beck's side.

"It looks like you came here at the right time. This doesn't happen often…"

He asked his aide to head back to the base.

"It seems we've lost a helicopter," he went on while the car, now gunning it, was bumping and zigzagging its way through the cactuses, taking a shortcut that strayed far from the path. "If there's a rebellion on our hands, things are about to get interesting!"

The forest opened onto a narrow clearing. Several stumps and two chopped-down trees at its edge signaled that troops had been through there recently. Theo and Marcos had crouched down behind a Mexican *yagrumo*, waiting for Huang to come back from where they'd sent him scouting. The small Vietnamese man appeared silently behind them.

"I heard voices, on the other side."

"Our patrols?"

"No. I did not move closer, but from the noise they made, it sounded like a good thirty of them."

Theo nodded his head.

"We're in the training area."

They skirted around the clearing and stationed themselves behind a natural hedge made up of sapodilla and white pine, keeping a lookout. The voices were reaching them clearly.

"We need to warn the others," whispered Marcos.

Theo felt his heart squeeze inside his chest. The thin tones didn't sound grown-up in the slightest. He tried to empty himself of all feelings. Only a few yards out, just on the other side of the bushes in front of them, he might find his daughter.

He straightened up.

"Let's follow them. They'll lead us to the camp."

The snap of twigs had them turning around. Huang's face had frozen. Before they could even make a move towards their weapons, two soldiers sprang up behind them, an M16 aggressively pointed at their chests. The children's closeness had made them utterly careless.

Marcos raised his submachine gun. With one move, Theo stopped him in his tracks. The men's fingers were on their triggers, their faces pinched with tension.

"What are you doing here?"

Theo lifted his arms in a conciliating gesture. He smiled and moved forward with confident steps.

"Congratulations, sergeant. You don't let anyone get the drop on you."

"I asked you a question. What are you doing here?"

"Colonel's orders," lied Theo. "We got dropped down close to the *rio* to check on your defenses. A surprise exercise."

The noncom frowned and shifted from one foot to the other. Uncertainty and astonishment were warring on his face.

"We weren't notified of any such exercise."

"Course not. How can it be a surprise if you get warned about it. Look at us. We're in the same uniforms as you."

"I did hear a chopper a few hours ago," put forward the second soldier.

The sergeant hesitated.

"You can never be too careful. No senior staff on base is supposed to be read into our existence. Where's your superior officer?"

Theo nodded his head.

"Not senior staff. Just a light patrol."

The NCO pointed his chin at Marcos and Huang.

"Grab their guns, we'll escort them back to the camp and check out their story."

Theo allowed himself to be patted down, and felt a pang inside when the soldier took his gun off him.

"A semi-automatic, an SMG, and a hunting knife," voiced the noncom. "You guys sure are carrying a lot of weapons for a patrol!"

He herded the three men together and signaled them forward.

"We'll be six feet behind you. Make even the slightest funny move and I shoot. And never mind if you're telling the truth."

The shrubbery gave way to a second clearing. Theo held his breath.

Several dozen children were sitting on the ground and watching them, their eyes open wide. They all had a cylindrical object between their legs, and they were just done digging a hole just wide enough to set it in. In the middle of the group, two soldiers turned around. One of them was a ranking lieutenant.

"Antipersonnel grenades," whispered Huang. "They're being taught how to allocate them."

Theo didn't hear the Vietnamese man's words. He was sweeping his gaze over the clearing, pausing on every little face there.

The children all wore that despairing and determined expression that characterizes deprived populations. Their hair was shorn like in juvie. At their feet, the dummy grenades were no toys, but there wasn't even a hint of foolhardiness flickering through their attitude. They were all in the same uniform, no concession made to their gender or age.

There were few girls, all the same, and their appearance was so masculine that it even drained them of their last remaining bits of childish charm. These were no longer children, but instead a troop of little soldiers, their miens hardened, their faces gaunt, their huge eyes opened onto a world stripped of all its innocence. Their tribulations could be read inside the hollows of their cheeks, and even more so in their disillusioned gazes.

Katia was not among them.

"We found these three in the bushes," explained the sergeant. "They're claiming they're on a mission for the colonel."

The noncom jabbered with his superior officer for a few seconds.

"Forward!" ordered the lieutenant. "We're making our way back to camp. Exercise over for today."

Theo needed a moment with his eyes closed. He tried to grab for his cool. To forget these images that had crowded in so close to him, like a highlight reel of the sort of cruelty he hadn't wanted to believe could be real, up until this day. Those photographs of radicalized children in Palestinian camps; the

Hitler youth, last defenders of a crumbling Germany; the small Cambodians, red headband circling their hair, ready to revile, to torture, to kill.

The children had put the grenades away in haversack and had lined up, calmly awaiting their orders.

Theo met Marcos's gaze. The Guatemalan was distraught.

"My children," moaned Marcos. "My two little boys. They did not recognize me."

Chapter 18

Joseph Feldman had always had a weakness for Amsterdam, especially at this time of year. For him, the Dutch capital embodied the full charm of old Europe, without the rigid social norms that bogged down other countries.

He enjoyed being able to wander along miles of canals without fear of being run over by a car when he crossed the street. Here, the grating sound of car horns had been replaced by the playful ding of bicycle bells.

The sober architecture downtown captured all the serenity that typified this singular northern mentality: neither heavy nor eccentric. It was the locals' kindness that was an especially nice change of pace. All told, he was pleased to be meeting his new contact in the Venice of the North, rather than in London, as tradition tended to call for in his line of work.

But why did his contacts always wish to rendezvous in dens of vice, in places where sex got sold like produce at the supermarket?

Feldman reached the edge of the Red Light district, the most famous quarter in Amsterdam, a little before nine in the evening. The bustle was already at a fever pitch, amidst hundreds of storefronts displaying the most diverse creatures, imported from all four corners of the world to cater to every taste.

There, tourists rubbed elbows with businessmen jonesing for an affair, with regulars, with perverts, and even with a whole family, a snickering father and a mother holding two little boys by the hand. Feldman shook his head in silent disapproval. He'd always been a prude.

A handful of streets down, niched between a coffee shop sporting a cannabis leaf logo and an Indonesian restaurant, he found the address he'd been looking for.

This time, there was no need for him to take his clothes off, nor to self-neutralize; that was a relief. The tazer burn had stayed behind on Feldman's skin for a long time, and he hated remembering that moment when darkness had overtaken him, his limbs paralyzed and shaken by aftershocks.

Three hundred million dollars. That was how much Cheston had asked him to put together, preferably before the end of the month. Feldman recalled that astronomical number as he reached the stairs of the building, its dilapidated walls making it look as inviting as a seedy hotel near a train station, and as dark as the entrance to Purgatory.

Three hundred million. This time, his contact wasn't Saudi. After Tarik and his associates had vanished, it was as if the network that had surrounded him had dissolved. Feldman had had the devil of a time tracing back his usual channels, tamed through heavy palm-greasing and built on the backbone of his reputation as outstandingly reliable as well as thanks to his acquaintances at the CIA.

The hallway, with its solitary yellow bulb glowing at the end, was heavy with the odor of Indonesian cooking, peanuts and curry over a backdrop of mutton, the staple ingredients of *rijstaffel.* Feldman felt slightly nauseous. His dinner this evening had been too rich and far too lavishly washed down. He hoped he'd be done soon and finally leave with some good news.

Off which he would, as usual, cash in his five percent commission, meaning a cool fifteen million bucks.

Preoccupied by the half-darkness that had him practically walking blind, Feldman felt around before firmly grabbing hold of the banister, hoping there was better lighting on the upper floors.

There was no time for him to notice, or even to suspect, the shadow of a man moving forward, before he felt something like a sting on his neck. Feldman wanted to cry out, but no sound could come out of his mouth. He'd gone dumb as well as blind.

Hand still clutching the banister, he felt himself pitch backwards. The spiral staircase started whirling around, and despite his fear of dying, that made him want to laugh. The last words he ever heard were delivered in a language he spoke to perfection.

"Lehitraot, haver sheli! Tissa nimah..."

Feldman was dead, succumbing to a massive dose of ricin before the Israeli had even run through the building entrance and vanished into the nighttime crowd bustling around the Red Light district outside.

The guards opened the double gates wide and let the row of children and their supervising instructors move through. Theo, Huang, and Marcos were rounding out the group, followed by the lieutenant. The officer motioned to the soldiers on guard.

"Call captain Khouri. We have an emergency situation."

They were led to the center of the courtyard. Camp B was like a scaled-down version of their base, one placed in a less-arid environment. The nearby forest provided it with a temperate climate, and Theo felt relieved that the children at least hadn't had to endure the temperature differentials of the high plateaus.

He took a long look at the faces of the men holding them in their sights. Two impassive, experienced soldiers, the embodiment of the Organization that had ripped Katia from him and hurled her into this soulless universe. A harrowing new wave of doubt assailed him. Had she truly survived? Had Meyrek not simply shown him some kind of doctored or prerecorded image?

Despite the ordeals he himself had gone through, he was having an impossible time imagining his child's fate in the hands of these mercenaries. And it was with a profound disgust towards himself that he was forced to face facts. They'd gotten busted like a bunch of cadets.

As though he'd read his mind, Huang whispered,

"All is not lost. There's still Will…"

Theo silently agreed. Now wasn't the time to lose hope. Will had six men with him. And the element of surprise could yet play into their hand. He took in Marcos, whose eyes were glued to the column of children marching into the building. Bitterness disfigured his face.

'How could his children have recognized him?' thought Theo. Dust mixed with sweat covered his features, his helmet was shoved down all the way over his eyebrows, and his uniform rounded out the full depersonalizing effect. He'd have liked to be encouraging, but one of the guards was already watching him curiously.

Out to the west, beyond the gorge, the sun was painting streaks of fire over the mountain peaks, a gigantic ball of flame distorted by the waves of humid heat rising up from the canyon.

They remained motionless for an indefinite length of time as darkness slowly fell. At this stage, the base had to already be on alert, and they had no way of warning their men. Their one shot was if Will's or Huang's group had already located the camp. *Before they got made themselves.* Theo turned his head towards the guard post. The gates had open to admit a second group of children. The slight figures were moving right towards them, two by two, in step. He stiffened.

Their faces all wore the same expression. They looked straight ahead, uncaring of the three men's presence. There were twenty-five, maybe thirty of them. The same walk, mechanical and steady, their chests forward like military academy cadets.

Theo scanned every face, every gaze. Impossible to make out anyone's identity. The instructing officers barked orders, stepped up the pace. Theo felt his heart leap inside his chest. His paternal instincts were screaming that she was among them.

The gates swung closed behind the troop. The section had come up level with them. He perused their faces, their figures once more, on the lookout for any gesture, any hint. His breathing turned harsh. His gaze froze along the sixth row. Tears sprang to his eyes…

Katia had grown, she was prettier than ever. Her doll-like face had matured. She was standing proudly, an immense sadness veiling her gaze. He felt his legs give out. The need to speak her name bubbled up in his throat like a sweet, tempting, forbidden taste.

310

'Katia!'

Not even the slightest sound had come out of his mouth. He forced himself to look away, to protect her, even if the need to take her in was stronger than anything, more powerful than the rifle pointed at his chest. He took a step back, hoping he could hide behind Marcos's bulk. Slowly, as though in answer to a silent call, the little girl turned her head.

Katia froze, amazement distorting her features. Then a flicker of joy lit up her whole face. Her lips parted. Theo could guess at her reaction more than he could see it. Inside of him, his prayer was at a howl.

'Don't speak, Katia. Don't say a word! I'm begging you, baby girl. Don't even look at me!'

The column moved beyond them. Katia wouldn't take her gaze off him, looking crazed, stuck between fear and relief. The main door to the building opened to spit out a band of officers. A young woman stepped away from the group and ate up the distance towards them with long steps. Theo noticed her worried demeanor and the great tiredness making her features drawn. Despite the tension, despite the uniform doing her femininity a disservice, he found her exceedingly beautiful. She was holding a machine gun in one hand.

"Meyrek didn't send you," she spat. "The base has no knowledge of this operation."

There was more surprise than anger in her tone. She came to stand between the two guards.

"Who are you?"

"I…" began Theo, tears clouding his eyes.

The young woman scrutinized him curiously, intrigued by his attitude. Her gaze slid over to Marcos.

"What on Earth is going on here?"

Theo was forcing himself to keep his gaze off his daughter with such obstinacy that it was making him sick. Once again, he could guess at Katia's movements more than he saw them. The child could no longer keep hold of herself. Overcoming her amazement, she was now only led by one desire, to burrow into her father's arms.

He howled inwards once more, hoping his mental strength would cut across the distance and persuade her not to move. But there was nothing for it. Katia broke ranks and sidled between the guards with hesitant steps.

Then she began to run. Fifty yards stood between her and her father. Fifty yards that she covered in a flash, fifty yards that seemed an eternity to a petrified, desperate Theo who was certain he had just lost everything he had. He fell to his knees.

When the little girl at last took refuge in his arms, the world ceased to exist for good. She smelled of soap and sweat. Her hair fluttered like stringy filaments. First prey to the most unspeakable terror, Theo suddenly felt that he'd become invulnerable. That moment of absolute happiness was something he'd just stolen from destiny, from death itself. Nothing and no-one could take it back from him.

He heard the young uniformed woman scream,

"Don't shoot!"

Katia burst into sobs and began trembling from head to toe while Theo peppered kisses all over her face and hair, mixing his tears with the little girl's while still feeling disbelief.

Disconcerted, the guards didn't know what tack to take. Katia's section had ceased its march, and all the children were looking at them in stupefaction.

The officers who'd been escorting Eliane rushed to the scene.

"Who are these men?"

"I don't know," replied the young woman. "I'm completely lost here."

"Estamos padres!" bellowed Marcos. "We're here to take back the children you stole from us."

Before Eliane or anybody else could move, one of the officers rushed Katia and unceremoniously tore her from her father's arms. Theo tried to hold her back for a moment, but there were several weapons pointed at him. To keep her safe, he had to resign himself to letting her go, his heart breaking at seeing her struggle and hearing her cries.

The officer had grabbed the little girl by her hair, and he let her collapse on the ground before dragging her like a sack of potatoes.

"Not like that!"

The barrel of her gun pointed mechanically at her men, Eliane had just stepped in. Stepping forward quickly, she moved level with Katia, who was howling in fear and in pain and writhing with all her strength to try and scratch and bite at the guard. The Lebanese woman took the little girl by the arm and pulled her gently but firmly away from her underling, spearing him with her glare.

"I still haven't been given any instructions regarding these men!" she thundered sharply. "Take those troops back to barracks and double their watch. As for you, follow me."

At a rapid glance, she took the measure of Theo and his two comrades in arms while their escort pushed them forward. As dangerous and determined as they might have seemed to her, these three men had pulled back the curtains on a mystery that made her sudden unease soar.

It couldn't be more clear that their familial ties with some of the children in the camp was not part of some stratagem. They belonged to Meyrek's troops and had come in from the High Plateaus. How they'd learned of their existence, and worse still, how they'd managed to reach them were the two leading questions that she'd love finding the answer to.

But their presence there, and the things she'd just heard, confirmed the suspicions that had been percolating in her subconscious for months. So all these children weren't orphans?

The officer who'd grabbed hold of Katia must have felt some hesitation in his superior officer's attitude. Before she could take one step to follow the group, he turned to the children, hitting them with a cruel smile.

"These men claim to be your parents. Do you know them? Are you going to let yourselves get taken in by some stolen uniforms? The enemy has just unmasked himself. Here's an opportunity for a new training exercise…"

"Lieutenant, what's gotten into you?" cried Eliane.

"All I'm doing is following the colonel orders, captain."

The irony in his voice chilled the Lebanese woman.

"I'm the only one who gives orders here!"

"Oh, really?"

The lieutenant stepped closer to Eliane while unsnapping the holster of his sidearm.

"I'm sorry, captain, but I'm under strict orders. No-one can come into contact with these children. All the more so if they claim to be their parents."

Fingers stiff on her submachine gun, Eliane took quick stock of the situation. The guards were hesitant to follow the lieutenant, but his behavior was so self-assured that they wouldn't take long to join forces with him. Even from afar, Meyrek had the gift of inspiring fear.

"You're not gonna force these children to fight their own parents. Don't come any closer, lieutenant, or I'm pulling this trigger."

"Won't the colonel find that a surprise."

"Let's call colonel Meyrek together and I'll comply with his instructions. In the meantime, holster your weapon…"

Before the young woman could even begin to make a move, the lieutenant dove to one side, while she was staggered to feel two arms encircle her. The second officer had silently sidled behind her and had only waited for the split-second when her attention slipped in order to act. With a skilled hold, he forced her to drop her SMG. Eliane couldn't bite back a short cry.

The rest happened at the speed of light, as though that had been the signal they'd all been waiting for. At first paralyzed by the scene, the children moved suddenly, in perfect harmony. Their coordinated motions looked like a magnificently synchronized ballet as they rushed the guards and the supervising officers.

The tide of small, frail, agile bodies, trained as they were in combat basics, took the men by surprise. They were five to one; they knew how to bite, how to kick, how to shove with their entire weight, and in a flash, their former instructors lost their balance. Some fell, others tried to fight back against the horde, not quite understanding yet what was going on. One of them came back to his senses quickly enough to retrieve his weapon and attempt to fire. Luckily, the burst of gunfire went wide.

That was the moment that Theo and Huang, followed by Marcos, chose to act. They had to move quickly, the gunfire had to have put the camp on alert by now. In a matter of seconds, they managed to turn the situation to their advantage, each neutralizing a guard.

But other soldiers were already running their way. From the barracks, from the guard post. Theo sought his daughter out with his gaze, ready to throw himself across her body to shield it. He froze, struck dumb. The little girl had grabbed a rifle and was aiming it at the arriving backup.

"Katia, don't!"

Right then, a burst of gunfire split through the air like a blast. The guards jerked, torn apart. The farthest of them threw themselves to the ground. A gigantic figure appeared between the bars of the gate.

"Will!" joyfully exclaimed Huang.

That was his last word. The lieutenant had dragged himself towards Eliane's SMG and had just shot it blindly from on the ground. The small Vietnamese man looked momentarily surprised before he crumpled.

The officer changed position and put Theo in his sights. Several methodical shots from Will tore through the gate lock, and he rushed inside with his men.

The lieutenant pulled the trigger once more. Theo dove to the side. The SMG fire missed him. The man didn't have the time to course correct. A rifle bullet had just struck him in the middle of his forehead. Katia watched him with the serious eyes of a child reciting a lesson, the barrel of her rifle still puffing out smoke.

She held the weapon out to Theo.

"That's not as nice as the Nintendo," she said with a grimace.

Before bursting into heaving sobs once more.

The Cayuse Little Bird had just circled Garroni's body like a vulture for the seventh time, pinning it with the beam of its side searchlight. It hadn't taken Meyrek a lot of time to widen the search once he'd understood this wasn't an accidental case of disappearance, but in fact an outright rebellion. Finding the sergeant out in the middle of the desert with no attempts made to hide his body only stood to confirm his intuition.

The second call caught him just as he was giving the pilot the order to land. There were only three of them in the cockpit: Beck, himself, and Novak. Meyrek thought for a few moments. He had a choice to either return to the base and organize a full-scale hunt, or take care of the issue himself before it turned into an insoluble problem.

"You seem to have brought us some bad luck," he told Beck in a voice loud enough to cover the rotor noise.

So, Collin had uncovered the second camp. That was the thorny side of this news. Garroni had most assuredly lied to him when he'd stated that he'd never let Theo out of his sight during the fire at the computer center. But with Garroni now dead, Meyrek wouldn't have the satisfaction of exacting his own payment for that mistake.

On the other hand, he liked Collin's audacity. One year's training was all he'd needed to turn a scrawny computer geek with barely a foolhardy bone in his body into a bona fide combat machine. Clearly, his search for his daughter was motivation enough to greatly increase his strength and talent as a soldier.

But it wasn't just that: Collin had persuaded hardened mercenaries to turn against their CO. He'd therefore found the chink in the Organization's armor. Few are the men who will consent to fight for money alone. Even the most obtuse of mercenaries like to see themselves as heroes.

314

In order to find his child, Collin had managed to counteract the fear that he himself instilled in his men, so as to give them a true reason to fight. Kudos to him.

The true good news was his imminent arrest. He had nevertheless gotten grabbed idiotically. And that, thought the colonel, was pretty irritating all the same.

"Some of the recruits seem not to care for the treatment they're subject to," he told Beck. "Has Langley already sent you out to visit hell?"

Howard stiffened. He disliked everything about this patrol, and Meyrek's announcement seemed still more threatening. Never would Cheston or his daughter have wanted him to learn this much.

"I've been to several Middle-Eastern countries," he retorted flatly.

"That was a joke, Mister Beck. Hell is when the highest level of civilization imitates barbarism!"

He immediately gave the pilot an order, and Beck understood that he would soon know much too much.

Inside every building, the children had followed the section's example. Captain Khouri had finally shown them the enemy. It was their own guards. Their instructors. The men who had taught them to fight and kill.

Things were made all the more confusing by the fact that some of them chose to ally themselves with their officers, obedience to the chain of command having been drilled into them down to the marrow, while others hadn't hesitated to defend themselves, shooting the swarms of angry little soldiers without remorse.

The children had grabbed all sorts of weapons. Stones picked up in the middle of the yard, chairs from their dorms. Someone had hit Eliane Khouri, their true leader, their only protector.

The mercenaries were quickly overcome by their sheer numbers.

In a handful of minutes, Will and his men had taken complete control over the situation.

They split up into two-man patrols, each one escorted by a group of children, and swept the camp looking for lone gunmen. Fifteen-odd mercenaries had been gathered together in the courtyard, face-down on the ground, hands clasped behind their backs. Standing square on his feet, alert to the slightest movement, Marcos was keeping them in his sights. Theo went to him.

"Let me take over for you."

"Later," gritted out Marcos. "I'm just waiting for one of these assholes to try and scratch an itch…"

"You'd be better off taking care of your kids," teased Theo. Marcos raised his head.

Two little boys stepped shyly forward. They were staring at their father, unsure, their features tense.

"*Mis niños!*"

He held the submachine gun out to Theo, not looking at him, then slowly stepped over to them.

"It's no surprise they didn't recognize you," said Theo lightly. "You haven't seen your face…"

The echo of the final gunshots had died down a few minutes ago. Quiet had descended over the camp once more, and patrols had begun coming back emptyhanded. If some mercenaries had managed to get away, it wasn't very likely that they'd risk launching a counteroffensive.

The camp was theirs.

Over on prisoner watch, Theo got relieved by Lochlan in turn. Assisted by Salinas, the Irishman had raided the weapons stock and had decked himself out like a revolutionary, mimicking Will. He'd strapped himself full of ammo belts and grenades and had slid the strap of a laser-guided riot gun onto his shoulder. A nervous tic had his mouth twitching, and excitement sparkled in his gaze.

"We swept over everything," he cried. "Ten to forty. We took them out. Elite, baby. The section damn sure lives up to its name."

Theo held back from noting that, without the children, liberating the camp could have quickly turned into a massacre. They only had one dead and about a dozen wounded, Huang among them. He'd been hit in the shoulder and side, but he seemed out of danger for now.

For his part, the Australian had mobilized the camp nurses and was organizing transport for the wounded. Three kids were a little worse off than the others. It was harrowing, seeing their little faces twisted in pain and astonishment. But Eliane Khouri had rushed to requisition the doctor, who was completely lost as to the situation.

"I'm going to need an explanation later," she said, coming to a stop in front of Theo.

"You're the one who owes us an explanation. But we have better things to do for now, don't you agree?"

Eliane stepped away to gather several children around her. With the help of several men who'd remained loyal to her, she made sure no-one was wounded. With the action waning, a sort of vertigo came over Theo.

That feeling again, that surreal impression, just like when he'd come to in that Mexican hospital to find Meyrek at his side, to comprehend that his world had crumbled, that Juliette et Katia were no longer there…

But Katia was there, alive, right by his side, peering at him with her frightened and astonished gaze. Still in shock, she wouldn't stop trembling, like a kitten torn from its nest. Theo was dying to know, to question her. How had she managed to escape the fire that had consumed the Dodge; was her mother, whose name didn't come up anywhere, whom the computer database couldn't identify, still alive?

The pictures kept flipping through his head faster and faster. The French army and Meyrek, then his civilian life, meeting Juliette, Katia's birth. Then

316

their deaths. And Meyrek once more. And the hellscape of all these world armies brought together. Then Katia brought back to life.

And Juliette?

He smiled at Katia, who was shooting him a questioning gaze, as impatient as he was, and he put a silent message in his smile. *'Not now, sweetie. Just a few more minutes. I need to deal with the people who helped me.'* He then took her by the hand and led her across the yard.

Will stood before them. He was holding his machine gun against his body and put his hand out to take Katia's. The little girl's fingers vanished entirely in the grip of his enormous fist. The giant smiled.

"If I had a kid like her, I'da laid siege to the camp all by myself, with my bare damn hands."

He'd crouched down low to get to her level, and he raised a serious gaze towards Theo.

"You've got a lot of things to talk about. You take care of her, I'll deal with the evac."

"Can the wounded be moved?" asked Theo, sidestepping his offer.

"Not all of them, but we've only got two choppers anyway."

Despite their sizes, the two birds could only take a small number of stretchers and supervising men on board. The black of night had fallen a long time ago. Theo looked at his watch. It would be midnight in less than two hours. And then the first minute of a new day... He just had to hope with all his heart that he'd set up his surprise correctly. And especially that luck would keep sticking with them from then on. Whatever happened, they had to act fast now.

"The real question is, how many men is Meyrek sending our way, and when will they get here," said Will.

On that matter, Theo was just about certain he knew the answer. The colonel had been notified of their incursion and capture, but he had no idea the situation had been turned around. And few men at the first camp knew about the second.

"He'll come alone, and it won't be long now."

From now until he got here, the base would need to look normal. Lights out, guards at their posts, wounded hidden inside the barracks.

"C'mon," went Will, patting his shoulder. "Stay with your kiddo, she's the one who needs you the most."

The first thing Theo would have liked to do was make sure that Huang was out of danger. His brother, Tran, had patched him up himself, declining all help from the nurses. He'd need surgery, but for the moment, he'd managed to stop the bleeding by applying pressure with his fingers at very specific spots. The Vietnamese man was alarmingly pale, but he still managed a smile when he saw Theo.

"It's tonight or never," he said in a weak, reedy voice.

"We don't really have much room for maneuver."

"Air, earth, water, fire... They're all just an illusion. You have the room, believe me. But now you leave me alone, and take care of your daughter. She has the answers you seek."

"I just hope I wasn't wrong about one thing."

"What's that?"

"The day of the week. When do you think we are?"

Huang hesitated before answering. Most of the men had stopped counting the days a long time ago.

"Thursday," intervened Tran. "For a little over an hour, it's still Thursday."

Theo felt at ease. He grabbed his daughter by the hand again and took her to the side, off to a secluded corner by the guard post.

When he set her down on the ground, away from everyone's looks, the child's face fell apart. She burrowed into her father's arms and hugged him with all her strength, digging her little fingers into his dust-covered utilities. Theo covered her in kisses and allowed her to let go, to be a little girl again. She'd just shot a man, and he could hardly dare imagine what she must have lived through to have gotten reflexes like that.

The outburst only lasted for a moment. When she finally calmed down, Theo asked her in a soft voice to tell him everything she remembered… To tell him about her mother and that long-ago day when the Dodge…

Katia looked at him in surprise.

"What accident?"

"When the three of us got separated, Katia. The policeman put me into his car, and you, you stayed with her. Then what happened…"

The little girl's eyes became so terror-filled that, for a moment, Theo thought she'd start screaming.

…The two cars had left the freeway, taking a tree-lined road. Katia couldn't take her eyes off her father, a few yards behind them. Then the road started turning. The surroundings became dryer. The police car slowed down and veered towards a gas station.

"Mommy, he's not following us anymore."

"I know, don't worry about it. They'll catch up to us."

The road was climbing up a steep slope, and the twists and turns became more frequent. That didn't mean the Dodge slowed down at all. Katia felt her stomach ripple queasily.

"Mommy, I'm sick."

Juliette shouted something at the policeman. The man laughed and shook his head.

"Please, honey. Hold on. We'll stop soon."

Too late. She reflexively leaned forward, and she got sick all over the interior carpet of the car. The policeman turned around and laughed even harder. Juliette pulled a tissue out of her handbag. She wiped at her mouth.

"There. All better now."

Despite the air conditioning, the stench was unbearable. Juliette opened her window. She pulled Katia across her knees and tenderly caressed her forehead.

They got to the top of the slope. A black car was pulled over on the shoulder. The policeman slowed down and parked the car a few yards over. Three men got

318

out of the other car. One of them was wearing military clothes. Before Juliette had time to protest, the Dodge door opened and the two civilians slid inside. The soldier exchanged a few words with the policeman. That was when Juliette felt her heart squeeze.

"No!" she howled. "Leave her with me!"

She gripped Katia and tried to shield her in her arms. The men separated mother from daughter none too gently. Katia burst into tears again. She struggled, tried to scratch her kidnapper. The man dragged her outside and threw her in the backseat of the black car while his accomplices subdued Juliette under the policeman's amused gaze. They hadn't counted on the immense strength of a mother whose child has been torn from her. Juliette fought so hard that she managed to escape.

Theo listened to her tale, hanging on his daughter's every word. So she hadn't escaped the car fire, but had instead been ripped from her mother's arms with a specific purpose, undoubtedly already meant for the second camp, guilty of nothing except having a certain father whose talents a certain colonel was interested in…

"After that, I don't remember…" moaned the little girl. "Daddy, I'm sorry, I don't remember…"

Theo bit back a sob. He'd held hope once more, and Katia was hurling him back into darkness. Now wasn't the time to push the issue. There may come one day, maybe, provided they managed to escape the camp. However, the little girl had other memories, and she wanted to confide, to tell her father about the months that she'd spent removed from his love.

…She'd woken up in a dorm, surrounded by children. She'd sought out her parents around her then screamed until a man in a white coat had leaned over her bed.

"I want my parents," had moaned the little girl. "Where are they? I want my parents."

After shooing the other children out, the nurse had grabbed a glass of orange juice off the side table and handed it to Katia.

"Drink this, you'll feel better."

"I don't want to drink, I want my parents."

The man had shaken his head, looking sorrowful.

"Something awful has happened. You're at the hospital, I need you to listen to me."

She'd pushed back the glass and slid down to the ground.

"I don't want to listen to you. I want to see my mommy."

The nurse had grabbed her by the arm.

"Relax! Let me take care of you."

"I'm not sick. I want to leave. I want my parents. Let go of me!" She'd started to stomp her feet, to screech, had tried to bite his arm, her cheeks a blotchy red from congestion. He'd waited for her to wind down a bit, picked up the glass again, and put it before her once more.

"I don't want to hurt you. Drink up, and I'll tell you all about where you are."

Katia was hiccupping. Her screams had scraped her throat raw. She'd ended up accepting the glass with a sob.

"It's all going to be OK now," said the nurse, stroking her hair.

She felt all funny, like a soft, sleepy feeling had wrapped around her. The nurse's voice seemed sweet, comforting.

"Your daddy did something bad. The police wanted to punish him. He didn't want to go to prison, so he stole a car and ran away with your mommy. They were in an accident."

It was like a story. One of those stories she was told when she was tucked in. She'd called out,

"Daddy!"

The nurse had kept on talking. His voice had gone far away. His face was disappearing into a fog.

Katia had fallen asleep once again.

The next day, they'd taken her to a different building. A young woman dressed like a soldier had seen her in an office. She'd asked her a lot of questions, but kindly. Katia didn't remember all that well anymore…

The woman had taken her to the base. They'd come across a group of children who marched like machines, a wooden rifle on one shoulder. She'd been shown the mess, where she would have her meals from then on, the classroom, where young boys were taking rifles apart.

Next, the woman had described what daily life was like at the camp, what sports she was going to do, their walks in the mountains.

"I'm sorry about what happened to you, kiddo. You shouldn't be here, but there isn't a lot that either of us can do about that."

She had advised her not to resist the orders she'd be given. At least the woman spoke the same language as her, but with an accent. She had added one last thing while she'd been caressing her hair.

"My name is Eliane, but here, they call me captain. If something really isn't going well, ask to see me."

Then she'd handed her over to a soldier.

During the months that followed, Katia had woken up screaming, calling out for her parents, every night. Eliane had ended up ordering her transfer into a solo dorm close to the guard's room. Then the fits had begun to abate. She was only a little girl, caught up in the most absurd of snares. All she sought was to live.

She had adapted to her new life, and had even reached a point where she laughed sometimes, not too often. She'd learned how to climb trees, how to fashion traps to catch wild animals in, how to shoot a rifle, how to march in lockstep. She'd been taught a new language, one she could now hold an almost flawless conversation in.

She'd stopped waking up in the middle of the night about eight weeks in. Her days were long, exhausting. She'd been issued a new bed inside a dorm, and her

320

teammates had been glad to take her in. Sometimes, when a nightmare got her in its claws again, the bigger children would slink to her bedside and talk to her so she could fall back asleep.

At the end of that interval, their training had changed. Gone were the paramilitary exercises made to look like children's games; instead, they had actual fights put together by their instructing officers.

A new teacher had showed up and was teaching them classes every evening. He'd explain to them how they were all orphans, and how they were all now one big family together. Their family had an enemy. When they were old enough, they'd know who that was.

The months had gone by. She'd learned judo, archery. The officers were almost never nice, unlike her teammates, and they always shouted their orders, even if they were a couple steps away. There'd been that dreadful exercise where she'd needed to crawl under a barbed wire net while bullets flew above her head. And her friend Matias, working himself into a panic, getting up just a few yards away from her...

In her nightmares, Katia would often see his face disfigured by terror, and the boy's blood would flow, and turn into a river, and stream over the whole entire world, and everything was colored red. The grass, the ocean, and even her mom and dad, whose faces she'd already forgot...

The sound of footsteps broke into the little girl's tale. Theo turned to Eliane, who was moving their way while wiping her hands, her SMG slung across her chest once more. She balled up the blood-soaked napkin and tossed it away.

"So you really are her father..."

"Why, were you doubting that?"

"Ever since you got brought in earlier, I've been having doubts about pretty much everything. Meyrek's gotten us used to surprise training exercises, all kinds of tests. But we've got better things to do than hash this out now. What's the plan?"

Theo looked at the young woman, whose features vanished in the half-darkness. Without the pilot lights and their dim halo outlining the barracks, they would have been in complete darkness. Most of the children had headed back into the dorms, awaiting new orders.

All those months of training had made some of them into actual small but discipline-oriented killing machines. Eliane's underlings had made a gross miscalculation when they'd assumed they could easily get the better of a chain of command that had been so rigorously impressed. They were paying for that now, and Theo, left empty by this excess of feeling, was eager to understand the meaning of this huge waste.

The attitude and the reactions on the part of the young woman standing before him were yet another mystery that he was dying to get to the bottom of. But that was as far as his plan went. After uncovering the existence of the children's camp, he'd been driven by one single, solitary, surreal goal, one that he'd nonetheless just carried out. Beyond that, he was putting himself in the hands of fate.

"I hadn't planned on our being captured," began Theo. "But what did you tell Meyrek, how come he's not here yet?"

The young woman kept silent. She was still having a hard time admitting that she'd just committed a betrayal, and even less so accepting the upcoming consequences for her actions. Still snuggled up against her father, her face a mess of tears, Katia stretched a finger out her in a gesture that held and displayed all of her ten-year-old innocence.

"That's her, that's Eliane. She's the one who was so nice to me."

Her words had the immediate effect of changing the young Lebanese woman's expression, which turned soft for the briefest second. She shook her head.

"Meyrek was unreachable, I could only talk to his camp leader. The colonel must have been notified by now, but he was hosting an official visit; that must be what's delaying him."

"He still believes we're being held prisoner, right?"

"The lieutenant who went against my orders and myself were the only ones who were in contact with the main base. So yes. And he will most likely come alone, or with minimal backup."

"That was my thinking, too. Can I ask you a question?"

"Go ahead," went-Eliane. "I think I already know what it is."

"Why did you agree to look after these children? And why did you change sides there at the last moment?"

Eliane smiled sadly, her gaze going unfocused.

"The children? You would need to know my story to be able to understand. Whatever they were put through here, that's nothing compared to what happens to them in Shia training camps, in Lebanon or Iran.

"I did not change sides. I merely got the war wrong. At the top of the command structure, there's always the same cowards everywhere, no matter what their intentions are."

No sooner had the young woman finished her phrase that they heard the sound of a rotor, still far-off, while a minuscule dot of light appeared in between the stars as though led in a dance by the wind.

Meyrek opened the Cayuse side door well before the helicopter had touched down. He needed to sniff at the air, and despite the exhaust coming off the turbines of the uncomfortable aircraft, he was still able to catch other odors, like a predator out on a hunt. Of course, this was all highly subjective, sensitive, unreal, but the waves of excitement sweeping over him were all so many signals that his instincts gave off.

For as long and as far back as he could remember, Meyrek had thought of the universe as a war zone, where everyone was entrusted with a mission. The enemy wasn't important: all that mattered was the way you survived it.

His duty, which he hoped he had upheld diligently and efficiently, was to train men for this enduring fight. Everything else was just empty words and wasted time. The rules had been written by savage gods who must have led numerous wars themselves, in order to have designed this merciless a world.

The Cayuse floodlight shone onto the moving surface of the tall grasses as they were flattened by the blow from the blades. A few dozen yards out, an undefinable figure was approaching at a run. With a cynical, almost mechanical gesture, Meyrek unsnapped the holster strap securing his sidearm. The exact moment that the aircraft gently touched down with a whistle of its turbines, he seized his weapon and pointed it at Beck.

"Sorry," he said, "but I'm afraid your vacation ends here."

Howard shook his head resignedly, a flicker of defiance sparking in his gaze. He'd had his chain yanked all day with that grand tour of the place, and he suspected Meyrek had taken an unholy pleasure in behaving like a proud and arrogant host, all the while knowing what was in store for him at the end. He'd been expecting the tide to turn like this, and the only thing he'd been wondering was what moment the colonel would pick to show his hand.

"I'm going to assume this isn't at your own initiative?" he said.

Not replying, the colonel asked him to turn around and nimbly zip-tied his wrists together. He then signaled Novak down before shouting at the pilot to cut off the rotor.

"You remain on board, and the minute anything goes wrong you send a code 140 out to the base. They'll know who to send out!"

Grabbing Beck by the arm, he led him to the edge before helping him down. The figure, now recognizable as Eliane, was less than ten yards out. Standing stoutly at attention, the young woman was waiting for the three men to approach her.

"Captain Khouri!" thundered Meyrek. "What a night!"

"Happy to see you, colonel. We've been expecting you. May I ask who this man is?"

With the whine of a dying engine, the helicopter's blades had slowed their spinning. Meyrek pulled Beck in towards him with a huge, theatrical gesture. The latter was trying to make out the young woman's features. Each new event was all the more intriguing to him as he discerned its impact on his own fate.

The last thing he needed to do was panic. Even trapped and bound, he'd been trained to calmly and logically work through the worst situations, and his nausea had given way to an all too familiar fear. But by keeping his breathing under control, he could hold that at bay. The small group was still a couple steps away from Eliane.

"There's no time for me to satisfy your curiosity, captain. I would, however, like you to answer a few of my questions."

Meyrek stopped moving forward, still holding Beck just as firmly.

"Why didn't the runway lights come on when my helicopter began its approach?"

"I was with the prisoners, Colonel. I was only notified of your arrival at the last moment."

"The prisoners? Very well. How many are there, exactly? Could you give me their names and ranks?"

"We've already reported…"

"I know that!"

Meyrek's voice had boomed out in the quiet left behind by the noise from the turbines dying out.

"You reported three men… Whereas my sections work in five-man groups. So I want their names, and I want them right. Now."

A hundred yards out, hidden behind an opaque wall of grasses and succulents, Theo could see the scene as though it was daytime thanks to the 338 Lapua Magnum's infrared scope that Will had dug out for him. Very close by, shielded behind a tree, Katia was watching him with the eyes of a little girl who'd been torn from a nightmare but still lived through the agony of her imaginary world.

Will wasn't far off, somewhere on his left, with the chopper in the sights of his .50-cal. Marcos, Lochlan, Tran, and the others had assigned themselves several other tasks, ranging from watching the prisoners to a Hail-Mary trap.

But, for right now, Theo's mind was preoccupied by his latest discovery, which was intriguing enough to prevent him from focusing on the current situation as he should.

The man who'd been dragged between Meyrek and Novak with his hands tied together wasn't unknown to him. Theo had only seen him once, in a picture, but he could have picked him up out of any crowd. Captured from a distance in Feldman's company, this was the target that the colonel had designated as his first mission.

"There's a Frenchman, Collin," said Eliane loudly enough for the colonel, but also Theo and Will, to hear. "And two Mexicans. One of them is called…"

She broke off when she saw Meyrek pointing his weapon at her chest.

"Go on," said the latter. "A mere precaution. Don't stop talking."

"I don't know their first names. Marcos… and then there's…"

"Why have you come here unescorted, captain? You're quite familiar with the SOP! Where are your guards?"

Despite the green cast, Meyrek's eyes shone with a fierce excitement through the infrared scope. All Theo had to do was move his rifle half an inch and he could sweep the scene from face to face. He could only admire Eliane's cool composure; she wasn't giving an inch despite the colonel's increasingly inquisitive tone.

The tied-up stranger, his designated target, seemed coiled in on himself like an animal getting ready to leap. Novak alone let his unease and his growing nerves show through. The memory of a time long ago rippled like an echo through Theo's head.

"Prone shooting position… Assume position!"

He'd been so afraid when his fingers had touched a weapon, that very first time! It had only been an old rifle, limited in precision, and yet. Between his hands, that rainy afternoon, that peashooter had turned out to be an instrument of fate with dark reverberations, the outcome of which might hinge entirely on his upcoming actions. It was the irony of a tumultuous fate that he so far hadn't been in control of for the slightest moment.

"I don't understand what's going on, Colonel," ventured Eliane again, her voice firm enough to be convincing. "We've got three captives. Procedures deal with regular situations only..."

Suddenly, Theo felt like an electric charge leave his entire spine feeling paralyzed for a split second, all the way to the small of his back. Camouflaged by the dense vegetation, he knew he was invisible. However, inside his infrared scope, the colonel's gaze had landed on him with such a level of intensity that it seemed like he could see him, despite the distance and the shifting, tall grass wall.

"Collin!"

The colonel's voice made him seize up. With a firm grip, Meyrek pulled Beck in closer to him to make him into a shield, his other hand keeping his weapon pointed right at Eliane.

"Collin, I know you're there. I can't see you yet, but I have a precise bead on your position. Who else is there with you? We have two five-man sections missing.

"Let me guess. If I was you, I'd have Will over to my left for a triangular shot, and what are you hiding behind that tree that's thick enough to shield a whole brigade...

"Oh, but of course. You've already got your daughter back, and you put her somewhere safe but not too far from you. Now that is a mistake I'd have never made. In combat, you should never have anything to sacrifice that you hold dearer than yourself!"

The colonel had said all this in English, in order for everyone present to understand him. Maneuvering lightly, Novak had sidled closer to Eliane, just enough to shield himself behind her if need be.

Through the infrared scope, Meyrek's eyes were staring dead into Theo's.

"Well played, Collin. I'm proud of you all the same. All I needed to do was give you a goal, you see, and the soldier came awake. I'm never wrong about what men are made of, deep down.

"We are all either fighters or cowards. Killers or prey. There are no other notes that compose the world's symphony, it is only civilians and politicians that turn it into dissonance..."

Meyrek was smiling the smile of a man who was living one of the most thrilling moments of his life. Theo suddenly recalled the ridiculous nickname he'd been saddled with so many years before. He knew that legends were often born from a detail, like the protruding canines in a perfect row of teeth, like those revealed by that smile. Meyrek abruptly changed his tone and shifted from English to French.

"You're going to do something for me now, Collin. And hurry it up, we've played around long enough... You can answer me, keeping quiet won't do you any good.

"One sign from me will have the pilot behind me calling the base. You wouldn't want to see three attack choppers spray the whole area with machine gun fire... The dorm walls aren't so thick as all that, you know. Come on, Collin, this has all gone on long enough!"

Theo took his face away from the rifle for one moment. Sticking close to the tree trunk, Katia looked less terrified than he'd feared. The little girl seemed to be focusing on something inside herself. He tried to shoot her a reassuring gaze. The rustle of leaves a few steps out told him that Will was changing position.

"Very well!" pronounced the colonel. "Keep quiet, if that's how you want to play it; you won't be silent for long. It must be thrilling for you to have me in your sightline, isn't that right? Where do you feel that excitement, hmm? In your stomach, lower down?

"You think all you need to do is pull that trigger and this nightmare will be over?… But you're gonna do no such thing! Quite the opposite. You're going to get up, and you're going to do exactly what I'm telling you to! The only way you'll get out of this is by telling everybody this was a mission, a training exercise!"

Theo started. A fresh rustle in the grass. Will's voice, very low.

"What's the *maricón* saying?"

"Hold on, something weird's going on. I'll translate afterwards."

An exercise? What was Meyrek alluding to? Fresh doubts gripped Theo. Even if the colonel's obsessions often dragged him to the edge of insanity, he was the kind of man who got a handle on himself in the most high-stakes situations. Like any good strategist, he knew he had no chance of turning the situation around to his advantage. How did he imagine he might manipulate him some more?

In the deep darkness that the halo from the helicopter lights could barely graze, the colonel's voice held the suggestion of a demented litany.

"It would only take one bullet, isn't that right? …And then? You'd spent the rest of your life asking yourself that one insidious question. The single question that's been hounding you since I gave you half your life back. What about the other half, Collin? Have you already given it up?"

The colonel's face folded into a terrifying rictus.

"Stand up, Collin. Tell them, they don't understand a word I'm saying. Tell them you were under my orders. You were the only one who knew. Be convincing, they'll believe you! I've just put an end to your mission, and your men will be nominated for military honors, same as you. The completion of this exercise will conclude your training.

"Tell them, and if you still want to take your shot, I'm holding on to your target. You did recognize him, didn't you? Do you like him better motionless, or should I shove him into a run? Give your men the good news and bring this circus act to an end."

Theo couldn't hold himself back anymore. Still lying low, eye stuck to his scope, he yelled out in the same language.

"And why would I do that, colonel?"

Once more that predatory smile in his fluorescent green sights.

"Because you've already figured it out! Your wife is alive, Collin. If you kill me, there'll be no-one left to take you to her. Her name isn't in any of the

326

computers. Your whole entire life wouldn't give you enough time to find the mother of your child!"

Theo felt his hands tremble. In the scope, Meyrek's face turned blurry as his eyes misted over. How could he have been crazy enough to think that his fate would let itself be tamed this easily? No amount of training could prepare you for these kinds of choices!

The focus of all his hatred was steadily disappearing from his sight, turning into a shapeless, greenish mass. He blinked, turned his gaze to Katia to gain some strength from her, and froze still.

The little girl was staring at him unblinkingly, her eyes wild, tears streaming down her cheeks. Slowly, she shook her head no. Then she moved even faster. No. And again: no, furiously, desperately. A silent no that rang out inside Theo's head like a bellow.

So then, eyes suddenly dry, Theo grabbed a firmer hold of his weapon. From this distance, in the middle of the night, even a particularly gifted sniper would need a scope, like the one mounted on the Lapua Magnum. But what was it Huang had said? *That he had the third eye?*

What was all that about, damnit! Some carnival crap. Why could he now see the scene as though it was daytime, no need for the IR scope or anything else! And the face of that man whose hands were tied, turning towards him, entreating, as though he too could see him. His target, his mission. Him or Meyrek? Believe, or go all the way?

Theo pulled the trigger. Three pops.

The very concept of coincidence is subjective by its very nature, since a plethora of simultaneous, interconnected events can only be awarded this definition by an interested conscious being, even if that interest is to observe only, to notice them. But there are other types of coincidence, of the kinds that remain forever unknown.

Although no observer was able to connect them due to the distances involved, three major and ruthlessly interconnected events occurred within the otherwise short span separating Theo's first shot and his last hit.

It was one minute past three in the morning in New York City. In the middle of a nightmare, Ellen Cheston felt like the stab of a knife in her sleep. The sharp pain woke her for a moment, just long enough to realize that she was alone in her room and that her heart had merely stopped beating, before she let herself fall with abandonment into this unconsciousness she'd been craving for so long.

A few blocks away, still in his office and busying himself with a multitude of tasks that would undoubtedly be keeping him up until dawn, Cheston got a call from Langley. The CIA director himself wanted to notify him of Joseph Feldman's death after his body had been found in the hallway of a squalid building in Amsterdam the day before. The assassination method employed was a dead giveaway of the Mossad's involvement.

This wasn't the Cold War anymore. The KGB couldn't take the blame for a ricin hit. The CIA director's anger remained palpable throughout the conversation, and even Cheston's announcement of an imminent reorganization that he would be the first to know about wasn't enough to bank his fury. No words were spoken about Howard Beck's ongoing mission that, officially, neither man knew anything about.

But the most significant event had been programmed by Theo himself a few days before, and it was occurring a scant few miles from there, although it involved repercussions at the other end of the planet, and by extension all over the world.

All it had taken was an encrypted instruction several lines long, skillfully hidden inside the program encoding the Umbrella's time management. Gradually, like an octopus pulling its tentacles back in, the main computer of the base's stealth instrument began withdrawing, ceasing its infiltration of the thousands of computers whose memories it had been discreetly piggybacking on for months.

Steadily, the data relayed to the satellites became unstable, and it was as though a movie had started playing back in reverse. The base and its men, just like the second camp, could now show up on any monitoring station, provided its observers were tasked with watching this part of the globe.

It was already ten in the morning in Tel Aviv. Near Kaplan street, not far from the by-now famous three large towers making up the Azrieli Center, the giant communication antennas assigned to surveil Iran and part of Iraq were spitting out a stream of pointless information. It was what they'd been doing ever since the geostationary D2 Eros B1 satellite had been temporarily diverted from its orbit some 375 miles above the Earth to capture any and all images to the immediate north and south of the United States.

The order to scramble its optical sensors, the 70 mm resolution of which was capable of picking up a fly on an Ayatollah's ass while he performed his prayers, had come in straight from the Mossad. The operators were already chortling at the thought of the first reports on the pastures of the Sierra Madre high plateaus and the Cancun beaches that were already piling up.

The computer, however, picked up an anomaly in this area that held no strategic interest for Israel, and it relayed the information to a zealous operator that instantly forwarded it to his supervisor, scratching his head in incomprehension all the while.

Why was there a radius of several square miles in the Western Sierra Madre where it looked like it was high noon? It was really only something like a minute past midnight in Mexico.

That Friday, on the *Shabbat* eve…

…The first bullet struck the helicopter's radio antenna, preventing any form of communication from leaving the small aircraft.

The second bullet struck Novak in the shoulder, throwing him backwards with the full concussive force of a battering ram.

328

The third bullet, meant for Meyrek's forehead, was diverted at the last moment by Theo's hand, going on to hit the gun that was pointing at Eliane. The weapon flew away, tearing off the colonel's forefinger and shattering his left hand on impact. His grimacing face was instantly back in Theo's scope.

As one, Eliane and Beck had thrown themselves to the ground. The echo of the three bullets gave way to silence. Theo heard the characteristic snick of a slide right where Will was stationed, indicating that his friend was ready to spray .50-cal rounds all over the area, if need be. Then came Meyrek's exclamation.

"What a shot, Collin! What precision! How self-sacrificial. But why spare me now, it won't get you anything…"

The colonel wasn't going to the trouble of holding onto his mangled hand, nor of looking for shelter. Pain and fear had no hold on him; he seemed ecstatic. Theo stood up straight and dropped the sniper rifle, which landed at his feet. Meyrek's voice rang out.

"All that's left for you to do is to finish your task! You'll explain to your daughter later how you sentenced her mother to death!"

The situation was easier to assess now that Theo was standing. Inside the helicopter cockpit, the pilot was motionless. What was there for him to do, all alone, against an undetermined number of assailants?

Beck and Eliane had moved closer together to take cover behind one of the taluses that lined the runway. On his knees, Novak was holding his dislocated shoulder, grimacing in pain. Theo couldn't stop himself from admiring Meyrek's conceit.

"No, colonel, it's over! It would be a shame to kill you now."

Meyrek snickered.

"What difference will it make? Are you hoping that, if you keep me alive, you'll force me to talk about… What was her name? Juliette? That was it, wasn't it?

"Come on, come closer. You have no idea who I am. I've withstood worse things than you could possibly imagine. And in a few hours, when no-one sees me come back to the base…"

Theo came to a stop a yard away from the colonel.

"Nothing else will happen. There'll be no-one coming. For a few minutes now, your base is as clear to the satellites overhead as a Taliban training camp!"

He was expecting a fit of rage, a sign of defeat, but the same triumphant expression remained on the colonel's face. His hand was bleeding profusely. Theo perceived, more than he saw, Eliane crawl out to retrieve her weapon, which had fallen close to the talus.

"The results are in, Collin," gritted out Meyrek. "My training is the best. Only a true soldier is capable of sacrificing a loved one for a strategic purpose."

He turned to Beck, who had gotten up in turn.

"When you know where this man comes from, you'll understand what I've made of him!"

What happened next spanned a fraction of a second. With all the dexterity of a carnie, Meyrek snapped a commando knife into his able hand. He leapt in that same motion, and he could have hit Theo in the stomach, as he'd aimed, had a burst of gunfire not mowed him down halfway there.

The colonel kept his gaze steadily on Theo, without even the slightest flicker of surprise. He collapsed, knife still in hand, before he could even know where the shot had come from.

Out of sheer precaution, Eliane sprayed a fresh burst through him.

"You didn't manage anything at all, colonel," murmured Theo, leaning over Meyrek.

He had no idea if the man could still hear him, but it didn't much matter. He was mostly talking to himself.

"You didn't even manage to make me into a killer."

The generators were running full power. The camp was lit up like it was the middle of the day. Beck was having a hard time believing that such a place could exist right in the middle of the western world.

Lending a hand to Eliane Khoury and these men he hadn't known until a few hours ago, he knew his nights would be haunted for years by these children's numb faces and some of their near-catatonic states.

A children's training camp. How could Cheston's Organization have gone to such abominable lengths? Who was responsible for that? What was the end goal of this horror that couldn't be named?

Meyrek alone would obviously never have been able to put together, or even implement, such a Machiavellian plan. And, further still, to what suicidal end?

It was three in the morning when he could finally, with Eliane's assistance, make telephone contact with Langley, and then immediately after with Avi Haim, who'd been back in Israel for a few days.

The three hours he'd spent dealing with the children had enabled him to gather together some of the pieces of the puzzle, and to make some sense of them.

Despite all appearances, the base had never been a private operation, but the result of an idea that had been gaining ground inside Langley since September 2000. Creating commando units that the government could disavow – and even attack and destroy – in the event of diplomatic unrest was not the result of a strategic reorientation.

Instead, it was the implementation of old principles that had governed Langley back in the sixties, when Dulles's leadership had had the CIA running as a state within the state. A loss of independence that a lot of nostalgia revolved around. With the growth of Islamism and its attendant string of terrorist attacks, it had seemed necessary to slip off all institutional constraints. To bring the *politically correct* to an end. One hand tied behind your back is no way to fight.

But they hadn't been counting on Gregory Cheston's delusions of grandeur or his callowness once the project's financing had been entrusted to him.

330

A hugely complex power game had then begun between the CIA and the founder of the all-powerful E.C.Tronics, with the aim of having control over the training camps and, beyond that, the assassin cells being produced there.

But how do you gain the upper hand over an organization you can't locate?

By interfering with the system, Howard had violated the sacrosanct principle of separation between operators, but he'd opened a potential door at the same time. A minuscule pawn placed on the chessboard, he could be sacrificed while enabling a strategic attack. Either Cheston took him out, and that had been next on the agenda, or – and the odds of success had been astronomical – he managed to locate the main base, and thus put the ball back in his bosses' court.

Fifteen years in service to the CIA enabled Beck not to get emotional about such proceedings. The world he moved in had long ago gone beyond the stage of festering cesspit. These were no longer duels between valiant knights over a woman's lovely eyes, but fights between dying civilizations vying for the supremacy of a cultural order.

Anything went.

But it was the most cutting-edge machinery that was the most susceptible to the smallest grains of sand. The Organization had self-destructed because it had itself sucked up this young computer engineer in its cogs, a man whose presence and even more so involvement Beck was having a hard time figuring out. He would make sure to question him, but later. He had no doubt that Collin would be able to help him piece together the elements he lacked.

Beck smiled on picturing the panic that had to be spreading through the upper floors at Langley, not to mention the NSA headquarters, since the images from the Israeli satellite had come up on their screens. Haim had done his job, and pretty well at that.

Persuading his bosses to divert the orientation of such a strategically significant satellite – even for a few days – couldn't have been a cakewalk, especially when he'd done it off a simple hunch. But unlike the CIA, which was drunk on its own technical prowess, it was tradition for the Mossad to trust its field operators foremost.

He'd managed to move his own little pawn forward in turn.

Instinctively, he looked up to the sky, and couldn't stop himself from winking up at the stars, hoping, but not believing it could happen, that Haim would come across this sequence over any other. One in a million odds…

The men and the children had come together. The prisoners had been locked in the basement, the children gathered in the mess. All that was left was to wait for the end of the talks that had to currently be monopolizing an avalanche of diplomats, military experts, and attorneys from the American and Mexican governments. By all accounts, they'd see the first uniforms show up at dawn. The men in charge of the main camp, who'd been left puzzled by Meyrek's disappearance, were in for the surprise of a lifetime.

Beck went over to Theo and Eliane, who had been joined by a massive Black man around a stretcher bearing an Asian fellow.

"You'll need to prepare for one heck of a hoopla," he stated gravely. "I just hope the Mexicans will be decent enough to send out help before they send in the infantry. You understand that, victim status aside, you'll certainly be treated as conspiracy suspects. Especially you, Miss; you're a ranking officer."

Improbably, the huge Black man was the one who answered for them all.

"Hey, *hombre*! Don't look so glum. This is Mexico; the only thing we're in danger of being accused of is littering paper and empty cans in a natural reservation!"

Beck shook his head. He'd have liked to have believed him. As a CIA agent, he was running a huge risk himself just by being in this camp. He swung his gaze over them all in turn, these men and this woman on the fringes of a civilization that had nearly ground them into dust. They nevertheless managed to keep optimistic, almost joyful looks on their faces at the end of a fight they'd lost either way. Not far off, a little girl was sleeping right on the ground, wrapped up in a blanket.

"That your daughter?" he said to Collin, no real question in his voice.

"Yes. And it's a long story. A very long story."

Behind the slightly tense yet altogether radiant smile shining from the Frenchman's exhausted features, Beck thought he could make out a sharp pain. The kind of suffering that years cannot erase. Or if they do, only too slowly.

"I'm going to need several days if not weeks to wrap my head around everything that happened out here," continued Beck. "But what I'm most curious about are the colonel's last words. Was there some kind of a personal connection between you and that man?"

Eliane and Theo looked at the CIA agent in surprise.

"You can speak French?"

"Yes, and a half dozen other languages. It's part of my job. What happened to your wife? Meyrek tried to blackmail you to turn the situation to his advantage."

Nothing but pain remained on Theo's face when he answered.

"I still have no idea if my wife is alive. For months on end, Meyrek tried to get me to believe that she and my daughter had been killed in a car crash. I now know it was all staged, but Katia's blacked out the moment where she was torn away from her mother; she can't remember anymore."

Beck gazed tenderly at the little girl. He could hardly venture to imagine what her father had to be going through, and especially what he must have gone through when, in a final Machiavellian twist, Meyrek had attempted one last manipulation.

"I thought I saw something in my daughter's eyes," Theo went on, his voice trembling. "I needed to make a decision."

At the heart of the inferno that had enveloped his soul, the malevolent voice of doubt had begun its sabotaging niggles. By forcing him to make such a choice, hadn't Meyrek actually won the game? The colonel was right about one thing: from then on, Theo would never know rest.

"You made the only decision you could," asserted Beck. "If your wife is alive, then the Organization took her in at one level or another, and we will track her down.

"If you'd given in to Meyrek, you wouldn't have given her any kind of a chance, and the rest of us either. You chose hope, Theo. Your daughter is living proof of that. Look at her, sleeping like an angel…"

Theo looked. He moved away from Beck to go sit next to her and watch her still. He'd have liked to spend the rest of the night and the end of his days doing nothing except watch her, all while banishing the image of her little face seized by the terror of a sudden memory.

Yes, there was undoubtedly still a little hope. But assuming Juliette was alive, and that he hadn't read the look in his daughter's eyes right, what would be the price to pay to find her?

Through the barred windows of the mess hall, a gold-tinged light had gradually replaced the deep dark of a night that had seen a succession of so many events. It was a new day, a Friday, the day that Theo had picked, through luck or foresight, to unveil before the free world one of its most terrible and least forgivable transgressions. *A conspiracy!* Inside this CIA agent's mouth, the word rang fake, but it rolled with full piquancy off of a thundering Will's tongue.

Deep down inside, just like Huang, Eliane, Beck, and Will, he knew that a door had been opened to the unacceptable. And the thing peculiar about the unacceptable, once it's been designated necessary, is that it ends up being accepted.

EPILOGUE

Three months had gone by, and not the slightest hint of information had trickled through since the large-scale operation that had brought together the Mexican army and US secret agencies, and which had been meant to clean up the two bases and enable certain social services to bring a throng of orphans into their care.

A handful of American stations at the most had broadcast a report on the Mexican mob making use of children, akin to similar organizations in Columbia. The blame had been placed on a local mob boss, Pedro Tamazula, who had since been assassinated during a revenge attack.

The piece could go nowhere except on top of an existing multitude of similar documentaries that dealt with child abuse around the world, particularly in African warzones, but also in Iran and inside Islamist organizations ranging from Hezbollah to Hamas, where a human being had no rights as long as they hadn't reached a marrying age so they could procreate in the name of Allah.

Except for the right to fight and die a martyr, occasionally a key to Heaven hanging around their necks.

Howard Beck hadn't returned to Iraq. No more than he'd seen even the hint of another field mission being sent his way since the Cheston affair. After several weeks spent poring over meaningless files dealing with inconsequential cases that involved the governments of exotic countries taking up as much space on a map as a pinhead, he'd taken several months' unpaid leave, which he intended to invest in evaluating his career, and all the more so his life.

Theo Collin, Eliane, Will… had merely been a cog. The last time he'd seen them had been when they'd been boarding a Hercules chartered by the CIA, destination unknown.

According to certain rumors around the Agency watercoolers, Gregory Cheston had quit the Organization and bowed out of his business not long after his daughter's death. He'd publicly announced he was starting a new humanitarian foundation endowed with his own annual share of E.C.Tronics profits. From then on, the company would be run by a board of directors from which he'd recused himself. The stated mission of the Ellen Cheston Foundation was the rehabilitation of child soldiers from conflict zones. How ironic.

This time, Howard Beck was on vacation. For real.

He landed at Ben Gurion airport in Tel Aviv, where Avi Haim was to be waiting for him as the world remained in a state of dramatic turmoil since the Iranian government had issued its announcement that they had attained the status of a nuclear power.

"For civilian purposes only!" kept proclaiming President Ahmadinejad's successor, an Islamist seen as a pragmatist and boasting an expertise in economics. Things that would, according to most observers, enable him to succeed where Ahmadinejad had failed. That didn't make him any less rabidly anti-Western, nor any less prone than his predecessor to herald the Apocalypse for this small Middle Eastern country where Beck had just touched down.

For civilian purposes only...

The modern and functional facilities at Ben Gurion airport took Beck by surprise. He cleared security in a matter of minutes and came to stand before the luggage delivery conveyors. He was instantly intrigued by the huge clamor going on inside the concourse. Cell phones wouldn't stop ringing, and the Israeli passengers from his plane were excitedly calling out to each other in Hebrew, a language he didn't speak.

A few seconds later, Beck understood that something had genuinely happened when he saw Avi Haim's face, looking more tense than he'd ever seen it. He barely had the time to thank him for his invite.

"Let's hurry back to my car," said the Israeli. "You need to see this!"

Two bodyguards – dark shades, Israeli-style shaved heads, dressed to the nines – unobtrusively escorted them to the armored Mercedes double-parked outside the terminal exit. Embedded in the passenger seat headrest, a small TV set was looping the same few images, clearly originating from an attack. Swearing, Haim rooted around for the remote and pointed it at the screen to switch from the second Israeli TV station to CNN.

Murder of the new Iranian president Mahmoud Hachemi in the vicinity of the UN headquarters in Geneva, just as Iran has officially announced it has become a nuclear power, read the news channel's ticker.

"Holy shit!"

Haim nodded his head.

"Wasn't our doing! And that's not all…"

According to the CNN, the deed had been carried out by a commando unit belonging to an unknown organization. The means that had been deployed to position a sniper at just the right place and time defied the news station analysts' imagination.

The news anchor broke off while the Breaking News splash screen filled the frame. He came back on a moment later to hurriedly reveal a second assassination. This time, it was one of the senior leaders of Hezbollah, killed in similar circumstances right in downtown Beirut.

Instantly, images of a furious crowd filled the screen, all of them brandishing fists, fingers, and thousands of green flags.

The two men's gazes met. Avi's held inside it all the terror that the generations before him had overcome. "A man dies, one universe disappears": so went the words somewhere in the prayer book he'd long ago stopped going through before going to sleep.

The surviving universes, for their part, keep on clashing.